NECTAR OF THE GODS

www.noexit.co.uk

NECTAR OF THE GODS

Gwen C. Watkins

NO EXIT PRESS

First published in 2008 by No Exit Press,
P.O.Box 394, Harpenden, Herts, AL5 1XJ
www.noexit.co.uk

A CIP catalogue record for this book is available from the British Library.

ISBN 978-1-84243-249-5 (Trade paperback)
ISBN 978-1-84243-281-5 (mass market)

2 4 6 8 10 9 7 5 3 1

Typeset by Ellipsis Books Limited, Glasgow
Printed and bound in Great Britain by Cpod, Trowbridge, Wiltshire

For Richard

Press Clipping from
SamSomers@newsday.com

9

Best
Buy

Macquarie Hawke Coonawarra Shiraz

'Nectar of the Gods'

Macquarie Hawke, one of Australia's most colourful and dynamic winemakers, recently released a shiraz to die for, the Macquarie Hawke Coonawarra Shiraz. From the very first sip, I fell in love with this dramatically rich, sensuous wine's spectacular fruit intensity, unforgettable complexity and seamless harmony.

Coonawarra, a magical name in Australian winemaking circles, is renowned for producing shiraz of depth and flavour, but in Hawke's hands, Coonawarra Shiraz has been elevated to the pinnacle of its powers.

Hawke's newest vintage is a deep ruby-plum in colour with crimson hues. The bouquet displays a complex array of spicy, ripe shiraz with pepper and plum fruit characteristics. The full-bodied palate is rich and well rounded, combining sweet berry fruit with new oak complexity and a long lingering finish. This is an outstanding wine, which will age gracefully for ten years or more. It is truly a Nectar of the Gods.

Prologue

The Pylon Lookout entrance for Sydney Harbour Bridge yielded no good prospects, so 'Thunder' Malloy Stout sauntered down Argyle Street and turned left at the Orient Hotel on George Street. Where were all the sightseers? The few people about this afternoon were in too much of a hurry to be anything other than locals. Thunder slowed as he approached Lower Fort, where Bradfield Highway became the bridge, whose massive underpinnings cast dark shadows on the buildings below. He knew that tourists interested in the bridge often began here, then proceeded to Gloucester Walk, a brick pathway that rose to a high point affording interesting views of the historic Rocks and ending directly across the street from the Pylon Lookout.

He wiped the sweat off his upper lip. Even with sunglasses on, the pavements shimmered. The heat must be keeping the tourists inside, knocking back a few stubbies in one of the many pubs maybe. That was where he should have been. Or maybe he should pay his little sister a visit . . .

He was about to call it quits, when he glimpsed an elderly Japanese couple on the other side of the street. The old man was guiding his wife towards Gloucester Walk. He followed them at a distance, watching them start up the slope. Once they were well on their way, he increased his pace, so intent on his prey that he failed to notice the two young men peering into the window of an opal shop across the street.

Midway along the path, he came to an abrupt halt under

a shady tree, lifted his sunglasses and wiped away the sweat that was trickling into his eyes. The couple had paused at a staircase that descended into a seldom-used tunnel leading back to the Rocks. He observed the woman remove a brochure from her handbag and point something out to her husband, who nodded. Keeping his eyes on them, Thunder lifted his trouser leg and reached for his knife, in a sheath at his ankle. At that moment, something metallic flashed in the sunlight, catching his eye. It seemed to be coming from the stairwell. He straightened as the elderly couple strolled off, arm in arm, down the path. 'Lucky bastards,' he muttered to himself, then strode to the stairway and peered into the shadows at the bottom.

'Bugger it!' he swore, as a young man with a buzz-cut stepped into a patch of sunlight. It was Wicky Riley, second in command of the Kings Cross gang. 'Goddamn Pom! What the bloody hell are you doing here?' he raged, flying down the stone steps as Wicky retreated into the gloom.

Entering the tunnel, Thunder ripped off his shades. In the moment it took his eyes to adjust, he missed seeing the two people hiding on either side of the entrance. 'Answer me!' He swaggered towards Wicky, silhouetted by the bright light at the opposite end of the passage.

'You were warned, but you couldn't keep it in your pants, could you?' Wicky snapped, and began to move towards him.

Thunder's knife was in his hand. 'It's none of your business. She's my sister.'

Just then, he heard footsteps. Out of the corner of his eye, he saw something long and thin swinging towards his head. There was a searing pain at the base of his skull. His legs buckled and he fell into darkness.

When Thunder came round, he was flat on his back, the surface beneath him hard and damp. His head was throbbing.

He remembered being struck. How long had he been unconscious? He opened his eyes and realized he was still in the tunnel. Something was covering his mouth. Craning his head, he saw that silver duct tape had been wrapped round his upper torso, immobilizing his arms. His ankles were strapped together. His head snapped to the left at the sound of heavy footsteps. Wicky appeared above him, holding a serrated knife. Another man materialized on his right. It was Ian, their leader.

Ian's eyes glittered beneath bushy black brows as he stood over Thunder, tyre iron in hand. 'There's a price to be paid for disobeying a direct order, cobber,' he said, in a low, hoarse voice, then nodded to Wicky.

Wicky's first kick caught him squarely on the left side. He howled, squirming and thrashing, as the other man continued to kick him, each blow accompanied by the sickening crunch of breaking ribs. Suddenly he stopped and knelt beside him. Thunder closed his eyes, fighting the urge to throw up. There was a tug at his trousers and a ripping sound. A knife bit into his flesh. Something warm ran down his leg. When he tried to jerk away, the knife sliced deeper. He raised his head, tucking his chin to his chest. Wicky was cutting away his trousers, exposing his genitals. He shrieked and shot upright, trying to head-butt him, but a fist smashed into his nose, breaking the cartilage.

"That one's from me, scunge." Ian grinned.

Blood gushed from Thunder's nose, filling his throat, choking him. This was the sickest thing they'd ever done. Well, he'd got the message. It was time to take the tape off his mouth before he suffocated. But Ian had disappeared. No! Don't leave me here!

A moment later, Lee came into view, pushing Wicky aside, and his fear faded. He relaxed as she leaned over him, her long hair hanging down in ringlets, tickling his face. She was so beautiful and only sixteen. She rose and turned towards Wicky, reaching for his knife. Thank God. She was going to cut him loose.

Holding the knife firmly, Lee knelt beside him. Her soft lips touched his ear as she whispered, 'So, big brother, now you know how I feel when you sneak into my bedroom night after night and fuck me till I bleed. I begged you to stop. I warned you this would happen. Why didn't you listen?'

Chapter One

Five years later: Alpharetta, Georgia

Ensconced behind a well-worn mahogany desk, Sarah Bennett gazed across the car park to a low-slung, red-brick building, a mirror image of the one that housed her company, Cornerstone Wine Imports. Above it hung a canopy of heat and humidity so thick, it trapped the fumes of the rush-hour traffic inching its way south to downtown Atlanta and turned the sky a dismal dish-water brown.

March, and it was already too hot to bear. Sarah took off her sage-green cardigan and draped it over the back of her chair. She picked up a pink highlighter pen and continued to work on a thick printout of accounts payable. She paused at an unusually large distributor invoice for a Bluestone Cellars wine-by-the-glass promotion. Could she let it slide until next month?

She glanced at the laminated map of the United States, studded with ninety multi-coloured pins, fixed to the wall on her right. Each pin represented a distributor who purchased one or more of the wines she imported from Australia, Chile and New Zealand, then sold to shops and restaurants. That was down from last year. She'd lost two distributors to bankruptcy after a London-based multinational conglomerate had moved their brands elsewhere.

Cursing, she hurled the highlighter at a group of pictures on the opposite wall. With a sharp ping, it hit her target. The eyes of her husband and business partner, Elliott Nichols, admonished her silently. 'Damn you, Elliott,' she muttered

Her eyes moved to a Peachtree International Wine Festival poster, framed in black metal and autographed by Sam Somers, *'To my good friend Elliott Nichols'*. It had been the last festival Elliott had attended before his death two years ago. Sarah felt like ripping it off the wall and smashing it.

In a few hours, Somers would arrive in the Barossa Valley to taste the latest releases from Bluestone Cellars, the Addison Group brand that represented seventy per cent of her sales. Sending him there had been either the best idea she'd ever had or the worst, depending on whether or not the chief winemaker, Andrew Dunne, heeded her warning not to play any of his practical jokes on the world's most famous wine writer.

She rested her elbows on the desk and lowered her aching head into her hands. She'd asked Dunne to forgo having Somers taste the liqueur muscats and tokays, dessert wines well out of most people's price range, in favour of Bluestone's latest release of the Coonawarra Shiraz. Last night, at the Peachtree Diner in Buckhead, she had shown the same wine to Judy Russo, owner of Atlanta's premier wine shop and the diner's wine buyer. She'd known Judy for at least twelve years, and while they weren't quite friends, they were more than business acquaintances. Perhaps that was why she hadn't seen what was coming.

After the feast of Southern comfort food, including her artery-clogging favourite, chicken-fried steak with black-eyed peas and mashed potatoes in thick gravy, she'd been ecstatic when Judy had pronounced the wine 'spectacular', without her usual caveats. It was lavish praise from a woman known for her fine palate and incisive opinions.

As expected, Sarah had presented her Georgia distributor's best pricing for upcoming in-store promotions. Last night's dinner had been specifically geared to the Coonawarra Shiraz, and she'd thrown in a few extras at her own expense, including two cases of limited-edition wines and a dozen denim shirts with the Bluestone Cellars logo. Inevitably, after the good-natured haggling, Judy would agree to the deal, which the distributor would ship, making everyone happy.

But last night, Sarah had listened as her friend described how Macquarie Hawke's Coonawarra Shiraz was flying off the shelves after a best-buy rating from Sam Somers, who'd awarded it ninety-eight points out of a hundred. It was impossible to promote more than one Australian shiraz, Judy had explained apologetically. She had confirmed a token Bluestone Cellars order.

Suddenly Sarah's fingers were on the keyboard, typing a password into *Newsday*'s premium Internet service. Waves of anxiety washed over her as a photograph of Somers materialized beside a piece of text that extolled him as the world's leading authority on Australian wine. She snickered in disbelief that he could pass himself off as the expert when he'd never set foot in the country before this trip. She shifted her attention to the section where the column would appear and groaned. The countdown showed two minutes remaining.

A light knock on the door made her jump. She punched off the monitor and called, "Come in."

The operations manager, Jim Barnes, hair brushed off his forehead in crinkly waves, came in, and flopped into a tweedy chair. "I have good news and bad news. Which do you want first?"

"I could use some good."

"We got our first choice for the Wine and Spirits Wholesalers of America convention. The two-bedroom suite at the Orlando International."

"Too late to change it for a smaller one, I guess." Sarah glanced at the accounts payable still laid out in front of her. "So, let's have the bad."

"The bank manager called." Barnes fished a yellow pencil out of his trouser pocket, avoiding Sarah's eyes. "He won't increase our line of credit."

Sarah struggled to maintain a neutral expression. "It was always going to be a long shot. But we're owed around a hundred and ninety thousand dollars, which should cover Bluestone Cellars."

"Don't forget about the fifty K for the Chilean container. It's due the week after." Barnes was tapping the pencil on the chair's wooden arm.

"We can put the Chileans off for the time being, but Bluestone Cellars has to be resolved before I go to Australia. I can't have anything interfering with the contract renewal," Sarah said. "Would you email Phillip Dwyer and ask for an additional ninety days on the first container and a hundred twenty on the other? Remind him that Taylor promised to extend the payments because she wanted to clear out all the old-label Coonawarra Shiraz."

Barnes's eyebrows rose. Taylor Robbins had a black belt in bitchiness even though he had yet to hear his boss say a word against her. "Should I copy her?"

"No. Phillip's her boss. Let him deal with it." Sarah's hand went to the back of her neck. A knot the size of a walnut had sprung up and she rubbed it gently. "Make sure you attach a copy of Somers's rating."

Barnes snapped the pencil in half. "We never had any trouble selling that wine until he trashed it. What does he have against Bluestone Cellars?"

Sarah exhaled. She knew exactly why Somers continually found fault with Bluestone Cellars. It had nothing to do with the quality of their wines.

Chapter Two

Barossa Valley, South Australia

The majestic three-storey façade of Bluestone Cellars's main building featured a covered veranda, wide balcony and balustraded parapet fashioned in the Romanesque Revival style popular in the 1850s. The winery's equally impressive side entrance faced the Misener family homestead across a grand courtyard paved with crushed stone, where a neo-classical fountain served as a gathering place for busloads of visitors keen to tour the winemaking facilities and sample wines in the Cellar Door tasting room.

The courtyard gravel crunched beneath Sam Somers's cowboy boots as he stepped into the porch of the old administration building behind the Addison Group's chief winemaker, Andrew Dunne. He felt a sneeze coming as they went into the public tasting room. He took a handkerchief from his jeans pocket and held it to his nose as he moved past the fifty or so people crowding up to the bar to collect their free samples. The air was charged with good humour and the aroma of fine wine.

He sneezed, blew his nose and replaced the handkerchief in his pocket. Keeping his head down so that no one would recognize him, he skirted a flock of tourists studying the show awards and silver trophies. The room was filled otherwise with family memorabilia, and sepia photos of the Miseners contrived to create a sense of warmth for the sole purpose of loosening a customer's wallet.

He cut through a labyrinth of waist-high wooden wine racks, and scanned the room for Dunne. A moment later, he spotted the Chief Winemaker halfway up the stairs to the second floor.

Just then, a chubby woman lugging two bottles of wine and a rolled-up poster grabbed his arm and asked for an autograph. He gritted his teeth, brushed past her, and made for the second floor, which was off-limits to everyone except winery personnel and special visitors. Taking the stairs two at a time, he arrived on the landing in time to see Dunne fling open the door to the private tasting room where, earlier that afternoon, they'd sampled fifty wines. Somers followed him in, greeted by a mélange of pungent aromas. He joined Dunne at the only clean counter, where a selection of wines had been opened for them. The other surfaces were strewn with dirty glasses that held varying quantities of wine, from celery green to plum red, and several half-empty bottles.

Dunne waved at the freshly opened wines and the clean glasses. "So, mate, do you want to have a go at these beauties?"

"I thought you were going to lock the door." Somers indicated an ultra-thin black laptop that lay on the countertop where he'd left it. It was warm. His brow furrowed. "Someone might have stolen it. What is it with you winemakers?"

Dunne tugged at his sweater, stretching it over his protruding belly. "No need to get your knickers in a knot."

"You'd think I'd learn," Somers said. He lifted the laptop's lid, and stroked a few keys. As far as he could tell, no one had touched it. "All right. Let's get on with it."

Dunne filled a glass with inky red wine and handed it to him. "This is the Bluestone Cellars Coonawarra Shiraz. You're familiar with the area, right? Terra Rossa strip of ten miles long and a mile wide, south-eastern part of the state."

"Very funny." Somers snorted as he accepted the glass, promising himself that Dunne would pay for the insult. Anyone who had anything to do with Australian wines knew Coonawarra, a magical viticultural area producing legendary shiraz and cabernet sauvignon with prices that equalled their reputation. He'd had the pleasure of spending a day there – incognito for a change – tasting wines without a winemaker in tow, hanging on his every word.

Somers studied the wine's colour, then took a sip and swished it round his mouth. It had none of the superb flavours of the Macquarie Hawke Coonawarra Shiraz. He spat it into a bucket, resisting the urge to let his lip curl, then placed the glass on the counter, angled his computer away from Dunne's line of sight, entered the wine's name, a brief evaluation and a tentative rating. It was a pain to have to carry a laptop around with him, but it saved him an enormous amount of time. From now on, he wouldn't let it out of his sight.

"Only a handful of wineries own a piece of Coonawarra and the Bluestone Cellars vineyard is the largest," Dunne said. "The wine is a hundred per cent Coonawarra shiraz, estate-grown on ten-year-old vines, matured in new and one-year-old French oak barrels."

Somers lifted his eyes from the screen. "What's the US retail?"

Dunne told him, then asked, "What do you think?"

Somers continued to type. "I thought Sarah Bennett warned you. I never discuss my opinion of a wine before publication," he said, and heard Dunne curse softly.

At that moment the door opened and both men looked up. Gerry Marks, one of Dunne's three assistant winemakers, came in. She smiled tentatively at Somers then said to Dunne, "It's getting late. If we're going to the mausoleum, we need to leave now, so Sam can get that photo for his column."

Ten minutes later, Somers stood at the foot of a crumbling pathway leading to the Misener family tomb, perched at the summit of the highest hill for miles. Dunne and Gerry Marks, who'd gone ahead in a dusty black truck, were already halfway up.

The summer heat made the climb arduous, but at forty-two, Somers was fit and reached the summit without breaking a sweat. There, his initial impression of the structure's elegant white columns and balustraded terrace changed. Graffiti defaced it and iron bars protected cracked, dirty windows above once beautiful, hand-carved wooden doors. Clearly, the Addison Group had neglected it.

Somers strolled to the balustrade, dug a digital camera from his pocket and took a number of shots while Dunne and Marks attempted to wrest the lock off the door. The view was indeed spectacular. A short distance away, the Bluestone Cellars winery sat in a thick stand of trees and parkland, beyond which rows of perfectly parallel vines snaked into the foothills of the Barossa. In the distance, the vineyards appeared as patches of green set against light brown soils. He put the camera away as Gerry sidled up to him.

"Beautiful, isn't it?" Gerry shaded her eyes with a hand. "Over a third of the early Barossa Valley settlers were Silesians, like the Miseners. Many of their descendants still live here, running wineries founded by their ancestors. It's a charming area. You'd be surprised how many of the old traditions have survived."

"You're right. I would," Somers responded, and wrenched himself away from the panorama. "As I understand it, most of the family-owned wineries have been taken over by corporations, as Bluestone Cellars was."

"A few, perhaps." Gerry's mouth tightened.

"More than a few," he retorted, and turned back to the view. "Ten companies produce ninety per cent of your country's wines. At the rate the big boys are gobbling up family-owned wineries, they'll be soon be extinct. No more than a name on a label. A marketing ploy like Bluestone Cellars."

"With all due respect, without companies like the Addison Group, the old wineries and vineyards wouldn't have survived. We work hard to preserve each winery's individuality."

"Of course you do. It sells your products," Somers snapped. "But we both know that the Addison Group bottles the same blends under a number of its twenty labels. Individuality at its best."

"Gerry," Dunne called. "Get over here, will you? I need help with this blasted door."

As they continued to fiddle with the lock, Somers stared into the distance. At least one person was bucking the takeover trend, he mused. Macquarie Hawke's wines had been in the US for only four years, but he was selling five hundred thousand cases annually, a rare achievement in the mid-to-upper price bracket. His sales in Britain were equally phenomenal. Even Stephen Randall, vice president of Oskar Hallgarten Vineyards, had been interested in discussing his amazing success. In fact, Hawke had been the main topic of conversation everywhere Somers had gone over the last two weeks.

Dunne gave a whoop and Somers spun round. The door to the mausoleum stood open. He sauntered across the stone terrace and went in. Inside it was cool and smelled musty. White marble plaques lined the walls. Each bore a gold-engraved epitaph, naming the Misener family member whose ashes were interred there. One space remained, a large, black hole.

Now Dunne reached inside it and brought out a plastic jug filled with grey material, the top loosely secured with masking tape. Striding to the door, he inverted the jug, angling it to catch the rays of the late-afternoon sun. With a grin, he read the note attached to the bottom: "'Waldemere Misener, fourth generation'. Too bad no one saw fit to give him a proper burial. Looks like we have a leak, damn it!" A trickle of something that resembled a very fine-grained OK sand floated to the floor. Fumbling, Dunne swung the jug upright too fast and the lid flew off.

Somers gasped, and jumped away from the cloud of ash that threatened to envelop him.

Eyes dancing, Dunne shook out the last from the jug,, "No worries, Sam. It's just sand."

"Good one, Dunne." Somers let out a short bark that sounded like laughter. "You really had me going there. Speaking of which, I have an early flight home tomorrow morning." He strode out of the mausoleum.

Dunne passed him on the five steps that led from the

balcony to the pathway and came to a halt, cutting off Somers's escape. He was still holding the jug. "I won't let you leave without giving us your opinion of the Coonawarra Shiraz."

Somers shook his head. "All I can say is, the quality of your Coonawarra Shiraz is consistent from year to year." Then he bounded down the steps to the path. Halfway to the bottom, he skidded on a chunk of gravel, lost his balance and fell backwards, hitting his tailbone. All at once he felt dizzy. After a moment, he stood up and dusted off his jeans, wincing in pain. Maybe he'd let little too much wine slip down his throat over the last several hours, but certainly he hadn't had too much to drink. Had he? .

"Hey, are you OK?" Dunne called.

When he turned to wave, Somers saw the smirk on the winemaker's face.

Chapter Three

Somers sped out of the car park and turned on to Sturt Highway. Almost immediately, he spotted a sign for Southern Valley Winery, where Macquarie Hawke's wines were produced. Sighing, he pulled up on the hard shoulder: he was heading north, away from Adelaide, where he was bound. He was about to U-turn, when it struck him that perhaps this wasn't a mistake after all.

Before he'd left for this trip, he'd purchased two cases of Macquarie Hawke's Coonawarra Shiraz before he'd released the ninety-eight, best-buy rating, although his home was full of wine samples waiting to be reviewed. Suddenly he was transported back to the night of the party he'd planned around his purchase, the scent of the lamb Stroganoff simmering on the stove as he'd grasped the stem of a crystal glass. He had twirled it in a tight circle, then lifted it to his nose, expecting a deeply aromatic bouquet. Baffled, he had taken a sip.

This can't be the wine I rated ninety-eight! He checked the label. It was definitely Hawke's Coonawarra Shiraz, but there were no mouth-puckering tannins, little oak, and virtually no peppery, spicy flavours. With deep foreboding, he opened a second, third and fourth bottle from the first case. They were weak, thin and colourless. He opened the second case and wrenched the corks out of four more bottles. Without exception, they were flavourless and dull. At the first opportunity, he'd called

Hawke, who'd confided that a bottling-line problem at Southern Valley had been discovered, affecting a limited number of cases, which they were in the process of tracking down.

Suddenly his stomach began to rumble, bringing him back to the present. He wasn't far from the Tanunda Bistro, the famous Barossa Valley restaurant where yesterday he'd enjoyed a meal with the owner, Gustaf, who'd had some rather uncomplimentary things to say about Macquarie Hawke.

A noisy truck barrelled past, rocking the car. Should he return to Adelaide, or stop at Southern Valley? It was getting late. He hated driving on the left, especially in the dark on unfamiliar roads, on the other hand, if only a few of the things Gustaf had said were true . . .

A few minutes later, he parked in a bay at Southern Valley and stepped out of the car. The breeze was freshening. He reached inside for his suede jacket, shrugged it on, then headed for the vast three-storey bluestone structure trimmed with red brick, its central tower reminiscent of a British castle. Majestic date palms lined the path. He went up the steps, and attempted to open the double doors. They were locked. He rang the bell.

A short time later, a young woman opened the door. "Sorry, sir, we're closed to the public," she said.

Somers introduced himself. "I write a wine column for *Newsday*. I'd like to speak to Macquarie Hawke's winemaker or to Angus Kennedy, if he's here."

She gave him a hesitant smile, then stepped back and pulled the door wide. Its hinges creaked. In the foyer a round mahogany table held a crystal vase filled with flowers. Above an antique chandelier cast sharp slivers of light on to the marble floor. "Take a seat." The young woman pointed to four wing chairs. "I'll be back in a moment."

"I'm a little short of time," Somers said impatiently. "I have to be back in Adelaide soon."

As the young woman left through another set of double doors, Somers ran through what he knew about Southern Valley, most of which he'd learned from Macquarie Hawke himself over lunch last September at an Atlanta restaurant. Owned by Angus Kennedy, Southern Valley was a co-operative that accepted grapes on a consignment basis from local growers, then produced whatever style of wine was deemed suitable for the market. Kennedy set prices for the bulk products, which were shipped in huge tanker trucks to Southern Valley's customers, domestic wineries of all types and sizes. When he'd been paid, he settled with the growers. Whatever was left over comprised Southern Valley's profit. Its customers added the bulk wine to their stock, and sold it as their own. What surprised Somers was that the red wine shortage in Australia was forcing even huge conglomerates like Oskar Hallgarten to buy from Southern Valley.

The door opened again. The young woman was back. Davis Hart, the chief winemaker, would see him, she said.

Somers rose and followed her. As they walked along a maze of corridors, he was reminded of his first visit to a winery at the age of ten. He had escaped from his father, and the young woman conducting the tour, and ended up talking to an elderly winemaker. He'd been enthralled by the tale of the angels who waited patiently for wine ageing in wooden casks to evaporate and rise to heaven as their 'share'. If not for that day, Somers might have become a truck-driver, like his father.

The woman led him into a glass-walled office where an emaciated young man with light hair and a pasty complexion sat hunched over a computer. An Aboriginal man was disappearing into a passage on the far side of the room.

"What's going on?" the young man asked, pushing his glasses up to the bridge of his nose.

"This is Jason Findley, our assistant winemaker," the woman said to Somers. She turned back to Findley. "Mr Somers is a wine writer from America. I'm taking him to meet Mr Hart."

Findley shook his hand, then said, "Julianna, let me know if you need help. Oh – and I left some documents on Mr Kennedy's desk to be signed. Would you make sure he does it today?"

Why would she need help? Somers wondered, as he followed her into a tasting room. On a table in the centre, a long line of tulip-shaped glasses containing remnants of wine stood in front of half-empty bottles identified by handwritten labels. A burly man with a large red stain on his shirt smiled as they approached. "Sam Somers!" he said. "It's good to meet you! I'm Davis Hart. Mac speaks highly of you."

He walked towards Somers, one hand outstretched, the other holding a half-empty wine glass. He ran straight into a stainless-steel bucket attached to the table, righted himself and continued as if nothing had happened. "Julianna, get us some fresh glasses, please."

Her face showed dismay. "I'll see if Mr Kennedy's meeting has finished. Maybe he can join you." She left the room, closing the door behind her.

Somers grunted as Hart mashed his hand in a bone-crunching shake. The other man was six feet tall, with thick grey hair and a complexion Australians referred to as 'expensive'. It took a lot of alcohol to produce a face so red and blotchy, lightening one's wallet significantly. "Call me Davis." He finished the wine, put down the empty glass, and stepped closer to Somers. The stench of stale wine hung about him, "What brings you to Southern Valley, mate?"

Somers inched backwards, "I needed some information on Mac Hawke's Coonawarra Shiraz, but I see you're busy. I'll talk to Mr Kennedy about it."

"That's not necessary. I make all Mac's wines. What do you want to know?"

"He told me there'd been a problem with the line when you bottled the last vintage of his Coonawarra Shiraz. I'm interested to know if you identified the lot numbers and, if so, how many cases were affected."

"You must be joking." Hart's bloodshot eyes glittered.

"No, I'm not," Somers assured him. "Mac said he intended to have the cases destroyed. He did speak to you about it, didn't he?"

"We've never had a problem with the bottling line," Hart wiped his mouth with the back of his hand.

"If Mac said there was a problem, there was a problem."

"How dare you accuse me of lying?"

Hart reminded Somers of his father, whose drinking had been a nightmare for the family before he had quit ten years ago. Until then, the slightest thing would trigger violence and the next day his father would have no idea of what he'd done. Somers had not immediately recognized the signs in Hart and cursed himself inwardly. He needed to find out about the wine. He folded his arms and looked the man in the eye. "Why do I get the feeling there's more to this than you're letting on?"

"Who are you to question my integrity? I come from a long line of winemakers and you're a bloody parasite – just a damned wine writer!"

"Take it easy," Somers said, unfazed. He'd spent years fielding far worse from his father. "I must have misunderstood. If you'll tell me what you know about the situation, I'll be on my way."

Without warning, Hart grabbed Somers's lapels. "It's Angus's fault. He's in on it. Don't let him fool you." His eyes rolled back in his head, but he held fast to Somers.

"Let go!" Somers snapped.

Hart released him, lost his balance and fell. His head struck the edge of the counter and he toppled to the floor. Blood poured from a head wound, mixing with a pool of red wine.

Chapter Four

She screamed and woke, terrified, sitting up in bed, her nightdress drenched with sweat. Disoriented, Sarah's heart beat wildly until she saw the red numbers on the alarm clock. She was in her own bed. It was two o'clock on Thursday morning.

Shaking, she groped for the bedside lamp and switched it on. In the dim light, she could see the imposing Georgian bureau, the corner TV cabinet, the antique dressing-table and her treasured Bahktiar rug, an heirloom from Elliott's family. She got out of bed, went to the bureau and opened one of its heavy drawers. After taking off her nightgown, she selected a fresh pink one, put it on, then went into the bathroom. She turned on the light and filled a glass with water. As she drank, she studied her reflection in the mirror. If only those who insisted she looked younger than she was could see her now, pale with dark smudges round her green eyes, limp auburn hair falling in clumps to her shoulders. She sighed and returned to bed.

A rush of wind rattled the pine trees outside, then rain pelted the roof. She turned on to her stomach and pulled a pillow over her head, but Elliott's face was still in her mind. He had never been one to talk about his feelings, but he'd been so distant over the last few months of his life that she'd worried about him. Eventually, one night, she'd refused to let his mood deter her. Was the pressure of running the business getting to him? she'd asked. Did he need a holiday? His answer had shocked her to the core. A week later, he'd left for Lyme Regis and moved in with his father after thirty years in the US.

She threw aside the pillow and climbed out of bed again. Going to the window, she parted the heavy curtains. An outdoor light illuminated the sheets of rain beating down on the wooden deck that jutted into her back garden.

Three months later, Elliott had died of a brain aneurysm. She'd been at her North Carolina distributor's trade show when his father had called with the news. Although she'd raced back to Atlanta and booked the first flight out, weather delays had caused her to miss the funeral. By the time she'd reached England, her husband's body had been cremated.

On her return, the house had seemed so empty, she'd taken to sitting on the deck for days on end, wondering how it would feel to just let go.

The red glow of the clock caught her eye again. It would be after five o'clock on Thursday afternoon in the Barossa Valley. She'd begun to represent Bluestone Cellars at about the time Andrew Dunne had been appointed chief winemaker, long before the Addison Group had entered the picture.

She sighed with relief when Dunne answered his office line on the first ring, and got straight to the point. "How did things go with Sam Somers?"

"Buggered if I know. I think he was pretty well pissed."

"Pissed as in angry, or pissed as in drunk?" Sarah's fingers tightened on the receiver.

"Both. I called one of my mates at Oskar Hallgarten

after Somers left. He said Somers had been there all morning before he came to us, swallowing more than he spat." Dunne paused, then explained how angry the wine critic had been to discover his laptop unsecured in the tasting room. "Apparently, the same thing happened at Hallgarten when he found his computer in my friend's office with the door wide open. We decided to revoke his wine-writer credentials for conduct unbecoming," he joked.

Sarah could hardly believe what she was hearing. "What else happened?"

"We put on a fancy lunch with wines from our library stocks, some real beauties, but he didn't say a word about any of them. Getting an opinion out of him is like trying to spear an eel with a spoon. Then at the mausoleum –" Dunne stopped, recalling his promise a second too late.

"God, Andrew! You didn't!" Sarah's stomach lurched and she leaned back into the pillows.

"No worries. The fake ashes got a laugh out of him. But he took exception to being asked his opinion of the Coonawarra Shiraz. I know, you warned me, but I couldn't resist having a go at him after what he did to my friend."

"The one who went bankrupt?"

"Yes. Krup finally found a job in a California 'wine factory'." Dunne's bitterness was clear. "Listen, Somers is entitled to his opinion, but he didn't review Krup's wines, he massacred them. Five vintages in a row. I wouldn't piss on Somers if he was on fire."

Sarah felt sick. "So, what did he say about the shiraz?"

"He said, and I quote, 'The quality of your Coonawarra Shiraz seems very consistent from year to year.'" Dunne cleared his throat. "Faint praise, considering he gave the last three vintages the kiss of death by rating them seventy-five. I'm sorry, Sarah."

There was a long pause. "I tasted that wine last night," Sarah said. "I think it's one of the best you've ever made. Air-freight ten cases. We'll send a bottle to every wine writer with national coverage and bury Somers in good press."

"No worries. I'll even pay for it out of my budget. But you've got a kangaroo loose in the top paddock, if you think that'll make a difference," Dunne said. "I like the idea of burying Somers, though. Let's hire someone to do it for real before he publishes another stinking, and, may I say, undeserved Bluestone Cellars review."

Chapter Five

Davis Hart sensed someone standing over him. When he opened his eyes, he was in Southern Valley's tasting room, seated on a chrome stool. The room pulsated with light. Half expecting to see Sam Somers, he was surprised to find Julianna Porter dabbing something on the back of his head. "Bloody hell! That hurts." He gritted his teeth against the sting, then glanced at his watch. He was glad to see it was five o'clock.

"At least you won't need stitches." Julianna threw the bloody cotton ball into the bin. "What were you and Mr Somers talking about?"

Hart shrugged his shoulders. "Not much."

"He seemed upset." Julianna frowned. "Mr Kennedy would like to know why."

"Then tell him to get down here and ask me himself." Hart slid off the stool. Blood trickled down his neck. He saw that Julianna's shoulders were shaking. Was she crying? She was an attractive girl, but not very bright. "Sorry I snapped at you, but my head hurts like blazes. Now, call someone to clean up this mess – we don't want Mr Kennedy to see it, do we?"

"Of course not," Julianna said. "He'd very cross."

You should know, my dear. Hart pulled out his handkerchief to stem the fresh flow of blood from his wound.

Much later on Thursday evening, in a tiny house not ten minutes from Southern Valley, Hart sat on a ladder-back chair in his cramped, sparsely furnished bedroom, a bottle of vodka in hand. He hadn't washed the dishes or taken out the rubbish for weeks. He got up, tottered to the bedroom door and slammed it, then went to the dresser and picked up the US itinerary Julianna had organized for him. Of all the times to start drinking! The day after tomorrow he was leaving for America. He couldn't afford to lose control now, not like last time when he'd passed out at the wheel of his car and woken up when it crashed into a tree. Until now, that was the last time he'd had a real drink. Tasting wine in the normal course of business didn't count.

One more, then he'd pack. He dragged himself to the narrow bed in the corner of the room, sat down and took a lengthy swig from the bottle. The vodka worked quickly, but rather than making him feel good, the pain in his head expanded. A glimmer of what he'd revealed to Somers flitted at the back of his mind. Then, in a rush, the entire scene emerged from the fog in his brain. Horrified, he gulped the vodka.

The next morning, Hart arrived at Southern Valley as a pallid sun rose above the horizon. He raced through the chilly corridors, relief overwhelming him when he reached his office. He unlocked the door and switched on the overhead lights. Banks of black filing cabinets lined the walls on either side of the room. Behind his desk was an old brick wall, part of the original 1850s building. He sank into his leather chair and turned on his computer.

Moments later, he entered a password and opened the files that specified the composition of the wine blends in each of Southern Valley's stainless-steel tanks.

Holding just over 114,000 litres each, they were identified by the letters SV, followed by a unique number. Information contained in the files included the name of each grape varietal in the blend, its cost, the year harvested, and a grower's code. In addition, the varietals were shown as a percentage of the total blend, in terms of litres and dollars. A duplicate record-keeping system existed in the form of handwritten cards posted on each tank.

Hart pulled up tank number SV888. Sixty-three per cent of the blend was a three-year-old grenache owned by Grower (GRW) 3 and thirty-seven per cent was a two-year-old shiraz owned by GRW 12. It was hard evidence he needed. Even so, his finger shook as it hovered over the print key. Only he and Kennedy had access to the real blend profiles, which allowed them to track actual costs. An entirely different set, doctored to match the tank cards, had been set up for the staff. Those were the ones that were printed out, signed by either Kennedy or himself for verification, then cross-referenced on their customers' sales invoices. He wavered. Once he followed through with this, his life would be ruined, but there was no turning back, not after what he'd revealed to Somers. He'd print out a few hard copies, just in case the discs got corrupted. He pushed the key, printed out the first record and threw it on to the desk behind him. It fell to the floor and floated under a filing cabinet. After that he printed several more, and added them to a growing stack.

Next, he inserted a disk into a CD drive, then began to copy the tank files for the last three years as well as Southern Valley's sales records, which contained customer invoices. Rubbing sweaty hands on his trousers, he willed the computer to go faster. Finally, it was done. Davis popped out the disk, put it into his briefcase and changed the password.

With shaky arms, he propelled himself out of the chair and went to the wall safe hidden in a corner of the room. He opened it and took out the code book that matched the growers' names and addresses with the codes used in the computer files, a duplicate of the one Angus Kennedy kept in his home safe. Dropping it into his briefcase, Davis congratulated himself on a job well done, then took a flask of vodka out of his desk drawer and drank. The liquid burned as it slid down his throat and his eyes wandered to the wall clock. It was almost nine. In the few minutes before he had to leave, he contacted the Stamford Hotel in Adelaide to check his reservation for that evening. He always stayed there on the night before an overseas trip. Finally, it was time to make the call. With unsteady hands, he dialled the familiar number.

"Australian Wine Board, Inga Wismar speaking. May I help you?"

Startled by the crisp voice, he barked, "Davis Hart. I must speak to Karl Kingsley immediately."

Moments later, a resonant voice boomed, "What can I do for you, Davis?"

His throat seized. Was this a mistake? But what choice did he have now that Somers was on to them?

"I need your help. I'm in a fair bit of difficulty at work. But I say anything more, will you promise me immunity from prosecution, if it comes to that?"

"I'll help you in any way I can."

Hart's voice steadied. "Get a search warrant. Access the tank files in my computer. Compare them with the cards on the tanks and the sales records. They won't match. Listen, I'm supposed to go to America tomorrow, but perhaps I should cancel my trip."

"Davis, these things don't happen overnight. It'll be at least a week before I can get an investigator out there." It was common knowledge that the Australian Wine Board's serious understaffing had slowed down investigations into all but the worst alleged code violations. "In the meantime, go about your business. By the time you get back from America, we'll have seized the records and begun an investigation, if warranted. And don't discuss this with anyone. It could hamper the investigation and jeopardize your position."

"Whatever you say," Hart flinched as he detected Julianna's scent near by. She must be outside his door, which was open a crack. He slammed down the phone.

Kingsley's office door flew open. "Inga!"

"Yes?" She fought the impulse to flee.

"Come in here – now!"

Trembling with apprehension, she gathered a notebook and pen, berating herself for having inadvertently activated the speaker phone when she'd transferred Hart's call. How many times had she done that now? Ten? Twelve? But this time, although she'd punched it off the moment he and Hart had hung up, the light had remained on for a few seconds, which didn't make any sense.

She stepped on to the Oriental runner and went towards the door, feeling like Marie Antoinette on her way to the guillotine. She'd been hired three weeks ago to help with the Australian Wine Board's move to temporary accommodation while their Adelaide offices were refurbished, and had stayed on to work for Kingsley. Her lack of wine-industry knowledge meant everything took twice as long as it should, so she hadn't had time to get to know the telephone system properly. Now Kingsley was angry and she couldn't afford to lose this job, not with two little boys and an unstable ex-husband who didn't pay child support.

She sat down in front of Kingsley's desk and rearranged her pleated navy skirt to cover her knees. The room was panelled in the same acorn-coloured wood as the reception area, and the carpet co-ordinated with the one outside. The early-morning sun was streaming through the large windows, hitting her directly in the face. She directed her gaze to her feet.

"You were listening to my telephone conversation with Davis Hart." Kingsley's stark Prussian features were tight. He set down his tea cup.

"I'm sorry. It was an accident," she said, her voice feeble with anxiety.

Kingsley continued as if she hadn't spoken: "This is the second time he's called me with that story. First time it was the Western Australian winery where he was chief winemaker. I sent investigators, but apparently Hart was dead drunk when he made the call and couldn't remember a word of our conversation. It was an embarrassment to the AWB. The chairman was not pleased."

Inga risked a glance at him. His salt-and-pepper hair, cut in a short, military style, was highlighted from behind by the sun, making his head look fuzzy.

"Of course, we both know Hart was drunk when he called this morning, so we won't be taking action on his allegations – at least, not at the moment." Kingsley's cloudy grey eyes were cold. "You would be well advised not to discuss this incident with anyone, especially your colleagues. If I find out that you have disclosed this, or any other confidential information, you will be fired. Have I made myself clear?"

Chapter Six

Inga hurried through the spacious lobby of the restored winery building, happy to be going home still employed. If only the last two wine inspectors would finish their evaluations, she could close up the AWB offices for the weekend, which promised to be warm and sunny. Maybe she'd pack a picnic lunch and take her boys to the park by the River Torrens for a day of rollerblading.

She passed the ornately carved mahogany bar, where visitors from all over Australia had once flocked to taste the finest champagnes of the early 1900s, then headed left, towards the tasting room. The marketing manager, Graham Blackwell, had been so kind clarifying the export-approval process. Where would she be without him? Kingsley had shown no inclination to train her, which worried her.

Pushing aside her anxiety, she went over Blackwell's latest lesson. Domestic wineries sent the Australian Wine Bureau two bottles of the wine they wanted to export, with a fee and an Analysis Certification. Since no scientific test could prove a wine's grape composition, region of origin or vintage year, including DNA testing, which was useless after grapes had been processed into wine, wine inspectors evaluated them blind. Rejects were re-evaluated by different inspectors.

A crack as sharp as a gunshot echoed through the lobby, and Inga jumped. A man in a green shirt and brown trousers had flung open the tasting-room door, which had hit the wall, followed by another in a black sweater and jeans, shouting. She'd met them this morning: Stephen Randall, vice president of Oskar Hallgarten, and Andrew Dunne, chief winemaker of the Addison Group. She slid behind the bar, crouching to avoid notice.

"Remember what happened to the Austrians? The antifreeze they added to their late-harvest wines bloody well killed people!" Dunne was furious. "You're a few stubbies short of a six-pack if you think that can't happen here! This isn't some game, mate. The entire Australian wine industry could go belly up if you let plonk slide through."

Randall faced him. "The wines you rejected today wouldn't win any awards, but they didn't deserve to have their Certificate of Approval denied. You're costing those wineries a fortune, simply because their wines didn't suit your palate."

"Let me get this straight. You think the chardonnay with some cheap sultana grapes added to bulk it up was OK? How about the Riverina Shiraz labelled as Coonawarra? Where the hell do you draw the line?"

"The evaluations are subjective," Randall barked. "I disagree with your opinion. End of story." He headed for the door.

"They're subjective all right." Dunne raised his voice towards Randall's retreating back. "But anyone with a trained palate can tell Coonawarra fruit from Riverina, and sultana from chardonnay."

Unexpectedly Randall laughed. He turned, hands on narrow hips, face alight. "Why don't you admit what this is really about? Hallgarten is trashing the almighty Addison Group. Get used to it, mate. That number-one spot of yours will be Hallgarten's before too long, mark my words."

Chapter Seven

With a start, Davis Hart realized he was talking. From a great distance he heard 'Mac's samples', 'tank files', 'computers' and 'America' spewing from his mouth. The babble of conversation and shouting in the background became louder. There was a disgusting taste in his mouth. He emerged from a dense fog to find himself leaning on a circular bar made of highly polished wood, talking to someone he didn't know.

He gazed up at the wooden podium rising a few feet above the bar and acknowledged the friendly nod of a rotund, red-headed man working the controls. It dawned on him that they'd been having an intense discussion. But who was the man and what had they been talking about?

The man's hand moved and a buzzer went off. The fifteen or so people at the bar began to hoot and holler at the brunette in the centre. She was holding a small paddle and staring unhappily at two coins on the floor. The man standing beside her bent to pick them up while another gyrated around the inside perimeter of the bar, shouting at people who were placing coins on the pads in front of them.

Shaking, Hart peered at his pad. There was a rectangle with a red 'H' in it, one with a yellow 'T', a square with '10' and another rectangle with 'Five Odds'. It was like reading hieroglyphics. His teeth began to chatter and chills moved up and down his back. He needed a drink. As if on cue, a waiter placed a glass filled with clear liquid, garnished with an olive, in front of him. Hart pulled money out of his pocket and threw it on to the bar. The waiter took some and left. Hart almost drained the vodka martini in one gulp.

As he set the glass on the bar, he realized he was in the Adelaide Casino, standing at the circular Two Up gaming table. He'd been talking to his friend Ray, the gaming manager, who was filling in for a Two Up inspector. He'd come in on Friday afternoon, but had no idea how long he'd been there. Glancing at his watch, he saw it was eleven o'clock but was that Friday evening or Saturday morning? If it was Saturday, he'd missed his flight to America.

He ran out of the casino into an elegant lobby, part of the renovated railway station building that the casino shared with Adelaide's transit station. Built in an era when grandeur was in vogue, the Great Hall had a taupe marble floor polished to a high gloss. Impressive white marble columns rose to the second of three floors open to the lobby. People were lounging on an octagonal bench that enclosed a long-case clock. As he ran past, he noticed their stares. He made himself walk and stepped outside as the clock chimed.

It was Friday evening. He hadn't missed his flight. Come to think of it, he should have known Two Up would never have been so busy on Saturday morning. Relieved, he headed for the Stamford Hotel.

Five minutes later he was unlocking the door of his room. He walked in, wrenched open the mini-bar and took out a bottle of vodka.

Chapter Eight

The young woman's long, coppery hair fell in cascades down the front of her navy sweatshirt. She had fallen asleep fifteen minutes into the flight from Honolulu to Los Angeles. Directly in front of her, in row twelve of business class, Davis Hart accepted another vodka martini from the flight attendant, whose name-tag identified her as Susan.

Across the aisle a casually dressed American was playing video games with his two rowdy teenage sons. They'd been on the Sydney to Honolulu flight too. When Hart had realized they were continuing to Los Angeles, he'd tried to switch seats, but the Honolulu gate agent claimed the flight was fully booked. He'd decided that the noisy family was his punishment for greed: he'd added an unnecessary stopover so that he could rack up more frequent-flyer miles.

Looking for distraction, he was rummaging in his briefcase when he spotted the tank-file code book. Bloody hell! Without it, the AWB inspectors would be lost, unless the police managed to get Angus Kennedy's copy from his home safe before he had a chance to destroy it. He could have it couriered to Karl Kingsley, but what if it went missing? He began to panic – until he was distracted by a faint hiss that seemed to be coming from beneath his seat. He wondered what it was. The sound got louder, waking the redhead behind him. He heard her ask someone what the problem was. She sounded scared.

The hiss stopped. Hart closed his briefcase, finished his drink and tightened his seatbelt. The man seated beside him was snoring. The hiss started again, much louder this time. Then, as before, it stopped. He heard a call button chime. Moments later, a high-pitched voice asked about the strange noises. Twisting round, he saw Susan crouched a little behind him, speaking to the redhead in soothing tones, assuring her that everything was fine.

The flight attendant had just stood up when there was a deafening tearing sound. The plane shuddered, then listed to one side. The girl screamed and snatched Susan's hand. The aircraft righted itself, but the tearing sound was closer to Hart now. He was clutching his armrests as it escalated into the screeching, gut-wrenching groan of metal being torn from metal. Hoping this was a drunken hallucination, Hart scanned the faces of those around him for comfort, but everyone seemed as terrified as he was. The redhead had gone quiet, apparently shocked into silence.

The intercom let out an ear-splitting squeal. Then: "Ladies and gentlemen, this is your senior flight attendant. Please remain in your seats with your seatbelts fastened. Everything will be fine."

The announcement was cut off by an explosion, which sounded like a bomb detonating. Moments later, a whoosh of freezing air filled the cabin with fog. Overhead bins opened and baggage toppled out. Briefcases, shoes and spectacles flew through the air, striking people about the head and face. Oxygen masks fell from their compartments.

The plane's ominous groans became a horrendous ripping sound. Blue sky appeared above and below Hart. Wind whipped against his face. Something hit his mouth and he tasted blood. A second later, Susan was sailing overhead. One of her shoes dropped off, landing on his forehead. Blood gushed into his eyes, blurring his vision as he twisted sideways to see where Susan had landed and stared blindly into swirling whiteness. A swoosh of air cleared the cabin and he screamed. He couldn't see anything because there was nothing to see. Not only was the window in his row gone, but so was the man seated beside him. Hart was gazing into a vast space where there was no longer an aeroplane wall. Susan and the man had been sucked out of a vast hole in the fuselage.

With growing terror and disbelief, Hart sensed his seat splitting away from the aircraft. If he could get to the other side of the row, he might save himself, but he dared not unbuckle his seatbelt, fearing he'd be sucked out instantly. Then he looked down. A rupture in the floor was widening and a deafening roar filled his ears. All at once, he was calm. This is it. At least he'd done one thing right in his life. He'd told Karl Kingsley about Southern Valley.

Then, still strapped to his seat, he was flying through the fuselage into thin air. Dazed, he saw his briefcase float away into the clear blue sky. A second later, he was heading straight for a huge object with whirling blades. Seconds before he was dragged into the starboard engine, Hart lost consciousness.

Chapter Nine

The automatic coffee-maker sputtered as Sarah dragged herself into the kitchen after another sleepless night. She flipped on the lights, rubbed her eyes and tightened the belt of her black-and-gold bathrobe against the early-morning chill. Her suede slippers made little sound as she crossed the floor and stopped the machine mid-cycle. She poured some coffee into a bone-china mug, then went to the refrigerator and added two ice cubes from the door dispenser. When they had melted, she gulped the coffee, poured another mug and repeated the process. She had to wake up, fast.

She went into the sunroom, punched off the alarm, unlocked the French windows, and stepped outside on to the wooden deck. She crossed to the railing and peered out at the tangle of wild vegetation that was her garden. It was still dark, but she could hear the rush of water in the rain-swollen stream at the edge of her property and the tall pine trees swaying in the brisk breeze. There was an earthy smell of damp and decay. She was about to go inside when her mobile phone rang, startling her. She took it out of her pocket and flipped it open. Suddenly she was wide awake. "Taylor, thanks for calling. Sorry to interrupt your Monday evening, but this couldn't wait."

"What can I do for you?" Taylor Robbins didn't bother to hide her irritation.

Clearly this wasn't the time for polite conversation. Sarah put her mug on the railing and plunged in. "I'm sure it's nothing more than a misunderstanding, but your shipping department swears you authorized the old labels for those five DI orders we just sent in. I'd appreciate it if you'd straighten it out."

"I did authorize it."

Sarah's heart began to pound. She counted slowly to ten. "I don't understand. When I agreed to buy the last two containers of Coonawarra Shiraz, you assured me that was the end of the old packaging."

"I didn't know the warehouse was holding nine thousand dollars' worth of old labels." She didn't sound concerned.

Sarah kept her voice calm. "Regardless, we can't change the timetable at this late date."

"We can and we will," Taylor replied. "That money comes out of my budget. I'm not about to waste it by throwing out perfectly good labels."

"Have you discussed this with Phillip?" Sarah asked, even though she knew the answer. Dwyer would never knowingly allow Taylor to screw up the global-repositioning plan he'd spent two years developing.

"I'm the brand manager now. We'll use up the old labels. End of story."

Sarah slammed her fist into the railing. When the pain subsided, she said, "It might be worth talking to Phillip about this. A good chunk of the marketing budget was spent on distributor-depletion allowances to get rid of the old labels. We have incentive programmes in place, sales meetings set up and ads running in major markets to introduce the new ones. If we don't ship as promised, the distributors may cancel their orders until they can get the new labels. We can't afford to let that happen for the sake of nine thousand dollars."

"If that amount of money means so little to you, you can pay to have the old labels destroyed and we'll go straight to the new packaging. You have forty-eight hours to decide." Taylor hung up abruptly.

Sarah folded her phone and returned it to her pocket. The situation would have been laughable, if it wasn't so serious. With shaking hands, she reached for the coffee mug, but it flew off the railing and smashed on the stone patio below.

Ten miles south of Sarah's home in Dunwoody, the golden glow of the rising sun seeped through the wooden blinds at Sam Somers's bedroom window, jolting him awake. Yawning, he stretched under the covers, then rolled over and looked at the clock.

"Oh, shit!" He'd forgotten to set the alarm. If he wanted to some coffee, he'd better get going. Atlanta traffic could be murder at this time of the morning.

He slid into his brown leather slippers and a Paisley silk dressing-gown and went down to the kitchen, where creamy cabinets with etched-glass doors showed off his collection of vintage wine glasses. He turned on the coffee-maker, then stepped outside and ran up the driveway for his morning paper. Somers's house was situated below street level, obscured from view by a heavily wooded garden filled with pine trees that stood at least forty feet high towering over dense stands of azalea and dogwood.

At the top of the driveway, Somers spotted his newspaper wedged into the juniper bushes surrounding the mailbox. As he picked it up, he heard a sharp crack, a car backfiring, he thought. He turned to the front page. "Seven

Confirmed Dead. Bomb Suspected As Cause of Jet Ripping Open Over Pacific". "My God! If I'd come home a day later, that could have been me. That's the flight I took on Friday!" He sprinted back down the driveway, and went into the house, kicking the front door shut. The aroma of freshly brewed coffee greeted him as he ran into the kitchen. He poured a cup, added milk, then sat down at the oak table. As he began to read the article, he wondered what else he'd missed by shutting himself off from the outside world since his return from Australia. He gasped when he read that Davis Hart of Tanunda, South Australia, had been on the plane and was among the dead. He flipped to the photographs of those who'd perished and recognized Southern Valley's chief winemaker.

He leaped up from the table, grabbed his mug and strode down the hall to his study. The blinds were open, and the sunlight streamed in. Behind him, black wrought-iron racks were filled with wines waiting to be reviewed. To his left, several boxes of samples sat unopened on the floor. Mindful of the leather on his cherry-wood desk, Somers placed the mug on a coaster, then sat down and turned on his laptop. He scrolled through his Australian trip notes to the section on his conversation with Hart.

Before he had become completely incoherent, Hart had said, 'It's all Angus's fault. He's in on it. Don't let him fool you.' Had he been too hasty in dismissing the man as a paranoid alcoholic? he wondered.

As was his habit, Somers typed as thoughts came to him: 'Hart implied something illegal was going on at Southern Valley. Two days later he was killed in an aeroplane accident. Are the two related? No. That's ridiculous. Yet, what if someone overheard us arguing and decided to silence him because of his drunken revelations? Who was there that day? His fingers flew over the keys. 'Julianna Porter, Jason Findley, an Aboriginal man. Angus Kennedy, owner of Southern Valley. Kennedy had the most to lose. His winery. His reputation. His livelihood. Who else would be affected? Macquarie Hawke.' Somers pressed the backspace key, deleting the last words. Damn it. There was no getting round it. He rubbed his eyes and resumed typing. 'Macquarie Hawke. His wines are made at Southern Valley. The two cases I purchased weren't even close to the quality of the samples he sent me. Hawke insisted it was a bottling-line problem. Hart said otherwise. At best, Hawke's telling the truth and nothing illegal is going on, or if there is, he doesn't know about it. At worst, Hawke and/or his wines are involved."

His fingers froze. Whatever was going on at Southern Valley, it was beyond absurd to think that someone would down a commercial airliner to get rid of one man. He saved the file, intending to delete most of what he'd added later, then transferred everything relating to his Australian trip to the desktop computer. That done, he deleted the files from his laptop.

The Westminster chimes of the grandfather clock in the hall reminded him that it was getting late. He stood up and left the room. A short time later, showered and dressed, he jumped into his black Lexus. He headed for downtown Atlanta and the first session of the Peachtree International Wine Festival competition.

As soon as the car had turned out of the drive, a man with buzz-cut hair wriggled out of the bushes in Somers's front garden and raced to the back patio, where he jacked the door off its tracks and entered the house.

Chapter Ten

At exactly twelve thirty on Tuesday morning, Sarah Bennett parked her Jeep on Peachtree Boulevard, directly in front of the red-brick building where the Peachtree International Wine Festival was being held. Given the unpredictable nature of Atlanta's traffic, she'd allowed an hour to get downtown from her office, but the journey had taken only twenty minutes. She switched off the engine, but made no move to get out. Sam Somers was running the event, which was reason enough not to go in. Eventually, reluctantly, she got out, locked the car and went through the battered front door.

Inside, hundreds of crystal glasses were arranged on folding tables covered with white cloths. Little buckets of clean sand were positioned on the floor next to each chair, six to a table. Shafts of midday sun poured through the huge picture windows, adding to the glare of the overhead fluorescent lights. The room was deserted.

Sarah unbuttoned her blazer and went to the corkboard fixed to the wall by the front door. She reviewed the panel assignments, then moved past the tables to the back of the room. Hesitantly, she pulled aside the brown velvet curtains, exposing a long, narrow space that served as the staging area for the competition. Open wine bottles stood ready on folding tables, which lined both sides of the area. She was expecting to see Somers, but there was only a woman volunteer opening bottles. She let the curtain fall back. The tasting was blind and she didn't want to be accused of cheating.

" Sarah!" a man called.

One of her closest friends, the US importer for Oskar Hallgarten Vineyards, was standing a few feet behind her, his blue eyes crinkling as he smiled, clearly delighted to see her. He was wearing a hand-tailored navy sports jacket, French-blue shirt and grey trousers. His black hair was swept back from a tanned face. It was totally unfair that any man could be as handsome as Jake Malone, she thought.

"Getting a preview of what we'll be tasting today, then?" Jake asked, the smile widening into a grin as he strolled up to her.

Smothering a laugh, Sarah flashed him a disapproving look. "Two thousand labels and counting."

"This I have to see for myself." He brushed past her, tugged the back curtain, and whistled.

"Get out!" the volunteer exclaimed.

He dropped the curtain.

Sarah burst out laughing at his expression. Few saw Jake's lighter side. He'd inherited one of the country's largest wine and spirits importers on his father's death a little over six years ago. "We're on the same panel," she said. "Australian fortifieds."

"I know. I asked Sam to put us together," Jake said, unbuttoning his jacket. "We may need something to soothe our palates afterwards. How about going for beer and pizza?"

"Sounds good. Which reminds me. I've decided on a restaurant for our dinner in Adelaide, the Jolley Boathouse. Have you eaten there?" She smiled mischievously. They'd wagered dinner and a night at the Adelaide casino on the outcome of their Sunday golf match and she'd beaten him with a convincing margin.

"Great choice," he said. "I'll look forward to it."

"Jake! Sarah! Is Peter Vine there?" It was Sam Somers, uncharacteristically flustered and out of breath, as he ran through the front door with a laptop bag over his shoulder.

"I haven't seen him." Jake shrugged.

"Someone broke into my house while I was here yesterday. Peter agreed to fill in for me while I get my patio door replaced and a burglar alarm installed." Somers shook Jake's hand.

As he took hers, Sarah was hit by the stench of stale wine on his breath. She felt herself flush as she pulled away her hand and stepped back. The room retreated. Jake and Somers were mouthing words she couldn't hear. She was in quicksand, sinking, and she gasped for breath. She could feel his hands on her thighs, pushing her skirt up. She was pounding his chest with her fists. Then, in a flash, it was over.

Somers was still talking. "They stole my desktop, nothing else. The police said something must have disturbed them. Just as well the wine competition files are on my laptop or we'd be dead in the water." He moved aside the curtain and disappeared.

Jake turned to Sarah. "Are you feeling OK? What's wrong?"

"Nothing. Really. I'm fine." She averted her eyes. "Just tired."

Before Jake could question her further, the door banged open and several people came in, chattering and laughing, all chosen by the celebrated Sam Somers to judge wines. Melissa McNair, the San Francisco-based importer of Macquarie Hawke wines, was among them. In a peach suede suit and movie-star sunglasses, she stood out from the crowd, who were pausing to study the panel assignments. She made a beeline for Sarah and Jake. As she neared them, she whipped off her sunglasses, smiled at Sarah, then cooed, "Jake, darling, it's been far too long. How have you been?" She stood on tiptoe to kiss him.

"Hello, Melissa. I didn't expect to see you here." He twisted to avoid her lips but wasn't fast enough. He ended up with a blob of lip-gloss at the corner of his mouth.

"Sam begged me to come. How could I say no?" She threw the sunglasses into the leather bag slung over her shoulder. "I'm here for a few days, staying at the Peachtree Plaza. We should get together."

Sarah saw a flicker of irritation in Jake's eyes as he took out a handkerchief to wipe his lips. In a way she felt sorry for him. Every woman in the room was sneaking glances at him, drawn by his heart-stopping good looks and undeniable sex appeal.

The babble of conversation was gathering strength as the judges, from all walks of life, filled the room, dressed in everything from formal business attire to jeans and T-shirts. The experienced among them headed immediately for the tables overflowing with cheese, hunks of bread, crackers and fruit, knowing that if they didn't load up now they would miss their chance. The aroma of wine crept underneath the curtain and into the room. The atmosphere reminded Sarah of a party, but she wasn't in a party mood.

"Excuse me, ladies, but I see my sales manager waiting outside." Jake indicated the windows overlooking

Peachtree Boulevard. "I need to speak to him before we get started."

Sarah watched him go, then said to Melissa, "You, Jake and I are on the same panel. Australian fortifieds."

"Don't you just love it? Three Australian importers judging their own wines! Sam has a sense of humour after all." Melissa chuckled. "I hope you're not too angry about Beverage Warehouse."

"What are you talking about?" Beverage Warehouse, a New Jersey-based retail operation with stores in fifteen states, had recently selected the Bluestone Cellars Coonawarra Shiraz as their September wine-of-the-month. Her distributors were already sending in orders to cover sales, which promised to be six thousand cases or more, depending on the programme's success. The boost would go a long way towards alleviating her current financial situation, and boded well for the brand's future.

"Oh. I thought you knew." Melissa's shocking-pink lips turned down. "The buyer called me. He wanted to know if we had enough Macquarie Hawke Coonawarra Shiraz to cover their September wine-of-the-month programme."

"Did you say September?" Sarah felt as if she were trapped in a lift on the top floor of a skyscraper and had just heard the cable snap.

"Yes. He didn't mention we were replacing your wine until after we'd reached an agreement. By then, it was too late to back out."

"I see." The lift was plummeting down the shaft. Retail programmes often skirted the letter of the law, which meant that nothing was ever confirmed in writing. If she confronted the buyer, she would only infuriate him and ruin any chance of a future deal.

"He didn't have much choice after Sam rated our wine a best buy with ninety-eight points." Melissa unzipped the outside compartment of her bag and took out a mirror to check her makeup. "Especially with your scores being well below that." She touched her lips with her middle finger, smoothing an imaginary flaw.

"If the buyer changed his mind, there's nothing much I can do about it, is there?" Sarah gritted her teeth. The lift hit the bottom of the shaft, along with her six thousand cases.

A thirty-something woman in bell-bottomed blue jeans, clogs and an embroidered white tunic approached them. "Hey, Sarah, Melissa, looks like we're on the same panel today."

"Hi, Bobby." Sarah infused the greeting with as much warmth as she could muster. Roberta Wagner, wine-sales manager for Coastal Beverages of South Carolina, was one of her favourite people. "I didn't know you two had met."

"Yeah. Melissa did a sales meeting for us not long ago," Bobby said.

"Right." Plainly Melissa had no memory of the woman. "Well, I'm off to the ladies' room. Save me a seat." She vanished behind the brown curtain.

"So, when did you put on Macquarie Hawke?" Sarah asked. Mentally she added Coastal to the list of those who'd defected after Macquarie Hawke's all-out attack on her distribution network. Was it ten or eleven now?

"I can't believe Matt didn't tell you," Bobby said, referring to the company's owner. "It happened about six weeks ago."

"We've known each other for sixteen years, so I won't lie to you. I'm not happy about this," Sarah said.

Bobby reached behind her head and tightened the rubber band round her straggly ponytail. "Trouble is, Macquarie Hawke is so hot that Matt couldn't bear to let another distributor get it, and Melissa offered him a ten-day trip to Australia with the first container order. For two people. Business class."

"Really." A container held twelve hundred cases at most. Two trips could cost upwards of ten thousand dollars. That was what she was up against. It was worse than she'd thought.

"Yeah," Bobby glanced around, then lowered her voice. "But he didn't reckon on having to deal with Melissa. Lordy, that woman is a piece of work. She upset almost every retailer she visited. Don't worry, Sarah, the salespeople won't let you down."

"Thanks, Bobby. That means a lot." Sarah knew her friend meant well, but in every instance where the two brands were in the same house, Macquarie Hawke was winning the battle for the sales team's attention, thanks mainly to Somers's over-the-top rating. Damn the man.

Bobby looked at her watch. "It's almost one thirty. Let's get over to the table so we can sit together. I want to tell you about our trip to the South of France. You'll never believe the jewellery the supplier gave us. It was wild!"

Forty minutes later, the event had yet to begin. Sarah was sitting at the end of a table six feet from the centre of the curtain, a subdued Judy Russo to her right. She and Judy hadn't spoken since their dinner at the Peachtree Diner in Buckhead, and the underlying tension made her uncomfortable. To her left, Bobby was working up to her favourite subject: wine-industry consolidations. As she launched into a heated diatribe, Judy's eyes glazed over.

Sarah had heard most of it before and her attention wandered to the opposite end of the table where Jake was being subjected to Melissa's ceaseless chatter. He looked strained. George Knox, a mental-health counsellor who seemed totally out of his element, sat across from Melissa, talking on his mobile phone. Just then Sarah heard the door slam.

A moment later, Peter Vine entered the judging area. "Hello, folks. We'll be getting under way shortly," he said, into the silence that had greeted his arrival. He waved away the bevy of questions that followed as he slipped through the tables, stopping briefly to lay a hand on Jake's shoulder, and disappeared behind the curtain.

That was when the shouting started. With her back to the curtain, Sarah heard Somers laying into Vine, complaining that he was late. The curtains flew open. Somers emerged and stalked through the room to the exit. He walked out, slamming the door behind him. The judges' voices rose in a swell of annoyance.

Then Peter Vine was swearing. From the raised eyebrows and appalled expressions of those nearby, she presumed they'd heard him too. Her eyes shifted to Jake. She flicked her head backwards and shrugged. At first he looked confused, then, apparently, he heard Vine, because he stood up and slipped behind the curtains. He reappeared almost immediately and took his seat, evidently troubled.

Sarah was about to ask him what was going on when Vine drew the curtains and entered the judging area, his blond hair askew and his eyes angry. He began to recite the standard speech for new judges and Sarah tuned him out. After he had finished, volunteers filed among the tables, handing out rating sheets and pencils.

Melissa waved hers in the air, "Can you believe it? After all that time, Peter still mixed up the panels! This is ridiculous. Australian shiraz under fifteen dollars. Eight flights of five wines each? Forty-five wines? We'll be here all night."

Sarah stifled a groan. Although she intended to spit every wine, some always trickled down her throat, which meant that by the end of the evening, her tongue would be bright purple tongue and her stomach full of acidic young wine. A beer afterwards would provide welcome relief.

Standing in the middle of the room, Vine raised his voice. "As I was saying, you'll be evaluating each wine in terms of colour, clarity, bouquet, flavour and finish, using a scale of one to ten, with ten being the top score. When all the wines in a category have been judged, those with the highest scores re-poured, and the panels will be responsible for awarding bronze, silver and gold medals. Best-of-show will be selected from the gold-medal winners by a special panel."

As the afternoon progressed into early evening, Sarah's panel reached the eighth and final flight of wines, when a volunteer let slip the white napkin that concealed the wine's identity as she filled Melissa's glass. Sarah saw the bold splashes of the Macquarie Hawke Coonawarra Shiraz label. From Melissa's expression, Sarah realized she'd seen it too. However, the other judges seemed too engrossed in tasting and making notes to notice the blunder.

"This wine tastes like cat piss," George remarked.

Sarah's eyes slid towards him. His white shirt was stretched to the limit by an enormous belly that hid his belt buckle. His florid face and unfocused eyes piqued her curiosity. Unobtrusively, she glanced at the floor beside his feet. His spit bucket was bone dry, a bad mistake for a novice judge.

"You're suffering from palate fatigue, George. After eight flights, it wouldn't be unusual for someone as inexperienced as you are." Melissa flipped her blonde hair over her shoulder.

"I beg your pardon?" George slurred.

"Folks, please." Jake held up a hand to Melissa, who suppressed the retort that was forming on her lips. "It's probably corked. I'll ask Peter to open another bottle."

Sarah propped her elbows on the table and watched the others finish their notes as she waited for the wine to be re-poured. It was quiet in the room, the last of the smaller panels having left an hour ago. A glance outside confirmed that the sun was setting and the street-lights were coming to life. She was exhausted. She had been up at all hours last night, checking the office email from her home computer for a response from Phillip Dwyer about the payment extensions and Taylor's dead-line on the old labels. There had been nothing.

Peter Vine appeared and poured the replacement wine. When he left, Sarah swirled it in her glass, sipped, then promptly spat it out. OK. So she was prejudiced against the Macquarie Hawke Coonawarra Shiraz, but there was no denying that this wine was terrible, lacking in flavour, thin and weak with no character. What was she missing? How could Somers have given it a ninety-eight?

George proclaimed. "This one tastes like cat piss too!"

"Oh, for God's sake! That's a phrase people use to describe sauvignon blanc, not shiraz. You're drunk," Melissa snapped, jumping to her feet. Her chair fell backwards and she overbalanced. Arms flailing, she knocked the table, sending the glasses flying. Red wine shot across the table and drenched George's white shirt.

"You stupid bitch!" he yelled, holding his shirt away from his chest as he leaped out of his seat.

"Prick!" Melissa shot back.

Half an hour after George had left, Sarah and Jake stood outside the building as Judy Russo drove away a little red sports car with Bobby Wagner in the passenger seat. Melissa had remained inside to talk to Peter Vine. The night air was cool. Sarah shivered. Through the window, Melissa was leaning over a table and Vine was nowhere in sight. "Jake, what's Melissa doing? Is she erasing something?"

He peered though the window, "I don't know. I can't see what she's doing."

"Isn't that where you left the tasting sheets after you'd wiped off the wine she'd spilled on them?" Sarah asked.

"Yes, but I thought Peter picked them up before we left."

"I hope so." Sarah wouldn't have put it beyond Melissa to change what had to be some fairly low scores on her Macquarie Hawke Coonawarra Shiraz. Medals from the Peachtree International Wine Competition were rewarded with substantial sales. A best-of-show wine would sell out within days. "Speaking of Peter, what happened when you went behind the curtain to help him? You haven't been yourself since."

"You know me too well." He sighed, then linked her arm and guided her towards the Jeep. "I caught him looking at a file in Sam's computer."

"What kind of file?" Sarah asked. She unlocked her vehicle, then turned back to him.

"Personal. He had no business looking at it. I wish I hadn't seen it either. Anyway, I'm famished. I'll follow you to TJ's."

Sarah hesitated. "I'm so tired I can hardly keep my eyes open and Sam roped me in to judge again tomorrow. Could I take a rain check on the pizza?"

"Anytime." He smiled. "Cassie'll be happy. I'll be home in time to tuck her into bed. Do you realize she'll be seven soon?"

"Of course! Have you forgotten she invited me to her birthday party?" Sarah found it hard to believe that almost seven years passed since Jake's wife had died in a car accident, leaving him with a three-month-old daughter. "Give her a goodnight kiss from me." She grazed his cheek with her lips. Was it her imagination or did he pull back ever so slightly? Out of the corner of her eye, she saw Melissa emerge from the red-brick building. Jake opened her car door for her. She climbed inside and lowered the window.

Melissa's strident voice pierced the cool evening air: "Either of you interested in going for a beer and something to eat?"

"Thanks, but I'm going home," Sarah replied, rather sharply. "Good night, Jake."

"Jake, I won't take no for an answer. I'm here alone, and I don't want to go back to my hotel – at least not yet."

Sarah drove off before Jake could reply. Stopping at a red light a block away, she glanced into the rear-view mirror. Melissa was pressing herself against Jake, laughing and tossing her hair as they headed for his black BMW.

* * *

The next day, Sarah entered the red-brick building with little enthusiasm for judging wines, especially after yesterday's fiasco. She'd been up most of the night, waiting in vain for Phillip Dwyer to contact her, and had a blinding headache. To top it all, she'd miscalculated the traffic again and arrived in record time.

The spring sun was beating through the windows of the empty judging area, bouncing off the white tablecloths and crystal glasses, throwing dazzling shafts of light round the room. Somewhere behind her a door slammed. Startled, she jerked, and felt a searing pain as a ray of sunlight pierced her eye. Spinning away, she prayed that her headache wouldn't escalate.

She headed for a dark corner, unbuttoned her beige leather jacket and hitched up her black wool trousers. She'd lost a few pounds over the last few weeks and nothing fitted properly. She sat down, retrieved a bottle of ibuprofen from her briefcase and shook out two tablets. She popped them into her mouth and reached for the water jug. It was empty. She swore softly and swallowed them dry, gulping as they stuck halfway down her throat.

In the stillness, she detected faint noises behind the curtain. They turned into angry words. She recognized Somers's voice. He was berating someone. A woman retorted – Melissa McNair. The argument escalated.

"Answer me!" Somers demanded, his voice radiating hostility. "Where were you last night?"

Sarah rose, tiptoed to the curtains and parted them. Melissa was standing toe to toe with Somers, holding a wine bottle – Hawke's Coonawarra Shiraz by the look of it. His face was contorted with anger. A corkscrew dangled from his fingers.

When Melissa didn't respond, he pointed it at her. "You were supposed to call me."

She strolled over to his makeshift desk, put the bottle down, then twirled round. She picked up another bottle from a nearby table and turned back to Somers. She smiled. "I was busy."

"All night?"

"Yes, all night! Since when do you care? Get out of my way! I'm leaving." She walked past him and headed for the back exit.

Somers followed her. They were still arguing when they disappeared through a doorway at the far side of the long, narrow area.

Melissa had been out all night? With Jake? Sarah returned to her table, took off her jacket and draped it over the back of her chair. It was none of her business who Jake slept with – but why Melissa of all people?

The silence didn't last long. The back door slammed again and there was more shouting. This time it was two men. Although she tried to block them out, fragments of the altercation broke through: "You'll never get away with this. I won't let you."

There was a scuffle, then the sound of glass shattering. Sarah ran to the curtains and pulled them apart. Somers had his back to her and a blond man was fleeing out of the rear door. Peter Vine? There was a thick puddle of wine, and the shards of broken bottles, on the floor at Somers's feet – she could smell the unmistakable scent of the liqueur dessert wines that Australians called 'stickies'.

She let go of the curtain. Somers was lucky that more bottles hadn't been broken. Those flimsy tables weren't meant to carry such a weight, as Melissa had discovered yesterday.

Out of the corner of her eye, Sarah caught a movement behind the curtains where they met the wall. Was Somers coming out? She dashed to the table, grabbed her jacket and briefcase, then fled. Only when she'd opened the front door did she risk a backward glance. Somers hadn't come into the judging area. She was safe. She closed the door behind her, raced to the Jeep and leaped in, head pounding.

The curtains moved and a man raced to the windows on rubber-soled shoes. The woman was driving away in a Jeep. She'd had the most startling green eyes he'd ever seen, the colour of chartreuse, a drink his mother liked. She had stared directly at his hiding place, then left in a hurry. Had she seen him? There was no way to know and, in his line of work, loose ends were not acceptable. He rubbed a hand over his buzz-cut hair, went to the front door and locked it.

"Oh, shit!" Somers mumbled, as the cork he was removing from the umpteenth bottle broke. At least he had two more of the same wine. And to think people complained at having to submit three bottles for each entry! If only they knew how many were scrapped due to bad corks. He stowed the unusable bottle in a cardboard box under the table, took the broken bits out of the corkscrew and threw them into an overflowing wastebasket. He laid the corkscrew on the table, pushed the sleeves of his khaki shirt up to his elbows, then reviewed the list of wines required for the first flights, checking it against what he'd opened so far. He glanced at his watch. He'd never be done in time without help.

Muttering to himself about lazy volunteers, he went

to the desk, picked up his phone and punched a few keys on his laptop to access their names and telephone numbers.

"Hello! Anyone here?"

Somers spun round. A powerfully built man in a short-sleeved black shirt, loose black trousers and rubber-soled black shoes was at the door. The man ran a hand over his head, then scratched the stubble on his unshaven chin. Somers was suspicious. "Who are you? What are you doing here?"

"I'm sorry if I startled you." The man enunciated his words carefully. "I'm here to help with this tasting."

Something about him put Somers at ease. He placed his phone by his computer and picked up the corkscrew. "OK. You can start by clearing up the broken glass and that wine, then I'll show you which bottles to open. Here's a corkscrew. Don't lose it. They're hard to come by."

As the man drew closer, Somers saw he was somewhat dishevelled and instinctively withdrew his outstretched hand. But it was too late. The man seized his hand, and spun him round. In a practised move, he bent Somers's arm behind his back and slammed him face first into the wall. The impact split his lip. Tiny drops of blood splattered across the wall. The man pressed his body against Somers, immobilizing him.

"You can have anything you want. Just let me go!" Somers moaned.

The man leaned forwards until his lips almost touched Somers's ear. "Shut up! We're going outside. If you come along nicely, I won't have to hurt you."

The odour of onions on his assailant's breath made Somers gag. He struggled to twist his head away, but his cheek was pinned to the wall.

"If you understand, nod." The man backed off a fraction.

That was all Somers needed. His father had often attacked him in a drunken rage and he'd learned how to fight someone bigger and stronger. He lifted his leg and slammed the heel of his boot into the man's shin. He was rewarded with a satisfying snap.

The man screamed. His grip on Somers's arm loosened.

Somers threw himself hard to the right and slipped his leg behind the man's knee, levering himself into a position in which he could pull him over backwards. For a moment he feared his own arm might break, then the man let go to break his fall. There was a sickening crack as his head hit the wooden floor.

Somers bent over him. He seemed unconscious, but he was breathing. He straightened and surveyed the room for something to tie the man up. There was nothing. He grabbed his phone, punched 9 to autodial 911, then made for the back door and the safety of his car.

Almost immediately, he slipped on broken glass, teetered and skidded. About to lose his balance, he flailed for a table to steady himself and dropped the cell phone. He didn't hear it hit the floor.

He righted himself then began to run. Something tangled in his legs. He looked down. The man was tackling him with his foot. Somers fell head into a table, which collapsed. The bottles toppled, smashing into one another, shattering and raining glass on his head and upper body. Then, like dominoes, the remaining tables collapsed, one after another, the bottles crashing to the floor. Champagne exploded, shooting bullets of glass. Red and white wine spread everywhere, mixing with Somers's blood.

The man groaned and got to his hands and knees. Glass caught in his clothing tinkled as it hit the floor. His shirt and trousers were soaked with wine. He realized how lucky he had been. A few more inches, and he, too, would have been under the table, cut to pieces.

He stood up and hobbled across to Somers's body. Wine dripped over the critic's face and his legs were splayed at an odd angle, resting on an overturned table. A tiny moan escaped his lips.

Sarah was angry with herself for not having kept an eye on the time. She'd been eating chicken salad at a downtown bistro and had started making phone calls. One had led to another, and before she knew it, she was late. Careening round the corner of Peachtree Boulevard in the Jeep, she was startled to see a grim-faced policeman waving at her to keep moving.

The traffic slowed to a halt near the red-brick building. Police cars with flashing lights were parked everywhere, with ambulances, fire and rescue trucks and other emergency vehicles. Then she spotted a restless crowd at the front door, which appeared to be cordoned off with yellow tape. She inched past several network TV-station vans with satellite dishes and antennae. By some miracle, she found a parking space round the corner. Once her feet hit the ground, she broke into a sprint. Nearing the crowd she spotted Judy Russo.

"Hey, Judy," Sarah said, shocked to see streaks of black mascara zigzagging down the other woman's cheeks. "What on earth happened?"

"It's terrible, just terrible!" Judy sobbed. "Sam's dead," she gasped and collapsed into Sarah's arms.

Inside the red-brick building, two detectives with the Atlanta Police Department crouched over Sam Somers's body to view the neck wound. Around them, rivers of wine flowed through mountains of broken glass. Shards in all shades of green and brown covered everything in sight. Heaps of soggy cardboard boxes had disintegrated, disgorging their contents. Only a few folding tables had remained upright, their bottles intact. The rest had collapsed or tipped over, dumping everything on the floor. The brown curtain blocked the view of curious reporters.

The pungent fumes of wine mixed with blood made Lieutenant Bernie McDermott feel nauseous as he studied the corpse through silver-rimmed bifocals. A piece of glass protruded from the neck. "Hell of way to go." His voice carried the distinctive inflection of his home-town, Chicago, where he'd worked undercover before he'd tired of grey skies and black snow, and headed south. "What do we have so far, Watson?" he asked the man crouched beside him.

Careful not to soil the edge of his jacket, his sergeant stood up. "One dead celebrity. Outside, circling like vultures, we have every network TV crew in town, and breathing down our necks, we have one very anxious deputy chief."

"Nobody likes a smartass." McDermott ignored the creaking of his fifty-nine-year-old joints as he stood up to face Leroy Watson.

"Right, boss." Watson smiled, his eyes serene.

Sucking in his stomach, McDermott buttoned his grey

herringbone blazer and straightened his club tie. He was in better shape than most of the officers on the Atlanta Police Force, but time was taking its toll. His thirty-four-inch waist had recently blossomed to thirty-six: his fondness for Oreo cookies was responsible. If he wasn't careful, he'd end up with a bigger neck and have to buy new shirts, white, of course, from LL Bean. He did a slow rotation, searching every inch of the room, his shiny black shoes crunching on slivers of broken glass. "What do you make of it, Sergeant?"

Watson shrugged. "Could be an accident. Guy gets drunk, trips, loses his balance, crashes into a table. It collapses, bottles break, he falls. His artery's punctured by a broken bottle and he bleeds to death." To make his point, Watson gave one of the few upright tables a shove. The bottles clanked together, then one tipped. He caught it before it crashed to the floor.

"Good save, Sergeant," McDermott said drily.

Chapter Eleven

Rain pounded on the roof of his black rental car. The man with the buzz-cut had been there for hours, waiting for the Bennett woman to leave her office. In case she happened to glance outside, he'd angled his car so it was partially hidden behind a van, the only other vehicle in the parking lot. A jagged bolt of lightning was followed closely by rolling thunder. The rain was coming down in thick sheets. He flexed his muscular arms and yawned. He could be patient. He had nothing else to do on a wet night in Georgia.

Inside the office, Sarah sat at the computer, rereading Taylor Robbins's email. It was terse and to the point. The new labels would be used on all orders, effective immediately, and the cost of destroying the old labels would be billed to the US marketing budget.

She rubbed her eyes with her fingertips, then stared at the screen again, amazed by the woman's arrogance. The budget, equally funded by the Addison Group and Cornerstone Wine Imports, was earmarked exclusively for marketing and promotions. In effect, that meant her company would end up springing for half of the labels if she let Taylor get away with this. As for the payment extensions, the email made clear that none would be offered. Sarah didn't want to believe that Phillip Dwyer hadn't intervened on her behalf, but the proof was in front of her.

The telephone rang, interrupting her thoughts.

She swivelled away from the computer and picked up the receiver. "Cornerstone Wine Imports."

"Sarah? I've called everywhere looking for you. What on earth are you doing there on Saturday night?" Clare Robertson asked.

Her friend's voice lifted Sarah's mood. "I was just tidying up before my trip to Australia. Where are you?"

"In the car. We're on the way back from Tybee Island. We bought the house with the studio so I finally have a place to paint." She sounded happy. "And the hotel chain bought my abstract prints."

"Congratulations. But that means you'll be moving to Tybee Island and I'm not sure I like that. Then again, I have only myself to blame."

"You have my eternal gratitude for convincing me I could make a living selling my water-colours," Clare told her. "And it's only a five-hour drive to Tybee. I expect you to visit us often."

"You bet!" Sarah agreed, already beginning to feel unbearably sad at the thought of her friend being five hours away. Things would never be the same, but she didn't want to think about that now.

Clare's voice changed. "I found out this morning about Sam Somers and remembered you were supposed to judge wines at his event this week. Are you OK?"

Somers's death was still front-page news, although most of it was a rehash of the first accounts written by a reporter who'd snuck into the building and taken a few photos of the body before being forcibly removed. The police had yet to release an official statement other than to say that the wine writer's death was under investigation. "Well, Sam and I were never friends." She decided not to mention she'd been in the building on the day of his death.

"As I recall, he was rather unpleasant when you refused to go out with him."

"Something like that." Sarah was uncomfortable with the white lie she had perpetuated for several years. "Elliott was still alive then."

"How did that golf match with Jake go? You played at his club this time, right?"

"Well, he loves to bet and once we discovered we'd be in Adelaide the same weekend, we agreed the loser would pay for dinner and a night at the casino. I'm happy to report the evening's on him."

"So, the two of you will be in Adelaide at the same time?" Clare had a smile in her voice.

"Coincidence," Sarah said a little too quickly.

"Really?"

"Please, don't start that again."

"Oh, for heaven's sake, don't you think something else might be going on? Why not see where it takes you?"

"We've had this conversation before." Sarah hadn't forgotten how Jake had pulled away when she'd kissed his cheek a few nights ago. Had he thought Melissa might get the wrong impression? "It's absurd to think he's interested in me in that way."

"So it has crossed your mind!" Clare laughed. "It's all right to just let things happen once in a while. Anyway, have a wonderful trip and good luck with the Bluestone Cellars contract."

Sarah stood up and stretched. Deciding she was too

tired to reply to Taylor's email, she shut down the computer, then gathered the reports she'd prepared for her trip and stuffed them into her briefcase. She went to the window, lifted a blind and peered outside. It was pitch black and raining sideways. She punched in the alarm code, hurried out and locked the door. Rain pounded on her back as she sprinted to the Jeep. Once inside, she placed her briefcase on the passenger seat, then took a moment to run through her mental checklist. Satisfied she hadn't forgotten anything, she started the engine and drove off, unaware that a black car with its headlights turned off was following her.

On Holcomb Bridge Road, she stopped at the lights, beyond which was the southbound entry ramp to GA400. Within a quarter of a mile, the four-lane ramp would merge into one. In spite of the need for caution, drivers often jockeyed for position at high speed. Tonight, long lines of cars on both sides of the lights were waiting. The glare of their headlights, combined with the steadily increasing downpour, made it hard to see what lay ahead.

The lights turned green and all hell broke loose. Cars raced for the ramp, seemingly oblivious to the danger of the wet road. Sarah joined the mêlée, rain sheeting down. She flipped on her indicator, but no one slowed up to let her merge.

She tapped the horn lightly, trying to catch the attention of the person driving parallel to her, on the left, then glanced sideways. Headlights from behind lit the black car and its driver, a man with an old-fashioned buzz-cut. She honked once more, but he ignored her. Irritated, she speeded up, intending to slip into the small gap in front of him. He accelerated, closing the space. "Idiot!" she muttered, as she slowed down to move in behind him. The driver dropped his speed to stay parallel. What was wrong with him? She had to get over now! And so did the van in front of her!

The van raced ahead to squeeze into the tiny gap created when the black car slowed, but there wasn't enough room. The black car braked, causing a cacophony of horns. Skidding, the van wedged itself into the opening. There was a space behind it. Sarah floored the accelerator and swung over, narrowly clearing the black car's front bumper. "Back off!" she shouted, when the vehicle's lights flashed on and off, inches from her bumper. She pumped her brakes as a warning, but the car moved closer. She glanced in her wing mirror, then veered left into the next lane.

The headlights behind her created pools of wavy light, making it impossible to see clearly. Suddenly the black car was directly across from her and inching into her lane. Couldn't he see her? He was going to hit her!

Praying there was enough room, Sarah wrenched the steering-wheel and swung into a minuscule space in the next lane. A second later, there was another gap, so she kept moving left, crossing one lane after another, head throbbing. She'd lost the black car. Ahead, the traffic was densely packed and moving at a fierce pace. She eyed the rear-view mirror. A car was dodging the traffic, whipping across the lanes, coming up behind her fast. She watched anxiously as the black car sideswiped a white pickup truck. Both vehicles spun on the slippery road, then struck each other again and broke apart. A moment later, an orange van smashed into the pickup. Their bumpers locked and they slid sideways, spinning crazily. Then an eighteen-wheeler smashed into them, locking them in a three-way death-dance. The thunderous noise grew. There were flames. People were running from burning vehicles. A car flew through the air.

Sarah was appalled. Wanting to stop, she looked for a place to pull over, but to her left there was a narrow strip of pavement and the central concrete barrier. She'd have to cross to the right. She looked in the rear-view mirror and gasped. Another eighteen-wheeler, which must have ploughed through the mangled vehicles blocking the road, was heading straight for her.

She punched the accelerator to the floor. In front of her, a lake of water appeared, blocking the road. Suddenly twin sprays of water surged up, covering the side windows in a thick film. The Jeep hydroplaned, drifting left as waves hit the windscreen and streamed down it. It was as if she'd suddenly gone blind. She lost control. How far away was the central barrier? Where was the eighteen-wheeler?

In an instant, the water fell away from the windows. She screamed. The barrier was inches from her left bumper. Braced for impact, she tapped the brakes and whipped the steering-wheel in the direction of the skid. Miraculously, the tyres found purchase. The rear end missed the barrier by no more than six inches.

She looked into the rearview mirror again. The chrome grille of the eighteen-wheeler filled it. Sarah stamped on the accelerator and the Jeep lurched forwards sluggishly, sliding on the wet road. She'd never be able to outrun the truck. When her eyes went to the rear-view mirror once more, the eighteen-wheeler was veering dementedly to the left. She felt rather than heard the impact as it slammed into the barrier. With sparks flashing and tyres squealing, it rebounded off the concrete and jackknifed. It was going to hit her –

Chapter Twelve

Lieutenant Bernie McDermott's office, painted a dull blue-grey like the rest of Atlanta Police Headquarters, was tucked away off a corner of the squad room on the second floor. McDermott was on the telephone, the receiver resting on his hunched shoulder. "If I don't get that Somers autopsy report within the next hour, I'll come over there and cut you a new asshole." He hung up on the medical examiner. God, he hated Monday mornings.

McDermott stood up and stretched his aching back, then walked round his grey metal desk and the two dilapidated chairs that faced it to the windows on either side of the glass door. Few of the detectives' desks were occupied. He closed the blinds, returned to his swivel chair, and looked out into the bleak, dingy daylight.

The blinds rattled and McDermott swung round. The imposing figure of Sergeant Leroy Watson filled the doorway. He was wearing a filmy plum shirt, black trousers, and a black belt with a big silver buckle. "I have coffee and doughnuts." He held up a large white bag. "You interested?"

"Me? I never touch those things!" McDermott deadpanned, and enjoyed the consternation that creased his new sergeant's face. "On the other hand, if you have chocolate-covered doughnuts in that sack . . ."

"Need you ask?"

McDermott shoved aside the papers on his battered desk top. Watson took a box out of the bag, laid it on the desk and sat down opposite his boss. "What's with Somers's autopsy?"

"The report should be here momentarily." McDermott opened the box, helped himself to a chocolate-covered doughnut, placed it carefully on a napkin, then took the lid off the single polystyrene cup of coffee and added creamer and two sugars. "If I were a betting man, I'd wager that bastard was murdered. Too many things don't add up. Like the locked front door and the shard of glass that conveniently sliced his artery. Besides, plenty of people had it in for him."

"Such as?" Watson slicked back the straight hair he had inherited from a distant Cherokee relative, then took a sip of sweet tea from his ever-present plastic mug.

"The question might be who didn't." McDermott ate his doughnut in three large bites, then reached into the box and took another. "Sarah Bennett, the daughter of a good friend of mine, invited me to a wine-tasting a few years back. Her Bluestone Cellars Shiraz was the hit of the evening, but she was upset because Somers had just printed a review saying it tasted like a sweaty saddle or some such idiotic thing."

"What's shiraz?"

"A grape. Makes spicy red wine."

" It got a lousy rating. So what?" Specks of powdered sugar dropped on to Watson's shirt as he picked up a doughnut.

"So people followed Somers's advice like a bunch of sheep and her shiraz sales plummeted. Turns out Somers had asked her out and she'd said no. The review was payback. Bastard."

"You aren't saying she had a reason to kill him, are you, boss?"

"Jesus H. Christ, Watson! She's like family to me. Watch your goddamn mouth!"

"Sorry, boss." Watson brushed the sugar off his shirt. "So why did she put up with it? Why not expose him?"

"Believe me, I wanted to give the bastard some of his own back, but she said there was no way to prove he'd targeted her wines. Wine evaluation isn't an exact science – it's totally subjective – and all he'd have to say was that in his opinion an inferior wine got the review it deserved. If she tried to out him, the reviews would only get worse."

"But you said her business was already suffering." He sipped his tea. "How much worse could it get?"

"He could have taken her to court for defamation of character, slander, libel, you name it. Call her a vindictive bitch who was trying to discredit him because the reviews were hurting her business." McDermott sounded unnaturally calm. "I figured she probably wasn't the only one he went after so I checked him out. He didn't have a sheet but his father was a drunk, got pulled in a few times for punching his wife, but she wouldn't co-operate so the charges were dropped. After Sarah, Somers's game escalated. He'd get drunk at wine events and go after women suppliers, implying that if they didn't fuck him he'd trash their wines in his columns."

A languid grin spread across Watson's face. "Screw me or I'll screw your wines?"

"Put a lid on it, Sergeant," McDermott snapped. "Not one of the women I talked to would admit it but I suspect he blackmailed a few into bed."

Chapter Thirteen

From the front seat of Andrew Dunne's pickup truck, Sarah Bennett admired the beautiful panorama of the distant Barossa Ranges framing the valley's intricate patchwork of vineyards, wheatfields and date palms. The sun was out, the sky was bright and clear, and the breeze had picked up considerably since Dunne had collected her forty minutes ago from the Stamford Hotel. She opened the window wider and breathed in the fresh air. Dunne's truck wasn't the cleanest vehicle she'd ever ridden in.

Her eyes slid sideways. He was in black jeans and a stretched black cotton sweater, talking away, oblivious to her silence. Didn't he ever get tired of listening to himself? Perhaps that was unfair. Just now she wasn't exactly the best company.

The trip from Atlanta to Adelaide had taken thirty hours. On her arrival yesterday, she'd checked into the hotel, then raced to Victoria Square to catch the tram for Glenelg, where she'd strolled along the beach for hours. The sunshine had done wonders. That evening, she'd fallen asleep the moment her head hit the pillow. Even so, in the middle of the night, she'd woken up on the floor, screaming as the eighteen-wheeler rammed her vehicle into the barrier where it burst into flames, trapping her inside. A few long seconds had passed before she'd realized it was a nightmare. In reality, she'd escaped unscathed. Her mind had gone completely blank, as if someone else had taken control of it. When the truck had hit the barrier, she'd accelerated and shot across the highway, missing the vehicle by a narrow margin. However, five people had died in the forty-vehicle pile up.

"I need to stop at Southern Valley." Dunne's wrap-around shades shielded his eyes from the bright morning sun. "We'll only be a few minutes."

"Will that leave us with enough time at Bluestone Cellars?" Sarah asked, hoping he'd take the hint that she wasn't in the mood for a detour. It would be hard enough to stay focused on tasting wines all day.

"No worries." Dunne turned into the wide cobble-stone drive leading to the building. Magnificent date palms lined the path from the car park to the main entrance at the foot of a three-storey tower.

He parked and pulled up the handbrake. "Why don't you come inside? You can have a look at the competition. Macquarie Hawke's wines are made here."

"I understand he recently released his wines in Australia. Have you tasted them?" she asked. George's 'cat piss' popped into her mind.

"Yes. He entered them in a competition I was judging. They fitted in as well as a pickpocket would at a nudist camp." Dunne jumped out of the truck. "I don't get it. Why are they so popular in the US?"

Rolling her eyes, Sarah put on her cardigan, then climbed out of the truck and hitched up her jeans. "Have you read Somers's reviews? You'd think Hawke wrote them himself. The consumers are in love with the brand. Now Hawke's dumping the mom-and-pop distributors that got him started in favour of the power-house guys, throwing money at them like you wouldn't believe." She followed Dunne along the path. "How he's staying in business is anyone's guess."

"Yeah, well, Hawke plays by Rafferty's rules. At least with Somers dead we won't have to read any more drivel about his bloody awful wines. It evens things out." Dunne was whistling as they walked up the steps to the front door.

Sarah raised her eyebrows, but said nothing as he rang the bell. After a short time, the sound of a key in the lock was followed by a screech as one side of the tall, oak double doors opened.

A young woman with waist-length tawny hair stood before them. "Andrew! How're we going?"

"Julianna," Dunne beamed.

She stepped outside and kissed his lips. Then she noticed that someone was standing behind him and instantly assumed a demure smile. The transformation was not lost on Sarah.

After the introductions had been made, Julianna said, "Jason mentioned you might come in. I'll take you to his office."

They crossed the foyer, passing an antique table with a crystal vase of dead flowers, and went through a second set of double doors that opened on to a gloomy corridor. A cloud of sickly perfume wafted from Julianna, who giggled at everything Dunne said. Sarah was glad when they arrived at their destination, a darkened, glass-walled office in which a young man was staring intently at a computer monitor.

"Jason," Julianna called from the door. When she flicked on the lights, the young man jumped. "Andrew's here to re-taste SV556."

They went into the spacious office, which was decorated in a shade of oyster-shell grey. The young man's desk faced the window to the corridor, with a visitor's chair positioned next to it. Another desk was pushed against the wall to the left. There were piles of paper everywhere, on top of the desks, the filing cabinets, even on the floor. Across the room a door appeared to lead to another office. There were no outside windows.

"Sarah, meet Jason Findley, chief winemaker." Julianna pulled a set of keys out of her pocket. "He'll take you to one of our empty offices – it'll be more comfortable for you to wait there while they taste the wine." She handed the keys to Findley, then said, "Andrew, we'll catch up later."

Dunne watched appreciatively as she sashayed out of the office, then turned to Findley, who was half sitting on the edge of his desk. "Mate, you look knackered! How's it been going since Davis's death?"

The chief winemaker's shoulders sagged. "Everyone's finding it hard to deal with the way he died."

"Sarah can commiserate with you. Someone we all knew – or, at least, knew of – died recently in a freak accident – Sam Somers."

"Sam S-S-Somers is dead? Wh-what happened?" Jason stammered. He had paled visibly.

"The newspapers are saying he tripped and fell while he was getting ready for a wine competition," Sarah said. "A piece of glass pierced his carotid artery. Did you know him personally?"

"I met him once. He was in the country, visiting winemakers, of course, and came here the day before he went back to America. He and Davis tasted some of

Macquarie Hawke's wines." Hand shaking, Findley pushed his wire-rimmed glasses up his nose.

"Right," Dunne checked his watch, "we'd better get to it then. We're in something of a hurry."

"Of course." Findley led them through the second door into a passageway. A few yards on he ushered Dunne into the all-white tasting room. It reeked of disinfectant and Sarah had to hold her breath. How on earth would Dunne be able to taste wines? Thank God it wasn't her problem. Two open bottles and four glasses stood on a counter beside two tall stools. Dunne went in and sat down while Sarah and Findley continued along the corridor.

In front of them a door opened and a man in a brightly coloured shirt slipped out and began to walk towards them.

"Hi, Bluey, how's the cabernet?" Jason pushed up his glasses again. The lenses were smudged with fingerprints.

"Good," he responded, after a pause. "And who's this?"

"Sarah Bennett. She's with Andrew Dunne. I was showing her to the empty office while he re-tastes SV556." He made to move on, then stopped abruptly, mumbling, "Sarah, this is Bluey Kubaku, our new assistant winemaker."

"I just saw that cat of yours heading for the front of the building," Bluey remarked. "That OK – or do you want to fetch her?"

"Take Sarah to the office for me, will you? Here. You'll need these." Findley flung the keys at him and set off at a run.

Bluey shrugged. "Follow me, Ms Bennett." He walked to the next door along, unlocked it and held it open.

It was a spacious room with a high, beamed ceiling and a flatscreen computer monitor, flashing 'Davis Hart'. Uneasy suddenly, Sarah moved past the banks of black filing cabinets. The desk and the two armchairs facing it were covered with paper. What was it with these people? How could they work in such chaos?

"Please excuse the mess," Bluey said, coming up behind her. "We're in the process of shredding old files. Before I go, may I get you something to drink?"

"No, thank you." Sarah leaned against one of the armchairs. "But I'd like to ask you a question. Are you involved in making Macquarie Hawke's wines?"

A brief frown darted across Bluey's face. "No, that was Davis Hart's job. He did everything, down to selecting the final blend. Mr Hawke was adamant about that. Now, if you'll excuse me?"

After Bluey had left, Sarah wondered if she dared move the papers off one of the armchairs. At the top of one heap, a document indicated that tank SV888 held wine made of 63 per cent grenache and 37 per cent shiraz. The grenache, which was three years old, and the shiraz, which was two years old, came from the Riverina area. With neither grape type making up at 80 per cent of the blend, or more, by law it couldn't be called shiraz or grenache and would probably be used for blending. The elaborate signature at the bottom was Angus Kennedy's.

Deciding it was best to leave the papers alone, she went behind the desk and sat in Hart's black leather chair. Instantly she felt queasy: the last person to occupy that chair had died a violent death . . .

After the nightmare about the eighteen-wheeler, she'd been plunged straight into another from which she'd woken in a cold sweat. Elliott's death haunted her dreams – she was for ever arriving at the funeral she'd missed as the empty hearse left the crematorium car park. Now she was assailed again by grief, loss, and wondered for what must have been the thousandth time what he'd meant by the message he'd left on her recorder. If only she'd seen him one last time maybe she could accept he was dead, that it had all been over between them . . . A tear trickled down her cheek. She wiped it away, then took out her compact and powdered over the streak it had left in her makeup. This was ridiculous. She had to put Elliott's death behind her, try to forget the past.

Taking a deep breath, Sarah closed her compact and put it away. She looked at the paperwork stacked haphazardly on every inch of the desk. It never ends, even when you die. *Enough. Let it go. Get a grip.*

She read the document closest to her, perched at the top of a teetering pile. It was a 'statutory declaration', required by the government, guaranteeing that the wine being purchased by the Addison Group had been made in accordance with the standards set out by the National Health and Medical Research Council, Food Standards Code, and the Label Authentication Programme. The wine was 100 per cent cabernet sauvignon from McLaren Vale, cross-referenced to Southern Valley's tank records for SV556, signed by Jason Findley, chief winemaker. She sat up straighter. That was the wine Andrew Dunne was interested in buying.

From the corner of her eye, she saw a ginger blur, jumped, and twirled her chair to get out of its way, knocking her knee on the desk. "Damn!" she yelped, as a tortoiseshell cat skidded to a halt a few feet away and stared up at her. She reached out to stroke it but it skittered out of the door.

Sarah sighed and rubbed her knee, which was red and throbbing. There'd be a fine black bruise tomorrow, she mused. Turning back to the monitor, she saw that the screen saver was no longer running. She must have jarred the mouse when she hit her knee. For lack of anything better to do, she read the file on the screen. It was a record of SV556, composed of 60 per cent cabernet sauvignon, with remaining 40 per cent made up of chenin blanc and riesling, all from the Riverina viticultural area. She did a double-take. That couldn't be right. No one blended white with red grapes.

A noise outside the room startled her. A glance at the monitor confirmed that the screen saver was active again and when Julianna came in, Sarah was facing the door.

"Do you know where Andrew is?" the woman asked, stopping beside one of the armchairs.

"Isn't he with Jason Findley?" Sarah wondered why she was no longer smiling.

At that moment, Dunne came into the room with Findley. "Julianna! We've been looking everywhere for you," he exclaimed. "That McLaren Vale Cabernet's a real beaut! We'll take all of it."

"Great." Julianna rearranged her face into a smile. "I happen to have the paperwork right here." She went to the desk, picked up the statutory declaration for SV556 and handed it to him.

"You had me pegged!" Dunne laughed.

"It's such a great deal, I knew you wouldn't pass it up." Julianna cocked an eyebrow at him flirtatiously. "Why don't we go to my office so you can sign it off?"

After they'd left, Sarah sank back in the chair, her

mind in a whirl. She swivelled to face the monitor. Dunne had to see this. She was preparing to print the file, her fingers poised over the keyboard when she heard foot-steps. Before she could swing away from the screen someone came in. Had they seen her snooping? Now she turned, her face flushed with embarrassment.

"They've finished," Findley said. "I'll take you to Julianna's office."

"Fine." Sarah stood up, relieved he hadn't asked what she'd been doing.

He stepped aside to let her pass. "Take a left. Cut through the tasting room and my office, then up the stairs. It's quicker."

On the way into the hall, Sarah glanced back. Jason had bent to pick up a piece of paper from one of the armchairs.

"Oh, my God!" She had collided with a man who'd been hurrying down the corridor. "I'm so sorry. I didn't see you."

He was tall and silver-haired, with wide shoulders and a narrow waist but the pockmarks of adolescent acne marred his skin. "No worries." He gave her the once-over, obviously pleased with what he saw.

Findley came out of Davis Hart's office. "Mr Hawke! I didn't know you were back." His phone rang as he slid round them. He fumbled in his pocket, pulled it out, and flipped it open. "OK. I'll be right there." He closed it. "Sarah, I'm needed in the winery."

"No problem. I can find my way to Julianna's office. You go ahead," Sarah said, and watched him lope off.

"He needs to learn some manners," the other man observed. "Let me introduce myself. I'm Macquarie Hawke and you must be Sarah Bennett." He grasped her hands. "I ran into Andrew Dunne and he mentioned you were here. Your eyes are every bit as beautiful as I've heard. Blue-green, like the Aegean."

"Thank you." Hawke's hands were warm, yet when he stared into her eyes, she shivered. They were ice blue, with an Arctic chill.

"I've heard so much about you," Hawke went on, "that I feel I know you. Just a few weeks ago I visited Federated, our new Florida distributor. Donald Stoilas spoke highly of you – as did everyone else I met there." He grinned.

"I'm surprised you let your other Florida distributor go. They seemed to be doing such a good job for your brand," Sarah said, as his eyes searched hers. Federated was one of the first distributors she'd ever appointed. Recently, Stoilas had promised he wouldn't take on any Australian brand that would compete directly with Bluestone Cellars. Disappointment washed over her.

"They weren't getting many on-premise placements so we had to make a change," Hawke responded. "Luckily it was easy. All we had to do was re-file our state label approvals."

"Well, Florida is the exception, not the rule," Sarah said, grateful for once that the franchise laws in many states dictated that a supplier couldn't take a brand from a distributor without a major legal battle. That should slow Hawke up for a while.

"Sarah, you live in Atlanta," Hawke said. "What's the latest about Sam Somers's death? There's been speculation here that he died in suspicious circumstances because the Atlanta police haven't released a statement."

"Everything I've read points to an accident." The last thing she wanted was to exchange gossip with him about Somers. She checked her watch – and found her reason to get rid of him. "Now, if you'll excuse me, I really must find Andrew."

But Hawke, it seemed, wasn't ready to let her go. He continued to talk: "God, I'll miss that man. He was a great fan of our Coonawarra Shiraz. Did you know he awarded it a ninety-eight rating and best-buy? 'Nectar of the Gods' he called it. It was the highest score he'd ever given." He shook his head. "Too bad he never had a chance to taste our newest release. It's spectacular. He would have loved it."

Sarah raised her eyebrows. "I sampled some recently," she said, then wished she'd kept her mouth shut.

"What did you think of it?"

Again, 'cat piss' popped into her mind. She bit it back. "It wasn't what I'd been expecting."

Hawke seemed satisfied with her answer. "It's much spicier than any previous vintage."

But she wasn't prepared to let him go without drawing a little blood. "I should extend my condolences to you on Davis Hart's death. I understand he was responsible for making your wines."

She guessed Hawke would deny that Hart's death might affect his brand in any significant way. However, the truth was that winemakers were artists, each with a unique approach. Once a winemaker put his stamp on a brand, it was hard to duplicate it. Losing Hart could prove disastrous for Macquarie Hawke, since the taste, texture and quality of his wines were likely to vary when someone else took over.

"We were all devastated by Davis's death, especially Angus," Hawke replied soberly. "But the wines are made to my specifications and I do the final blending. They won't be affected."

"Really?" He had spoken evenly, but she could tell from the tightening of his lips that she'd made her point. And if he wanted to continue telling that tale, he'd better have Bluey and Findley on board or the press would get wind of it.

From behind someone grabbed her arm from behind, startling her. She snatched it away as Dunne's voice said, "I hate to take Sarah away from you, but we need to get going. I'll catch up with you later, Mac."

Hawke saluted Sarah. "I understand you'll be at WSWA. Come to our suite and taste some of our new releases."

She smiled. In your dreams, asshole.

At the other end of the winery, Julianna Porter headed for the operations area, to which she rarely ventured. She took a hard hat from a shelf by the door and placed it carefully on her head so that it didn't wreak havoc with her hair, then went through a set of double doors to the 'farm' of stainless-steel tanks that seemed to stretch for ever. If only people knew how unglamorous winemaking could be, she thought, avoiding a puddle. With all the hoses and machinery, this place looked the canning factory where she had worked on the assembly line. It was wet, noisy and smelt of must.

Ten minutes later, Julianna's dainty high-heeled shoes were soaked and her head ached with the pressure of the helmet. Finally she found Findley, talking to one of the workers. She butted in, "Jason, I can't find the blend profile for SV888. I left it in Davis's office. Do you know where it is?"

"Can't you see I'm busy? I'll be with you in a minute." He turned back to the worker who was clearly frantic.

"The temperature in the tank is way too high. The fermentation's stuck. We need you. Now," the man said.

"What's going on?" Julianna barked. "We've never had a stuck fermentation."

Findley continued to talk to the man as if she wasn't there, which incensed her. Nothing had gone right since Hart's death, and Findley wasn't capable of running this operation. Why didn't Angus Kennedy replace him before he did real damage? She'd acquired enough knowledge to be aware that bacterial infection was a dangerous possibility when fermentation got stuck. And once a wine was infected, it was almost impossible to save it.

"I'll be with you in a minute," Findley said, and the man left him. At last he turned to Julianna. "Don't worry, I can handle it. The cooling mechanism for the tank wasn't working properly. We'll get it going again." His words belied his anxious expression.

"You'd better, if you value your job," she answered. "Now, tell me where the blend profile for SV888 is."

"What's wrong with you? If you lost it, just print out another. Kennedy can sign it if you need it right now. I'm busy. I don't have time for this nonsense." With that, Findley walked away, leaving Julianna alone in the storage area.

Bluey moved further into the shadows of the tanks hoping his bright shirt wasn't visible. His face glistened with sweat as he watched Angus Kennedy appear out of nowhere and grab Julianna's arm. "You were supposed to shred it. Why the hell didn't you tell me it had gone missing?" His face was red with anger as he shouted over the roar of the machinery.

"Let go of me!" she snapped, and deliberately rubbed

her arm when he released it. "Last time I saw it, it was in Hart's office, on top of a pile of papers. When Andrew showed up with Sarah Bennett, I put her in there to wait while we finished up. After they'd left, I went back to shred it, but it wasn't there."

Chapter Fourteen

The early-afternoon sun beat down on the Bluestone Cellars Barossa Valley winery, and visitors awaiting the next guided tour moved into the shade. Some sought refuge beneath the covered veranda of the main building while others headed to the Cellar Door for a refreshing taste of chilled wine. A few stalwarts, drawn to the tinkling waters of the neo-classical fountain that graced the grand courtyard, formed a line, their shoes crunching on the white gravel.

Across from the fountain, the Misener homestead's brick façade was set off by shiny cucumber-green door and window shutters. Inside, to the left of the front door, was the family dining room, where the intricately carved spires of an antique sideboard soared to the ceiling. Dark wood framed the simple room's white walls, on which hung sepia photographs and daguerreotypes of the family, stretching back five generations.

Seated across from Andrew Dunne at the long narrow dining table, Sarah watched his eyes narrow to slits as he swished red wine in his mouth. To his right a watercolour, painted by a second-generation Misener in 1871, depicted the winery compound as viewed from the family mausoleum. Sarah was struck by its resemblance to present-day Barossa Valley. Seemingly time had stood still.

She picked up the heavy silver fork, emblazoned with the Bluestone Cellars crest, and stared at her half-finished roast pork with *spätzle*, the thick German noodles. The mouthwatering aroma should have sparked her appetite but she wasn't hungry. After spending the last several hours with Dunne, tasting the Bluestone Cellars new releases, she'd just screwed up the nerve to tell him about the file in Davis Hart's computer. His lips were compressed, showing his anger. She speared a piece of meat and put it into her mouth.

"Rubbish!" Dunne slammed down his glass on the white linen cloth. A few drops of red wine splashed out. "Complete and utter rubbish!"

Although it was moist and succulent, the meat stuck in Sarah's throat. She reached for a glass from the line-up of wines in front of her and gulped a few mouthfuls. "I'm simply telling you what I saw. According to the file, that wine isn't a hundred per cent cabernet sauvignon. It's not even close. Forty per cent of it is chenin blanc and riesling."

Dunne stood up. "Listen, Sarah. I've worked in the Barossa Valley since I was sixteen, when Angus Kennedy gave me my first job. His family's been making wine in the Barossa for more than a hundred and fifty years. Not only does he have an impeccable reputation, but also he's a good friend of mine. It's absurd even to contemplate that he'd try to trick me into buying cheap wine at an inflated price based on a file you saw in a computer!"

"Andrew, I haven't accused him of anything. For all I know, you're right. The file may well be a worksheet. But isn't it worth looking into?" Sarah watched Dunne as he stalked to the window, and drew aside the curtain. Outside, the courtyard was filled now with visitors who had finished their tour and were making their way to the Cellar Door, where they would sample wine and purchase mementoes. Around the fountain, the queue for the next tour was three deep and growing. A curious few wandered towards the family homestead.

Dunne let the curtain fall. "It seems like only yesterday I was the new Chief Winemaker for Bluestone Cellars and you'd just started Cornerstone Imports." He shrugged, releasing the tension in his shoulders, then returned to the table. "We had some good times, travelling around America flat out like a lizard drinking, promoting Bluestone Cellars."

Despite her anxiety, she couldn't help smiling at Dunne as he slid back into the heavy mahogany chair and rested his forearms on either side of his plate.

"We've known each other for a long time," Dunne went on, "so I'm saying this to you as a friend. You have a great imagination – it's what makes you such a marketing whiz – but it's working overtime here. Trust me, nothing illegal is going on at Southern Valley. As a favour to me, just drop it. OK?"

A polite cough silenced them. Gerry Marks was standing in the doorway.

That evening, Sarah hastened down the corridor of the Stamford Hotel, her eyes on the blue-and-gold carpet. She passed several room-service trays of dirty plates and left-overs before she checked the room number on a door. She still had a long way to go. Ahead, the corridor seemed to stretch endlessly into the distance. Suddenly uneasy, she pivoted round. No one was there.

She picked up her pace, her thoughts reverting to Andrew Dunne. He was probably right. It had to have been a worksheet. Who would be idiotic enough to think they'd get away with mixing cheap white grapes and cabernet sauvignon, then selling it as a premium wine? The Australian wine laws were among the toughest in the world. She felt foolish now for having mentioned it. Dunne had tasted the remaining wines with her in a wary truce, then asked an employee who lived in Adelaide to drop her at the hotel on his way home.

Glancing at her watch, she was surprised to see it was after ten thirty. She'd lost track of time, working on her notes in the hotel dining room after a steak and a baked potato with sour cream. She hoped it wouldn't keep her awake. Tomorrow was the first day of the contract meeting.

As she neared her room, Sarah took the key card from the outside pocket of her briefcase and swept it through the lock, which clicked open. She stepped inside and groped for the light switch with her left hand as the door closed behind her. Before she could flick it on, someone grabbed her right shoulder and hurled her to the floor. She landed heavily, the wind knocked out of her. Then she heard a metallic rasp, and a shaft of light struck her face. A tall man was silhouetted by the light in the corridor as he opened the door and raced through it. The door closed again and the room was black.

On wobbly legs, Sarah got up, blood roaring in her ears. She inched across to the door and turned on the lights. She gasped.

A category-five hurricane had swept the room. All the drawers had been yanked out and thrown on top of the clothes they'd once held. Her suitcase had been hurled across the room, its lining ripped to shreds, and her cabin bag had suffered a similar fate. The mattress had been stripped bare and tipped off its springs. The bedspread was on the floor, covered with feathers from pillows that had been torn apart. Her eyes flew to the desk beneath the window. Her notebook computer was there, seemingly untouched, but her manila folders had been upended, the contents scattered. She took a few minutes to gather herself, then grabbed the phone and dialled hotel security.

Early the next morning, Sarah was on the phone in the Stamford Hotel's elegant penthouse suite. Eventually she said goodbye to Inga Wismar, secretary to the Australian Wine Bureau, hung up and riffled through her briefcase for her diary. She opened it, flipped the pages to Monday and made a note that her meeting with Graham Blackwell, the marketing manager, had moved back an hour to nine o'clock. Yawning, she returned the diary to her briefcase, picked up the phone again and dialled a local number. When Jake Malone's voice came on the line, she brightened, but it was only a hotel voicemail. Disappointed, she left a brief message with her new room number and hung up, wondering where he was so early in the morning.

She stood up and went across the room to an invitingly plump maroon sofa, unbuttoned her jacket and sat down. She kicked off her shoes and put her feet up on the sturdy coffee-table. At three o'clock this morning, having given a statement to the police, she'd been moved to this luxurious two-bedroom suite on a floor with limited access. Ten minutes later, she'd crawled into bed, far too troubled to sleep.

Now she leaned back on the sofa and closed her eyes. How was she going to get through an entire day with

Taylor Robbins? If only Elliott were alive. He had been so much better equipped to deal with that woman than she was, with his uncanny ability to anticipate what people would do or say before they knew it themselves. It was an annoying trait in a husband but useful at times like this . . .

Sarah's eyes opened to bright sunshine streaming through the windows. She checked her Tissot watch, which had been an anniversary present from Elliott. Her meeting was at nine thirty and it was already a quarter past! She leaped off the sofa and raced into the bathroom.

The taxi dropped her in front of the Addison Group's offices on Wakefield Street at exactly half past nine. She went in through the thick glass doors and walked across the ultra-modern reception area, a sea of beige walls, carpet and chairs. It reminded her of the dentist's surgery where she'd recently had root-canal work. The dread she'd experienced that day welled once more in the pit of her stomach as she introduced herself to the young receptionist.

A few moments later, Sarah heard low thuds coming from the stairs to the executive offices, then she spotted chunky patent-leather shoes. She smiled when Taylor Robbins came into view, wearing an orange tunic that co-ordinated with newly dyed hair. She was holding a manila folder.

"Sarah. Good to see you." Taylor squared her shoulders as she came across the carpet. "Phillip will be joining us in a few minutes. Let's go into the conference room."

It was oak-panelled and dominated by a rectangular table surrounded by green leather armchairs. The walls were covered with award certificates, framed magazine articles and winery posters. A faint odour of stale wine lingered in the room, mingling with the scent of fresh coffee.

"We need to go over a few details before Phillip gets here." Taylor threw the folder on to the table and yanked out a chair. Her horsy face radiated ill-will.

"Is that fresh coffee I smell?" Sarah asked, silently cursing Dwyer for being late. Her gaze rested on the woman's wide-spaced eyes, smallish button nose and sallow skin. "I wouldn't mind a cup before we start."

Taylor's eyes flared. Then, with ill grace, she turned and beckoned. They entered a short passage to a tasting room, where mirrored cabinets filled with hundreds of wine bottles and trophies lined the walls. Sarah joined her at a bar-height counter. Three trays heaped with pastries had been laid out beside a stainless-steel coffee urn, along with ceramic mugs and plates marked with the Bluestone Cellars logo.

"We need to clear the air." Taylor picked up a plate and selected an almond Danish. "I was disappointed you felt it necessary to involve Phillip in the label changeover."

Sarah stared at the woman's scrawny back, then moved to the coffee. "Maybe I missed something, Taylor, but didn't he retain control of global repositioning? I thought we'd both be better off if he was kept in the loop about any proposed changes."

The china plate clattered as Taylor put it on the counter. She angled herself towards Sarah, who was filling a cup. "I'm responsible for thirty-two Bluestone Cellars importers around the world. I can't have them going directly to my boss every time they disagree with one of my decisions. I'm sure you understand. Anyway, to finish what I was saying, you misunderstood my plan for dealing with old labels." She folded her arms across her concave chest and glared.

Sarah focused on the urn's spigot. In a way, she felt sorry for Taylor, who was out of her league and didn't know it. How long would it take the Addison Group's upper management to realize that putting an inexperienced person in charge of an international brand might not be the best idea? Before or after she ruined Bluestone Cellars?

When the cup was full, she turned to the other woman and said, "Last I heard, you were going to write off the cost of destroying them to the US marketing budget." She blew on the coffee to cool it. "However, I'm afraid that isn't going to work. The budget is strictly for US promotions, like distributor sales incentives. Besides, all of the money currently in the account has been committed to pay for the promotional allowances to help our distributors sell through their old label inventory before the new stuff comes in. I'll need every cent to pay for those programmes."

Taylor shrugged, and went back to the counter for some coffee. "You'll accrue more money with the next container orders."

Sarah's hands were unsteady as she took a sip. "I'm afraid you're missing the point. No one has the authority to appropriate those funds for anything other than US promotions."

"I damn well can." Taylor clamped her mouth shut as a tall man with the physique of a dedicated bodybuilder strode in. She busied herself putting cream and sugar into her coffee, her pallid face colouring.

"G'day! It's been far too long since we've seen you!" Phillip Dwyer bent over to kiss Sarah's cheek. "How'd things go with Andrew?"

"Great." Sarah smiled, trying not to stare at him. He'd undergone a complete transformation since his promotion to upper management. His shaggy chestnut hair had been cut short and his previously full beard reduced to a neat goatee. Instead of his usual casual attire, he wore a midnight-blue jacket, a white shirt, open at the neck, and tan trousers. She barely recognized him. He'd always prided himself on not fitting into the corporate culture. "Some of the estate-bottled single-vineyard wines would be perfect for the US, provided you can allocate enough cases for us to justify bringing them in."

"That shouldn't be a problem." Dwyer's eyes slid to Taylor, whose complexion had resumed its normal colour. "Now, if you don't mind, Taylor and I have a few things to discuss. If you'd like to go ahead, we'll join you in the conference room shortly."

The sound of his voice reprimanding Taylor for having misappropriated the US marketing budget followed Sarah as she drifted into the conference room and sat down. Just another nail in the coffin of their relationship, she thought, glad that the contract renewal was merely a matter of updating the existing document with a Letter of Agreement confirming the annual sales targets and other relevant issues. She was counting on Dwyer to support her more realistic numbers against the outrageous quantities Taylor had proposed.

"Sorry to be so long." Dwyer came in, deposited his mug on the table and took a seat across from Sarah. Taylor had flopped into a chair at the head of the table.

"Bluestone Cellars will be covering the cost of destroying the old labels and the funds will go back into the US marketing budget. So, Taylor, it's your meeting. Let's get started."

Taylor faced Sarah. "Before we do, I'd like to clear up the confusion regarding the payment extensions you requested. I know you contacted Phillip about them. I'm sorry, but Corporate turned them down again."

Dwyer's head jerked round so fast that Sarah could have sworn she heard his vertebrae crack.

"I approved the extensions. Perhaps you didn't receive my memo." Dwyer's steely response resonated round the room.

"I did. So did Pym Noonan. He called me when he couldn't get in touch with you. The procedures have changed. He'd like you to call him immediately."

Sarah was stunned by the woman's insolence. Something was seriously wrong, and she had an inkling of what it was. The Addison Group's general manager, Paul Burnside, had been manoeuvred by the board of directors into appointing Noonan as his second in command. The latter's ruthless cost-cutting measures and focus on the bottom line were supposed to offset Burnside's more people-oriented management style. The widening rift between the two men was common knowledge. It appeared to Sarah that the payment extensions featured in their power struggle, pitting Burnside and Dwyer against Noonan and Taylor.

Dwyer stroked his goatee. "Let's move on to the contract."

Taylor's narrow shoulders lifted. "Corporate kicked it back on a wording issue. The attorneys promised to have it here this afternoon."

Sarah's stomach flip-flopped.

"I won't have anything delay signing the contract on Thursday." Dwyer said, his voice low and unnaturally steady. "Under the circumstances, I'd like you to babysit them until they produce both the contract and the Letter of Agreement. That means you'll have to be in Sydney first thing Monday morning to hand-deliver the instructions. If there are any hitches, contact me immediately and I'll take care of them. Understood?"

Taylor nodded, her face flaming.

Over the next few hours, Sarah began to think that Taylor was purposely sabotaging the meeting, exacting her revenge on Dwyer for countermanding her decision to pay for the old labels out of the US budget by disagreeing with everything he proposed. It was nearly four in the afternoon and they still hadn't established sales targets. More ominously, the preliminary contract hadn't arrived.

Chapter Fifteen

Sarah and Elliott left their suite at the Alexandra Hotel in Lyme Regis, and walked down to the Cobb, a stone jetty that curled into the sea. The beach had just come into view and it was a warm, sunny day. A rescue helicopter on a training exercise was hovering above the water. Suddenly she knew something terrible was about to happen. Elliott clutched his head and fell to the ground. In the distance, a bell rang insistently –

Sarah woke up screaming, her nightgown soaked with sweat. Her heart was pounding and it was several moments before she realized she was in the penthouse suite at the Stamford Hotel in Adelaide.

The telephone was ringing, which must have been what woke her, but she couldn't bring herself to answer it immediately. She hadn't yet let go of the dream. It stopped. Seconds later, it started again. The bedside clock's luminous dials showed it was six thirty. She pulled herself together and picked up the receiver. "Hello?"

"Good morning, Sarah. It's Phillip. Sorry to call so early, but I wanted to speak to you before I left."

Now Sarah was wide awake. "Does this have anything to do with the phone call you took at lunch yesterday?"

"Nothing gets past you, does it? Yes. I have to get back to Sydney, urgently. I'm sorry I won't be at the meeting today. Pym Noonan will be sitting in for me."

"Phillip, we're old friends – you can tell me the truth. Why is the company axeman chairing the meeting?"

Dwyer laughed. "He's a pussycat in disguise – besides, everything's under control. See you Thursday."

The afternoon sun shone brightly in an azure sky as Sarah left the hotel and headed for the Addison Group offices, which were only a few blocks away. For the meeting, she'd selected a sophisticated suit of tissue-thin wool gabardine in a buttery yellow with darker chevrons creating a subtle pattern. The feminine outfit was part of a plan to lure the notoriously chauvinistic Noonan into thinking she was easy prey, then catch him off-guard. The way things were going, any edge was worth pursuing.

When she'd read the preliminary contract, delivered to her hotel at eight that morning, she could no longer delude herself as to why Noonan was attending the meeting, which had been postponed until two this afternoon.

On entering the Addison Group's office at one forty-five, Sarah ignored the receptionist, veered left and went down the corridor to the conference room. As she approached the open door, she heard a ringing telephone and a low, gravelly voice said, "Stop her. I don't want her in here now."

"Hello." Sarah paused in the doorway. Taylor was seated near the centre of the conference table while Noonan stood to her right, facing the door, a telephone glued to his ear. Although she was not one to believe in auras, Sarah decided that Noonan's was so palpably brutal it was frightening, matched by his appearance: he had an enormous, misshapen nose and wiry grey hair that resembled steel wool. Although he was wearing a hand-tailored suit, he looked dishevelled, his tie askew. However, his stern expression relaxed as she swept into the room, smiling.

"Hello, Ms Bennett." He put the phone down. "Pleased to meet you. I'm Pym Noonan. Why don't you take a seat?" He waved at the chair across from him.

Sarah offered her hand, holding it out until he was forced to shake it. His own was clammy. She acknowledged Taylor with a curt nod, then sat in the chair Noonan had indicated.

"Now, Ms Bennett, I assume you've read through the contract and found everything satisfactory. We were pleased to offer you the same contractual terms as last time for representing Bluestone Cellars, the next great global brand in our portfolio."

With Noonan continuing to spout corporate bullshit, Sarah glanced at Taylor, whose refusal to meet her eyes answered one question. She knew about the new clause hidden in the contract. Gathering courage, Sarah concentrated on Noonan's nose. If Elliott were here, he would be questioning her sanity, but if she didn't execute her plan, chances were she'd lose her company anyway.

"Pym." She'd stopped him in his tracks. "Before it's too late, I'd like to review the contract. My company met the terms of the last one, obligating the Addison Group to renew them for another five years. However, I discovered a new clause that allows your company to break the contract, without cause, at sixty days' notice. It needs to be removed. Once that's done, I'd be happy to sign."

"Our attorneys insist it's included in all new contracts as a safeguard for everyone involved. If you read it carefully," he went on, condescending now, "you'll see it works in your favour too, since it gives you the same rights."

"My position is non-negotiable." Sarah clenched her teeth to stop her jaw quivering.

"I'm afraid there isn't anything I can do. It's company policy." Noonan sounded sincere. "I'm sorry."

"I'll leave you to think it over and be back at four." Sarah rose and walked out of the office.

On the street, she took several deep breaths, then set off to find somewhere to sit and wait. A café with a bright awning caught her eye and she discovered she was hungry. She went in and sat down at a table near the back. When the waiter appeared she ordered a pot of coffee and apple pie with chocolate ice cream, which arrived in record time.

Had she miscalculated in refusing to sign the contract? Most major Australian wineries were establishing their own import companies in the US and it was only logical to assume that the Addison Group would follow suit, but as far as she knew, they were a long way from doing so. In the meantime they needed a US importer. She was gambling that Noonan was smart enough to understand that calling her bluff might come at a high price.

For one thing, she had solid grounds for a lawsuit, based on the Addison Group's failure to meet the terms of the original contract. Although that wouldn't stop them appointing another US importer, they'd find it almost impossible to appoint a reputable one that was not already locked up by a competitor. And even if they achieved that, the hostile transition would undoubtedly result in a major loss of business, if not permanent damage, to Bluestone Cellars. Which was exactly what had happened two years ago when the Addison Group had switched US importers for one of their other brands. Presumably Noonan would have been told of the disaster when, despite assurances to contrary, the existing distributors terminated their agreement to represent the brand and sold off their inventory at rock-bottom prices, assuming the new importer would take it from them anyway. Afterwards, no decent importer would touch it. Sales plummeted and the Addison Group had been forced to pull the brand off the market.

Although she was confident that she'd correctly assessed their options, she had now seen Noonan at work and was beginning to have second thoughts. He might decide to let the Bluestone Cellars brand rot in hell rather than give in to her demands. It all depended on how much the Addison Group was willing to risk.

What bothered her most was Dwyer's role. He'd sworn the contract renewal was a formality. Had he been lying or had he been duped too? She'd considered calling him after she'd read the contract, but what was the point? Noonan would have his way regardless of Dwyer.

She was going in circles and getting nowhere. At four o'clock she'd know whether or not she still had a company because, without Bluestone Cellars, she'd have to close Cornerstone Imports.

The apple pie and ice-cream had made her sleepy. She put her elbows on the table and rested her head in her hands.

When the man sitting alone at a nearby table saw Sarah's eyes close, he stood up and sauntered past her as if he was on the way to the men's room. He was almost past when his hand snaked down to seize her briefcase.

It was after five when Sarah rushed into the Addison Group offices, wondering if she'd find everyone gone. "Are they still here?" she asked the receptionist,

The girl was on the phone and didn't look up. Sarah considered going down the hall, then thought better of it. Noonan probably wasn't there anyway.

The thief who'd snatched her briefcase had made it as far as the restaurant door when a man at a front table had lunged at him and ripped it out of his hands. The thief had hesitated, plainly considered fighting for it, then changed his mind when the man's two friends made a move on him. He had fled and no one had bothered to chase him. After that, she'd had to work hard to convince the restaurant manager not to call the police, explaining that she had to get back to her meeting.

The receptionist hung up. "Mr Noonan's waiting for you in the conference room."

He was standing beside the table, alone, once again talking on the telephone. Sarah entered and took a seat directly opposite him.

Eventually he disconnected his call. "Taylor left to catch a flight to Sydney and I'm on a tight schedule, so I'll keep this brief. You'll get your contract, without the clause you find objectionable. However, failure on your part to live up to any of part of the agreement, especially the sales targets, will result in the immediate revocation of your right to represent Bluestone Cellars. Now, if there's nothing else, I, too, have a flight to catch."

Chapter Sixteen

Friday afternoon, and Jake Malone was swatting at the flies that swarmed round his face and watching his golf ball veer into the rough on the eighteenth hole at Bottle Brush Creek, a few miles outside Adelaide. The insects might be driving him crazy, but it was no excuse for a poor tee shot, he thought. If he hadn't been playing with one of his major suppliers, he might have worn one of those wacky hats with lightweight balls attached to the brim by thin strings. Any head movement made them dance, keeping the flies at a distance.

"It's all yours." He stepped aside to let Stephen Randall, vice president of Oskar Hallgarten Vineyards, have the tee box.

Randall made a fast, slashing move with a driver and his ball hit a tree, then ricocheted into the middle of the fairway. "Rather be lucky than good any day." He chuckled, slinging the club into a lightweight bag strapped to a two-wheel trolley. Tucking his tropical-print shirt into the pea-green trousers that hung loosely on his wiry frame, he said, "By the way, the old man won't be coming to dinner tonight. He's feeling a bit off. They're considering bringing his surgery forward."

"I'm sorry to hear that." Jake said, concerned. He enjoyed time spent with the winery owner, who had a calming effect on Randall.

Jake found his ball in tall grass, took a penalty drop, then put his next shot on to the green close to the pin.

"Well done." Randall pulled a long iron from his bag. "Listen, son, I have a proposition that could make us both a lot of money, but it's confidential. Once I tell you about it, you won't discuss it with anyone. Agreed?"

Jake studied the gaunt face and the sharp set of the angular jaw. "I'm intrigued, but if it requires that much secrecy, I'm not sure I want to know about it."

"Believe me, you do, my friend." Randall slashed wildly at the ball. It flew into the bunker, short of the green. "Damn!" He dropped the club into his bag, grabbed the trolley and trotted away.

Jake wondered why the old man had appointed Randall, rather than his son Oskar the Sixth, as temporary president while he underwent a quadruple heart bypass. Randall was the last person Jake would have trusted with the company cheque book.

He was waiting for Jake to catch up. "What do you say?"

Jake hesitated. In the last few years, he'd made too many promises he'd lived to regret, but those had been personal and this was strictly business. "If it's above board, legal and doesn't involve putting my first-born up for adoption, tell me about it."

"Oskar Hallgarten is buying the worldwide rights to Macquarie Hawke." Randall said.

Jake stopped dead. "No kidding!"

"We want your company to be the US importer."

"B-but . . ." Jake stuttered, taken by surprise ". . . Southern Cross Traders is doing a tremendous job. Why not work with Melissa McNair? She's in place and it would reassure the existing Hawke distributors if you kept her on."

"Melissa has no say in the matter. Hawke owns Southern Cross and we opted out buying it in favour of having your company represent the brand."

"Whoa, wait a minute." Jake threw up his hands, shocked not only that Melissa didn't own the import company, as she'd led him to believe, but also at Randall's presumption. "I'm not sure we're in a position to do justice to a brand like Hawke's."

"Jake, my boy, this is the chance of a lifetime!" Randall began to walk, pulling his trolley. "Last year Hawke sold half a million cases. We plan to double that number in three years, with your company as importer. And that's just the beginning."

Jake trailed after him. "Why didn't the old man mention this on Thursday?"

"We weren't at liberty to divulge the details before our final offer was accepted. As of this morning, that document is in hand," Randall called over his shoulder.

"I thought the old man was adamant about purchasing tangible assets." Jake parked his trolley next to Randall's and pulled out a putter. "Hawke doesn't own a winery or a vineyard, does he?"

"The old man changed his mind." Randall was stone-faced as he searched for a particular club. "Mac's wines are made under contract at Southern Valley. Of course, when we take possession of the brand, they'll be made at our facilities. That's also confidential."

"Goes without saying," Jake responded automatically. Randall must have worked like the devil to convince the old man to buy Hawke's brand, then advised him Malone Brands International was already on board as the new importer or they would have bought the US import operation. Randall was a vindictive son-of-a-bitch. What would happen if he turned the brand down? He had to apply the brakes until he could make sense of it.

"We'll be announcing the acquisition of Macquarie Hawke and that your company is the new importer, at WSWA." Randall was watching him closely for a reaction.

Jake put on his best poker face. "That's only two weeks away. It doesn't give us enough time to evaluate the impact of including Hawke in our portfolio."

Face tight, Randall walked to the bunker with his sand wedge and putter. "The damned ball's embedded in the face."

Jake moved to the shade of a nearby tree as Randall entered the bunker and slashed at the ball, which flew across the green. He threw his club after it, then swore loudly.

Jake squatted, pretending to study his putt. Macquarie Hawke's sales exceeded those of every other start-up brand ever, in the above-ten-dollars-a-bottle category. The potential profits, even if sales remained flat, were enormous. But taking on the brand meant restructuring his company, creating a new sales division to keep his main suppliers happy and Hallgarten's sales on track. Was it worth the risk? Did the brand possess the staying power required to justify the changes once Hawke was out of the picture? Randall's putt missed the hole by three feet. His curses brought Jake back to the present. "Pick it up," he said. "I know you can make that one."

A few minutes later, they were sitting at a table on the clubhouse patio overlooking the eighteenth green.

An umbrella angled over the table provided some shade and the cold pints of West End bitter, a local brew, were refreshing.

"Getting back to Macquarie Hawke, I'm counting on you to come through for me." Randall swigged his beer. "I think you'll find your agreement to represent Hawke will be important to your company's future relationship with Oskar Hallgarten."

That was a threat if ever Jake had heard one.

Chapter Seventeen

Clare Robertson glanced at the wall clock in the yellow and white kitchen of her Duluth, Georgia, home, then returned to the spicy shrimp, green pepper and tomato dish she was preparing for dinner. It was just past five. Hank should be home in an hour or so, provided Atlanta's Friday traffic wasn't any worse than usual.

She set the gas burner to simmer, went to the refrigerator and selected a bottle of the Bluestone Cellars Chardonnay Sarah had dropped off a few weeks ago. She uncorked it, poured a glass and took a long, slow sip. As she had hoped, the flavours would complement the shrimps perfectly. Reluctantly she put the glass on the granite counter, then picked up the telephone and dialled.

"Hello?"

"Hi, Sarah. I hope I didn't call you too early for a Saturday morning."

"Hardly! I've been up for ages, getting ready for my big day at Cleland Park. Off to pet the kangaroos and koalas. How about you? Everything OK?"

Clare paused for a fraction of a second too long, "Fine. How are the contract negotiations going?" She listened as Sarah brought her up-to-date.

"So that's it," Sarah concluded. "No matter what Noonan tries, I'll sign that contract before I leave Australia."

"I'm sure you will." Clare responded. "When's your dinner with Jake?"

"Sunday night."

Clare didn't miss the note of warning in her friend's voice. She laughed. "I just wanted to say have a wonderful time – and remember it's OK to let things happen."

"Would you please stop telling me that?"

"You'll thank me later for reminding you." Clare replied sweetly. As she spoke, her eyes fell on the headline that blared at her from the *Atlanta Journal*, spread out on her kitchen counter. "Sarah, I hate to bother you when you're travelling, but I thought you should know there've been some disturbing developments. Atlanta Police think Sam Somers may have been murdered."

"Good God!"

"According to the newspaper, a piece of glass was pushed into his carotid artery to cover up a knife wound."

"Are there any suspects?"

"Not yet," Clare said. "By the way, I tried your cell first, but all I kept getting was your voicemail. When I called your office to get the hotel's number, Jim Barnes mentioned that Bernie McDermott had been there, looking for you."

"Did he say why?" Sarah asked.

"Only that it was something urgent to do with Somers's death," Clare said, troubled now. McDermott was a lieutenant in the Atlanta Police Department's homicide division and a good friend of Sarah's late father. "What's this about?"

"Don't worry. I'm sure it's just routine."

But Sarah's voice had faltered.

* * *

Later that morning, Sarah was sitting in the front row of a modest, twelve-seat bus winding its way up to Cleland Park, located in the Mount Lofty Ranges outside Adelaide. Its generous picture windows provided an all-too-perfect view of the sheer drop down the mountainside off the two-lane road's left shoulder, which was unprotected by guard rails. Ahead, vehicles clogged both lanes, coming to a virtual standstill as they encountered the treacherous twist known as the Devil's Elbow. Behind her, the two families taking up the remaining seats were having a hard time controlling their exuberant children.

"What a bloody idiot!" the bus driver exclaimed, his eyes directed at the rear-view mirror.

Sarah shifted round. A motorcyclist in black leather, his black helmet sporting a jagged red emblem, swerved over the centre line, his machine whining as he accelerated to pass a battered blue car that had tailgated the bus for miles. Her eyebrows rose almost into her hairline. Where did he think he was going? There was a two-second gap in the traffic before a truck barrelling down the mountain would reach them. The car's driver pounded on the horn, then ripped off his sunglasses and gestured rudely out of the window. Horrendous images of another pile-up appeared before Sarah's eyes as the motorcycle slid back into position behind the car, narrowly avoiding a collision.

As the bus drove on, Sarah's pulse slowed. She was entranced by the stunning scenery. All too soon, though, they were pulling into Cleland Park, followed by the car, the motorcycle and a few other vehicles. She alighted and made her way towards a cluster of low, dark buildings that blended into their surroundings.

Inside, she picked up a park brochure, then headed

for a counter that sold food for ducks, kangaroos and wombats. A little girl of seven was standing there, sucking in her lower lip to stop herself crying. She was wearing pink and white gingham shorts, a pink T-shirt, pink socks and white tennis shoes. Her hair was in a ponytail, tied with a pink ribbon.

"Hello. My name is Sarah." She knelt down and smiled. "What's yours?"

"Regina." The child's big blue eyes brimmed with tears. "A bad 'roo took my bag of food."

She was from England, that much Sarah could tell. "I'm sorry about that, honey. Where's your mother?"

"Feeding the 'roos." She was sobbing now. "I – I – was afraid she'd be cross with me so I came to buy another b-b-but I don't have any money."

"Tell you what. I'll buy you another bag and we'll ask the park rangers to help us find her. How does that sound?"

"OK," Regina said, and the tears stopped.

Sarah explained the situation to the woman behind the counter, who assured her they would find the mother. After she'd bought two bags of food, she handed one to Regina and they went to a bench next to the counter. Now that the little girl had recovered, she chatted away about everything under the sun, reminding Sarah of Jake's daughter, who was terribly grown-up for seven. Absorbed in the child's conversation, she was slow to notice that a man in sunglasses was observing Regina far too closely.

A uniformed park ranger and a young woman in her early thirties, dragging a small blond boy, rushed through the door. "Regina! I was so worried!" The woman scooped the little girl into her arms. "Promise you'll never do that again?"

Sarah accepted the mother's heartfelt thanks, then said goodbye to the little girl and headed for the park's northern quadrant. It was turning out to be a beautiful day and she was soon caught up in its tranquillity. The only disturbing note was that the man in the sunglasses appeared to be trailing her.

Sticking to the paved pathway, she spotted a gaggle of red kangaroos piled on top of each other in the shade of a large tree. A few people were feeding the smaller ones. The park brochure warned that kangaroos or, for that matter, any other animals, should not be surrounded. Kangaroos protected themselves in various ways, the most lethal being with the long, sharp claw on each back foot, which they used to disembowel their enemies. Sarah decided to keep going.

She glanced around to get her bearings and something moved behind her. The man in the sunglasses was bending to offer a kangaroo a handful of food. Startled, it leapt away. He was giving her the creeps, she thought, and set off briskly for the koalas.

Soon she spotted a thatched structure resembling a tree-house sprouting from a thirty-foot eucalyptus. She selected a spot well away from the three people standing at the surrounding railing and peered inside to where four koalas clung to branches under the roof. Heavy boots crunched on the gravel behind her.

"Cute little buggers," a man in black leather said. He spoke with a thick Australian accent.

"Yes," Sarah murmured, then backed away from the railing and went on along the path at a fast clip. She paused after a few hundred yards, took a map out of her handbag and pretended to study it. The man who'd spoken to her was heavy-set and held a black helmet with a jagged red bolt in his hand. He was the motorcyclist who'd almost caused the accident at the Devil's Elbow. She decided she was becoming paranoid and went on toward the dingoes. The pathway to their enclosure crossed a small stream and led to a small, wood-shingled building. Sarah looked back to make sure she hadn't been followed, then went inside. An exhibition told her that dingoes were somewhere between the size of a wolf and a jackal. They had sharp, pointed muzzles and oversized teeth. Carnivorous, they hunted kangaroos, wallabies and rabbits, but they would eat more or less anything, including insects, rats and vegetation.

She stepped outside, on to an elevated walkway made of wide wood planks, suspended fifteen feet above the ground. It overlooked a field enclosed by a steel mesh fence attached at intervals to vertical steel beams and horizontal bars. In the distance, two dingoes were asleep under a tree. Moving along, she came to a gate leading to a platform that jutted out over the enclosure. The gate was ajar. An open padlock hung from the latch.

Someone jostled her elbow and she felt a prick on the side of her neck. Whoever it was now pushed her from behind so that she was crushed against the railing. She screamed as her left arm was bent back and pulled up between her shoulder-blades, stretching the joint almost to breaking point. "Stop screaming or I'll slit your throat!" a man whispered, and pressed the point of the knife a little deeper.

The stench of his unwashed body engulfed her. His breath was hot on her neck. She started to shake.

"Keep still!" he hissed.

Sarah couldn't breathe.

"All I want is the paper you stole. Give it to me and

I'll let you go." He pulled the knife back. "Try anything funny and I'll slice you from ear to ear, then throw you to the bloody dingoes."

If she screamed, who would hear her? There hadn't been anyone behind her on the path and the dingo hut was deserted. The only park employees she'd seen were at the entrance, miles away from where she was now. She angled her eyes along the path.

"Bitch!" He pushed the knife harder into her throat, drawing blood this time. "Tell me where it is!"

"I – I –" Sarah stuttered, as blood trickled down her neck. What was he talking about? She hadn't stolen anything. Would he kill her when he found out she didn't have what he wanted? "It's in my bag!"

"I'll let go of your arm. You drop the bag. Try anything stupid and you're dead. Understand?"

Nodding, Sarah made a fist with her right hand and bent her elbow. The instant the man released her arm, the self-defence training on which Bernie McDermott had insisted took over. She slammed her elbow into his solar plexus. With a whoosh of air, the man doubled over in pain, but not before his knife had sliced through the strap of her bag. Acting on instinct, she twisted round, snatched it up and hit him squarely in the face. Its large brass buckle connected with the bridge of his nose.

He swore as he tottered backwards, his free hand going to his bloodied nose.

Sarah bolted for the gate to the platform. The man chased after her and lunged, slashing the back of her cotton jacket with the knife. He tripped on a loose plank and went down hard on his knees, dropping the knife, which hit the planks and spun out of reach.

Sarah threw her weight against the gate. It opened. She rushed on to the platform, ran to the end, and took a flying leap. Screaming, she flew through space, landing hard inside the dingo enclosure, smashing the side of her head on the ground. The man raced after her, stopping short at the end.

In the distance, a dingo howled. Its companion joined in.

Stunned, Sarah lay motionless, wondering if she'd broken something, afraid to move. At that moment, the dingoes' eerie cries broke into her consciousness. She tested her arms and legs, then rolled over and pushed herself on to her hands and knees. When she stood up, her head was swimming and she was overcome by dizziness.

She swung round and peered into the distance. The dingoes were on their feet, their eyes fixed on her. When they began to lope in her direction, she raced for the fence, the ground tilting beneath her. Looking up, she saw that the man had left the platform, but she had no idea where he'd gone. Grabbing the fence, she turned again. The dingoes were moving closer. She threw herself at the fence and began to climb, shoving her toes into the narrow diamonds in the fence as her fingers curled round the wire.

"Sarah! Sarah!"

Her eyes snapped towards the wooden building. The little girl she'd met earlier was leaning over the railing. Sarah groaned. "Regina, go back inside the building! Find your mother!"

"Sarah, the dogs!" Regina pointed to the now frenzied dingoes.

Twisting round, Sarah saw that they were no more

than two hundred yards away. When she turned back, the man was at the edge of the walkway, peering down at her, holding her bag. He opened the clasp and dumped the contents on to the planks. His menacing smile disappeared. "Bitch!" he roared. "Where is it?"

For a moment, Sarah thought he might climb down after her, but then he registered Regina's screams. Sarah dropped back to the ground and raced towards the wooden building. Regina's hands were laced in the metal fence as tears ran down her cheeks.

Sarah took a running leap and grasped the fence, forcing herself to hold on. It vibrated with every movement as she inched towards Regina, who was directly above her. A high-pitched scream pierced the air. Her eyes flew to the child as the man lifted her off the ground with one hand. As he backed away from the fence, he brandished the knife in the other. "Tell me where the paper is or I'll kill her." Blood from his nose splashed on to Regina, who hung over his arm like a rag doll.

"No! Oh, God, no!" Sarah shrieked, scrabbling at the fence. She had only a few feet to go. "Stop! I'll tell you where it is!"

At that moment, the dingoes hit the wire, which buckled, violently waving forward, then whipping back. Sarah hung on, her head swimming. She could almost feel the sharp teeth biting into her calf.

"Tell me now, bitch!" the man snarled.

The fence swayed with another dingo assault and Sarah lost her foothold. Now she was hanging on to the wire by her fingertips. Flashes of light appeared before her eyes and she despaired. Finally, when she felt she couldn't hold on any longer, her toes found purchase. She risked glancing up. Regina was kicking the man, screaming and crying, trying to wriggle away. The pink ribbon slid off her ponytail and drifted on to the wooden planks.

In a burst of strength, Sarah crabbed up the fence and slung one leg over the top. For a split second she was balanced precariously, hoisting the other leg over. In that instant, the dingoes charged and the fence rebounded. Sarah lost her balance. A hand slipped and she began to fall back towards the dingoes.

Chapter Eighteen

It was Sunday evening, but Southern Valley winery was running full tilt, the night crew stretching the machinery to its limits. A lone man stood by the entrance to the offices, a wrench in his right hand. Silently, he opened the door and slipped through. The motion detector blinked red as he glided past, but the alarm remained silent.

Faint night lights illuminated the murky corridor and adrenalin coursed through his veins as he peered round a corner. The hall was empty. The only sounds were the heavy thudding of his heart and the far-away hum of machinery.

Stopping at the next intersection, he craned his head round another corner. A sliver of light from an open door snaked across the floor and up the opposite wall. He heard clicking, raised the wrench to shoulder height and approached the door. His heart skipped a beat as he peered inside. Someone was at Davis Hart's computer, typing furiously. The contrast between the light from the computer screen and the darkness of the office made it difficult to see who it was. Wrench raised, muscles tensed, he ran towards the figure, ready to strike.

"Bloody hell!"

"Jason!" The man dropped the wrench, which hit the floor with a clang.

"Bloody hell!" Findley repeated, glaring at Bluey. "You could have killed me!"

"I heard the alarm being turned off and thought someone had broken in." Bluey picked up the wrench and pointed it at him. "Next time, let me know when you're planning a late-night visit. What are you doing here anyway? You should be at home, getting some rest."

"I couldn't sleep." Findley stood up, rubbed his bloodshot eyes, then made a clumsy attempt to block Bluey's view of the screen. "I came in to get some work done."

"It might be easier if you had some light." Bluey went to the door and flicked the switch. Findley had half turned towards the computer, one hand on the keyboard. Davis Hart's name gyrated across the monitor. A few filing cabinets drawers were open and the desk was covered with manila folders. Bluey tilted his head to read the tabs. A chill shot through him. "I'm sorry if I scared you," he said. "I'm a little on edge tonight."

Findley came round to the front of the desk and eyed him. "Why? What's going on?"

"You remember Sam Somers? The wine writer?"

"Of course." Findley's eyebrows rose over the top of his glasses. "He died recently. Some sort of freak accident."

"The police are now saying he was murdered. And he was here tasting wines with Davis not so long ago. Now they're both gone." Bluey headed for the door. "I need to get back to the winery and you need to go home. You look like hell."

As the door closed, Findley collapsed into the black-leather chair. A blur of ginger caught his eye. He reached over and lifted Pauline on to his lap, stroking her absently. She began to purr.

"How could I have been so bloody stupid?" he

murmured to the cat. "I never questioned a damn thing. The inconsistencies after the bottling line was put in? The problems with the statutory declarations? The sales invoices? No worries, all bookkeeping adjustments. I signed everything – so I'll take the fall."

Pauline jumped to the floor and ran under the desk. Findley gathered the manila folders and went to the filing cabinets. Contacting the authorities now would land him in jail. Destroying the trail of paperwork that implicated him was all but impossible. He'd have to act as if nothing was wrong until he could get out of this place.

The stack of manila folders he'd rested on an open drawer slipped and tumbled to the floor, spewing paper. Findley's shoulders shook with silent sobs.

Chapter Nineteen

The expansive windows of the Jolley Boathouse provided Jake Malone with a magnificent view of the River Torrens, its rippling waters alight with the crimson rays of the evening sun. His eyes drifted inside the restaurant, decorated in a nautical style with a knotted pine floor. Everywhere he looked, tables were filling with families enjoying Sunday evening, reminding him of how much he missed his daughter.

He drained the glass of Bluestone Cellars fino sherry. It was austere and biting, one of Sarah's favourites. The glass he'd ordered for her remained untouched. He checked his watch for the hundredth time. It was nearly eight. Where the hell was she? The question resonated in his brain, dredging up fragments of long-buried memories.

One night seven years ago. His first dinner out with Marissa after Cassie's birth. A call from work to tell her he was running late. Her anger at being left alone with the baby. Keeping his father's lung cancer a secret from everyone, including his wife and mother. The apprehension when his wife didn't show up at the restaurant. His collapse after discovering her body in the twisted wreckage of her car, a block from their home . . .

Jake leaped to his feet, colliding with his waitress. "I have to leave. Here's some money for the drinks." He pulled out his wallet. "Keep the change."

She smiled, about to say something, when a woman with emerald eyes came up beside them. She wore a striking green dress and strappy high-heeled shoes. Her auburn hair hung in soft waves to her shoulders. The waitress pocketed the money and retreated.

"Jake Malone, you weren't about to welsh on your bet, were you?" Sarah sensed her lame attempt at humour had fallen flat when he whipped round to face her. Her eyes followed the waitress. Jake's wife had been blonde. "I hope I didn't interrupt anything."

"Interrupt?" Jake's voice was filled with indignation as he returned his wallet to his breast pocket. "You're an hour late! I was coming to look for you."

"I left you a message. I guess you didn't get it." She bit her lip. The last thing she wanted was upset to Jake, especially since he habitually assumed that every minor annoyance was the forerunner of horror.

"I'm sorry. I'm doing it again, aren't I? It's just that you're almost never late. Let's sit down and order some dinner, OK?"

Sarah nodded, and her hair fell away from her neck, revealing a flesh-coloured plaster.

He was pulling out a chair for her when he noticed it. "What happened to your throat?"

She didn't answer straight away, wanting to make light of it but knowing that with Jake she couldn't: they'd always been honest with each other. "There's no easy way to tell you this. Yesterday, at Cleland Park, a man held a knife to me and threatened to kill me. Jake, don't look like that! I'm fine. It's just a scratch."

He let go of the chair, came round to her and enveloped her in a tight embrace. She was shaking a little. "Why didn't you call me?" he asked. It came out more forcefully than he'd intended.

"Please, Jake." She pulled back to look him in the eye. "I knew you'd be upset. That's why I waited till now to tell you. I'm fine, really I am, but a little girl was involved too. That was the worst thing. She was terrified."

"I don't know what I'd do if anything happened to you. Or Cassie," He touched her cheek, then released her. "Tell me what happened – from the beginning."

"I need to sit down." She sank into a chair facing the river, and waited for her heart to slow. The smell of the dingo enclosure seemed to hover around her, and she could still feel the point of the knife as it pierced her skin.

Jake sat down beside her, reaching for one of her hands. It was icy. He leaned forward and picked up her glass of sherry. "Here. Have some of this. Take your time."

Sarah sipped some, then told him everything, from the moment the tour bus had left for Cleland Park to the point when a ranger had shown up. "The man dropped Regina and took off." Sarah shuddered. "She's fine, but they're keeping her in the hospital overnight until she's over the fright."

"Did they get the bastard?" Jake asked

"The rangers searched for hours, then the police arrived, but he was long gone." She shook her head. "I spent all afternoon looking through mug shots but it was useless. He never took off his shades."

Jake rubbed her hands. "This is crazy. I should take you back to your hotel. We can talk there. Order room service maybe."

"Do you really think I'd let you off the hook that easily?" She pulled her hands away to tuck a stray hair behind her ear and grimaced. Her body felt as if it had been used as a punch-bag.

"I don't think you should push yourself. Really. Let's go back."

"I'm staying," she said.

They reached for the wine list at the same time, then fell into their regular routine, debating whose wine to order, his Oscar Hallgarten or her Bluestone Cellars, both content to pretend that all was well.

"I'm having barramundi. The Bluestone Cellars Sauvignon Blanc would be perfect with it," Sarah said, relieved to see Jake's dazzling smile. It reminded her of his mother, an aristocrat whose family had lived in Atlanta for four generations. With elegant features, a straight nose and sensuous lips, he was every bit as handsome as Anna was beautiful, but his brilliant blue eyes and dark lashes had come straight from his Irish grandfather, founder of Malone Brands International.

After the waiter had poured the Bluestone Cellars Sauvignon Blanc and taken their order, they spent a good fifteen minutes talking about the attack. Finally, Sarah said, "And I swear to God, the detective assigned to my case could be a Bernie McDermott clone, but more intense – if that's possible. His name's Danny Doolan. Another good Irish cop. He was fixated on the paper the man was after. If he asked me one question about it, he asked me a thousand. But neither one of us could figure it out."

"Maybe it was a case of mistaken identity."

Sarah took a sip of wine. The waiter was serving the barramundi, a mild yet flavourful local fish. "That's what Doolan thought at first, but once I told him about the other things that had happened, he changed his mind."

Jake put down his fork. "What other things?"

Sarah described the ransack of her hotel room and the attempt to steal her briefcase. "He believes the incidents are related, but I don't see how, with three different men involved."

"It's not safe for you to stay here. You do know that, don't you? You should go home. Tomorrow," he said.

"Damn it, Jake. Cornerstone won't survive without Bluestone Cellars, and you know it," Sarah spluttered. She decided not to tell him that Detective Doolan had recommended exactly the same thing. "I can't leave without signing the contract."

"Then I'm not leaving either." He folded his arms and stared at her defiantly. A vein pulsed at his temple.

"Yes, you are. Cassie needs her daddy and you have a business to run," Sarah said. "I'll be with people every second until I get the contract signed on Thursday. I'll be fine."

"Sarah, you are one of the most stubborn people I know. At least think about it," Jake pleaded. "Let's run through it again. Has anything else out of the ordinary happened since you arrived in Australia that you haven't told me about?"

Immediately the file in Davis Hart's computer sprang to Sarah's mind. She believed Andrew Dunne: it had been a worksheet. That was the only logical explanation. It had had nothing to do with the attack on her. She hadn't told the police for the same reason. "Nothing I can think of," she responded, then steered the conversation elsewhere. But his question lingered in her mind.

Half an hour later, a giant pavlova and two coffees were delivered to their table. Sarah dug into the meringue filled with tropical fruit and cream, and handed a plateful to Jake. He rewarded her with a smile and she envied his ability to let things go. She'd remained on edge, distracted by something that tugged at the edge of her memory.

Chapter Twenty

Lieutenant Bernie McDermott checked the clock on the high-tech stove in his Peachtree Hills condominium. It was seven o'clock on Sunday morning, so approximately nine on Sunday evening in Adelaide. Maybe he could catch Sarah at her hotel. He'd call as soon as he finished dinner, then try to catch up on some sleep. Yeah, right. Even if he had time, there was no way he'd get any shut-eye until Somers's case was solved. He might as well get used to sandpaper eyes and shooting back pains.

He went into the pantry and was greeted by wire shelves filled with canned soup, salted snacks, Oreo cookies, Hershey's Kisses, a few cases of beer and an assortment of wine, courtesy of Sarah. He loved this condo. It had been completely renovated by its former owner, an Atlanta chef, so the kitchen was a work of art, all black appliances and wood cabinets. The gas stove had six burners and an oven big enough to roast three turkeys at once. The refrigerator was the largest he'd ever seen in a private home. And the black marble countertops were the last word in elegance and style.

He grabbed a package of Oreos, then returned to the stove to check the cheese on toast, which was browning and bubbling in the pan nicely. On the next burner, tomato soup simmered in a heavy aluminium pot. There was just enough time to make dessert. He ripped open the Oreos, took some out, dropped them one by one into a tall glass, poured the last of a carton of milk over them and put it into the refrigerator.

He returned to the stove, flipped the cheese on toast into a thick blue bowl and poured tomato soup over it. Then he sat on a bar stool at the kitchen counter. He was savouring the first bite when his phone rang. "Not now!" McDermott groaned. He drank some beer, grabbed the phone and flipped it open. "Hello!"

"Boss, it's Watson. We've had a break in the Somers case. Traced his phone to a woman on the south side. I just got a call. She rolled on her boyfriend. Name's Wicky Riley. Says he was bragging about killing Somers. She swears he's holed up in a house off Camp Creek Parkway. I've got to get moving."

Sergeant Leroy Watson threw a lightweight black jacket over a shirt the colour of fresh raspberries, then ran down the steps of Atlanta Police Headquarters to his unmarked car. He jumped in, gunned the engine and drove out on to the road. Fifteen minutes later he reached the dilapidated house off Camp Creek Parkway as the uniforms were preparing to go in after the occupant.

Watson pulled his car to a halt next to a group of squad cars. The house wasn't far from Atlanta airport, aeroplane noise a part of gritty everyday life. The front door opened. An emaciated man with dirty salt-and-pepper hair emerged, wearing a loose black jacket and jeans. Shoving his hands into deep pockets, he walked towards the officers, who were crouched behind their car doors, guns drawn on the man they presumed to be Wicky Riley. Watson stripped off his jacket and removed the gun from his shoulder holster. He opened his car door quietly, and crouched, poking his head up for a better view.

"I'm out, man, I'm out," the man shouted, prancing towards the street as if he were high.

"Stop right there!" the officer in charge roared. "Let's see those hands. Raise 'em up high, motherfucker!"

Weaving from side to side, the man stopped, swaying gently, mumbling to himself. Snot dripped from his nose on to the ground, but he didn't bring his hands out of his pockets to wipe it away. "OK, OK! Don't shoot!" he called. Then he pulled something out of a pocket.

"Gun! Gun! Motherfucker has a gun!" someone shouted, as the man aimed at Watson's bright shirt and pulled the trigger, getting off a clean shot.

Chapter Twenty-one

The twinkling lights scattered around the ceiling of the Adelaide casino muted the gold-flocked wallpaper and patterned carpet. The smell of spilled whisky and stale bodies permeated the air. The canned music in the background was punctuated by the sound of slot-machine arms being pulled. Occasionally ringing bells and coins dropping into metal trays inspired the capacity crowd to cheer the lucky gambler who'd hit the jackpot. Yells of delight and groans of despair rose above the din: at the Two Up game, sixteen players gathered around a circular mahogany bar to live or die on the toss of two coins.

"I don't why I let you talk me into this." Jake stood beside the last two vacant spots at the Two Up game. "How do we know the man who attacked you didn't follow us here?"

"With the entire Adelaide police force looking for him? I don't think so. Come on, Jake, be a sport." Sarah slid on to the bar stool and ordered diet Coke from a waitress.

"Fine. This covers our golf bet. Knock yourself out." Jake handed Sarah the equivalent of fifty US dollars in Australian currency and sat down beside her. "By the way, I demand a rematch."

"No worries." Sarah laughed, pressing a palm to the pain in her ribs. A woman was leaving the area enclosed by the circular bar and the two men running the game remained inside. They were looking for the next player.

"Hey, spinner, come on in!" One pointed at Jake.

He shook his head. "I'll just watch."

"Come on, mate. We'll show you how it's done. Come on in, spinner!"

"Jake," she whispered. "There are security people everywhere, watching everyone. And you saw all the video cameras. Please. Go ahead. It looks fun."

Jake took off his jacket, handed it to her and entered the circle through a gap in the bar. Sarah noticed that most of the women players' eyes followed him appreciatively – and, indeed, he looked so handsome and youthful in the cobalt shirt, which intensified the blue of his eyes, but she could see weariness in his tense shoulders. Perhaps she should have listened to him and gone back to the hotel, but she felt safe here.

"Heads or tails, mate?" the "boxer" asked.

"Heads," Jake replied. The gamblers round the packed bar were debating whether or not a first-timer could get the job done.

The boxer gave Jake an eight-inch wooden paddle with a rectangle of green felt at the end. "This is the kip. I'll put the two coins on the end, one heads up, the other tails up. Throw them in the air by moving your arm straight up and flipping your wrist to make them spin." The boxer demonstrated with the kip, minus the coins. "Like twirling a door knob, cobber. Land both coins heads up three times, and you're a winner. Head 'em up, spinner!"

On the outskirts of the throng, a man in a brown windbreaker and white polo shirt scratched his eyebrow, then pushed his way towards Sarah Bennett. His fingers twitched in his jacket pocket and curled round a switchblade.

Jake sent the coins twirling into the air. They landed side by side, heads up. Looking pleased, he glanced at Sarah.

Sarah gave him a thumbs-up. Her tokens were on the H, for heads, on the pad in front of her where bets were placed. Every position at the bar had one. The crowd pressed closer to the players, wanting to snatch the first open position. Normal conversation became impossible. Everyone was hooting and hollering, copious amounts of alcohol fuelling the noise. Caught up in the excitement, Sarah rested her elbows on the bar. She didn't notice the unusual pressure on her back until it was too late. All at once, she couldn't move and something sharp was poking into her. She struggled against it, but she was trapped. The sharp object took on definition. Now the knife stabbed into her. Twisting to one side, she screamed for help, but no one heard her.

"Stop pushing or I'll have you thrown out, sir!" a man with an Australian accent shouted near her ear.

Instantly, the pressure was gone and Sarah spun round to find herself face to face with a short, fat man. He appeared mortified. She slumped against the bar. She'd met the gaming manager during a brief visit to the casino on the day of her arrival. "Oh., Ray. It's you."

"Things get a bit rough sometimes. Are you all right?" He sucked in his gut.

"Yes, of course. I'm a little jumpy, that's all," she said, glimpsing the metal clasp on his clipboard. To think she'd mistaken it for a knife!

Ray wiped sweat from his upper lip. "I was hoping I'd see you again. I'd like to talk to you about a friend of mine, Davis Hart. He died recently, in a plane crash – he was here the night before he died. Some of the things he told me were disturbing. He was chief winemaker for Southern Valley, and since you're in the wine business . . ."

The rest of Ray's sentence was lost as Jake prepared for another throw. He flashed Sarah a smile, which disappeared almost immediately. He rushed his last throw, but the coins still landed heads up, winning the game. Sarah watched him return to her. He seemed anxious but all he said was, "I think I've had enough. How about you?"

She introduced him to the gaming manager, then said, "I'd like to talk to Ray for a few minutes, if you want to take another turn."

After a boxer had cashed her chips, she folded Jake's jacket over her arm and followed Ray, who used his bulk to part the crowd. They sat down at a table with a reserved sign. A waiter appeared instantly. Ray ordered coffee with extra cream, while Sarah settled for another diet Coke.

Ray raised his voice over the hubbub. "I was filling in for a Two Up inspector when Davis arrived that night. He'd had a fair bit to drink." He paused, then cleared his throat. "Actually, he was very drunk. He was complaining about Southern Valley's owner, Angus Kennedy, cutting corners. He kept mumbling something about varietals and blends. Varietal's just a fancy word for grapes, right?"

"Yes." Sarah thought of the file in Hart's computer.

"I got the impression there'd been a serious problem,

something he was going to report to Karl-somebody. You have any idea who that might be?"

Sarah's attention was diverted momentarily by a man in a brown windbreaker wandering aimlessly among the tables in their vicinity. She didn't like the look of him and followed his progress until he was out of sight. "I'm sorry, Ray. Did he mention Karl's last name?"

"No, he didn't. He also kept on about Macquarie Hawke. He said some day someone would see the red dot and then it would be all over. Does that make sense to you?"

Sarah frowned. "No."

"One last thing. He was upset about an argument he'd had with a guy called Somers about Macquarie Hawke. Davis made all Hawke's wines." Ray was sweating. "I don't suppose you know who Somers is?"

Later that evening, the lights in the Stamford Hotel's Sky Lounge were low, the music soft and Jake was holding her close. They were dancing in a small circle to avoid the other couples on the crowded floor. Sarah felt as if she was in a dream, listening to a trio of musicians, their lead singer crooning an old fifties ballad. Jake caressed the back of her neck as they swayed in time to the music. His body seemed to radiate heat. Elliott had never felt like this. Sarah opened her eyes. It wasn't a dream.

She willed herself to break away. Instead, she moved closer, pressing against Jake. He was hard. What was wrong with him? At forty-two, she was much too old for this.

"You smell delicious." Jake's lips touched her ear.

"Time to go," she whispered. His hand was almost burning the skin on her back through the thin fabric of her dress.

Jake slowed, and kissed her. "Please. Don't say anything," he murmured, when he paused, and kissed her again.

At five o'clock the next morning, Sarah woke in her hotel room, the covers on the king-size bed tucked under her chin. Had she been dreaming or had Jake been in bed with her? She threw back the covers and picked up the pillow beside her. It smelled of him. He'd insisted on accompanying her to the suite, for her safety, he'd said, then invited himself in for a nightcap. After pouring a glass of tawny port, he'd made himself comfortable on the sofa. She'd started pacing, confused, wanting to know if they were still friends, and if they were, what had he been doing, kissing her like that? When he'd refused to discuss it, claiming they were tired, she'd asked him to leave.

Assuming he'd find his way out, she'd thrown herself on to the bed. All sorts of disparate images were whirling through her mind at a dizzying rate – the traffic accident, the smell of the man who'd attacked her in Cleland Park, Regina kicking him, Pym Noonan's face, Davis Hart's name flashing across the computer screen, the man stealing her briefcase, Jake's body pressed against hers . . . and Elliott's icy calm on the day he left for England. "Goddamn you, Elliott!" she'd cried, pounding the pillow. She'd felt the bed tremble, rolled over and found Jake sitting beside her, concern etched on his face. "Goddamn you too, Jake Malone." Jake had lain down beside her and gathered her into his arms. They'd fallen asleep, his front to her back. She had no idea when he'd left.

It was too early to get up, but she did anyway and took off her green dress. She put on her dressing gown and went into the kitchen to make coffee.

Chapter Twenty-two

Raindrops splattered the windscreen of Sergeant Leroy Watson's unmarked police car as he pulled into the Atlanta Police Department's car park. He unfolded himself from the cramped car, stretched his arms over his head, and shook out his legs. The traffic had been backed up for miles and it would only get worse. Heavy thunderstorms, with the possibility of tornadoes, had been forecast. At the moment, the sky was a sickly greenish-yellow.

Inside the building, Watson loped up the stairs, carrying his container of sweet tea and a thick manila folder. Striding down the centre aisle, past a few detectives filling in reports, he was blasted by the tantalizing scent of pepperoni pizza. Ravenously hungry, he stifled a groan of disappointment at the sight of an empty box sticking out of a bin. At his desk, he took off his black windbreaker and draped it over the chair. Tucking the folder under his arm, he grabbed his tea and went to Lieutenant Bernie McDermott's office.

"I don't fucking care. The man drew his gun. End of story," McDermott growled, the phone tucked between shoulder and chin as he plucked at something on the sleeve of his camel-hair jacket. "The body's at the morgue now. No, it wasn't Wicky Riley. That's your goddamn problem. It's why you get paid the big bucks!" He slammed the phone down. "Sergeant, get the fuck in here."

Watson lowered himself into one of the chairs facing McDermott's dingy grey desk. Balancing the manila folder on his knees, he gulped some tea, then put it on the floor. From his shirt pocket, he removed a dilapidated leather notebook, then looked at his boss. McDermott was giving him the evil eye.

"OK, Sergeant. What did you find at the house?" McDermott snapped.

"Somers's laptop." Watson said, a smile tweaking the outer corners of his lips. "I had the tech print out copies of the emails between Somers and his attorney. Seems our victim was tired of sharing the big bucks from the *Newsday* column and the Peachtree International Wine Festival. He was going to give Peter Vine the old heave-ho, right after this year's event. According to the attorney, Somers wouldn't owe him a dime. Vine had no contract, no agreement, no nothing."

"Doesn't mean a damn thing unless Vine knew about it." McDermott leaned back in his prehistoric government-issue chair. It protested with a screech. His back was killing him, sending waves of acute, stabbing pain down his legs. Once Watson left, he was going to eat the entire bag of Oreos in his desk drawer. Maybe get some milk from the machine in the canteen to go with them.

Watson's eyes brimmed with enthusiasm as a bolt of lightning bleached the industrial-blue office walls. He raised his voice against the thunder, "I went back through the judges' statements. One afternoon Peter Vine showed up to run the competition while Somers went home to get his patio door replaced after the burglary. Somers gave Vine his laptop – and get this! He didn't password protect his files! There's no doubt in my mind what Vine was doing behind the curtain, and it wasn't figuring out how to run the wine competition . . ."

As Watson continued, McDermott spun round to face the Peachtree Street window. A bolt of lightning struck so close that the hair on his arms prickled. Ominous clouds hovered over Atlanta's skyline. The thunder sounded like cannon fire. When the sergeant had concluded his theory, McDermott pushed up his glasses and rubbed his eyes. Without turning, he said, "Pick Vine up for a friendly chat. Shake his cage. Let's see what happens."

The minute Watson's enormous frame dipped to clear the door frame on his way out, McDermott's hand went for the desk drawer, but the phone rang. "Damn it," he muttered, then picked up the receiver. "McDermott," he barked.

Chapter Twenty-three

"Hey, Uncle Bernie." Sarah sensed she'd caught him at a bad time. Pushing back her desk chair, she stood up and peered out of the window of her Stamford Hotel suite. North Terrace Street was bustling with traffic. "I just wanted to let you know I got your message. Could we set up a time to talk tomorrow? I'm a little short on time this morning."

"I'm fine," McDermott growled. "How are you?"

"I'm sorry," she said. "What's up?"

"I assume you know Sam Somers was murdered?" His voice had softened.

"Oh, God, Bernie, I know I should have stayed to talk to the detectives, but Sam was alive when I left the building."

"Jesus H. Christ! You were inside the building?" McDermott asked. "Tell me everything that happened, from the moment you arrived until the moment you left."

Sarah went over how she'd arrived early and heard Somers arguing, first with Melissa McNair, then with someone else. "When I got to the curtain, I saw a man rushing out of the back door. Sam was fine. I left just after that, around eleven forty-five, and went to a diner for a bite to eat."

"Did you recognize the man?"

"I only saw him from the back"

"That's not what I asked."

She took a deep breath. "It might have been Peter Vine, but I'm not absolutely sure."

There was a long pause. "The body was found at one o'clock. It's possible the murderer was in the building, waiting until you'd left to kill Somers. I'm glad you're in Australia. You'll be safer there."

The angry throbbing behind her eyes intensified. "If only that were true."

"What do you mean?"

"It's nothing," Sarah said. There was a crackling on the telephone line from McDermott's end, then what sounded like thunder. "Listen, I have to go. I can't be late for my meeting."

"Oh no you don't!" He'd raised his voice. "I promised your father I'd watch out for you. Don't make me into a liar."

Sarah ran her fingertips over the knot at the back of her neck as she relayed the events of the last few days, concluding with the attack at Cleland. "I have to get my Bluestone Cellars contract signed. Besides, you said I was safer here, so don't even try to convince me to come home."

"Only if you agree to let a friend of mine in the Sydney Police Department arrange protection for you. You may have heard me mention his name, Sebastian O'Connor. I met him in Northwest Traffic School. He's a detective superintendent now. Promise me you'll do everything he says. No questions asked."

"This is one time I'll be happy to follow instructions," Sarah said.

"I don't know if O'Connor will be able to get someone to you tonight, so be extra careful," McDermott cautioned. "More likely he'll pick you up in Sydney tomorrow morning. I'll have him call you. Now, I know there's something you're not telling me. Spit it out."

Even as a little girl, she'd never been able to get anything past Uncle Bernie. "There's one thing. The day after I arrived Andrew Dunne and I stopped at the Southern Valley Winery on the way to Bluestone Cellars. I saw something in Davis Hart's computer."

"You're fading. I can't hear you. Sarah? Are you there?"

"Mixing red and white grapes," Sarah continued, a little surprised that McDermott wasn't interrupting with questions. "Andrew thinks it was just a worksheet. I suppose he should know. Uncle Bernie? Are you there? Can you hear me?"

The phone went dead. McDermott slammed down the receiver. He stood up slowly and hobbled to the window, fighting the pain in his legs. Atlanta's skyline had disappeared. The storm had knocked out all power, plunging the city into a total blackout.

Chapter Twenty-four

On Monday morning at eight o'clock sharp, Angus Kennedy staggered into his office on Southern Valley's second floor. He threw on the overhead lights and viewed the room with distaste. It was stuffed with Edwardian antiques, courtesy of his wife, Beatrice. The amount of money she'd spent was shocking, the dark oak panelling as oppressive as their marriage. He had a sudden vision of his wife, her face contorted in a sneer, mocking him, calling him a loser. She was the boss, she owned the winery and she loved rubbing his nose in it. Soon he'd have enough money to buy his own winery. That was the day he'd serve her with the divorce papers he'd already had drawn up.

Kennedy paused at the mirror, fogged with age, which hung on the wall next to his desk. Who was that old man staring back at him? The silver streaks were encroaching in his chestnut hair at an alarming rate. He began to pace back and forth in front of the desk, its leather top worn by generations of English aristocrats.

The shrill ring of his private line startled him. He went to the desk and picked up the receiver. "Kennedy." His voice trembled noticeably.

"Hello, Angus. I got your message." The man sounded as though he was in a wind tunnel. "What can I do for you?"

"It's about bloody time you called! Did you get it?"

"Relax, mate. We'll have it in hand soon."

"You don't understand, do you?" Kennedy's stomach turned. "It's not your signature on that damned paper! There's nothing to tie you to it."

"I told you, we're in this together," the other man purred.

"The hell we are!" Kennedy lifted his head as a heavy scent wafted into the room. The door to his office was ajar. He covered the receiver with his hand. "Is that you, Julianna?"

As she came in and sashayed towards him, he wondered if she'd been listening to his conversation, but her face was expressionless as she approached. A movement in the corridor caught his eye – Bluey's bright shirt. He pointed to a manila folder, "File that and make sure you close the door on your way out."

The lift at the Stamford Hotel reached the lobby. Sarah waited until the last passenger had departed, then wheeled her bulky suitcase across the threshold. As the others rushed away, she came to a standstill. The lobby resembled an obstacle course littered with mounds of baggage and its owners. Sarah turned around to the mirrored wall directly behind her, slung the strap of her briefcase over one shoulder and straightened the lapels of her black Gianni jacket. It was two hundred yards to the North Terrace Street exit and the safety of a taxi. Sooner or later she'd have to walk through the lobby. At least she didn't need to check out – the management had taken care of her bill in recompense for the intruder.

After a fortifying deep breath, she straightened her shoulders and stared once more into the mirror. A man in a faded, olive jacket was making his way through the crowd. He lifted his head, revealing feverish eyes framed by bushy black brows. Fear struck her. She had to escape. But she was trapped by the bank of lifts and the mirrored wall. The only way out was through the lobby.

A ping announced the impending arrival of a lift. The man was pushing his way through the crowd, holding something by his side. A knife?

With a sigh, the lift doors parted. A single man got out. She stepped in and jabbed the button for the penthouse. The doors didn't budge. Of course! She needed a key, but it was somewhere in the bottom of her briefcase. She mashed another floor number at random, then pressed 'door close' until her finger hurt. Her sigh of relief as they slid shut became to a gasp of horror as hairy fingers thrust themselves into the almost non-existent space between them. The hand gained purchase, inching the doors apart. When a sliver of olive sleeve appeared, she swung her briefcase at the fingers, hard. There was a bellow and they disappeared. The doors closed.

Ten minutes later, Sarah was in the back seat of a taxi parked outside the hotel's service entrance. The security guard who'd escorted her there rapped on the boot after he had loaded her suitcase in it. She gave the driver an address, then asked him to step on it. She was in a hurry.

He gunned the engine and drove away, narrowly missing a heavy-set man on a colossal black motorcycle. Encased in black leather, the man was holding a black helmet with a red diagonal strip on his lap. Sarah frowned and twisted to look out of the back windscreen. Before he jammed on his helmet, she saw his face. It was the same guy who'd spoken to her at the koala pen. She faced the front, visualizing the journey to Cleland Park as the bus had approached the Devil's Elbow, the motorcyclist attempting to pass the battered blue car tailgating the bus. In a show of anger, the driver had whipped off his sunglasses, revealing bushy black eyebrows. Later, he'd attacked her and that poor little girl at Cleland Park.

Her hand flew to the plaster on her throat. Those eyebrows. He was following her, waiting for the perfect opportunity to kill her. He'd been in the casino last night, wearing a windbreaker, and in the hotel lobby this morning, in the olive jacket. She turned in her seat: out of the back windscreen, the motorcycle was weaving through the traffic, pursuing the taxi.

At the Australian Wine Bureau's temporary headquarters, Inga Wismar was struggling to move the chenille sofa and club chair around her cubby-hole. Finally she left them against the wall across from her desk, where at least they were out of the way. As she returned to her desk and sat down, a woman in an elegant black trouser suit was dragging a large suitcase toward her. She looked haggard and pale.

"Good morning. My name is Sarah Bennett." She stopped in front of the receptionist's desk. The taxi driver had been convinced he'd lost the motorcyclist, but she wasn't so sure. "I have an appointment at nine o'clock with Graham Blackwell."

"Right. I'm Inga. We talked on the telephone," she responded with a smile, her hand moving towards the telephone as it began to ring. "He should be here shortly. Why don't you leave your suitcase over there by the sofa? I'll show you to the upstairs conference room in just a moment."

Sarah wedged her suitcase between the sofa and the wall. Then, straightening, she found herself facing two men who had obviously been enjoying a view of her backside. She groaned silently.

"Sarah, good to see you again!" Macquarie Hawke took her hand and air-kissed it with a flourish. "I read about your ordeal in the newspapers. How dreadful it must have been." He let go and stepped away, eyes raking her body. They came to rest on her bandage. "I understand the man escaped. Do the police have any leads yet? "

"I really can't discuss that." Sarah was careful to hide her dislike behind a neutral expression. She moved backwards, colliding with the arm of the sofa.

"I have the greatest respect for our police, but if I were you, I'd head for home before something else happens." Hawke's pale blue eyes never left her face. "Oh, forgive me. Have you met Stephen Randall? Vice president of Oskar Hallgarten?"

Maybe she was over sensitive, but Hawke had sounded oddly menacing. She turned to Randall.

"Hello, Sarah." His hands hung loosely at his sides. "I understand from our importer, Jake Malone, that you live in Atlanta. He's in Adelaide this week, but I guess you already know that."

His smirk made her wonder briefly if he and Jake had been talking about her. She dismissed the idea. Jake would never discuss his personal life with a business associate.

A door opened behind her and a big-chested man emerged from an office. In a way, he resembled the Silesians in the sepia family photos at Bluestone Cellars, although his silvery hair was cut short, military fashion. He strode towards the group beside the reception desk.

"Karl, how are you?" Hawke clapped him on the back, then introduced him to Sarah as the Australian Wine Bureau's general manger.

Karl Kingsley appraised her politely. "To what do we owe the pleasure of your company, Miss Bennett?"

Everyone was startled when Inga spoke up, "If you recall, Mr Kingsley, she has an appointment with Mr Blackwell this morning."

Sarah caught the contemptuous glance Kingsley cast at the woman and wondered what she'd done to merit it. "I need to make a call before my meeting. Is there a telephone I can use?"

"Inga, will show you to the conference room," Kingsley told her. "You'll find one in there."

"I was about to make some coffee anyway," Inga said. "Please follow me."

Kingsley walked across the lobby with Randall and Hawke, passing the long mahogany bar. When they reached the stairs, he said, "Andrew Dunne and the owner of Smyth and Hawthorne Vineyards should be here soon. Go ahead and get set up. I'll join you in a few minutes."

When Inga reappeared, he bellowed, "Where the hell is Blackwell?"

"I imagine he's on his way," Inga said, her face reddening.

"You advised him that his meeting with Ms Bennett had been moved to nine o'clock, didn't you?" Kingsley snapped.

Inga cocked her head. "You insisted on giving him that message yourself."

His voice hardened. "That's your job, not mine. Can't you get anything right?"

Upstairs in the cramped conference room, carved out of a low-ceilinged attic, Sarah heard Kingsley berating Inga. She closed the door against the tirade, then sat down and placed a call to Detective Danny Doolan. Ten minutes later, she hung up. The light on the line she'd been using didn't go out immediately.

She wandered to the window, which overlooked the car park, and lifted the dusty blinds. A cherry-red Rolls Royce convertible caught her eye. Fleetingly she thought of Elliott. He'd always dreamed of owning a Rolls. In that instant, the door opened and Inga came in, carrying a coffee pot and cups on a tray.

"Sorry this took so long." She put it down. "Ms Bennett, I'm sorry, but there's been a mix-up regarding the time of your appointment. It's possible Mr Blackwell thinks it's still at ten o'clock. I've left a message on his phone to find out if he can get here any earlier."

"Please, call me Sarah. And don't worry, I can always discuss my business with Mr Blackwell on the telephone," she said, observing the younger woman closely. In a pretty lilac suit, she was like a flower that would curl up and die at a withering glance. It must be hell to deal with a boss like Kingsley. "I couldn't help overhearing Mr Kingsley talking to you. Just between you and me, I think he was completely out of line."

"He's under a lot of pressure," Inga explained, risking a glance at her. "And being a single mother with two small boys, I can't afford to lose my job so I put up with his moods."

"I understand," Sarah said, sensing Inga was about to lose her composure. "Good jobs are hard to find." She paused. "Is something wrong with your telephone? The light on the line I used stayed on after I hung up."

"As far as I know, it's fine. But we have do have several new wine inspectors here today. It's possible someone punched it by accident," Inga said, then excused herself, promising to return once she'd heard from Blackwell.

Sarah sat down at the conference table, facing the door to the hall. The coffee smelled good, so she poured herself a cup. As she sipped it, she wondered if someone had listened to her conversation with Doolan. So what if they had? No one in this building could have been involved in the attack. Her mind wandered back to last night and Jake playing Two Up at the casino. Then Ray was telling her about his conversation with Davis Hart. She was forgetting something important . . . She racked her brain. Think! Suddenly it came to her. Davis Hart had telephoned someone named Karl to discuss the problems at Southern Valley. That was Kingsley's first name.

Inga poked her head round the door. "Sarah, are you OK?"

"What? Oh, yes, I'm fine."

"Are you sure? I hate to say this, but your face is white." She came in and sat down across the table. "I hope you don't mind me bringing this up, but I admire you for carrying on with business after what you went through at Cleland Park. I know it's not easy. My ex-husband attacked me once. With a butcher's knife. You think you'll never get over it, but you will, I promise."

Sarah studied her with fresh eyes. Earlier, Inga's self-confidence and inner strength hadn't been apparent. "I can't even imagine how difficult that must have been for you, especially with two little boys, but you've obviously come out the other side just fine. How did you get past it?"

"Put one foot in front of the other, just like you're doing now. When you get home, find a support group. They'll help you through it. One day you'll wake up and it won't be the first thing on your mind. But it will always be part of your life. It never goes away entirely."

"Thank you." Sarah glanced at her watch. "I wish I could stay. I'd like to talk with you some more, but I have another appointment at ten thirty. Now, would you mind telling Graham Blackwell to expect a call from me later this week? I sent him a list of Western Australian wineries and want his opinion on their ability to service the US market."

"Of course. Is there anything else I can do for you?"

Sarah stood up, but made no move to leave. "I need some information, but I'd rather Mr Kingsley didn't know I was asking. If that's a problem for you, I'll understand."

"I've only been here a few weeks, so I may not be able to help, but I'll try."

"It's a long story, but I'd like to know about a telephone call Mr Kingsley received within the last four weeks from the chief winemaker of a Barossa Valley bulk producer," she said. "I don't want to get you into trouble, but this might be really important. That call should have resulted in an investigation, but when I was at the winery it seemed like business as usual. If what I suspect is true, it could damage the reputation of the entire Australian wine industry." And especially Bluestone Cellars, she added silently, thinking of Andrew Dunne blending the bulk wine he purchased from Southern Valley into a variety of Bluestone Cellars products, something almost all the big wineries did on a regular basis.

"I can't discuss it," Inga said dejectedly. "It wouldn't be right."

Although Inga hadn't actually confirmed the call, Sarah had her answer. She'd guessed correctly. Hart had called Inga's boss.

The door knob rattled and Inga jumped. A second later, Karl Kingsley entered the conference room.

Chapter Twenty-five

Blackwell arrived at the Australian Wine Bureau offices at a quarter to ten and ran straight into Karl Kingsley, who was standing by the lobby wine bar.

"Where have you been? You had a nine o'clock appointment with Sarah Bennett. She's already come and gone." Kingsley frowned. "The least you could have done was to call and let us know you'd be late."

"There must have been a mix-up," Blackwell said, not sure why he bothered to defend himself. Kingsley was always right, at least in his own mind. Besides, he didn't have time this morning to listen to his boss rant and rave. He took off up the stairs, calling back over his shoulder, "I'll look into it."

He walked past the conference room and went into a cluttered office the size of a linen closet. He flung himself into his chair, and a moment later Inga Wismar appeared in the doorway. "Mr Kingsley was supposed to tell you that Sarah Bennett had agreed to meet you at nine o'clock. But I should have known better. Next time I'll call you back one way or the other." She shook her head, sat in a chair across from him and stared at the floor.

"Don't worry about it. It's not your fault." She was flustered about something, wringing her hands. He wondered why. "Something else is bothering you, isn't it?"

After a few seconds, she said, "Two weeks ago, Davis Hart called Kingsley and told him something illegal was going on at Southern Valley. He hasn't done anything about it. If he finds out I told you, he'll fire me."

"I'll do my best, but if it's as serious as it sounds, that might not be possible. I may need you to confirm that the conversation took place. Tell me about it."

Inga explained how she'd accidentally listened in on a number of calls, including Hart's. Uncrossing her legs, she leaned forward, "After they hung up, the light stayed on. I think someone else was on the line, but I have no idea who it was."

Blackwell put his hands behind his head, elbows in the air, and leaned back in his chair. "Why bring this up now?"

"I wasn't sure what the procedures were until this week," Inga faltered. "Then today Sarah asked me about it."

Blackwell sat upright as she explained what had happened. "Worst of all, I think Kingsley overheard us talking," she ended.

"If he had, you'd know it by now," Blackwell reassured her.

Some time before noon, Blackwell went down to the lobby and nudged open the tasting-room door. Andrew Dunne and Nathan Smyth were swirling, sipping, and spitting. As far as he could tell, they were almost finished. He left them to it and tiptoed across the lobby to the room where Stephen Randall and Macquarie Hawke were working. He peered in, and was relieved to find it empty. They must have taken a break – three-quarters of the way down the line of bottles, labels hidden beneath white cones, the glasses were clean. He slipped into the room and closed the door.

He went immediately to the untasted wines, lifted a cone and checked the label. He replaced the cone and repeated the process until he came to the last bottle, a Macquarie Hawke Coonawarra Shiraz with a red dot on the label. He set it aside, took a duplicate bottle without the red dot out of his briefcase and put it into the line-up.

Chapter Twenty-six

Thirty minutes north-east of Adelaide, the never-ending stream of small towns had changed to a more rural landscape of dun-coloured, rolling hills dotted with green patches of vines, the beginning of the Barossa Valley. Traffic was light for a Monday afternoon. The weather was clear, if breezy, not a cloud in the sky.

The Kawasaki's powerful engine surged as the motorcyclist, in black leather, closed in on Sarah Bennett's tomato-red rental car less than half a mile ahead. Despite the taxi driver's efforts, he hadn't lost her in Adelaide and wasn't about to now. He glanced into his rear-view mirror and was startled to find a battered blue car on his tail. He slowed down and waved it past. Instead, it accelerated and rammed his rear bumper. The Kawasaki swung wildly, fishtailing from side to side. It struck the first in a long line of orange cones, positioned on the hard shoulder, which bounced off the handlebars and smashed into his face.

The bike listed and he shifted his weight to counterbalance it. He needed a bail-out area, but to his left there was a sheer drop and to his right, the car was driving exactly parallel to him. He looked ahead and cried out. He was heading straight for roadworks and a piece of machinery the size of a two-storey house. He hit the brakes and the bike skidded, tipped over and went into an unstoppable slide, trapping him. The mirror flew off. The rough concrete ripped his jacket and trousers, then sandblasted the skin on his left leg and arm. He felt nothing. When the bike collided with the machinery in an explosive crash of metal on metal, he let out a roar of terror. The impact propelled him up, towards a V-shaped metal prong. His neck wedged in it and the bones snapped.

Sarah's rear-view mirror reflected a car travelling in the other direction past the roadworks. It puzzled her. There had been no slip roads and she didn't remember seeing it drive by. If McDermott had known she was travelling alone, he'd have stopped her, but this was the only way she could see Nathan Smyth's new winery in the Barossa, and still catch the flight to Melbourne this afternoon. She wasn't looking forward to walking through yet another winery, pretending to be interested in crushers, fermenters, row upon row of stainless-steel tanks and stacks of imported oak barrels. However, if she wanted to put an end to the stranglehold the Addison Group had on her company, she had to start adding new brands to her portfolio. She'd wanted to for years, but Elliott had fought against it, thwarting her efforts, insisting they wouldn't be able to meet the Bluestone Cellars sales targets if their efforts were diluted by minor brands.

Fifteen minutes later, she was seated in the Tanunda Bistro, a well-known German restaurant in the heart of a Barossa Valley village. It was quaint, with pretty lace curtains, carved wooden tables, and cushioned armchairs.

"*Guten Tag, Fräulein*. Are you waiting for Herr Nathan Smyth?" A man with a heavy accent had approached her.

Sarah put down the menu she was studying and smiled up at a rotund, elderly man with snow-white hair. He wore a rumpled button-down shirt, a stained tie and a tattered sports jacket with a chef's apron tied over the top. In his hand was a bottle of Smyth & Hawthorne wine. "*Guten Tag*," she replied, in her best school German. "Yes. I am. My name is Sarah Bennett."

He made an old-world half-bow. "I'm Gustaf, the owner of this establishment. Herr Smyth called from his car. He apologizes that he is late, but he stopped to help a man who had crashed his motorcycle. The poor fellow died."

"How terrible."

"Ach, it is. A man who had been working in the field nearby had seen the accident and gone to help – a car hit the motorcycle, he told Herr Smyth, and drove off without stopping." The old man shook his head. "Such dangerous machines, I tell my grandson. These young men and their motorcycle clubs. *Mein Gott*!" He remembered the bottle in his hand. "This wine is with Herr Smyth's compliments. He also wanted you to know he has ordered the Königsberger Klopse. It's a dish from East Prussia and, if I say so myself, it's *wunderbar*. What may I get for you?"

"I'll have the same, thank you," she murmured. The colour had drained from her face. Gustaf had put the wine on the table and was plodding towards the kitchen when she called, "Excuse me. How did you know the man was in a motorcycle club?"

Gustaf stopped and turned. "Herr Smyth was afraid for my grandson or someone from his club. But, *Gott sei dank*, it wasn't his club's insignia. The young man's helmet was black with a diagonal red stripe." He continued on his way.

Sarah reached for her water and nearly knocked it over. Calm down! She gulped some – it was ice-cold – then closed her eyes. After she'd left the Australian Wine Bureau, she'd met Detective Doolan to tell him what she'd remembered about the motorcyclist who'd followed her from the Stamford Hotel. When she'd described his helmet, Doolan had informed her it belonged to an unsavoury group who'd dubbed themselves the Kawasaki Kamikazes.

So, the taxi driver hadn't lost the motorcyclist, after all. He must have followed her from the hotel, to the Australian Wine Bureau, then into the Barossa Valley. Now he was dead. Her stomach ached as she replayed what she'd seen in her rear-view mirror. The car driving in the other direction was blue. A beaten-up blue car, like the one Clive Slattery drove – at least, that was the name he was using at the moment, according to Detective Doolan, who'd identified him from an artist's sketch based on her description. Born and raised in a Sydney suburb, Slattery had done time for rape and assault. Recently, he'd been tried in a murder-for-hire case, accused of stabbing a woman to death. He had been acquitted on a technicality.

That's it! Sarah jumped up from the table and dashed to the ladies' room. She pulled out her phone, dialled the Adelaide Police and asked for Doolan.

"I'm sorry," the operator said. "Detective Inspector Doolan is out. I'll put you through to his voicemail."

"No, it's –" She'd been about to say it was an emergency, but the operator cut her off. Seething, she stated her name for Doolan's voicemail, then described what she knew of the accident. "It's possible Slattery killed the motorcyclist. I'll be at the Tanunda Bistro for an hour or so. Please call me as soon as you get this message."

Next she dialled McDermott's home number, calculating it was around ten o'clock on Sunday evening in Atlanta. She had tried to reach him several times since they'd been cut off earlier this morning. Surely by now the problem with the phones had been fixed. But an automatic message answered her: "All circuits are busy. Please try your call later."

Sarah returned to the table and collapsed into her chair. She should never have come to the Barossa Valley alone. But the motorcyclist was dead and Slattery had fled after murdering him. Or had he? What if he'd circled back? Maybe she should leave. Or was she safer here?

Gustaf was lumbering towards her. He picked up the bottle of Smyth & Hawthorne Coonawarra Shiraz, opened it, then poured a small amount into her glass. "Herr Smyth mentioned you are from Atlanta. A few weeks ago, a famous wine writer from your city was here. Ach! He loved our food and promised to feature us in his column. Sam Somers. Do you know him?"

"Yes, I knew him." She lifted the glass to study the colour of the wine. It was a brilliant medium-red with purple highlights. She twirled it round in the glass, inhaled its aromas, then took a sip. It was exceptionally spicy, loaded with fruit, and had a long, lingering finish. "This is excellent."

"Pardon me." Gustaf looked perplexed. "You said you knew Sam Somers. Please tell me nothing has happened to him."

Sarah paused, unsure what to say, "I'm afraid he passed away recently."

"But he was so young! What happened?"

Sarah felt sorry for him. A glowing review in Somers's column would have turned this sleepy bistro into a money-spinner. "I'm sorry you didn't know. He was murdered in Atlanta a few weeks ago."

He sat down heavily, the rosy colour draining from his face. "He seemed such a gentleman. We had a glass of port together. Who would want to murder a man like that?"

Who wouldn't? Sarah itched to say it, but held herself in check. "The police haven't found the murderer yet, but they have a few leads."

The waitress appeared with an open bottle of Macquarie Hawke Coonawarra Shiraz. "Excuse me, Herr Gustaf, but one of the customers says this is 'bloody awful'. His words," she said.

"Take them a bottle of Smyth & Hawthorne Shiraz, compliments of the house. Leave that one here and please bring me two more red-wine glasses," he instructed her.

When the waitress returned, Gustaf poured a glass of the Macquarie Hawke wine. He sipped. "Pffft! Just as I had suspected. Thin and weak. Nothing like the sample Hawke brought to me. This wine is an outrage!" The old man's face was crimson now with indignation. "You will taste it?" He poured a glass and handed it to her.

Sarah took a tentative sip. Ugh! "There's not much to it," she said, knowing it was a gross understatement.

"We started serving it the day Mr Somers was here for lunch. We had three returns. I asked him, 'Can this be the wine you rated ninety-eight? A best buy?"

Somers's usual response to those who questioned his ratings ranged from merely unpleasant to downright vicious. "What did he say?"

"He explained that he'd bought two cases that weren't right so he'd called Mr Hawke. Supposedly it was a bottling-line problem." Gustaf sounded disgusted. "But all the bottles we get are poor. Mr Kennedy should never have involved himself with that man."

"Sorry to interrupt, Herr Gustaf, but the customer who returned the wine would like to speak to you." The waitress helped him to his feet.

"Please excuse me," he said to Sarah.

As he left to placate the customer, Sarah tasted Hawke's wine again. It had been decanted, which in a good wine enhanced the aromas and flavours. However, in a wine as poorly made as this, it only accentuated the faults. She spat it into an empty glass and pushed aside the bottle.

A terrifying thought surfaced. Somers had suspected something was wrong with Hawke's wine before he left Atlanta. He had called Hawke, who had told him it was a bottling-line problem. That must have pacified him until his lunch with Herr Gustaf, because later he had arrived unannounced at Southern Valley, where he had argued with Davis Hart. The next day, if she'd read Inga correctly, Hart had called Karl Kingsley and asked for immunity from prosecution. The day after that Hart was dead. And then Somers had been murdered. Fear surged in her.

There was a rustle and Sarah was startled to find Gustaf at the table again. God! She had to stay alert. He might have been Slattery.

"The Smyth & Hawthorne wine went down well. Now, where were we? I remember – Herr Kennedy." He hunched over and rested his liver-spotted hands on the table. "I suppose there's no harm in my telling you this story. I told Herr Somers too, God rest his soul. I overheard Herr Kennedy and his wife quarrelling one night, here at my restaurant. She threatened to shut down Southern Valley if he couldn't make a profit on her investment."

"Mrs Kennedy owns the winery?" Sarah asked.

"Yes," Gustaf confirmed. "Then that Englishman, Macquarie Hawke, joined Herr Kennedy. His wines are made there, you know. Suddenly there's money to buy new crushers, new tanks and a new bottling line. Frau Kennedy left to live in Sydney. All that money went to Herr Kennedy's head."

"Excuse me, but did you say Hawke is English? I thought he was Australian."

"He is English," Gustaf stated. He paused to sample the salad the waitress had served. "I don't know what is going on there, but I ask you, where does Southern Valley get all those grapes to make premium red wine, when our last two vintages were so short?"

"Good question." Sarah was not prepared to share her growing suspicion that if Southern Valley was mixing top-quality red grapes with cheap white ones, it wouldn't be a problem to produce an over-abundance of 'premium' red wine.

She moved her salad out of the way and the waitress put a plate of *Königsberger Klopse* in front of her. It looked like meatballs. She cut off a piece, chewed it and tasted minced pork and beef, combined with onions and anchovies. The sour cream sauce had a hint of lemon and a sprinkling of capers. It was good, but Sarah's appetite had deserted her. She put down her fork on the plate.

Once the waitress was out of earshot, Gustaf pointed

to a booth that was all but invisible to the rest of the restaurant. "I do not like to gossip, but Herr Kennedy often sits there with his personal assistant. Too close. She is half his age and he is married."

Chapter Twenty-seven

"Damn you, Nathan!" Sarah swore as the tail lights of Smyth's black BMW convertible disappeared into Southern Valley's driveway. She followed and pulled up beside him. Ahead, the palm trees that lined the path to the entrance swayed violently in the stiff breeze. She jumped out of her car and approached him – he had remained seated, the top of his car down, talking on his car phone. She waited until he had hung up, then said, "Nathan, I wish you'd said something about stopping here. If you recall, I have a flight to catch later this afternoon." Her eyes darted to the driveway. Had anyone followed them from the Tanunda Bistro? She focused on him and glared.

"No worries." He smoothed down his curly black hair, then adjusted his rectangular glasses. "We'll be out in a flash."

Ten minutes later, Sarah had had enough of the idle chit-chat between Smyth and Jason Findley and headed for the ladies' room, feeling a little queasy. Had the Königsberger Klopse upset her, or was it the thought of driving back alone to Adelaide airport? If only Doolan had returned her call.

Findley's directions took her past Davis Hart's office. She stopped by the door, scanned the corridor in both directions, then slung her briefcase over her shoulder and peered in. Hart's computer was still spelling his name across the monitor. She reached for the door-knob, then heard scrabbling. She spun round and pressed her back to the door. Findley's cat ran past, disappearing into the dim recesses of the corridor.

She continued through the labyrinth to an immaculate white-tiled cloakroom. There, she rested her brief-case on the basin, took out two indigestion tablets and popped them into her mouth. A huge bottle of Oceana *eau de parfum* stood on a shelf. She sprayed some on a paper towel and sniffed, then threw the towel into the bin. It was almost certainly the cloying scent Julianna had been wearing the other day, quite an extravagance for a personal assistant, at three hundred dollars a bottle, she thought.

When something rubbed against her leg, she started, knocking the perfume off the shelf. It fell to the floor and shattered, sending glass flying and liquid splashing across over the floor. "Shit!" Sarah cursed as the cat skit-tered away – she hadn't seen it follow her in. She wondered whether she should clear up the mess of glass shards, but the scent was so overpowering that she had to leave. She'd let Findley know to get a cleaner in here and leave some money for Julianna, to cover the cost of the perfume.

On the way back to Findley's office, she heard voices coming from the tasting room. The two men were probably sampling wine by now, she thought, and went in. It was empty. She moved across the room to the passageway. "The varietals and vintage dates aren't close enough to the real blend as it is. It's too risky. I don't give a damn what Smyth wants. I won't change the declaration again," she heard Findley snap.

"What's your problem? You did the same thing for

Dunne's order so you'll sign off on this one too." The menace in the other man's words was clear.

Sarah backed away, almost unable to comprehend what she'd heard – and someone grabbed her arm, squeezing it so hard, it hurt. *Slattery!* her brain screamed, and swung round to confront her captor.

Chapter Twenty-eight

"What the hell do you mean my Coonawarra Shiraz didn't pass?" Macquarie Hawke raged into the speakerphone. He swung the Rolls-Royce into the circular brick driveway at his palatial home on Adelaide's north side. "That's impossible."

"Not only is it possible, but it was you who rejected it. You and Randall." Karl Kingsley took pleasure in relaying this news to the normally imperturbable Hawke. "I thought you'd want a heads-up on it."

"Fix it." Hawke manoeuvred the vehicle into his four-car garage.

"Why don't you call at my office tomorrow? We'll discuss it then."

"I don't have time. I'm in meetings all day." Hawke pushed a button on the wooden dashboard.

"Make time." Kingsley slammed down the phone.

Astonished, Hawke remained in the leather seat as the motor whirred, raising the convertible roof. "Goddamn Prussian!" he exploded. "What the fuck does he think he's doing?"

Infuriated, he stepped out of the car and seized the two sample bottles of Coonawarra Shiraz from the back seat. "Nectar of the gods, my ass," he said, then flung them out of the garage door. They shattered, splashing blood-red wine across the immaculate driveway.

Chapter Twenty-nine

With vehicles lined up two and three deep in the departure area, the rental car company's van dropped Sarah a couple of hundred yards from the entrance to Adelaide airport. She was much too early for her flight to Melbourne, thanks to Bluey, who'd scared her to half to death, sneaking up and grabbing her arm. He had escorted her to Findley's office, where she'd made her excuses to Smyth, then raced out of Southern Valley, breaking the speed limit all the way to the airport, one eye glued on the rear-view mirror. The battered blue car hadn't materialized. Slattery wasn't tailing her. But she wouldn't feel safe until she'd gone through security.

A tug at the suitcase handle stopped her in her tracks. She turned. A wheel was wedged in a crevice. A crowd of people enveloped her as she stooped to dislodge it. When she stood up, a man was helping Taylor Robbins out of a car a few lanes over. Her orange hair appeared to be on fire in the bright sunlight. What was she doing here with Stephen Randall, of all people? Now she was wrapped in his arms, kissing him passionately. Sarah joined the swarm of people entering the terminal, hoping the couple hadn't seen her.

Somewhere between Melbourne airport and the Pyrenees Mountains, Sarah's head jerked up. The monotony of the landscape and the drone of the charter aircraft's single engine had put her to sleep. From the cramped back seat, she saw the pilot staring into the distance as his co-pilot, an older man, read a map. Dead tired, she closed her eyes again. It was hard to believe it was still Monday. After everything she'd been through, it felt as if an entire week had passed.

The aircraft banked and Sarah's eyes opened. The cloud formations were picking up the fiery scarlet of the setting sun. In the distance, the rolling hills and gentle slopes were covered with perfectly spaced rows of vines.

"You weren't dreaming of falling down a cliff, were you?" the pilot asked her, his eyes mischievous. He was rugged, with fine lines round his eyes from squinting into too many sunsets.

"Not really," Sarah shouted, above the roar of the engine.

"No? Well, if you were, it would feel like this!" The pilot turned the plane wing over wing, then slipped down the tallest slope.

Sarah's stomach nosedived, but she grinned and gave him a thumbs-up.

Not long afterwards she recognized the sprawling buildings and rows of steel tanks coming up on their right as the Bluestone Cellars Pyrenees Winery, now the Addison Group's main bottling facility. The pilot buzzed the building, swooping low and flying so slowly that she feared the engine would stall. Someone ran out and waved. The plane veered off and circled a pasture a short distance away.

"That's where we're going to land. Look out for cows!" The pilot circled, then landed on the bumpy grass.

As the plane rolled to a standstill, a vehicle approached.

Gerry Marks climbed out and the pilot hopped down from the cockpit to envelop her in a bear-hug. She laughed at something he said and slapped him on the back. Ten minutes later the plane took off again, roaring towards the flaming sun as it dipped below the horizon.

"How was the flight?" Gerry asked, as they sat in her vehicle, the hint of a smirk in her friendly smile

"Smooth as glass." Sarah laughed. On Elliott's last trip to the Pyrenees with a few of their distributors, photos showed them standing beside the plane, holding airsickness bags, the pilot grinning triumphantly.

"Let's get you over to the Rose. You can relax until our meeting tomorrow morning."

Five minutes later they arrived in 'town', a group of quaint buildings that dated from the 1850s. There was a filling station, a tiny grocery store, a run-down hotel, a hardware store, and the Rose bed-and-breakfast. A few cars whizzed past as Gerry pulled into a wide concrete parking area. Luggage in hand, the two women walked into a small garden enclosed by a white picket fence. The house stood in front of them, trailing vines filled with masses of blue flowers climbing round the front door.

Sarah went inside, carrying her briefcase. Gerry followed with the suitcases. The front door opened into a kitchen with a compact refrigerator, a small stove, a table and four chairs.

Gerry picked up a white envelope. "The owner lives in the other half of the house. She won't be here tonight, so she left this for you. I'll jot my home phone number on it in case you need anything." As she was scribbling, she said, "I was really sorry to hear what happened to you at Cleland. I'm glad you and the little girl are all right."

"Thanks." Sarah sounded preoccupied even to her own ears. She was already wary at the prospect of spending the night alone in such a remote area.

"Why don't you get settled in while I fetch something from the truck?" Gerry suggested.

Sarah wheeled her suitcase through the sitting room, where a wood fire burned in a brick fireplace before a worn blue plaid sofa and a couple of armchairs. From there, a short hall opened into the bedroom, where a white wrought-iron bed was covered with a handmade quilt. There were plenty of pillows, a wooden wardrobe, and two bedside tables with reading lamps. She dropped her briefcase on the bed, then went into a modern bathroom. She looked longingly at the shower, but returned instead to the kitchen.

"I brought you some wine – chardonnay, cabernet and a liqueur muscat." Gerry put the bottles on the work surface. "If you're hungry, call the restaurant across the street. They'll deliver dinner and put it on our tab. I'll pick you up early tomorrow."

Once Gerry was gone, Sarah flipped on the heater in the bedroom, then went to the kitchen and opened the envelope. It contained instructions on operating the appliances, and asked her to leave the door open for another guest, which alarmed her. It was bad enough to be here alone, without leaving the door unlocked. She picked up the telephone to call Gerry, then decided she was being ridiculous. Slattery couldn't possibly have followed her here. Instead, she dialled the restaurant and ordered dinner.

Returning to the bedroom, she stripped off her trouser suit and had a long, hot shower. Feeling better, she put on a pair of jeans, a T-shirt and a crocheted sweater, then headed for the sitting room. The flames were roaring up the chimney, the room toasty warm. She sat on the sofa, put her feet up on the scarred old coffee-table and fell instantly asleep.

She woke groggy and confused. The room was dark, save for the firelight. She heard footsteps. A loud thump. Was the restaurant delivering her meal? The front door squeaked. Footsteps in the kitchen. Someone was headed her way.

Leaping up, she ran to the fireplace and grabbed the poker. When a man stepped through the doorway into the sitting room, she swung it like a golf club, aiming at his chest.

Chapter Thirty

"Exactly when can I expect the funds to hit my Cayman Island account?" Macquarie Hawke's frown made deep grooves in his pockmarked face. He changed position on the pale leather sofa in his immense living room and glared at Stephen Randall, blue eyes glacial.

"Once the inventory discrepancy is cleared up, I'll have the first payment wired." Randall adjusted his angular body, silently cursing the low-slung chair, a modern design clearly not meant for human use.

Wordlessly, Hawke rose and went to the fireplace, its marble mantel flanked by bronze metal racks jammed with leather-bound books whose spines had never been cracked. He warmed his hands at the gas flames, then went to a humidor on top of a small chest. "Care to join me in a cigar? They're Cuban."

"You know I don't smoke."

Hawke slid open the glass door and picked up one cigar after another, holding each under his nose, twirling and sniffing.

Randall reined in his temper. Hawke wanted to provoke him. It was old man Hallgarten's fault: instead of being pleased that Hawke had signed the contract, he'd gone ballistic. It didn't make sense. The ten-million-dollar purchase price fitted established parameters as far as earnings were concerned, and three million dollars for Hawke's existing inventory was equitable. He was mystified. Wasn't Hallgarten's goal to become the number-one Australian winery? Hawke's brand would take them over the top. Did the old man regret offering him a seat on the board of directors, the cash bonus? Or was it the other incentives, based on each quarter they retained the top ranking?

Hallgarten had refused to discuss the issue, using the discrepancies found by the independent auditors in the inventory report provided by Hawke weeks ago as reason to withhold Hawke's first payment. The position was indefensible. Hallgarten knew it. So did Hawke.

Hawke puffed his cigar, then moved to the bar where a selection of crystal decanters and glasses had been arranged. He poured some port, then returned to the sofa and blew a smoke-ring, which floated to the high ceiling. "Stephen, you have as much to lose as I have. The inventory issue is bullshit. The payment was due within forty-eight hours of my signing the contract. I want that money in my account by five o'clock on Friday or you won't like what happens next."

"Don't threaten me!" Randall erupted from his seat. "You'll get your money. And you'd better be damned sure you stick to your side of the bargain." He gritted his teeth and sat down again. "Now, let's go on to something more productive, shall we?"

Hawke glanced surreptitiously at his watch. It was half past ten. They had reviewed the transition plans country by country and Randall was getting on his nerves. The man was anal. So was his boss. A number of other wineries had offered Hawke vast sums for his brand, but Oskar Hallgarten's deal was the most lucrative, in spite of the extra 'costs' involved. If things hadn't gone awry over the last few weeks, he would have broken the contract and taken another offer.

"Would you like some port?" Hawke asked, simulating cordiality he didn't feel.

"No, thank you. I'd like to review the inventory report so we can sign it off tonight." Randall's eyelid twitched as he retrieved the document from his briefcase. "Here's an audited copy."

Hawke got up and took it from him, then returned to the sofa and compared it with his records. "I see what the problem is." he said. "Three US orders left the warehouse ahead of schedule, which accounts for the minor overstatement of inventory." Removing a Mont Blanc pen from his jacket, Hawke initialled each page, then returned it to Randall. "That should satisfy the bloodsuckers."

"Now, based on US inventories, we're going to need that new vintage of Coonawarra Shiraz shipped right away. Have you received the export licence?"

"I'm expecting it next week." Hawke lied.

"It should have been issued by now. Is there a problem with the wine?" Randall's voice was sharp with suspicion.

Hawke blew another smoke-ring and watched it drift away. "You tasted it this evening. You tell me."

"There was nothing wrong with it, but that wasn't what I asked."

Hawke stiffened. "I don't like what you're implying," he snarled. "If you had any reservations about my wines, why the hell did you buy my company? Let's tear up the contract and call it quits right now."

In a corner, a sleek bronze pendulum clock ticked off the minutes. Randall's eyelid continued to twitch, Hawke noted. The question had been out of line, but he'd over-reacted. He should have laughed it off. After all, he had nothing to hide, right?

The angular planes of Randall's face relaxed into a smile, "That won't be necessary, but we do need the licence. The Coonawarra Shiraz is a big percentage of US sales and Malone will need an inventory straight away."

Collecting himself, Hawke gave Randall a mock-salute. "Congratulations. The old man must be pleased his brands are with Jake Malone."

"Now that he's on board, we'll need a 'use-up' letter giving his company the right to the existing labels showing Southern Cross Traders as the importer. Make it good for six months," Randall said. "By the way, is the president of your import company on board with the changeover? Melissa McNair, isn't it?"

"No worries, mate." Hawke's mood had improved immeasurably. While he was contractually obliged to keep Southern Cross Traders open during the agreed transition period, nothing had been put in writing as to who would be running it. He was looking forward to advising Melissa that she was being replaced by Rent-a-secretary at a quarter of her salary.

Chapter Thirty-one

Jake Malone returned from the kitchen at the Rose B-and-B with the bottle of Bluestone Cellars Liqueur Muscat and two glasses. Placing them on the coffee-table, he glanced at Sarah. She was sitting lifelessly on the sofa, mesmerized by the flames. The firelight's glow turned her auburn hair a brilliant red, her pale face a ghostly white and her green eyes a glinting black.

"That carpet-bag steak was delicious, but I really didn't need a piece of chocolate cake on top of it." He sat at the opposite end of the sofa.

A whiff of Sarah's perfume drifted to him as he poured two glasses of the muscat and handed one to Sarah. Their hands touched and she jerked away.

"Are you still angry with me for turning up unannounced?" Jake asked, rubbing his upper arm where a colossal bruise was forming. "Do I need to hide the poker?"

"Jake, it isn't funny. If you hadn't backed off, I might have broken your arm – or worse." Sarah curled her legs beneath her, careful not to spill the wine.

"I don't think it's funny either. What if it had been Slattery instead of me?" He brushed something off his jeans. Sarah had been tense ever since he'd arrived, talking ceaselessly about Slattery and the motorcyclist he'd killed. "Please, fly home with me tomorrow. I'll get you a first-class ticket so we can sit together. Taylor can courier the contract to you."

"Right." Sarah rolled her eyes. "Like Taylor isn't doing everything in her power to screw me. She couldn't even have the contract ready for our meeting. If it wasn't for Phillip Dwyer, there'd be no contract. And who knows how long he'll be around, with Noonan gunning for Burnside and him? Anyway, Bernie McDermott arranged police protection for me. His friend Sebastian O'Connor is having someone pick me up at Sydney airport tomorrow. Now let's talk about something else."

Jake positioned a tattered, but scrupulously clean, needlepoint cushion behind his head and leaned back, resisting the urge to point out that signing the contract wasn't as important as staying alive. It would only start another fight. "Up to you. How did things go with Nathan Smyth?"

"They didn't." Sarah's lips tightened. "I've decided not to work with him."

Jake raised his eyebrows. "Why? What happened?"

She lifted the glass to her lips and took a sip of wine. The promise she'd made to Andrew Dunne about the file in Hart's computer had been rendered void by the conversation she'd overheard between Jason Findley and an unidentified man. "It started last week, when Andrew and I stopped at Southern Valley. While I was waiting for him, I accidentally accessed a file in the chief winemaker's computer. It indicated that the wine they were selling to Andrew as a cabernet sauvignon was actually forty per cent chenin blanc and riesling."

"You're joking!" Jake sat up. The cushion fell behind his back. "Why didn't you say something about this yesterday?"

"Andrew convinced me it was a worksheet, but I got suspicious last night at the casino after I'd talked to Ray. Southern Valley's chief winemaker, Davis Hart, was a friend of his," she said, "and Hart was at the casino the night before he was killed."

As Jake repositioned the cushion behind his head, Sarah explained how she'd come to believe that Southern Valley might be involved in something illegal. She omitted nothing from the narrative. A sharp crack made them jump as a wave of sparks flew up the chimney. When Sarah picked up her glass again, her hands were trembling. "Would you pour me some more muscat, please?"

"It's getting cold in here. Let me fetch you a blanket," he said, as he refilled her glass. He stood up, pulled a throw off a chair and spread it over her legs, picked up the poker and stirred the fire into a comforting blaze. He returned the poker to its brass stand. "What happened after Findley refused to make the changes?"

"The person he was arguing with – it might have been Macquarie Hawke – said, 'You fixed Dunne's order. You'll do the same for Smyth, if you know what's good for you.'" Sarah paused. "I don't care about Nathan Smyth. It's Andrew Dunne involvement that upsets me. He lied to me to shut me up."

Jake could see how angry she was now – she could barely contain herself. But what could he say? That he was as disturbed as she was? He lifted his arms and clasped his hands behind his neck. "First, why do you think the other man was Mac Hawke? Have you met him?"

"Twice. And, no, I couldn't swear it was him. It was just an impression I had." She tilted her head to one side.

"OK. So we aren't sure who it was. Now, neither Jason nor the other man actually said Dunne was in on it, right? Just that they fixed his order. Maybe they 'fixed' it without his knowledge."

"It's possible," she said, a note of desperation creeping into her voice. "But that doesn't change what Southern Valley's doing. Imagine what's going to happen when people find out Australia's most prestigious wines have been blended with garbage from a bulk producer. Remember when the sorbitol scandal broke a few years ago? Australian wines all but dropped off the face of the earth. And that was one producer using an illegal but harmless additive to sweeten one product. Someone has to stop them!"

Jake held up a hand. "Wait a minute. You said Davis Hart had already reported the problem to Karl Kingsley. These things take time. Give the Australian Wine Bureau a chance to do something about it, all right?"

For a long while they sat in silence, sipping muscat, watching the dying embers of the fire. Finally Sarah got up. "I have to go to bed." She picked up the throw, folded it and laid it across the back of the chair. "I know I haven't been the greatest company tonight, but thanks for going out of your way to stay with me. Wake me up before you leave, OK?"

"I will. Sleep well. When we get home, we'll sort things out."

Sarah went into her room, both relieved and disappointed they'd avoided talking about last night. She washed her face, put on a warm nightgown and collapsed into the antique bed. It creaked as she reached for the lamp on the bedside table and switched it off. The wind picked up. The window rattled. There was another noise. Pipes clanking? Or something else?

She sat up and flipped on the light. The clanking stopped. The thought of going to Jake's room crossed her mind, but she dismissed the idea. Eventually she drifted into a half-sleep, picturing Jake as he'd been seven years ago, eyes glazed, tie half undone, leaning over the waist-high curtain dividing their booths at the Peachtree International Wine Festival. It had been noisy, the crowds pushing up to the tables, holding out their glasses impatiently. Sarah had been expecting a quick hello from a casual acquaintance, but had been appalled to discover Jake was drunk. He had been rambling incoherently – saying over and over again that he was responsible for his wife's death and how hard it was to cope with the baby – so she'd dragged him outside for some fresh air. They had sat on a bench in the cool night air while he'd poured out his heart. That was when Sarah had discovered he had kept his father's cancer from his mother, who had stumbled on the truth that day, and had denounced Jake, calling him a poor excuse for a son. Elliott had driven him home. The next morning, they'd gone back to offer whatever help he needed.

She didn't know how long she'd been staring at the ceiling when she threw off the covers and got out of bed. She put on her black-and-gold dressing-gown and went into the sitting room. It was cold, the fire almost out. She was shivering as she walked through the kitchen, then into the hall to Jake's bedroom. The door was open, but she knocked anyway.

"Come in."

Jake was standing over his suitcase, a white towel wrapped round his waist. His hair was damp. The room was warm. "I just had a shower. Let me move these things off the chair." He smiled at her, picked up his T-shirt and jeans and threw them on to the bed.

He was lean and muscular, with broad, square shoulders and a narrow waist, more beautiful than she'd ever imagined. She sat down, her eyes at the level of his thighs. "Couldn't sleep?" he asked, taking a shirt out of his case and shaking it.

"I keep hearing things." She hesitated. "I should go."

"No. Please." He put down the shirt and scrutinized her in the low light of the bedside lamps, then walked over and knelt in front of her. Smoothing a few tangled strands of hair on her face, he asked, "Is this about Slattery or last night?"

His fingers were soft on her skin. She fixed her eyes on a spot over his naked shoulder. "Last night. For some reason, it started me thinking about the wine festival when Elliott drove you home."

Jake sat back on his haunches. "What does that have to do with last night?"

Sarah looked him in the eye. "It has to do with promises."

"As I recall, you and I had words about that." Jake stood up and tightened the knot in the towel. "You thought my mother was justified in asking me for an apology because I'd kept Dad's cancer from her."

"But you didn't apologize, did you?" she asked, gathering from his expression that even to this day, he'd stood his ground. "Keeping your word takes precedence over everything and everyone. You keep your word, no matter what. That's why I'm confused. The night you drove me home from the show in North Carolina, after I'd found out Elliott had died, you promised you'd always be there for me . . . as a *friend*. What's changed?"

"Nothing." Jake stood up and moved to his suitcase. He picked up the shirt again, went to the wardrobe and hung it up.

"I see. So we had a few drinks and shared a friendly kiss, right?" She stared at his bare back, all at once feeling foolish. She stood up. What on earth had she been thinking?

He turned round. "Do you have any idea how I feel about you?" he murmured, gazing directly into her eyes. Then he reached out, pulled her close and kissed her.

She kissed him back, pressing against him, her breathing ragged. He was hot, so hot, his fingers seeming to burn through her robe. He started to tug at the sash, but all at once it felt wrong. He was her best friend. She couldn't go through with this.

With an intensity that frightened her, he began to kiss her forehead, her eyes, her cheeks, her neck. It was as if he wanted to consume her. His hands moved feverishly up and down her body. She felt herself responding. All at once conscious thought was replaced by pure desire. She was spinning out of control. He undid her robe and slid it off her shoulders.

He moved back and lifted her nightgown over her head, "I've waited such a long time for you, Sarah. You're so beautiful."

For an instant, Elliott's face was superimposed on Jake's. The image faded and Jake's blue eyes were drilling into hers. Then he took her once more into his arms and kissed her deeply. At that moment, she wanted him more than she'd ever wanted any other man. She reached down and pulled his towel away.

Chapter Thirty-two

The smell of bacon made Bernie McDermott's mouth water. He walked over to the stove-top, spatula in hand, and prodded the four thick rashers sizzling in the pan. It was important the bacon didn't get too crisp. He propped himself against the black granite counter and stretched his back. He'd been working flat out since the storm had cut the city's power, returning to his Peachtree Hills apartment at seven o'clock that morning. Monday, he reminded himself, as he went into the pantry for a jar of peanut butter.

He opened it as the toaster pinged, ejecting two perfectly toasted slices of white bread, which he put on a thick blue plate. With a wide knife, he slapped a large glob of peanut butter on one piece and spread it to the edge. Then he arranged the bacon on top and covered it with the other piece of toast. He took his plate and a glass of cranberry juice to the far end of the kitchen counter, hoisted himself on to a bar stool and took a bite. He was still chewing when the telephone rang. "Not now!" he growled. He took a swig of the cranberry juice, leaned over and lifted the receiver. "McDermott!"

Sergeant Leroy Watson said, "Boss, we picked up Vine. He's at the station."

McDermott cursed under his breath. "I'll get there as soon as I can." He dressed hurriedly, took a last look at his unfinished sandwich, then left for Headquarters. Halfway there, he ran into rush-hour traffic at a standstill. Even with lights and siren, it would take some time to get to the station. He called Watson and instructed him to get started. He didn't want Vine to think about a lawyer.

An hour later, he joined Watson at the two-way mirror, a bleak interrogation room on the other side. Painted the same industrial shade as the rest of the building, the room's bright overhead lights reflected off Peter Vine's white-blond hair as he sat at a battered rectangular table. A young Hispanic homicide detective stood behind him, while an older man, with a shaved head and gold-rimmed aviator glasses, sauntered round the table and sat down next to him.

His nose practically in Vine's ear, he said, "Come on! A witness will testify that you were reading Somers's correspondence to his attorney. Somers was going to dump you. No more column, no more wine festival, your reputation in ruins, dropped by Sam Somers, wine guru of the Western world. No way to fight it because you never signed an agreement. It would certainly piss me off!"

Vine's face reddened and he clamped his jaws shut.

The detective's voice grew louder: "The next day, you decided to pay Somers a visit. How did it work? Your hired killer waits outside. If Somers agrees to keep you, he gets to live. If not, the guy goes in and –"

"That's absurd. I wasn't there!" Vine held a hand to his chest. "I want to talk to my attorney!"

"Damn it!" McDermott fumed. He punched off the sound, and turned to Watson.

Watson's massive shoulders were rigid with tension.

"Vine said Somers got blitzed at the Peachtree International Wine Festival two years ago and started badmouthing an exhibitor, a woman who'd apparently refused to sleep with him. Somers followed her into a storage area. Vine got worried and went after them. By the time he located them, Somers had her pinned to the wall, her skirt up to her waist. She was screaming. Vine reckoned he pulled Somers off moments before he would have raped her. Boss, it was Sarah Bennett."

Chapter Thirty-three

Jake Malone could almost see his breath in the damp, chilly air of his bedroom at the Rose B-and-B. It had been hard to get out of bed and pack for his trip, with Sarah still asleep under the quilt. She was wearing his black T-shirt, lying on her side, her arms round a pillow. Sitting down on the bed, he lifted a strand of Sarah's hair and curled it round her ear. As she woke, the peace left her face. He felt a stab of pain in his chest. "Goodbye, Sarah." He kissed her cheek.

She yawned. "What time is it?"

"Five o'clock," he said softly.

She shut her eyes and hugged the pillow to her chest.

"Take care of yourself. I'll call you when I get home."

"Fine. Have a good trip." she mumbled.

Jake stroked her hair. "I know that look. What's on your mind?"

She squirmed into a sitting position. "This is what happens when you sleep with your best friend. You can't hide anything because they know you too well."

He grabbed her. "Don't make a joke of this."

"I'm sorry. I didn't mean it to come out that way." She flung her arms round his neck.

He held her close and whispered, "I want us to be more than friends, you know that. Much more."

After he left, Sarah turned on to her stomach and put the pillow over her head. She found herself almost wishing that last night had never happened.

Chapter Thirty-four

The blinds in McDermott's office were closed, a sure sign he didn't want to be disturbed. Watson disregarded the warning and rapped on the door. "For fuck's sake, Watson, come in!" he heard.

"Sorry, boss. It's urgent."

McDermott stood by the window, which faced one of the city's busiest restaurants, popular with the business crowd. It was a fine day, and a long line of people would be waiting outside for the Monday lunch special, Watson thought, fried chicken, mustard greens and corn pudding, then sweet-potato pie for dessert. He'd considered ordering take-out.

"What it is now?" McDermott grunted.

"The lab finally got round to processing the palm print on the wall above the spatter of Somers's blood. It's Wicky Riley's," Watson told him, "real name Colin Riley, born in Chester, England, nicknamed Sticky Wicket, hence Wicky."

"Sticky Wicket?"

Watson's face lit up briefly. "Comes from the game of cricket. Means a tight situation."

"How the hell did you know that?"

"Brother-in-law's English," Watson answered. "He took my sister to the Cayman Islands to live. Don't see her much now."

McDermott was giving him 'the look' so Watson got

to the point. "Riley became a naturalized citizen a few years back, then took advantage of the free housing at the Florida State Penitentiary. Unlawful possession of a firearm, among other things. Last known address was Kissimmee. His mother lives there, in an old folks' home – excuse me. An assisted living facility."

"Sit down," McDermott barked, then returned to his desk and lowered himself gingerly into his chair. It protested with a loud squeak.

"Riley's prints are on Somers's laptop and a partial was on the piece of glass in Somers's neck."

"Sergeant!" That look again.

"I contacted Kissimmee Police. Riley was in a barroom brawl. Got sliced up pretty good with his own serrated knife. He's in hospital getting stitched up, as we speak."

Chapter Thirty-five

Early on Tuesday morning, Julianna Porter went into Davis Hart's office to do some filing. His name was still streaming across the computer monitor. Almost immediately, she spotted something white poking out from beneath a filing cabinet. Hoping it was the missing SV888 document that was supposed to have been shredded, she stooped to fish it out.

"My dear, you look delightful today." Angus Kennedy had come in and was standing beside her. "I missed you last night," he added, moving closer.

Julianna edged away a little, tossed her tawny hair and held out the paper. "I can't even take one day off. I found the office unlocked and this on the floor. Were you working in here earlier?"

"No. What's the matter?"

"This document is from Hart's confidential files and someone was using the computer. But yesterday, just before I left, I turned off the computer and locked the door," Julianna told him. "There are only three sets of keys to this office, yours, mine and Hart's. And Hart's are at the bottom of the ocean."

She yelped as something furry brushed against her leg. "Damn cat! I thought you told him not to bring it to work any more." Without thinking, she lashed out, the spike heel of her shoe connecting with the cat's belly. It screeched and ran off, leaving a trail of blood.

Moments later Findley was in the room. "What have you done to my cat?" he panted. "My God! That's blood!" He made to take off after the cat, but Julianna's voice stopped him.

"Just a minute, Jason. I want to know why you were going through Hart's confidential files." She shoved the paper under his nose. "I loaned you the keys to this office. You never returned them. Did you think I was so stupid I wouldn't realize what you've been doing?"

"I gave the keys to Bluey when Sarah Bennett and Andrew Dunne were here. He never gave them back to me. Now, get out of my way!"

"Liar!" she snapped.

"That's enough!" Kennedy said. "Jason, you and I are going to straighten this out right now. Julianna, go back to your office."

"Why didn't I think of it before?" Julianna stepped forward and pointed a manicured finger at Findley. "You took the blend profile for SV888, didn't you? Where is it?"

Chapter Thirty-six

Dressed in dirty work clothes, a yellow hard hat and thick-rimmed glasses that concealed his bushy eyebrows, Slattery stood in the hallway at the Addison Group Winery, located in the foothills of the Pyrenees. He caught his reflection in the row of windows and congratulated himself. He'd be indistinguishable from every other worker in the building.

The tasting room he was observing was flooded with light from the windows on the opposite wall. From his vantage-point, he had a perfect view of the rectangular work stations attached to the white walls, crammed with bottles and used glasses. Sarah Bennett was moving rapidly along a table, sipping wine and spitting it into metal buckets fastened to the counters. She was accompanied by a plain woman in faded brown trousers, a white shirt and brown boots. He shifted to get a better view. Shit! The winemaker had seen him. He moved away from the window and out of sight.

"This one is eighty per cent cabernet sauvignon, ten per cent shiraz and ten per cent cabernet malbec," Gerry Marks said. "Eighteen months in new French oak casks." She moved Sarah to the next wine and poured a sample. "This is a one hundred per cent cabernet sauvignon from the Yarra Valley."

Sarah scribbled a few notes on a spiral pad, stifling a

yawn. She wasn't used to sharing her bed, and Jake's tossing and turning last night had kept her awake. Struggling to maintain her focus, she took a sip of the cabernet. It was full-bodied with ripe fruit, hints of blackberry and a velvety finish. She puckered her lips and spat. "This one has possibilities. How many cases were made?"

"Around eight thousand." Gerry grinned. "I thought you might be interested. It's a single vineyard, plenty of oak, loads of flavour. I haven't shown it to anyone else yet."

Sarah consulted a price list, and made a few calculations, "I'll take all of it. I'll let Taylor Robbins know when I see her tomorrow."

"Excellent," Gerry said. "And this might be a good time to stop for lunch. We've gone through all the sparkling wines, the whites and this is the last of the reds. After we've eaten, we can taste the sherries, dessert wines and ports. We should be finished by three. Plenty of time to get you to the airport."

"Sounds good."

Strolling through the building, Sarah contemplated the changes the Addison Group had made to the former Bluestone Cellars site. Remote as it was, this winery had been a tourist destination until it was transformed into a bottling plant with clusters of industrial buildings containing state-of-the-art equipment.

A few remnants of the past had been preserved. The original winery now housed a small museum, and twenty feet beneath it underground tunnels had been excavated in the 1860s by out-of-work gold miners from nearby Ballarat. Once used as maturation cellars, the 'drives' kept wine at a constant temperature during the summer heat. Nowadays, only the most expensive products were stored there, due to the time-consuming nature of the process, resulting in prohibitive labour costs.

On the second-floor landing, Gerry's phone rang. She was still talking when they entered the sunny conference room, with its eight-foot walnut table and six armchairs upholstered in forest green leather. A matching sideboard tucked into a corner held trays of sandwiches and a selection of drinks, including coffee, which someone had just put on to brew.

Gerry flicked the phone shut. "I have to take care of a minor emergency. I'll be back as soon as I can. Andrew Dunne and Graham Blackwell are joining us for lunch."

Moments after Gerry had left, Andrew Dunne burst in. "G'day, Sarah! I just ran into Gerry. She said you were interested in that Yarra Valley cabernet. It's a real beaut!" He sounded unnaturally cheery. "There're some other wines I want you to try. Come into the drives with me to pick out a few bottles. We can taste them at lunch."

"If you don't mind, I'll pass. I've been down there plenty of times before," Sarah replied. There was no way she wanted to be alone with Dunne, especially in the drives, until she was convinced beyond a doubt that he wasn't involved in Southern Valley's fraud. "I'm not dressed for it. Besides, I'm famished."

"Oh, hell. I wanted to surprise you. A few pallets of Bluestone Cellars cabernet sauvignons going back forty years were unearthed when a section of the drives crumbled. If they're viable, we could do a vertical tasting in the US, using cabernets from our library stock, then finish with our new releases. It would generate loads of publicity for Bluestone Cellars. We could invite Som –"

Dunne corrected himself: "Some of the big-name wine writers. Come on, Sarah! You know I still think of Bluestone Cellars as my baby."

He was practically dancing with glee. It was hard to imagine he was in cahoots with a reprobate like Hawke and the crew at Southern Valley. Perhaps this thing with Slattery had coloured her judgement. She decided to trust him.

They left the building and walked across the courtyard, then down steel-mesh steps to a concrete-paved grape-receiving area where several crushers were going full blast. Next to them, oak barrels rested on wooden pallets, stacked five high. Another flight of steel-mesh steps brought them to the one original winery building that was still in use. Inside, Sarah's ears were assaulted by the grating noise of heavy machinery. She stepped round a puddle of water mixed with wine.

Suddenly Dunne reached out and pulled her away from one of the tanks as a fork-lift truck barrelled past close to where she'd been standing. "Bloody hell. Watch where you're going, mate!" Dunne shouted after the truck, making a note of the number on the back. "Sorry, Sarah. I don't recognize him. He must be one of temporary employees. The last of the grapes came in really late this year, as you know, and the place is still crawling with them."

Ahead, a group of workers spotted Dunne and scattered. A man wearing thick-rimmed dark glasses waited to open the door for them.

"Go on, mate," Dunne said.

He touched his hat, preceded them through the door, and veered left, while Sarah and Dunne headed right. As they went downwards, following a marked path, she noticed that light fittings were few and far between, creating pockets of shadows on either side of the wooden barrels stacked on steel frames reaching to the ceiling.

At a dead end, they made a sharp U-turn. Sarah estimated they were directly under the main winery. Massive overhead beams were held up by five-foot-thick posts painted red and white. Behind them, giant oak puncheons were supported by curved wooden structures. The puncheons were as tall as Dunne and held five hundred litres of port; dates burned into the wood indicated that the contents were more than a hundred years old.

After several more turns, Sarah and Dunne came to a five-foot-wide ramp descending at the steepest angle yet. Here, the once-white walls were covered with black and green mould. Ahead Sarah saw an arched entrance made of brick, with an elaborately carved door, above which hung a gold plaque placed by the National Historic Register. To one side of the door there was a blackboard with names, times and dates; on the other there was a no-smoking sign.

Dunne took a key from his pocket and unlocked the door. A yawning black cavern greeted them. He threw a switch and a series of naked bulbs attached to the ceiling provided a dim yellow glow that stretched into the distance. "After you." Dunne attached the door to a latch to hold it open. "Just a precaution. Never know when you might want to make a quick exit."

"That's a comforting thought." Sarah entered the cold, damp tunnel. "But this isn't the only way out. There's an exit on the other side, right?" She recalled a narrow set of spiral steps barely big enough for a person to squeeze up.

"Yes. This is Drive A. The other exit is in Drive C," Dunne said, "but without a map, they might be hard for you to find. There are five miles of tunnels, none of which runs perpendicular or parallel to another. Eighteen sixties technology."

Sarah's shoes crunched on gravel. She brushed something fuzzy off her face, then looked up. The ten-foot-high arched ceilings were covered with a trailing mould, like the Spanish moss that clung to the trees in south Georgia. Some of the walls had been patched with a stucco-like material. She shivered.

Dunne led the way along a series of tunnels, taking them a good distance from the main entrance. Suddenly he stopped. "Bloody hell. We're supposed to sign in and out so no one gets locked down here by accident, and I forgot to do it. No worries. We won't be here long."

Soon they came to an area where floor-to-ceiling cubbyholes had been carved out to make room for bottles stacked on wooden racks with their punts, the deep indentations in the bottom of the bottles, facing out. Sarah noticed they weren't labelled, but the thick layers of dust would have made them impossible to read anyway.

"The heaviest tanks are above us right now," Dunne said, pausing by a partially collapsed area held up by wooden brackets. He put out his hand and wiggled it. A few pieces of ceiling fell to the floor. "The cabernets I wanted to show you should be close by. This is the section that crumbled yesterday."

"Stop it, Andrew," Sarah said. "Let's just get what we came for and leave."

Dunne dusted off a sheet of paper encased in plastic hanging from the top of a stack. "Damn it. Someone's moved those cabernets. Wait here. I'll be back in a few minutes. I need to find out where they put them."

"I'm coming with you!" Sarah exclaimed, as he took off at a run.

"I'll be back in a flash. Stay there!" he shouted, as he disappeared into the gloom.

Sarah went after him, but her leather-soled shoes made the going treacherous. Rounding a corner, she was faced with an intersection of four tunnels. She had no idea which he'd taken so she'd just have to wait for him to return. There was nowhere to sit. She couldn't even lean against the walls – they were too mouldy. Should she try to find the way out? What if she got lost? It would take ages for someone to find her in five miles of tunnels.

Dunne had been gone for more than fifteen minutes when she heard something echo down the tunnel. "Andrew! Is that you?" she shouted. "I'm here!"

Was that a door slamming? She thought she heard a sharp clank, like steel on steel. Without warning, the lightbulbs hanging from the ceiling went out. Plunged into total darkness, Sarah gasped. She held a hand in front of her face. She couldn't see it – or, for that matter, anything else. This is what it must feel like to be buried alive, she thought. All at once the air seemed thin.

Dunne was sure to return soon, she consoled herself. He could be so childish sometimes that she wouldn't have put it past him to lock her in the drives and turn off the lights.

A terrible thought struck her.

Dunne had the perfect reason for stranding her in a tunnel that had collapsed only yesterday. Not only had she revealed her suspicions about Southern Valley to him, but also she'd been caught eavesdropping by Bluey, who must have known she'd learned the truth about the scam. Maybe he'd convinced Dunne to arrange an accident in this unstable tunnel.

She touched the cold walls and felt the damp strands of mould. It took every ounce of willpower not to run screaming into the darkness. She crossed her arms, seized the sides of her sweater and bent over, claustrophobia overcoming her. It was like being in a whirling vortex, rendering her irrational, unstable, unable to think, to move. "No!" she screamed.

The only way to combat it was to do something. With no clear idea as to which direction she should take, Sarah groped along the wall, steeling herself against the mould. After a few steps, she encountered a stack of wine. A bottle fell to the floor and broke. The air was filled with the scent of old cabernet. Then, all at once, her nostrils were filled with an entirely different smell. Fuel oil?

A rush of air made her whirl round. Where was it coming from? In the distance, she noticed a peculiar glow, which grew brighter as she watched. Wispy threads of smoke floated towards her. *Someone had lit a fire in the tunnel. She'd burn alive.* Her legs gave way.

"Think!" she told herself. "Where are the exits?" What did it matter? She'd never be able to find them, not in the pitch-black tunnels that twisted round like demented pretzels. Suddenly the luminescence in the tunnel directly ahead turned a brilliant, menacing orange. The dark retreated. Despite what the light heralded, she felt calmer now that she could see. She'd find her way out. The exits were in Drives A and C.

She stood up quickly, bumping into the wooden

supports holding up the collapsed ceiling. A shower of rocks rained down on her head and shoulders. There was a prolonged, low-pitched rumble, then more fell from the ceiling. Blindly she scrambled away, heading for the fire.

A crescendo of sound filled the tunnel as she ran. It was getting dark again and now dust clogged the atmosphere. She was choking. Then as suddenly as the noise had started it died. There was silence.

A few more rocks crashed to the floor as Sarah stopped and turned round. Through the thick, smoky particles that filled the air, she saw that an impenetrable wall of earth and rock had sealed off the tunnel. The hysteria she'd been fighting welled up in her. A sign on the brick archway above the blocked tunnel read, 'Drive A'. Her legs buckled.

Chapter Thirty-seven

Jason Findley stumbled along the corridors, following the trail of blood. Hearing voices, he ducked round the next corner and stopped to catch his breath. They were spreading out, searching for him. If only he'd defended himself to Kennedy rather than rushing out of Hart's office. The heartless bitch! How the devil had Julianna discovered he'd taken the blend profile?

All at once the searchers' voices rose, sounding angry. Dashing towards the next intersection, Findley veered right and almost stepped on Pauline, who was curled up in a ball on the floor. Bluey stood over her, "I'm sorry, mate." His eyes betrayed nothing. "She's gone."

As if he had been punched in the stomach, Findley sank to his knees. A moan escaped him as he reached out and turned his cat over. Pauline's belly was sticky with congealing blood.

"Forget her, mate." Bluey sounded on edge. "We have to get you out of here. Your life may be in danger."

"If it is, it's your fault." He clasped Pauline to his chest, then got to his feet unsteadily.

"My fault? Are you mad?"

"You saw me going through Hart's files! You reported me, you bastard!"

"Rubbish! You brought this on yourself." Bluey latched on to his arm and propelled him towards the door that led to the employees' car park. "You refused to change

Smyth's order, then dropped one of the bloody files on the floor, which Julianna found. When she accused you of taking the blend profile, you might as well have had a sign reading 'guilty' pasted on your forehead! To think I was convinced Sarah Bennett had it."

Findley wrenched away from Bluey's grasp. "You tried to have her murdered because you thought she's taken it?"

"You're daft, if you think I'm in with that lot." Bluey seized Findley's arm again. "Now get moving!"

Findley stumbled along in a daze. His beloved cat was dead. Davis Hart was dead. Sam Somers was dead. He himself was as good as dead. At the back door, he stopped and glared at Bluey. "I don't trust you. I'm not going anywhere with you!"

"Believe me, I'm the only person here you can trust." Bluey threw open the door, put his hand on Findley's back and shoved him outside. Shielding his eyes against the intense sunlight, he said, "We'll use your car. Give me the keys and put Pauline in the boot."

Wild-eyed, Findley clutched the cat's body to his chest.

"Just get in!" Bluey shouldered him into the passenger seat, slammed the door, then raced round the car and jumped in. He roared out of the car park, swerving on to Sturt Highway with one eye on the rear-view mirror. "The only way you'll be safe is by handing over the blend profile to the Australian Wine Bureau. Where the bloody hell is it?"

Chapter Thirty-eight

Gerry Marks selected a cucumber sandwich from the heavily laden sideboard in the Addison Group's second-floor conference room, then went back to the table, where Graham Blackwell was sitting in an armchair, eating crisps straight from the bag. He'd taken off his jacket and draped it over a nearby chair. His shirt cuffs had been rolled up, exposing his wrists and the golden hair on his arms.

"Is it getting stuffy in here, or is it just me?" She put her plate on the table and unbuttoned her white shirt to reveal an orange T-shirt. "I wonder what's taking Sarah and Andrew so long. Maybe we should go down there, see what they've unearthed," she suggested, sneaking a glance at him.

"Anyone who willingly goes into that death trap is completely mad." Blackwell crumpled the bag into a ball and threw it at the wastebasket. It hit the rim and fell in. He pushed a damp lock of hair off his forehead.

"Coward!" she teased, although secretly she agreed with him. Last year she and Blackwell had discovered a cache of ports maturing untouched in the drives for eighty years. In digging them out, they'd upset a ceiling support, dislodging chunks of rock. They'd been lucky to escape unhurt. She blamed the sorry state of the tunnels on Pym Noonan: the Addison Group's vice president hated to spend money on anything that didn't produce an immediate profit.

At that moment, a panting, red-faced man in denim overalls, carrying a yellow hard hat, appeared at the conference-room door. "I've been looking everywhere for you." he gasped. "There was an explosion – the drives are on fire!"

"Why didn't we hear the alarm?" Gerry burst out, then straight away took control. She barked a series of instructions and sent the man on his way. Then it was Blackwell's turn: "Find Andrew and Sarah. Try his office first. Tell him to meet me by the fire-extinguisher panel, and take Sarah somewhere safe, OK?"

"No worries."

As Gerry flew out of the conference room, her thick-soled brown boots thumping on the wooden floor, Blackwell slipped on his jacket, snatched his briefcase off the table and followed at a run.

In an instant, he was engulfed by a swarm of people shoving their way downstairs. Suddenly the congestion cleared, and he sped up the stairs to Dunne's third-floor office, his thoughts turning to the millions of dollars' worth of wine above and below ground, and the new high-tech bottling lines. All would be lost if the tunnels collapsed.

Dunne's office was empty. Blackwell ran over to the picture window and looked down at the hordes of people milling about in the courtyard. Smoke poured from the ground floor of the old Misener winery. He whipped round to leave, but Dunne's secretary, a stout woman in a pink-flowered dress, was blocking the door. She was frowning, her hands resting on hips, which were as wide as the new *Queen Mary 2*. After a moment, recognition dawned in her face. "Graham Blackwell! What are you doing in here?" Her manner was that of a teacher scolding a pupil caught in the principal's office.

Blackwell's jaw tightened. "The drives are on fire. I'm looking for Andrew and Sarah Bennett. Do you know where they are?"

The woman's jowls quivered. "Andrew was here fifteen minutes ago, looking for the foreman. He got a phone call. Next thing I knew he was gone."

"Was Sarah with him?"

"No. He was alone."

Blackwell told her to leave the building, then sprinted down the stairs and raced outside into a square courtyard paved with crushed white stone, surrounded by bluestone and brick buildings. The smoke billowing out of the Misener building had turned black. People continued to pour outside, joining the masses in the courtyard. The sight filled Blackwell with despair. It would take him a good ten minutes to get across the yard and into the bowels of the building. He'd never find Gerry before she sealed the exits and set off the fire extinguishers. His only hope was that she'd have the presence of mind to check the sign-in board first.

Hunching his shoulders, Blackwell plunged into the crowd. Even if he got to Gerry before she unleashed the extinguishers, he might still be too late. The drives were a diabolical maze, filled with dead ends. If Sarah was down there in a raging fire, she wouldn't make it out alive.

Twenty-five feet below the Misener building, Sarah stared into the distance. From the brightness of the glow, she sensed the fire was gathering speed, getting bigger and more powerful.

A tumultuous roar filled the tunnel. She cringed and put her hands over her ears, coughing. Her only option was to go forward, towards the fire, but her feet wouldn't move. Tears trickled from her smarting eyes. Soon the drives would become unbearably hot. The flames would eat the oxygen. If she was lucky, she'd pass out before they turned her skin to liquid.

She strove to block out her fear and get her bearings. But more crazed thoughts surfaced. She was suffocating. Her hair was on fire. She was burning to death. Shaken and disoriented, she reached out and touched the wall. It was damp and slimy. "Ugh!" She wiped her hand on her sweater.

At that moment, a boom was followed by a flash of light and she saw the archway of an intersecting tunnel sixty yards ahead. Time was running out. This might be her last chance to find the other exit. Still unsure that it was the right thing to do, she moved forward, towards the fire.

The smoke was thickening. Her throat tickled and she began to cough uncontrollably, tearing her abdominal muscles. Her heart was beating so fast it hurt. Dizzy, gasping for air, she dropped to the floor. Ignoring the sharp gravel digging into her knees and palms, she crawled forward. At the intersection, she turned, continued a few yards and stopped. The air seemed fresher here. Standing up, she saw a faint light some distance ahead. It appeared man-made. With a rush of adrenalin, Sarah dashed towards it, coughing.

The cry of joy she gave at seeing the word 'exit' on an illuminated sign died on her lips as another violent explosion echoed through the tunnels. She screamed and leaped for the stairs. Both hands on the railing, she climbed up, legs wobbly, shoulders brushing against the walls. The stairs were worn and uneven from more than a century of use and the darkness was solid again. She'd been climbing for what seemed like aeons when she bumped face first into a solid object. The door? She found a handle and tried to turn it. It wouldn't budge.

"Help! Help!" She pounded on it with her fist, then stopped. By now the building had been evacuated. No one would be looking for her, because Dunne hadn't entered their names on the sign-in board.

A dense cloud of smoke drifted up the stairwell, fuelling Sarah's claustrophobia. Soon they'd set off the fire extinguishers. If they used chemicals she'd suffocate. She had to get out. Twisting round in the tight space, she dashed down the steps and slipped. She made a wild grab for the railing, missed it and fell backwards, her skull hitting the stone step.

On the ground floor of the Misener building, near the entrance to the drives, the broad beams of the ceiling were supported by dull-red steel posts. Behind them five-hundred-gallon oak puncheons stretched as far as the eye could see. The fire extinguisher panel was tucked away in a corner. Workers circled Gerry Marks, who was having a heated dialogue with a technician, attempting to reroute the shorted circuit board. She flipped her phone shut and announced, in a cold fury, "That's it. The extinguisher isn't going to work. Damn Noonan to hell."

Blackwell appeared, put an arm round her shoulders, and described his conversation with Dunne's secretary. "Andrew's truck has gone and he's not answering his phone. But if Sarah had come upstairs with him, she'd have gone straight to the conference room, knowing we were waiting to have lunch with her. She must still be in the drives."

"I hope to God you're wrong." Gerry rubbed her hands on her white shirt, now smoke-smudged and filthy. "The main entrance is blocked and the worst explosions seem to be around the entrance at Drive C. It won't be long before the floor collapses into the tunnel. There's no way to get in or out. We'll have to wait for the fire brigade."

"I can't leave her there. She'll never make it out on her own." He ran towards the pathway down to the drives.

"Graham, it's suicide." Gerry shouted. "You don't even know that she's down there."

His face and clothing grimy with soot, Blackwell arrived at the entry to Drive C. The smallish door was padlocked. He reached up and ran his fingers along the top of the door frame and found the key he'd seen Gerry use during their last foray into the drives. Inserting it, he snapped off the padlock, threw it on to the floor, then stood to one side and opened the door. Hot fumes escaped, but there were no flames. He took a deep breath and went down into the inferno.

The width of his shoulders forced Blackwell to slide sideways down the twisting, worn steps. Fighting for breath, he stepped on something soft and nearly lost his balance. He grasped the railing and bent over awkwardly. Blinking away tears that the smoke had induced, he saw the outline of a body positioned at a strange angle. It was Sarah Bennett. She wasn't moving.

Chapter Thirty-nine

Heaving himself off the bed, Sergeant Leroy Watson rolled back the cover with its garish palm-tree pattern. At least the sheets looked clean. He made his way to the air-conditioner and turned it on full blast, hoping the cold air would reduce the room's stench. If he had to be away from his five children, he'd rather have been in a nice hotel and not this dive on the wrong side of International Boulevard close to Orlando airport.

He picked up the moon pie and the can of sweet tea he had purchased from a convenience store across the street and slid open the balcony door. He went outside to admire the dramatic colours of the setting sun while he ate his pie. He'd only had a few bites when his phone rang. He stuffed the remainder into his mouth, chewed, swallowed, and managed to answer on the fifth ring. "Lieutenant Cameron arrived?" he asked.

"Yeah. Meet us in the parking lot," McDermott barked.

Watson holstered his gun, put on a lightweight black jacket over his tangerine shirt and left the room. As he emerged from the hotel, he spotted McDermott standing by a navy car, talking to James Cameron, a fit-looking man with a runner's build.

Detective Superintendent Sebastian O'Connor and Cameron had been friends with Watson's boss since they'd roomed together during a course at the Northwest Traffic Institute. Even so, Watson marvelled at the speed with which they'd responded to his boss's call for assistance in the Somers case. He should be so lucky to have friends like that.

"Pleasure." Cameron shook Watson's hand. "I was just saying how that scumbag Riley escaped from hospital an hour ago."

His expression stoic, Watson shrugged his shoulders. The sole purpose of their trip had been to interrogate Riley.

Cameron turned to McDermott, a twinkle in his eyes. "However, your intuition paid off, Bernie. I've planned something else for your evening's entertainment – that is if you're game." He fished a set of keys from his pocket. "Ready to rock and roll?"

After driving south on an eight-lane highway for a quarter of an hour, they turned on to a rutted track lined with pin oaks in need of trimming. Cameron pulled up in front of an ancient building, designed in the old Florida style, with a tin roof and wraparound porch. The paint was peeling, and a shaky wheelchair ramp zigzagged to the ground from the front door.

"I guess crime doesn't pay," Cameron joked, "or Riley would never have left his mother to die in this shithole." As he spoke, two uniformed officers materialized. They exchanged a few words with Cameron, then slipped back to their posts.

"No sign of Riley," Cameron told McDermott and Watson, as they headed up the ramp into the building.

Inside, a girl with coal-black hair greeted the three policemen from behind a wooden counter. She put down the blue polish she'd been using to touch up her nails and checked their identification. Then she motioned them to follow her down a long, narrow hall.

The sickly-sweet smell of decaying bodies struck Watson as he passed an open door. On a bed, propped up by a large wedge of pillows, was a bag of bones with straggly white hair. He guessed it was a woman. His eyes met hers and veered away from the pain in them. He hoped Mrs Riley was in better shape.

Watson and Cameron took up position outside Mrs Riley's room while McDermott and the girl entered. It had been decided that McDermott would conduct the interview on his own.

"Mrs Riley," the girl said, in a sing-song voice, to a tiny woman sitting in a wheelchair facing the door. "This is Lieutenant McDermott. I told you about him. He's the police officer from Atlanta."

"Hello, Mrs Riley. May I come in?" McDermott asked, as the girl departed.

The old woman's watery eyes studied him briefly before she answered, her voice surprising strong, with an almost imperceptible English accent. "Of course you may, young man."

"Thank you, ma'am." McDermott took in the hospital bed and its threadbare, blue-cotton cover. On the pitted metal nightstand there were a few faded photographs and a cheap alarm clock. A box of Kleenex lay on a dresser that had seen better days. Attached by a metal frame to the wall, a small black-and-white TV droned in the background. Although the linoleum floor was cracked, it was spotlessly clean, as was the rest of the room. He pulled a stool close to Mrs Riley's wheelchair. "I'm here about your son – about Colin."

"Everyone calls him Wicky." she interjected, studying

her blue-veined hands. "You've come a long way to talk to me. That means he's done something terrible this time, doesn't it?"

"Well, ma'am . . ." McDermott trailed off, aware of the old woman's fragility.

"Don't even think of coddling me. I may be old, but I'm not stupid. I want the truth."

The vehemence with which she spoke caught McDermott off guard. "Your son is wanted for questioning in connection with a homicide. Do you know where we can find him?" he said, more bluntly than he'd intended.

"No, I don't." the old woman responded firmly.

"When was the last time you saw him?"

She lowered her head as if thinking, then looked up. "I want to know who Wicky murdered." Her voice faltered slightly.

"Actually, I'm here to find out if a call you received recently from Australia has any bearing on the death of Sam Somers," McDermott told her, softly this time. "I'd like to know who called and what you talked about."

Mrs Riley's face crumpled at the mention of Somers's name. "Wicky used to be such a loving boy, but he scares me now. You have to stop him. Please promise me you won't harm him if I help you."

"I'll do everything I can," McDermott promised, shifting in the uncomfortable chair. His back still hurt from sitting in the plane's cramped seats.

She began to talk as if in a trance. "We were living in England when my husband lost his job and began drinking. Wicky was ten when his father took a knife to him. He still has the scars." She shuddered. "Wicky and I moved to Australia. Alone. I thought he'd be all right, until he started running around with that gang from King's Cross. It took every last cent I had to get him to America."

She surveyed the shabby room, tears forming in her eyes. "But they wouldn't leave him alone. I overheard him on the phone that day, you know. Supposedly he'd come for a visit, but he was really waiting for that call. I haven't seen or heard from him since."

McDermott changed position again, ignoring the pain shooting down his legs. On a hunch he'd asked Cameron to check Mrs Riley's phone records. The call had originated from the Southern Valley Winery in South Australia. "Who called him?"

"I don't know. Wicky said it was a friend from Kings Cross. He asked me to wait outside. He wanted to talk in private."

"But you listened in, didn't you?" McDermott asked, his voice firm but polite.

"Yes." She was staring at her hands again. "Wicky kept repeating a name, as if to remember it. The name was Somers. Sam Somers." She began to sob. "That poor man. I read about him in the paper a few days later."

McDermott went to her dresser and pulled a handful of tissues from the box. He handed them to her and retreated to his seat. After she had stopped crying, he said softly, "Mrs Riley, tell me about his friends from Kings Cross."

Mrs Riley looked bewildered, then said, "There was a boy, part Aboriginal, and a girl he talked about incessantly. I warned him about her, but he refused to listen. Her people were trash. Her brother, he was murdered, was a friend of Wicky's. I can't remember their names.

They were terrible people." Suddenly she put a hand to her head and let out a high-pitched moan.

Later that evening, McDermott was ensconced at Lieutenant James Cameron's desk in the Orlando Police Department building, while Cameron and Watson went in search of something to drink. The offices testified to their proximity to Disney World, a fantasy police station with peachy designer walls, honey-brown desks, matching chairs and filing cabinets, colour-coordinated laminate floors and hundreds of commendations on the walls, flanked by American flags. McDermott felt as if Cinderella might waltz past at any moment.

Leaning back in the adjustable chair, he chewed the end of a pencil. He'd just concluded a phone call to the nurse, who reported that Mrs Riley was resting peacefully in hospital after a mild seizure. Sometimes his job sucked.

He glanced at his watch. It was late Tuesday afternoon now in Sydney, Australia. He picked up the telephone and dialled a number from memory. It was answered on the first ring. "Detective Superintendent O'Connor," a voice snapped.

McDermott's gut tightened. "Sebastian, my friend, aren't you supposed to be at the airport meeting Sarah?"

"Bernie." O'Connor hesitated. "First, Sarah's fine, but there was an incident at the winery." He described the fire and Sarah's rescue by Graham Blackwell, then the security measures that were being put in place. "We'll take care of her like she's family. Doolan's brother-in-law is on the detail. Listen, Bernie, I'm sorry this happened. I miscalculated. I don't know who they are, or how the hell they found her, but they damn well won't get close to her again."

"I know you'll take good care of her." McDermott coughed. "So, being the wine snob you are, what can you tell me about Southern Valley Winery?"

"Not much. They're a bulk producer. Their chief winemaker was killed recently, in a commercial airline accident. What's your interest?"

"Someone made a call from Southern Valley to Wicky Riley, one of the suspects in Somers's murder," he said, and gave him the gist of Mrs Riley's story.

"I have an old timer who's tracked those gangs for years. If anyone can figure out which one Riley belonged to, it's Geoff Stabler," O'Connor told him.

Chapter Forty

Late on Tuesday afternoon, a man with white-blond hair strode through the front door of the Australian Wine Bureau's temporary offices. He walked past Inga Wismar as if she were invisible, his footsteps muffled by the Oriental runner. "Kingsley, you cock-sucking Prussian prick," she heard Macquarie Hawke snarl in the corridor. "I want that export certificate for my shiraz or, as they say in America, you can kiss your ass goodbye!" He strode into the room and slammed the door.

Kingsley's measured response came to her clearly through the thin wall: "I suggest we sit down and discuss this like gentlemen."

When the men lowered their voices, she slid her chair closer to the door and strained to hear them. She nearly jumped out of her skin when someone coughed. Spinning round, she saw an emaciated young man in front of her desk, shaking, his eyes red. He pushed his glasses up the bridge of his nose. "Ma'am? I'm Jason Findley, chief winemaker at Southern Valley. I'm here to see Graham Blackwell." His eyes darted about as he removed a piece of paper from his inside jacket pocket. "It's urgent. I need to deliver this document to him."

"One moment." Inga stood up, wondering if he was on drugs. She went to Kingsley's office and rapped on the door, then glanced back over her shoulder. The specks on the young man's glasses looked like dried blood. When Kingsley opened the door, she whispered her concerns, then stepped aside.

"Hello, Jason." Kingsley moved forward, his hand outstretched. "Mr Blackwell is out of the office for a few days. If you leave that with me, I'll make sure he gets it."

Findley held fast to the document. Bluey's instructions had been specific. Hand it to Blackwell and no one else. But surely he could trust the general manager. He shoved it at Kingsley, who snatched it from him.

Kingsley held the document at arm's length, squinting to read the fine print without his glasses. His head jerked up. "Is someone using their horn in the car park? Inga, go find out what it's about."

Inga had been reading the document over his shoulder. Startled, she jumped back, then glanced at Findley. His eyes were directed at something behind her. When his expression changed from apprehension to terror, she whirled around. Macquarie Hawke was framed in the doorway. The look on his face made her shiver. When she turned back, Findley had vanished.

Much later that evening, in the cosy, six-table restaurant at the hotel across the street from the Rose B-and-B, Bluestone Cellars sparkling wine fizzed in Sarah's glass. Across the pedestal table, Graham Blackwell was finishing his soup. It was slow evening and they were the only customers, for which she was grateful. She took a sip of wine and put it down. Too warm in her green dress, she pushed up the sleeves, then set aside her untouched soup and scrutinized Blackwell. He was staying at the hotel and had changed his filthy clothes for a brown suede jacket, striped shirt and charcoal grey trousers. His mannerisms reminded her of her college art-history professor, a charming bachelor.

"Gerry won't be able to join us after all." He closed his phone and stowed it in his jacket pocket. "She wanted you to know that several sections of the drives were damaged, but it won't affect the bottling lines."

"That's good news." she replied, her head pounding. The doctor had insisted she didn't have concussion: the headache was the result of a nasty bump and smoke inhalation. She'd flushed the painkillers he'd given her down the toilet and was now regretting it. The lump on the back of her head had swollen to the size of an ostrich egg – at least, that was how it felt.

Clanking dishes announced the arrival of their waiter, who cleared their soup bowls, then served the main course of lamb, new potatoes and asparagus. He poured them each a glass of the Bluestone Cellars Coonawarra Shiraz, sent over by Gerry Marks, then left them alone.

Sarah pushed the food round on her plate, then looked at Blackwell. "So, what exactly was it you wanted to talk to me about?"

Blackwell swallowed a mouthful of lamb, then put down his fork. "Gerry overheard you and Andrew discussing a file in Davis Hart's computer. The one for SV556. I wanted to know more about it." When her already strained expression deepened, he hastened to add, "She told me in the strictest confidence. She was worried about the implications."

"Right. Like why Andrew was completely unconcerned about its contents?" Sarah bit her lower lip, cursing herself for not having the presence of mind to keep quiet. She didn't need to cast suspicion on the Addison Group's chief winemaker, or cause problems for the company, not with the contract renewal on the line.

Blackwell shrugged, then pulled apart a hot roll and slathered it with butter. "You must understand, Kennedy's family has been making wine in the Barossa Valley for four generations. He and Andrew have been friends for years. Andrew had no reason to be suspicious." He put the bread into his mouth. The butter had melted and dripped on his hand. He reached for his napkin.

Sarah lowered her eyes to hide her confusion. Why on earth would Gerry confide such damaging information to the marketing manager of the Australian Wine Bureau, and why would he defend a winemaker who might or might not be involved in a scam? "You and Gerry are friends, aren't you? Andrew too." It sounded like an accusation.

"Yes. Gerry and I went to college together. I met Andrew through her," Blackwell admitted. "But getting back to the file, Gerry seemed to think it indicated the cabernet sauvignon Andrew bought contained forty per cent chenin blanc and riesling."

"Yes. But Andrew's convinced the file is a worksheet. The paperwork guaranteed that the wine was a hundred per cent cabernet." It was strange that Blackwell had travelled all the way to the Pyrenees to talk to her about Southern Valley when Davis Hart had already reported them to the AWB. An unsettling thought struck her. Suppose Blackwell had been sent here to find out what she knew and whom she'd told, then contain the situation?

She pushed her chair back, stood up and slung the gold chain of her black leather clutch bag over her shoulder. "If you'll excuse me, I'm not feeling too great. I need to lie down. The constable's outside and he can escort me back to the Rose."

"I can't let you do that." Blackwell threw down his napkin, vaulted out of his chair and was at her side.

Her hand flew to the plaster on her throat and she backed away, eyes swivelling to the door.

"God, Sarah, I didn't mean that the way it came out." Blackwell threw his hands into the air and moved away from her. "Listen, I didn't want to get into this now but I have a real problem on my hands. Southern Valley sells bulk wine to every major winery. If it's ripping off its customers, supplying them with cheap blends of God knows what varietals as premium wine and the international press gets wind of it, our industry stands to lose millions – perhaps billions – of dollars. Every wine from every producer will be suspect. I'm talking world-wide problems. Think about it. In the US alone, our sales are well over seven hundred and fifty million dollars a year. That's ex-cellars. In US dollars. I won't even begin to speculate what'll happen to our economy." He shook his head. "Please, Sarah, stay and talk to me."

Sarah lost the battle against a tickle in her throat and began to cough. She held on to the back of the chair, hacking until her ribs ached. When the bout was over, Blackwell was staring at her neck with what she could tell was genuine concern. Touching the plaster, she realized it had come loose. She pressed it down. "I always heard you should never inhale."

Blackwell gave her a half-hearted smile, then poured a glass of water and handed it to her. She forced it down, still holding on to the chair. "You didn't touch your dinner," he said. "Maybe you'd feel better if you ate something." His voice was melodious and soothing. "How about an omelette?"

Sarah thought about returning to the Rose and slugging down a glass of the liqueur Muscat but she said, "With Cheddar cheese would be nice. And chips."

Blackwell leaned over and gathered up their plates. "I'll be right back."

As she watched him walk away, Sarah suspected he had probably been very fit at one time, but middle age had packed a few extra pounds on him. When he returned, Blackwell removed his leather jacket, draped it over the back of a chair and rolled up his shirt sleeves. "I understand your reluctance to talk to me. You're worried what you say might be used against the Addison Group." He gave her a disarming smile. "And you're upset with Gerry for involving me in this. Then there's my friendship with Andrew, whom you suspect, at the very least, left you alone in the drives deliberately. Am I right?"

"Close enough."

"As I'm sure you know, once a wine's been made, there's no way to prove what grapes were used in it, where they were sourced or when they were harvested. Since there's no way to prove that the wine Andrew bought was anything other than Southern Valley claimed, Gerry came to me for advice." Blackwell lifted his glass and sipped, taking time to get his thoughts straight. "Due to the fire, the order was cancelled and since Gerry consulted with me, the Addison Group's possible involvement is a non-issue." He took another sip, observing Sarah over the rim of the glass.

"Does that include Andrew?" Sarah brushed a strand of hair behind her ear.

Blackwell sighed and put down his glass. "He wasn't responsible for what happened to you in the drives."

"Oh? Was it just my bad luck I was alone down there when the fire broke out?"

"I'm not saying that either." Blackwell picked up the bottle of shiraz and topped up his glass, then Sarah's. "I talked to Andrew an hour ago. The police cleared him of any wrongdoing. He's devastated about what happened to you."

"Right." She wasn't convinced. "So what exactly was his excuse for leaving me down there?"

Blackwell frowned. "He had a call from the police saying his parents had been seriously injured in a car crash. He left in such a hurry he forgot to take his phone. On the way to Ballarat, he stopped to call his sister from a pay-phone and found out his parents were with her, having tea."

"And he'd just left? Without letting anyone know I was still in the drives?"

"No!" Blackwell was losing his patience. "He asked a worker to go after you."

"Is that right? So why didn't they?"

"No one knows. The man disappeared and Andrew couldn't remember his name."

"How convenient!" Sarah scoffed.

"Give him a break!" Blackwell snapped. Forcing himself to calm down, he continued, "With the number of temporary workers they've hired this year, Andrew couldn't possibly remember all their names. Anyway, the man wasn't an employee. Whoever he was, the police believe he may have started the fire."

"They think it was arson?" she asked. "What did the man look like? Did anyone see him other than Andrew?"

"A fork-lift driver," he replied. He described what he knew of the afternoon's events. "A special police unit is arriving from Melbourne later tonight. In the meantime, a local sketch artist is working with Andrew and the fork-lift operator." Blackwell's anger subsided. "For the record, I believe Andrew should have gone after you himself, but he wasn't thinking clearly. I do not believe he left you there on purpose."

"I hope you're right," Sarah said, weary now of bickering. She fiddled with her glass, twirling it on the tablecloth. "Graham, I'll help you in any way I can, but wouldn't it make more sense to investigate the winery?"

He nodded at the offered truce, paused until the waiter had served Sarah's omelette and departed, then said, "It's not my call, but from what I gather, it's a possibility some time in the near future. In the meantime, I'd like to know everything that happened at Southern Valley that day you saw the file in the computer. Who was there, what you saw, whatever you can remember."

"Why?" Sarah picked up her fork and poked at the omelette.

"Humour me." Blackwell grinned. "That's the least you can do for the person who dragged you to safety."

"I see." She arched her right eyebrow. "You saved my life so now I'm for ever in your debt?"

"Well, I have to confess," Blackwell said, the wrinkles around his eyes deepening as his grin widened, "I was searching for Andrew and I only helped you out of the stairwell because you were blocking the exit."

"Carried me is more like it." Sarah put down her fork, her expression sombre. "The firemen said it was pure luck you didn't die trying to rescue me. I'm in your debt."

"Anyone would have done the same." he said. "Let's get back to the file."

Over the next few minutes, Sarah reviewed her visit to Southern Valley. "That's about it. Jason came to fetch me when Julianna and Andrew were done." She paused. "I feel as if I'm missing something important."

"Try imagining yourself in Hart's office. What do you see?"

Sarah closed her eyes and visualized walking towards the desk. "Papers, piled everywhere. I remember a blend profile for SV888, signed by Kennedy, sitting on a stack of papers piled on a chair. The wine was sixty-three per cent grenache and thirty-seven per cent shiraz." Her eyes flew open. "It was sold to Nathan Smyth as hundred per cent shiraz."

"How do you know that?" Blackwell blurted out. "Never mind. Tell me later."

She picked up her fork. Nothing on her plate looked appetizing enough to eat. It made her think of the emaciated Jason Findley. "Wait! As we were leaving, I saw Jason stoop and stuff something into his shirt. A piece of paper from the chair! I must have forgotten about it because the next thing I ran smack into Macquarie Hawke."

"Do you think it was the SV888 document?"

"Yes." She cut a piece of omelette and stuffed it into her mouth. It tasted like soggy cardboard.

Blackwell's phone rang. Reaching round the back of his chair, he extricated it from his jacket. He answered, then went silent, his face pale. "Inga, please calm down! Tell me where they found him." Blackwell's grip on the phone tightened until his knuckles turned white. "What paper? What are you talking about?" A short silence followed, then Blackwell asked, "Who signed it?" Lips pursed, he listened to the response. "That paper is very important, but I don't want you looking for it now. It's too dangerous. Wait until tomorrow . . . No! Don't hang up! Bloody hell!" He hit redial several times, then gave up, returning the phone to his jacket. Resting his elbows on the table, he rubbed his forehead with his fingertips.

"I gather that was Inga." Sarah said. "What's the matter, Graham? What's happened?"

Blackwell raised his head. He appeared disoriented, his hazel eyes troubled. "Inga was watching TV when a live report came on. The police have found Jason Findley's body in the trunk of his car with his dead cat. He'd been stabbed."

Several hundred miles away, in the Barossa Valley home of Angus Kennedy, the flat-screen TV cast a blue-green light on Julianna Porter as she pushed aside the covers and climbed out of bed.

Her movements woke Kennedy. Groaning, he rubbed the back of his neck and reached over to switch on the bedside lamp. The room was another of his wife's creations, dominated by elaborate gold-leafed 'French' furniture with ornate carvings, swooping draperies and a red and gold silk bedspread. "Where are you going?" He had caught a fleeting glimpse of her buttocks as she disappeared into the bathroom. Her behaviour was worrying him. She'd arrived three hours late with several nasty scratches on her arms that she had refused to explain. At that moment, he heard the sound of rushing water. What the hell was she doing, taking a shower at this time of night? Suddenly his attention was caught by an image of Jason Findley on the TV screen. "Holy Mother of God!" he gasped.

He got out of bed, put on a dressing-gown and leather slippers, then hurried into his study and flipped on the overhead light. At the drinks cabinet, he poured Scotch into a crystal tumbler. After he'd drained the glass, he poured three more inches, then marched across the room to a painting above the fireplace. He swung it aside and entered a code into a keypad. The door to his safe clicked open. He took out Southern Valley's code book, a slim volume of handwritten names and numbers relating to their suppliers. He closed the safe and returned the painting to its original position.

Placing the glass on the mantelpiece, he began to rip pages out of the book and throw them into the fire. It was roaring by the time he tossed in the empty binding. He closed the screen, retrieved his drink, then sat at an oval desk and dialled an Adelaide number.

"Hello?" a voice muttered.

"Why did you kill Findley?" Kennedy slurred.

"Hold on a minute." Macquarie Hawke turned on the bedside lamp, got out of bed, and found his dressing-gown tucked into the folds of the grey coverlet bunched at the foot of the sleek brass bed. He put it on and went to kiss the naked girl pretending to be asleep under the covers. Her tawny hair was exactly the same colour as Julianna's. The comparison made him uneasy. "Stay put. I'll be right back."

Hawke shuffled into the living room, switched on a lamp and collapsed on to the sofa. The rhythmic ticking of the grandfather clock was replaced by two loud gongs. Hawke rolled his eyes. Speaking quietly, he said, "For your information, I was with Kingsley this afternoon. Findley delivered the blend profile to him, the one with your signature on it."

"I'll be damned. He had it all the time. What the hell are we going to do?"

The night was clear and the moon shone brightly in the narrow canyon of deserted buildings as Graham Blackwell and Sarah left the restaurant and headed across the road to the Rose. Sarah's heels clicked loudly on the pavement. "Did you hear that?" She twisted round to confirm that the police car was still parked in a side-street next to the restaurant. Blackwell detected the faint orange glow of the constable's cigarette and thought she seemed marginally more relaxed for having seen it too. When she turned back, her heel caught in a crack on the pavement.

"Hear what?" Blackwell asked, grasping her arm. Once she'd regained her balance, he let go.

"Thanks. If you don't mind, I think I'll hang on to your arm."

"No worries." Blackwell felt her shudder. He suspected it had little to do with the cool evening air.

Directly after Inga's call, the police had barged into the restaurant with two sketches, one based on Dunne's description of the man he'd asked to bring Sarah up from the drives, the other based on the fork-lift driver's. She identified Slattery from the driver's description, then related the series of events leading to the attack. The current theory was that Slattery had started the fire in the drives to finish what he'd started in Cleland Park.

"Tell me honestly, Sarah. How are you feeling?"

"I'll manage. But I don't understand how the police

can be so certain Slattery won't come after me tonight when he finds out he botched the second attempt," she said.

"It's their job to know these things." Blackwell disengaged his arm to unlatch the low wooden gate leading to the Rose's front garden. "Personally, I think he'd be crazy to try anything with so many police in the vicinity."

"But Slattery *is* crazy! Otherwise why would he be after me?" Moonlight highlighted her hair, leaving her face shadowed. "Graham, I meant to ask you earlier," she went on. "What paper was Inga talking about? Why were you so worried about her?"

"Let's go inside," he replied.

As they went into the kitchen, Sarah said, "I know it's late, but would you like some coffee?"

"Only if it's decaf." Blackwell cruised past her to the table. "I'm getting too old to drink high test so late at night or, rather, so early in the morning."

"Yes, I can see that." She played along, throwing up her hands in mock despair. "You probably need to sit down before you fall over."

"You didn't have to agree so readily!" Blackwell chuckled.

"I'm sure I saw some decaf," Sarah said, then rifled through the cupboards. Finding a full canister, she handed it to him. "Wait a minute. There's a piece of chocolate cake somewhere. It would go well with this liqueur muscat." She picked up the bottle, surprised to see she and Jake had drunk almost half of it. "What do you say to dessert?"

Blackwell's stomach growled and they laughed.

"I'll take that as a yes," she said. While Blackwell

made the coffee, she set the table with plates, coffee cups, glasses and silver.

A few minutes later, sitting across from her at the table, Blackwell stirred sugar and milk into his coffee. "If you like, Sarah," he began, "I'll stay here tonight, even if there is a policeman outside – if you'd feel safer, that is."

She sidestepped the question. "Tell me about Inga." she said, though a mouthful of cake.

"She said Findley was at the office this morning to deliver a document. It was the SV888 blend profile, signed by Kennedy."

"Really? It must have been what I saw him sneak into his shirt." She picked up her glass and sipped. "How bizarre. Why would anyone at Southern Valley print out the real contents of SV888? Why would Kennedy sign it? Why would Jason hand it over to the Bureau if he was involved in the fraud?"

"It is rather extraordinary," Blackwell answered thoughtfully. "The only thing we know for sure is that Jason handed it to Kingsley this morning. Now he's dead."

She shuddered. "Maybe someone found out and murdered him before he could do any more damage. If that's true, then how did the murderer know he went to the AWB? You don't suppose Kingsley . . ."

"Findley could have told any number of people what he intended to do." Blackwell pointed out. "What strikes me as odd is that he took the document a week ago. Why did they wait so long to stop him?"

"Because they didn't know he had it until he showed up at your office?"

"Or they thought someone else had taken it." Blackwell

set his fork on the side of his plate without taking a bite of the cake.

"Maybe they didn't know it was missing."

"Oh, I think they did." Blackwell clenched his jaw. "You were with Findley when he stuffed the paper into his shirt. Later that evening you interrupted someone ransacking your hotel room. The next day someone tried to steal your briefcase. Then Slattery attacked you in Cleland, demanding the paper you'd 'stolen'."

Sarah put the fork on her empty plate, her eyes widening. "You're implying that whoever murdered Jason thought I'd taken the document? So they came after me, but when Jason showed up at your office, they realized their mistake and murdered him instead?"

"Like you said, he was still a threat," Blackwell said.

"But why did Slattery try to kill me this afternoon?" Sarah asked.

"I'm not sure. Maybe they didn't have a chance to call him off." Blackwell shrugged, evidently puzzled. "Or you're still a danger to them, same as Jason was."

"No. It has to be a mistake. A terrible mistake!" Sarah exclaimed, her voice rasping. But even as she disputed Blackwell's speculation, she realized it fitted together all too seamlessly. "Who do you think is behind it?"

"Exposing the fraud would destroy Angus Kennedy's business," Blackwell said. "But I have a problem with his motive. His wife is one of the wealthiest women in Australia. Even if he or the company were found guilty of fraud the fines would be no more than an irritation to her. With the best lawyers, he might even get out of doing jail time. Murdering someone to protect his business doesn't make sense."

"Kennedy might have another reason. Gustaf, the owner of the Tanunda Bistro, told me about him and –" Sarah began to cough. "I need some medicine. Be right back." Her chair screeched as she stood up.

"I'll go outside and bum a cigarette off the constable," Blackwell said, taking the key to the front door off the table.

Sarah went through the sitting room, where the fire was little more than a dim glow, and into her bathroom. She uncapped the cough-syrup bottle and swigged. The liquid was sliding down her throat when she heard a noise in the bedroom. "Graham? Is that you?"

Chapter Forty-one

Graham Blackwell stepped into the front garden of the Rose. The night had turned chilly and damp. He wished he was in his Adelaide flat sitting in front of the fire, wearing his favourite cashmere cardigan and leather slippers. A sharp breeze tugged at his thin leather jacket as he surveyed the corridor of buildings stretching in either direction. When his eyes rested on the police car across the street, he remembered the cigarette and fought the craving briefly. Then, disgusted with himself for giving into the urge after twenty odd years' abstinence, he began to walk towards the officer.

His phone's shrill ring made his heart skip a beat. "Hello?"

"It's Inga. I'm at the office. I think I know what happened to the document, the one Jason Findley brought in." She described what she'd found.

Blackwell was beside himself. "Lock the front door this minute and call the police. Tell them everything you know, then insist one escorts you home." She promised to do as he'd asked and he ended the call, then went across the street to the police car, shadowed from the moonlight by the restaurant.

"Constable? Hello?" Blackwell's voice echoed up and down the deserted street.

Something wasn't right. It was too quiet. Coming to the driver's side, he peered into the open window, catching a whiff of stale cigarettes. The officer was leaning back, his mouth wide open, sound asleep. Blackwell was appalled. "Officer? Wake up!"

When there was no response, Blackwell shook him and felt something sticky on his fingers. He wrenched open the door. The overhead light came on as the officer's head rolled to one side, opening a wide gap below his jaw where his throat had been slit from ear to ear. "Oh my God!" Blackwell backed away. His hands were covered with blood.

In that instant, he heard a high-pitched squeal and recoiled, then realized it was static from the constable's radio. He reached inside and depressed a button. "Hello? Can you hear me? A police officer has been murdered! I'm across the street from the Rose bed-and-breakfast. He was guarding Sarah Bennett – bloody hell!" Blackwell took off towards the Rose, arms and legs pumping like pistons. He crossed the road at breakneck speed and tripped, crashing to the pavement.

Sarah closed the bathroom door, but it was too thick for the frame and wouldn't stay shut. There was an ancient dead bolt at eye level. She reached up and turned the thumbscrew, then went back to the wash-basin, where she'd left the cough syrup. The doorknob rattled. She whirled round.

"Police. Open up!"

Sarah recognized the voice, gasped and backed away. "I know who you are, Slattery, and I'm calling the policeman across the street. He'll be here in seconds."

There was a short bark of laughter, then the door rattled. She bit back a scream.

"Forget about the constable. But if you come out now, I promise not to slit your boyfriend's throat."

He must mean Graham, she thought. She glanced round the bathroom. There was one door and no windows. Another blow rattled the door, followed by a sharp crack. She whipped around. A wide fissure split the middle. "You're making a mistake," she said, shaking violently. "Jason Findley took the paper. He's dead. It's over. Can't you hear the sirens?"

"You fucking bitch," he snarled, and proceeded to describe, in terrifying detail, exactly what he intended to do to her.

Graham Blackwell crept into the empty sitting room, praying that the siren in the distance wasn't a figment of his imagination. He picked up the poker, then glided down the short hallway and stopped outside Sarah's bedroom. The door was open a crack. Brandishing the poker, he charged inside. There was no bloody body on the floor. The quilt on the bed was undisturbed. The only thing out of place was the open window, lacy white curtains flapping in the breeze.

He crossed the room and leaned out and scanned the gloomy street. It was deserted, aside from the squad cars pulling up outside. Not far away, a motorcycle revved and took off with a roar.

Blackwell hurried down the hall to the bathroom. Slivers of wood littered the floor. "Sarah, it's Graham. Slattery's gone. Open the door."

For a few heart-stopping moments there was silence. Was she dead? Then the battered door creaked open and Sarah emerged, emerald eyes wide with shock. Keeping the door between herself and Blackwell, she peered beyond him. "Where is he?"

"He must have climbed out the bedroom window. I

think he left on a motorcycle." Blackwell put the poker down and reached for her, but she backed away, staring with horror at his hands. "Whose blood is that?"

"I'll explain after I've washed."

She gave Blackwell a wide berth as he brushed past her to the sink.

Chapter Forty-two

The Vegemite sandwich, a childhood favourite, sat untouched on Detective Superintendent Sebastian O'Connor's utilitarian black-and-grey laminate desk in the ultra-modern offices of the New South Wales Police Headquarters in downtown Parramatta, a western suburb of Sydney. He considered going to the cafeteria for a bowl of vegetable soup, but right now he couldn't stomach its cold, institutional atmosphere. It was as if the building had been designed for a sci-fi movie. Anything with distinguishing characteristics or slight imperfections had been banished in favour of white, grey and black plastic with space-age sleek contours.

In sharp comparison his drab office was cluttered with personal keepsakes. The walls were covered with photographs, the largest being a snapshot taken during Northwest Traffic School, in which he stood arm in arm with Bernie McDermott and James Cameron. Next to it was a photo of last year's Christmas party at Danny Doolan's. He tore away his eyes and stared out of the window. Finally he picked up the telephone and dialled McDermott's home number.

"Who the hell is this?" McDermott said, glancing at his alarm clock, wishing he hadn't had those three beers before he'd turned off the lights an hour ago. "Don't you know it's past midnight?"

O'Connor snorted. "I didn't wake you up, did I, mate?"

McDermott felt a hippopotamus sit on his chest. "Talk to me."

"Sarah is safe and on her way to us," O'Connor said. "However, the man I asked to guard her overnight, Danny Doolan's brother-in-law, was murdered. Slattery slit his throat trying to get to Sarah."

"Jesus H. Christ, give me a minute." McDermott had heard the anguish in his friend's voice. Danny Doolan had been on O'Connor's team for ten years before he'd moved to Adelaide and the pair still celebrated all major holidays together. The Doolans were the family O'Connor had never had.

McDermott threw off the covers and sat up, letting his legs hang over the side of the bed as he flicked on the light that stood on his mission-style bedside table, part of a suite he'd purchased in Chicago. He rubbed his face. "I'm really sorry, Sebastian. Tell me about it."

O'Connor relayed the events leading to the identification of Slattery as the arsonist at the winery, the constable's murder and subsequent attack on Sarah, "The sirens scared him off. He hasn't been apprehended. Yet."

"Fuck!" McDermott slid his feet into the slippers on the floor beside the bed. "Slattery didn't tail her to the Pyrenees. He knows her schedule. A fire like that doesn't happen on the spur of the moment. He knew in advance she'd be going into the tunnels and got there before she did to set it up. The only way he could get that information is from someone at the Addison Group and Andrew Dunne's story sounds like bullshit."

Julianna raised her head from the desk in her second-floor office at Southern Valley and scanned the pale apricot room, painted to complement the new burnt-umber carpet. Another sharp tap on the door drew her eyes to the frosted-glass panel and the indistinct outline of a short person on the other side dressed in a multi-hued shirt. "Go away, Bluey," she muttered.

She laid her head back on the desk, resting her forehead on her folded hands. Her life had turned into a nightmare. In the wee hours of the morning, she'd snuck into Kennedy's study and called Beast. The proprietary manner of the woman who had answered his phone kept replaying in her mind. After everything she'd done for him, he'd betrayed her. If she knew where he was, she'd kill the bastard.

Worse, this morning she'd run into an impenetrable mass of reporters swarming round Southern Valley like Great White Sharks waiting to take a chunk out of a bloodied swimmer. The feeding frenzy had started in earnest when Kennedy had begun his press conference on the front steps, answering questions about Jason Findley's death. It was akin to throwing bait into the water. She'd rushed to stop him, but some photographer bumped into her, knocking off her sunglasses. If only she hadn't screamed at him. God, the flashbulbs!

"Julianna, the police are here. They're with Mr Kennedy. Open the door!"

Her first thought was to run. Instead she stood up, smoothed down her snakeskin-print skirt, then went to the door and flung it open. "Come inside and be quick about it." She locked the door behind him.

"Where are they?" she asked, the pattern on Bluey's shirt making her eyes vibrate.

"In Kennedy's office." Bluey clasped his hands behind his back. "I think they're arresting him."

"Shit. Shit. Shit."

"I punched the intercom on before the police kicked me out of his office." Bluey studied her, his black eyes flat. "We'll be able to hear them if you turn yours on."

Frowning, she went to the desk and pressed a button.

"Mr Kennedy," a man was saying, his manner straightforward and cool, "we have a man in custody who swears you paid him to go to Sarah Bennett's hotel room and find a document that was stolen from you. The blend profile for SV888 showing its real contents with your signature on it. Is that right?"

"That is a rather absurd accusation. Blend profiles are printed out every day, showing the tank contents, Detective Doolan," Kennedy responded calmly.

"Why would the police accuse Mr Kennedy of paying someone to get a blend profile back? They can't be that stupid!" Julianna babbled, to cover her rising panic.

"Oh, come on. You know exactly why he wanted it back!" Bluey scoffed, his eyes fixed on the intercom.

"You bastard." Julianna was livid. "You give me the creeps, always lurking around, listening to people's private conversations. Besides, if anyone would know why, it would be you! You're the chief winemaker now that Findley's dead. Remember?"

"Quiet!" Bluey hissed.

"Why? They can't hear us."

"We'll miss something if you don't shut up." The menace in his voice silenced her.

" . . . I wish I could believe you," Doolan was saying. "However, Jason Findley delivered the missing document to the Australian Wine Bureau. It proves you knew your company was fraudulently selling the wine in tank SV888 as one hundred per cent shiraz."

"We did no such thing." Kennedy was indignant now. "That document has to be a fake. Where is it? I want to see it!"

"I'm sure you do," Doolan agreed. "You went to great lengths to obtain it. When your thief failed to get it back, you hired Mr Fowler, a member of the Kawasaki Kamikaze Motorcycle Club, to do the job. When he failed, you hired Slattery, a known murderer. He cleans up by killing Fowler, then goes after Sarah Bennett. Twice. Still, no document. Then Jason Findley turns up with it so you decide to get rid of him too. Why? Because he can authenticate the contents."

"I want my solicitor," Kennedy said, in his most imperious manner.

"No worries." Doolan sounded a shade perturbed, but still under control. "Just one more thing. Tell me, who's lying about your alibi for last night? You or Julianna Porter?"

Later that evening, in Sydney's domestic airline terminal, Detective Inspector Geoffrey Stabler walked back to the gate area after he had purchased the late edition of *Sydney Evening Times*, a cup of black coffee and a jumbo chocolate cookie.

He sat down in an empty row, satisfied that the window's reflection provided him with an excellent view of the entire area. As he unfolded the newspaper, the loudspeaker clicked and the gate agent announced a further delay in Sarah Bennett's flight from Melbourne. Stabler sighed. He put down the paper and took the lid off the coffee. He should have been belting down a few stubbies with his mates, as he usually did on a Wednesday evening, he remembered regretfully. He added three packets of sugar, then sat back in his seat.

Although everything appeared normal in the gate area, he was on full alert. Sarah was a key witness in the high-profile murder of a police officer, as well as the 'niece' of O'Connor's closest friend. He'd already been warned that if anything happened to her, his life wouldn't be worth jack, a curious American expression but one he understood.

He let his mind drift. While he'd made short work of identifying Wicky Riley's Kings Cross gang, it was proving more difficult to determine who'd called the man from Southern Valley. So far, his investigation revealed that five gang members were serving life sentences, two were in jail pending trial in a drug-related stabbing, four had been murdered, and three, including Riley, had left the country. Slattery, as the object of a nationwide manhunt, was bound to be captured soon. That left three to trace, which shouldn't be too difficult. It was unlikely they'd gone on to become model citizens.

Stabler unfolded the newspaper and tilted his head to bring into focus the sketch of Slattery featured on the front page. "You despicable piece of rat shit! This time you're going down." Stabler was still annoyed that he hadn't made the first murder charge stick, the one involving a fellow gang member. If he had, maybe Doolan's brother-in-law would still be alive. He read the accompanying report about Slattery, the leader of Kings Cross's most infamous and now defunct gang. He finished it, then peeled the cling-film off the cookie and took a bite. It was dry and tasteless, definitely not worth the calories. He threw it into the bin, then picked up the newspaper again and opened it to page two, where he spotted a piece about Jason Findley's murder with an accompanying photograph.

He adjusted his glasses. The man speaking into the microphones had been identified as Angus Kennedy, owner of Southern Valley. Standing behind him was a flinty-faced Aboriginal and to one side a pretty woman, obviously in some distress. Neither the man nor the woman was named . . . but there was something familiar about the woman. He studied the picture more closely, then let out a whoop of joy.

He got out his phone and punched in O'Connor's number. "How ya going, boss?" He listened for a moment, then said, "No, the flight's late . . . Right, we'll meet you at the hotel. Before you hang up, I have good news. I believe the person who called Wicky Riley from Southern Valley is featured in a photograph on page two of the *Sydney Evening Times*."

Chapter Forty-three

The subdued façade of the hotel blended into the quiet residential area of Elizabeth Bay, just west of downtown Sydney, so effectively that when Detective Inspector Geoff Stabler pulled the unmarked police car into the hotel's unobtrusive driveway around eleven p.m., Sarah was taken by surprise.

At the hotel's rear entrance, she got out of the vehicle and Stabler whisked her inside while two uniformed policemen took her luggage out of the boot. Dead on her feet, she struggled up the back stairs to the second floor, the two officers leading the way, Stabler trailing behind. A short walk down a brightly lit corridor brought them to the three-bedroom suite where she would spend the night.

The officers entered first, calling to someone already inside. Stabler stayed with her, his eyes roaming up and down, then led her into a small foyer. A whiff of roses and lemon furniture polish hit her. Passing an opening to her right, she glanced in and saw a sleek kitchenette with a granite counter. A high-tech machine spluttered in the corner, sending out aromatic waves of coffee. She kept walking, the thick, blue-patterned carpet muffling her footsteps.

A few more paces brought her to the bedrooms, where the officers were checking what she gathered was a connecting door to another suite. Continuing, she came to a spacious rectangular room, where two blue and ivory striped sofas faced each other over a square mahogany coffee-table. A clear glass vase of yellow roses, her favourite flower, stood on a side table.

At one end of the room, a man seated in a blue leather armchair, positioned in front of a sliding glass door, was talking on a phone. A tall cinnabar lamp cast a harsh light on his ruddy hair and accentuated the deeply etched lines round his tired brown eyes. Although years older than he'd been in the photographs Bernie McDermott had taken at Northwest Traffic School, Detective Superintendent Sebastian O'Connor had retained a boyish, jaunty air. Sarah smiled as he flipped the phone shut and rose to greet her, arms outstretched.

Three hours, five cups of coffee and hundreds of questions later, Sarah's head was pounding. When she leaned back in the sofa, every muscle in her body screamed and her head was throbbing. The king-size bed she'd seen earlier was summoning her. O'Connor, however, seemed to be getting his second wind. He was on the phone again, while Stabler, sprawled on the sofa opposite, fiddled with his glasses.

O'Connor closed the phone and put it on the table in front of him. "That was one of my detectives. He double checked. You're still registered at the Rocks Hotel, but other than the message from Phillip Dwyer about your meeting tomorrow, no one's called or left any packages. Who was supposed to deliver the contract?"

"Taylor Robbins," Sarah replied, with a frown. "I suppose I shouldn't be surprised. Last I time I saw her, she was kissing someone goodbye at Adelaide airport on Monday morning when she was supposed to be in

Sydney, finalizing the details." Her pettiness surprised her.

Stabler laced his fingers, bowed his palms and cracked his knuckles. "Who was she with?"

Sarah turned to him. His pudgy face wore a vacant expression. She was having a hard time imagining him as an integral part of the Homicide Unit. "Stephen Randall, vice president of Oskar Hallgarten Vineyards."

"You sound disapproving," O'Connor commented.

"Do I?" Sarah picked up a glass of water. "He started a vicious price-cutting war aimed at the Addison Group. Randall's the last person she should be involved with yet she disregarded Dwyer's instructions to return to Sydney, then lied to Noonan, about taking a flight there on Friday, apparently to spend the weekend with him." Unexpectedly Jake came to mind. He represented Oskar Hallgarten too. But Taylor's relationship with Randall was different. Or was it?

"Excuse me." O'Connor's phone was ringing. He checked the display and flipped it open. "Doolan! It's about time we heard from you. Tell me about the thumbprint." He listened. "Thanks, mate." He looked at Stabler, who was adjusting his glasses again. "Doolan said the print they found on the inside of Jason Findley's trunk was Lee Stout's."

Stabler clucked. "So I was right, after all."

"Who's Lee Stout?" Sarah asked.

Instead of answering, O'Connor took a newspaper off the coffee-table, and folded it to the photograph of Angus Kennedy's press conference. "Someone made a telephone call from Southern Valley to a Mrs Riley who lives in a nursing home near Orlando, Florida. Her son Wicky was there to take it. During the conversation, his mother overheard Sam Somers's name mentioned several times. Later Wicky's fingerprints were found on the wall near some drops of Somers's blood." He held out the newspaper to her. "You recognize the people standing behind Kennedy?"

Sarah studied the photo. "Yes. That's Bluey, the assistant winemaker, and Julianna Porter, Kennedy's assistant." She thought of the woman's shattered three-hundred-dollar bottle of scent.

At a nod from O'Connor, Stabler scooted forward on the sofa. "I've been tracking Kings Cross gangs for fifteen years. When I saw that photo, I recognized the young woman you know as Julianna Porter. She was tight with the leader of Wicky Riley's gang. Ever since they disbanded a few years ago, he's used a number of aliases, one of which is Clive Slattery."

"Julianna was Slattery's girlfriend?" Sarah was appalled.

"Yes, although at the time he was calling himself Ian Murray," Stabler replied. "She was also involved with Wicky Riley. That girl's about as bright as a two-watt bulb. My guess is that someone else is calling the shots."

A disturbing image of Julianna and Andrew Dunne, laughing like old friends, forced itself into Sarah's mind. She dropped her head into her hands.

O'Connor dropped the newspaper on the table. "We may have another break where Julianna's concerned."

"What's that?" Sarah asked, lifting her head slightly, nausea threatening.

"The thumbprint inside Findley's trunk," O'Connor replied cryptically.

"I don't understand," Sarah said, mystified. "I thought you said it was a man's."

Chapter Forty-four

On Thursday morning, white-hot sunlight, unusual in its intensity so late in the season, beat down on the concrete sidewalks of Sydney, which were crowded with tourists heading for the Opera House. Slattery walked in step with them, then paused to admire his reflection in a shop window.

His oversized camouflage trousers fell in a straight line from his hips and bunched round his ankles, covering thick white trainers. His shabby shirt hung below a brown waistcoat. The morning sun struck his newly shaven head, making it glow. He pulled down the new rimless glasses to scratch his non-existent eyebrows. Shaving them off had been a good decision, but they itched. He pushed his glasses back up his nose, then dumped the *Sydney Evening Times*, which featured his face on the front page, in a bin. Just doing his civic duty to keep the city clean. With Sydney Harbour Bridge on his left, he continued along Circular Quay East to the last outdoor restaurant. The Opera House was a block away. He selected a seat next to the water, as a tourist would.

A young waitress, pierced navel on display, took his order, eggs over easy, sausage and potatoes. As she walked away, he took Sarah Bennett's schedule out of a pocket and unfolded it. Today she had a series of meetings at the Addison Group's Miller Point offices. From there, she was going straight to dinner with Taylor Robbins and Phillip Dwyer, then back to her hotel. The rest wasn't important. He returned it to his pocket, chuckling to himself, thinking of his plans for tonight.

The girlfriend of a former Kings Cross gang member worked on the front desk at the Rocks Hotel where Sarah was supposedly staying. Slattery had kept close tabs on his mate, who was in prison serving a five-year sentence. A quick telephone call to him and several hours later, he'd had the information he needed. Sarah had been hidden at an obscure Elizabeth Bay hotel where his mother had once been head chambermaid. When he had applied there this morning, he'd been taken on straight away. He would return to his former job as a room-service waiter this evening. He smiled pleasantly at the waitress as she set down his breakfast.

Chapter Forty-five

Detective Inspector Danny Doolan elected to interrogate Julianna in Angus Kennedy's office at Southern Valley while the place was turned inside-out by the Special Crime Unit. Kennedy's office had already been tossed, but they had found nothing of use. He peered down at Julianna, who was sitting in a leather chair facing him. At the back of the room, several police officers stood by a floor-to-ceiling bookcase, observing the interrogation.

"Of course my fingerprints were in Jason's car. He drove me back to the office after we'd delivered Mr Hart's car to his home," Julianna explained, as if Doolan were an idiot. "That was the day before he left for America. Ask anyone!"

"Julianna – or should I call you Lee?" Doolan was gratified to see her expression change. "As in Lee Stout?"

"My name is Julianna. I legally changed it. So what?" She pouted, tugging at the drawstring of her low-cut top. She crossed her legs and jiggled her foot, bringing attention to the black stilettos whose thin straps were entwined loosely round her shapely ankles. During Doolan's prolonged silence, she recrossed her legs, forcing her short skirt to ride up, exposing firm thighs.

Doolan smiled insincerely, eyeballing the exposed flesh. "Come on, Lee. There's no reason for your thumbprint to be inside Jason's boot."

Julianna returned his stare unblinkingly. "Mr Hart requested some promotional materials for his trip. We put them in Jason's boot and transferred them to Mr Hart's car later."

Doolan's grip on the armrest tightened. "I know all about you, Lee Stout. You grew up in Kings Cross where your brother, 'Thunder' Malloy Stout, joined a gang. He introduced you to two men, both of whom became your lovers. One of them currently uses the name Clive –"

"I don't know what you're talking about," Julianna interrupted, speaking haughtily as if he'd offended her.

"– Slattery and the other was Wicky Riley. Don't bother to deny it." He took a piece of paper out of his jacket pocket, unfolded it and thrust it under her nose. It was a computer printout of a photograph that showed a younger, heavier Julianna lounging on a street corner with Slattery and Riley. It had been emailed earlier this morning by Detective Inspector Stabler. "I want to know where I can find Clive – or maybe you prefer to use his given name, Ian."

"That photo was taken years ago. I haven't seen anyone from the old neighbourhood in ages. I hardly remember those two." She shook her head, then uncrossed her legs and studied her gold nail polish.

"Rubbish!" Doolan sprang to his feet, moved close to her and bent down so that their faces were almost touching.

She recoiled, swivelling her head to one side. Her long hair fell forward, shielding her face from Doolan.

"Why don't I believe you?" Doolan's voice was cutting." Is it because Clive and Wicky helped you murder your own brother that day in the Rocks? He liked to screw his little sister, didn't he? You ended up in hospital, what, four, five times? Broken arm, cracked ribs, ruptured spleen. Once you almost lost an eye. But you never let them do a rape kit. I think the reason's obvious. Tell me, did you get the same rush sticking Jason Findley as you did cutting off your brother's balls?"

Now Julianna's mask slipped. "You're crazy!" she screamed. "Get away from me."

There was quiet as Doolan walked to the wall, picked up an antique shield-back chair and moved it into the narrow space between Julianna and the desk. Straddling it, he rested his elbows on the back and folded his arms. As his narrow shoulders hunched, a lock of straight black hair fell on to his brow. His eyes, sunken from lack of sleep, were bloodshot. "Slattery murdered a police officer, Lee. That couldn't have been part of your deal with him. Tell me where he is and I'll see what I can do to protect you."

"My name is Julianna," she insisted, through clenched teeth. "And if you had proof, you wouldn't waste time insulting me. You'd arrest me. But you don't have proof because I didn't do anything wrong."

"Nothing wrong? You murdered your brother. You hired Wicky Riley to murder Sam Somers. You hired Slattery to murder Sarah Bennett, and in the process, he killed a police officer who happens to have been my brother-in-law. Add Jason Findley to the mix, and you've got one fucking cold-blooded murderer. I assure you, we'll find Slattery and when we do, he isn't going to protect your sorry arse."

Chapter Forty-six

Sarah emerged from the bedroom in a black and jade tweed suit. Her black sling-back pumps sank into the plush carpet as she walked down the hall and into the sitting room where Detective Superintendent Sebastian O'Connor stood by a room-service trolley. Sunlight poured through the glass doors.

"You're very smart this morning." O'Connor smiled as he removed the metal covers from their breakfast.

"Thanks." Sarah pulled out a chair and sat down at the table. "That looks good. I can't believe I'm actually hungry."

"Coffee?" O'Connor picked up the jug. When he leaned over to pour it, his jacket flapped open, revealing a gun.

"Where's Detective Stabler?" she asked, eyeing the weapon.

"At the Addison Group office interviewing Phillip Dwyer and Taylor Robbins. I'm afraid it'll delay your meeting." O'Connor sat at the table and splashed cream into his coffee. "Sugar?" he asked, holding out the bowl to Sarah.

"No, thanks." Sarah's appetite had vanished. O'Connor and McDermott believed that an Addison Group employee had given Slattery her schedule. Andrew Dunne was their top suspect. Had Taylor Robbins and Phillip Dwyer been added to that list? Before she could ask, O'Connor's phone sounded. He answered, and set it to speaker mode.

"Hey, Sarah, Sebastian." Bernie McDermott's voice boomed into the room. "I know you're on your way out so I'll keep this brief. We located Somers's computer in a pawn shop. You're gonna love this. It has every detail of his trip to Australia, as if he was writing his memoirs, everything but his bowel movements."

"Good on ya, mate," O'Connor said. "So, tell me, what did Somers get stuck into at Southern Valley?"

"Davis Hart." McDermott explained the chief winemaker's drunken fury when confronted about the quality of Macquarie Hawke's Coonawarra Shiraz. "Somers didn't think anything of Hart's claims that something fishy was going on, until Hart bought it in that plane crash. That got Somers thinking someone had overheard their argument and murdered Hart to shut him up. I suppose it's possible, but using a bomb on a planeload of people seems like overkill, if you'll pardon the expression."

"No worries, mate." O'Connor glanced at the newspaper folded up beside his plate. "Your National Transportation Safety Board just released a preliminary report attributing the accident to a defective cargo-door latch."

"I see. So, whoever's behind this must consider themselves lucky," McDermott said, his voice fading in and out as if he were pacing. "They lucked out again when they lifted Somers's computer. You won't believe what he'd decided to do after he found out Hart was dead. And get this – he didn't password protect his files."

When McDermott told them what he'd found, Sarah choked on her coffee and spat it all over the tablecloth.

Two hours later, her stomach in knots, she sat silently in the back seat of the police car, observing the historic Rocks section of Sydney as the two uniformed policemen, who'd been with her since last night, chatted quietly in the front. A right turn from George Street on to Lower Fort brought the Harbour Bridge Pylon Lookout into view and, beyond, the Sydney Harbour Bridge. Moments later, they were at the tip of Miller's Point, pulling into the car park at the new Addison Group headquarters.

The police officers made quick work of securing the conference room, then took up positions outside the door. The bump on the back of Sarah's head began to throb again as she walked to the far side of the rectangular walnut table and selected a padded chair facing the door. To her left, sparkling picture windows offered a panoramic view of Walsh Bay, where ships ranging from small sightseeing cruisers to ocean-going vessels were sailing the shimmering azure waters.

Suddenly there was a commotion at the door. A tight-lipped Taylor Robbins, her face red, slunk into the room and threw a stack of stapled documents on to the table. They slid across the surface to Sarah, who reached out to stop them before they landed in her lap. "You have a lot of nerve!" Taylor snapped, running a hand through her spiky orange hair.

"What are you talking about?"

"My relationship with Stephen Randall has nothing to do with your goddamn problems!" Taylor hissed. "You told the police you'd seen us together to cause trouble for me. You're beneath contempt." She slammed her briefcase on to the table and started to search through it.

"Police! Don't move!" Detective Stabler raced into the

room, flinging the door wide. He was followed by the uniformed officers. They froze when they saw Taylor's hand in her briefcase. "Take your hand out of the case, Miss, and do it very slowly," Stabler commanded. "Leave the case on the table and back away."

Taylor gazed at him, clearly bewildered. "I don't understand. What's going on?"

Stabler moved cautiously towards her. "Do it now!"

Wide-eyed, Sarah watched as Taylor inched her hand up until it was visible, then stumbled backwards until she bumped into the wall. One of the officers seized the case and handed it to Stabler while the other moved closer to Sarah. After a painstaking inspection, Stabler returned the case to Taylor, then instructed the policemen to escort her outside.

Once the woman had been hustled out, Sarah turned to Stabler. "Was it really necessary to treat her like a common criminal?"

"Unfortunately she slipped in without her briefcase being checked. We can't take any chances. Your safety is our primary concern," he responded. "Now, tell me, what was the dust-up about?"

Sarah stood up and went to the window. She stared out bleakly at Walsh Bay. Squinting at the sun's reflection on the water, she repeated Taylor's accusations. "I thought we'd agreed her relationship with Randall wasn't relevant. Did you have to bring it up?"

A tow-headed constable stuck his head through the door, "Phillip Dwyer's here for the meeting. He's been checked out."

Stabler stepped aside as Dwyer entered. "Don't plan on Ms Robbins being back any time soon." he said, then gave Sarah a curt nod and left.

"What on earth is going on?" Dwyer unbuttoned his jacket and took it off.

"It might be better if Taylor explained it to you." Sarah returned to her chair and sat down, eyes on the table.

Dwyer unsnapped his briefcase and removed a leather notebook and gold pen. He laid them on the table. After a moment's hesitation, he expressed sympathy over her misfortunes and said, "I suppose we may as well get on. I apologize on Taylor's behalf for not getting the contract to you last night. I gather this is it?" He motioned to the stapled documents.

Sarah picked up a copy, as did he. Flipping through the document, she said, with as little emotion as possible, "I see the clause we agreed to take out is still there."

"Bloody hell!" Dwyer fast-forwarded to the page she indicated. He stroked his goatee, grabbed his gold pen, then slashed through the clause and initialled it. He sent the contract flying across the table to Sarah. "If that's the only thing stopping you agreeing to the terms, then put your initials next to mine and sign it on the last page."

At first Sarah was too stunned to speak. Then she smiled radiantly. "Works for me."

Chapter Forty-seven

The setting sun filled the sky with hot magenta, vibrant crimson and intense plum as the water-taxi left Circular Quay in Sydney Cove on its way to the Wharf restaurant in Rose Bay where the premier wine event of the year was to be held. It sped out of the cove and into the harbour, passing close to the Opera House at the end of Bennelong Point.

Graham Blackwell moved to the rail, and studied the graceful winged arches of the Opera House, poised to soar into the evening sky. Beside him, Andrew Dunne's head was framed by the Sydney Harbour Bridge towering in the distance. Dunne was wearing a short-sleeved, brown and white striped shirt, brown trousers and brown lace-up shoes. He was carrying a lightweight tan jacket. It was hardly the correct attire for the evening that lay ahead.

From the tense expression on Dunne's face, Blackwell decided his friend needed time to settle. He watched the scenery change from the high-rise buildings of downtown Sydney to a series of low-rise apartments, then to breathtakingly luxurious and beautiful homes perched on the hillsides leading down to the bay. Long wooden staircases zigzagged to the boat docks and the small, isolated beaches that dotted the shoreline.

Dunne was first to speak. "The media crucified Angus on the news tonight. Did you see it?"

"No." Blackwell adjusted the sleeves of his black dinner jacket over the cuffs of his starched dress shirt. On his return he hadn't had time to do anything in Adelaide other than talk to Detective Doolan last night and again early this morning. After that he'd packed and flown straight to Sydney. When he'd checked into the Rocks Hotel, where Karl Kingsley was supposedly staying, he learned his boss had yet to arrive. Despite his misgivings, Blackwell had decided to go ahead with his plan to attend the Wharf's Winemaker Dinner. There would be a champagne reception on the pier, followed by a six-course meal assembled round limited-edition wines presented by Australia's most distinguished winemakers. Afterwards, the guests were invited to mingle with the winemakers, sampling port, liqueur wines and desserts served buffet-style in the foyer. Tickets for the event were as rare as the wines being poured, and cost a fortune. Blackwell was confident that the complimentary ticket Kingsley had received would guarantee his attendance.

He turned his head and was disturbed to see the recklessness in Dunne's eyes. During difficult times, his friend had a bad habit of reverting to impulsive, childish behaviour, and the situation with Angus Kennedy was enough to unhinge anyone.

"According to the news, the police suspect Angus is responsible for the deaths of Sam Somers and Jason Findley, the attempted murder of Sarah Bennett and the death of the constable guarding her." Dunne swayed as the water-taxi rocked in the wake of a huge boat passing close to them. "Murder Inc. That's my friend Angus!"

Blackwell squinted towards the coastline and spotted

the Wharf's pier, decorated with tiny coloured lights. A number of boats were tied up and more were arriving. His eyes trailed down to the restaurant, where masses of windows facing the bay showcased the gathering crowd. He moved to Dunne and put an arm round his friend's hunched shoulders. "I know this doesn't make sense now, but it will be sorted out eventually. In the meantime, I'd watch my step, if I were you."

Dunne shrugged off his arm. "What the bloody hell does that mean?"

Blackwell sighed. "Your friendship with Kennedy is common knowledge, that's all." He held on to the rail as their boat bumped into the rubber-covered docking area. Dunne scrambled up the steps, leaving Blackwell to pay the fare.

Dunne wove a path through clusters of fashionably dressed people sipping champagne from crystal goblets, as waiters passed between them with trays of elaborate canapés, and swaggered up to Stephen Randall. He was peering over the railing into the dark waters below, a glass of champagne in hand. "They'll let anyone into this event, won't they?" he said, and clasped Randall's shoulder.

Startled, Randall dropped his glass. It splashed into the water. With forced calm, he smoothed the lapels of his hand-tailored dinner-jacket, then eyeballed Dunne's ensemble. "Yes, I can see that."

"So, Stephen," Dunne smiled cockily, "I saw you lowered Hallgarten's front-line prices again. For the third time, was it? That was either a brilliant move or a bloody good way to go down the gurgler, mate." Dunne's resonant voice cut through the air, drawing curious stares.

"It'll make paying for those brand acquisitions we've been hearing so much about rather dicey, won't it?"

A group of wine writers had taken an interest in their conversation and Randall grinned as if he'd heard a joke. Then he seized Dunne's forearm, and murmured, "Mind your own business, arsehole, or you'll regret it. Now get the fuck away from me."

Before Dunne could respond, Blackwell arrived. "Hello, Stephen. I hate to interrupt, but I believe the dinner's getting under way. Come on, Andrew."

Grasping Dunne's arm, Blackwell ushered him firmly towards the restaurant's entrance, passing the elegantly clad Macquarie Hawke, who had been standing a few feet away, ogling women in low-cut evening dresses as they hurried inside for the opening ceremonies.

Hawke took a glass of champagne from a passing waiter and joined Randall. When the last few people had entered the restaurant, Randall said, "I want the truth. Are you involved in this Southern Valley cock-up?"

Hawke's face twitched, "Of course I am! I'm the goddamn victim! Kennedy was scamming his customers, and because I make my wines there I'm guilty by association." He gulped some champagne.

Randall's hooded eyes narrowed. "I hope for your sake you're telling the truth."

Hawke probed the other man's face and saw something other than the expected hostility. My God, if he didn't know better, he could have sworn the invincible Stephen Randall was scared out of his wits.

They started when a door slammed. A tall, lanky man had left the restaurant and was coming their way. His reddish hair was touched by silver and the air of authority he exuded was apparent even at a distance. As he neared them, the hair on the back of Hawke's neck bristled. Distracted, he placed his glass on the railing.

"Good evening, gentlemen. I'm Detective Superintendent O'Connor." He put his glass beside Hawke's, then shook hands with both men. "If you don't mind, Mr Randall, I'd like a few minutes alone with Mr Hawke."

After Randall had gone inside, Hawke leaned languidly against the railing and folded his arms. "You don't appear to be dressed for duty, Detective."

"Police officers are always on duty." O'Connor stared at him. "I'm curious about something. Detective Doolan says you considered Sam Somers a friend."

"Yes." Hawke's hair rippled in a light breeze. When he smoothed it down, he realized his hand was trembling. He moved away from the railing and clasped his hands behind his back. "Sam was a good friend. He loved my wines. He'll be sorely missed."

"Really? That's odd," O'Connor responded, as the tall lamps that stood along the pier came alive. "The Atlanta police found Somers's computer in a pawn shop. I understand he kept a diary of sorts on it. What I'd like to know is, if Somers loved your wines, why was he planning to rescind the ninety-eight rating on your Coonawarra Shiraz?"

Hawke's jaw dropped. "You've got to be joking, mate!"

"Come on, Hawke, admit it. You knew Somers was going to retract that rating. Selling your wine after that would be about as easy as pushing shit uphill with a toothpick."

"Are you absolutely sure Sam was referring to my Coonawarra shiraz and not someone else's? No offence,

Detective, but people who aren't in the business often get wine names confused."

"No offence taken. However, there's no doubt it was your wine." O'Connor's eyes glittered. "I don't think it was a coincidence that Somers was murdered before he could publish the retraction, do you?"

"I have no idea." Hawke turned to the restaurant. Someone had called his name. "Detective, this is all very fascinating, but I'm afraid I must go. I'm the keynote speaker."

O'Connor smiled pleasantly as he picked up his glass. "One last thing. Several witnesses in your neighbourhood report that Julianna Porter is a frequent overnight visitor at your home. Would you care to comment on that?"

Chapter Forty-eight

Alone in the lift at midnight, Slattery waited impatiently as the doors opened on to the second floor of the Elizabeth Bay Hotel, then pushed the heavily laden room-service trolley into the corridor of the recently renovated wing. He moved to the full-length gilded mirror opposite the lift, and adopted the weary expression he had honed to perfection during his previous stint in the job. Satisfied, he began to push the trolley, which rattled on wobbly wheels, along the carpet.

At the split in the main corridor, he bore left. Passing the stairwell exit, he came to an abrupt halt. The metal covers on the china dishes clanked. The corridor leading to Sarah Bennett's suite was empty. Where was the constable he'd taken pains to chat up this evening? Or his colleague?

He ran a hand over his shaved head and pressed on, slowing as he neared the suite. He glanced up and down, then pressed his ear to the door. The only audible sound was the low hum of a television. Slattery pushed the trolley forward and inserted a master keycard in the electronic lock of the suite adjacent to Sarah's. When the green light came on, he thanked his mother. The hotel's security system hadn't been changed since her retirement last year. He shoved the trolley inside, then closed the door behind him, taking care it didn't slam.

Intense moonlight shining through the trees outside

the glass door made spidery patterns on the carpet. This was his last chance to get rid of Sarah Bennett, who was booked on the Friday-afternoon flight to Los Angeles.

Leaving the lights off, he stowed the trolley in a corner, retrieved a pen-sized torch from his pocket and turned it on. Beyond the glass door there was a balcony with a view of the distant Elizabeth Bay. Noiselessly he opened the door and stepped outside. A thick brick wall divided this balcony from Sarah Bennett's. Aside from the TV's low drone, he heard nothing. Given the lateness of the hour, it was logical to assume she was asleep and, if his luck held, so were the cops.

Returning inside, he removed a serrated knife from the sheath on his calf, then crept to the connecting door and unlocked it with the master key. With great care, he inched it open, exposing a short hallway with three doors. He slithered in and stopped by the first. According to the head housekeeper, an old friend of his mother's who loved to gossip, this was the bedroom the woman was using.

The door was ajar. He peered inside, sending a tiny beam from his flashlight across the room. The door to the adjoining room was closed. He moved the beam to the king-size bed, playing it over the long lump under the pile of bedclothes. Dark hair sprouted from beneath a pillow.

As he approached the bed, the uncomfortable thought struck him that it was too quiet but he dismissed it, raised the knife and brought it down hard on the figure that lay before him. The first thrust hit something unyielding. A wide shaft of light set the room ablaze.

"Police! Don't move!" a male voice ordered. A man burst through the door to the connecting bedroom.

Slattery raced into the hall, banging into the opposite wall with his shoulder. Recovering swiftly, he ran into the adjoining suite, diving through the door on his stomach, then flopped over and slammed it shut with his feet. He leaped up and sprinted to the sliding glass door, reaching the balcony as gun shots slammed uselessly into the connecting door.

Not far from Elizabeth Bay, the presentations at the Wharf 's Winemaker Dinner had finally ended and Graham Blackwell went into the foyer, which was filled to capacity with well-lubricated men and women wandering around buffet tables loaded with a tantalizing array of bite-sized desserts. Waiters circulated, pouring ruby, tawny and vintage ports, sherries and liqueurs. Clusters of guests gathered round the winemakers, who had stayed to chat with them. Andrew Dunne was not among them.

Blackwell walked past a hissing cappuccino machine and spotted Karl Kingsley surrounded by a group of red-faced men. Sliding up next to him, Blackwell murmured, "The chairman has been looking for you since last Wednesday. He asked me to track you down. We need to talk."

"Track me down, you say?" Kingsley popped a tiny peach tart into his mouth, leaving speckles of powdered sugar on his fingers. He wiped them on a dainty napkin. "Tell him I'll call him tomorrow."

Blackwell's jaw pulsed. "Unfortunately that won't do. The Adelaide police were at the office, questioning everyone, including the chairman, about some irregularities."

"That's enough." Kingsley said, grey eyes glinting with

a hint of steel. "Outside. Now." Clutching a glass of port, Kingsley manoeuvred himself through the throng and stalked out of the room, Blackwell trailing him. Outside, he sped down a tree-lined gravel path illuminated by low-wattage ground lamps. Benches facing the water lined one side. A couple of hundred yards away, the pier's lights sent ribbons of colour skimming across Rose Bay. The laughter of guests enjoying a nightcap drifted to them over the water, which lapped gently on the shore. Thick shrubbery hid the restaurant's car park.

"This is far enough." Kingsley stopped beside a bench and turned to Blackwell. "Who the hell do you think you are, accosting me in front of my friends?"

"I'll get straight to the point. It's come to the chairman's attention that Davis Hart called you recently with allegations about illegal activities at Southern Valley and that no action was taken."

"I see. That bloody ignorant secretary told you about the call and you went to the chairman behind my back," Kingsley sneered. "You're a fool, Graham. You have no idea what you're talking about. Not that I feel any obligation to answer to a subordinate, but for your information, Hart was a drunkard. The last time we investigated a complaint he'd lodged, he was so intoxicated he didn't even remember making the call. Perhaps the chairman forgot about that. You can ask him when you report in."

"I'll take that as a yes." Blackwell fixed his eyes on the ramrod-stiff man. "As you know, that call should have been logged and evaluated for follow-up."

"How I handle things is my business!" Kingsley exploded.

"Actually, your decisions reflect on everyone at the

Bureau," Blackwell replied calmly. Kingsley's rudeness at being questioned by an underling, as he called them, was only to be expected. "He's also concerned that the Macquarie Hawke Coonawarra Shiraz didn't pass the sensory evaluation, yet it showed up approved. Can you explain how it received a licence without being retested?"

Kingsley downed his port in one gulp. "Talk to the person who entered the data. It sounds like a clerical error."

"Let me rephrase that question." Blackwell said. "Did the change in status have anything to do with Macquarie Hawke showing up at the office the day after it was rejected?"

"How dare you question my integrity?" Kingsley shook his fist in Blackwell's face.

"Maybe you'd prefer to discuss this with Detective Doolan of the Adelaide police?" Blackwell shot back. "From the questions he's been asking, it's obvious he thinks you're involved in Jason Findley's murder."

"What are you talking about?"

"Don't tell me you don't know!" Blackwell stared at him in disbelief. "A few hours after Jason Findley called at the office and gave you that Southern Valley document for safekeeping, he was murdered."

"Oh, my God!" Kingsley went to a bench and sat down heavily, placing his now empty glass on the ground beside him. "I left Adelaide directly after work that evening. I went deep-sea fishing with a friend. We turned off our phones, didn't listen to the radio. I only came back for this dinner. Why would the police think I'm involved?"

Blackwell marched to the bench and glared down at him. "The document Findley delivered to you is, or rather was, a crucial piece of evidence proving that

Angus Kennedy is involved in the alleged fraud at Southern Valley. It went missing. Kennedy's a childhood friend of yours, isn't he?"

"Go to hell!" Kingsley rose and brushed past Blackwell, purposely hitting his shoulder.

"You've been protecting Kennedy all along, haven't you? Blackwell grabbed the sleeve of Kingsley's dinner-jacket. The seam gave way where it met the shoulder.

Kingsley latched on to Blackwell's wrist and twisted viciously until the smaller man let him go. "Leave well enough alone or, I'm warning you, when I'm through with you, you won't have a pot to piss in."

Blackwell backed away, rubbing his wrist. "The first time was easy, wasn't it, Karl? When Hart called, you sloughed him off as a drunkard, thinking no one would be any the wiser. Then it got tricky. Sarah Bennett saw that file in Hart's computer. Your job was to make sure I missed my meeting with her in case, on the off-chance, she told me about it. How bloody brilliant to blame me for being irresponsible! Did you know they'd hunt Sarah down like an animal?"

Seeing Kingsley clench his fists, Blackwell backed away. "Your involvement didn't end there, did it? Kennedy was always teetering on the verge of bankruptcy, then Mac Hawke appeared, and suddenly Southern Valley was in the black. When you learned that the most popular wine of the man responsible for saving your friend's business had failed the sensory evaluation, you changed the record. You did it for free, didn't you? Then Findley showed up with proof of Kennedy's scam. Did you take it upon yourself to destroy it, or did Kennedy ask you to do it as a favour for an old friend?"

Quivering with fury, Kingsley came round the bench

and jabbed a finger into Blackwell's chest. "You're pissing in the wind. You have no proof!"

"On the contrary." Blackwell batted away Kingsley's hand and stood his ground. "You burned the document and flushed it down your own toilet. Inga found a piece floating in the bowl."

Chapter Forty-nine

One hand on the wheel of the unmarked squad car, the other holding a plastic mug of ice-cold sweet tea, Sergeant Leroy Watson drove past the Georgia governor's mansion on West Paces Ferry Road, then made a leisurely right into an area called Tuxedo Park where in the early 1900s wealthy Atlantans had built their 'summer' homes. Traffic was unusually light for a Monday afternoon. He was ahead of schedule.

The rolling hills and winding streets were filled with stately mansions nestled in heavily wooded grounds where lacy pink and white dogwood blossoms decorated the dense greenery. Watson was searching for a residence somewhere in the middle of the maze bordered by West Paces Ferry Road to the south, Blackland Road to the north, and Valley Road and Northside Drive to the east and west respectively. It was a beautiful day and he had the windows wide open, enjoying the scents of spring, despite the oppressive silence of his passenger.

He turned into a steep uphill driveway, which meandered through a leafy half-acre of dense pine, oak and dogwood mingled with masses of pink azaleas. As the car emerged into bright sunshine, he passed several majestic magnolias and eventually arrived at the Villa Verona, a cream Italianate mansion with elaborately carved marble decoration.

He whistled under his breath, then parked the car and

lumbered up a flight of steps to the front door. A small child with curly black hair and deep blue eyes opened the door and greeted him with a smile. In the background, a striking woman in her early fifties stood watching.

"Hello. You must be Miss Cassie Malone. I'm Sergeant Watson of the Atlanta Police Department." He grinned and bent to shake hands with her.

The child's mouth dropped open as her eyes travelled from Watson's knees, past his wool blazer and raspberry shirt, to the top of his head. She giggled when her hand disappeared in Watson's enormous paw.

Just then, a car door slammed and Cassie peeped round Watson's legs. A woman with shoulder-length auburn hair in a green sweater and black trousers was standing by the police car. Cassie gave a squeal of delight, then tore down the steps and leaped into Sarah Bennett's open arms.

An hour later, Sarah was comfortably ensconced on a chintz sofa across from Anna Malone, sipping Earl Grey tea and eating raisin-cinnamon scones with English clotted cream and strawberry jam. It was a charming room filled with antiques, family heirlooms and a collection of blue-and-white Old Minton china. Cassie was cooing over the stuffed koala Sarah had brought for her, which she'd set up in the corner with her other animals.

Sarah lifted the delicate china cup to her lips and took a sip of tea, stealing a glance at Anna. She was amazingly youthful, with delicate features, porcelain skin, honey-blonde hair and lovely smile.

"I'm so glad you're safe. Jake was worried when he couldn't reach you in Sydney." Anna kept her voice low so Cassie wouldn't hear them.

The gentle rebuke wasn't lost on Sarah, who'd edited her story, leaving out some of the more alarming details. "I'm sorry, but Detective O'Connor was adamant that I mustn't tell anyone where I was. As it turned out, it was all for nothing. Just as well I finished my business and left a day early."

"What do you mean?" Anna asked, as she placed her cup on the coffee-table and reached for the silver teapot.

Wishing she hadn't brought up the subject, Sarah glanced at Cassie, reassured herself that the little girl was still engrossed in her game, then said, "The police were convinced Slattery couldn't find me at the Elizabeth Bay Hotel, but they set a trap for him anyway. He managed to get into the suite and the bedroom where I was staying."

Anna's eyes widened. "Did they catch him?"

"No, which is why I have a police officer with me day and night." Out of the picture window, they could both see Watson leaning on the car, phone to his ear.

She couldn't help feeling that Anna had been studying her with more than mere concern for her ordeal. She guessed it had something to do with Jake. Had she worked out that they'd become lovers?

While Anna busied herself pouring more tea, Sarah mulled over her own deteriorating relationship with Jake. She'd taken a flight on Thursday and, crossing the International Date Line, arrived back in Atlanta the same day. McDermott had met her at the airport and driven her home. Friday and Saturday, she was either sleeping off jet-lag, or being questioned at Police Headquarters. During dinner on Saturday night, McDermott admitted he'd neglected to forward several urgent messages from Jake, who believed she was still in Australia.

She'd immediately telephoned him, but got his answering service. On Sunday night he had rung her from Chicago, overjoyed at her safe return. But once he'd learned she'd been at home for several days and hadn't called him, he'd become distant and withdrawn. After they'd hung up, Sarah had felt empty and confused.

"Sarah? You're miles away. Let's not talk about this terrible business, all right?

"What? Oh, of course." Sarah reached for her handbag, which was on the floor. Opening it, she reached inside and pulled out a small, gaily wrapped present. "Cassie, would you come over here, please? I have one more present for you."

"Yippee!" Cassie shouted, and knocked over the koala, which fell flat on its face. "Oh dear!" Carefully, she propped it up and smoothed its fur.

"Cassie is such a lovely child. I wish Jake would get married again and give her a little sister or brother, maybe both. It would be wonderful to have more grandchildren." Anna smiled guilelessly. "And she would be so happy to have a mother who could stay at home with her while Jake travelled."

Sarah stiffened. An unwelcome vision of Jake, wrapped in a white towel, materialized in her mind. The twelve-year age difference seemed vast suddenly, especially when his mother was only a decade her senior.

"I want Miss Sarah to be my mother!" Cassie ran to the sofa, climbed up beside her and gave her a hug.

"Cassie, that is so nice." Sarah hugged her back. She had Jake's blue eyes. "Anyone would be happy to have a little girl like you for their daughter, but I thought we'd decided to be best friends."

"We are best friends. For ever and ever." A moment

later she had torn open the package and was squealing with delight at the fourteen-carat gold earrings shaped like kangaroos. "Gramma, look! I love kangaroos!"

"They're beautiful. Come over here and I'll put them on for you." Anna said.

"Cassie, I don't know how you convinced your daddy to let you have your ears pierced. You look very grown-up," Sarah said, cloaking her growing apprehension with a smile.

"He didn't have much choice." Anna smiled. "All the little girls in Cassie's class at school have had it done."

"And, if I'm not mistaken, Cassie, you're wearing perfume too," Sarah said.

She giggled. "Daddy brought it back from Australia for Gramma."

Sarah's mind reeled. "Anna, it's Oceana, isn't it?"

"Why, yes, I believe it is. Jake said it was made in Australia. It's a little, uhm, dramatic, isn't it?" She wrinkled her nose.

"Daddy said one of his girlfriends wears it." Cassie giggled. "I think it smells lovely."

Chapter Fifty

From across the antique partner's desk in Angus Kennedy's Southern Valley office, Beatrice Kennedy dismissed her husband's concerns with a wave, ashes dropping from her cigarette. She was surprised when he made no comment. Leaning forward, she flicked the rest into the ashtray. Beside it lay the order suspending Southern Valley's operation until the investigation into the alleged fraud had been completed.

"You paid Bluey to spy on me?" Kennedy raised his eyes to his wife's face. Her cheeks were wrinkled, and her eyelids sagged over clouded grey eyes. Since he'd last seen her two months ago, she'd dyed her hair a ruddy brown, adding ten years to her age.

"He wasn't spying. He was looking out for my interests. I recruited him the day you hooked up with Macquarie Hawk." Beatrice adjusted the canary diamond cocktail ring she wore in place of a wedding band.

"But he's been with the police for hours. The smarmy bastard turned on me once, what's to stop him doing it again?" Kennedy protested.

Beatrice took a drag on her cigarette, inhaling deeply. "Actually, he didn't. It was my idea to have Findley hand over that document to the Australian Wine Bureau."

"Yours? But that was the only evidence against me!" Kennedy bellowed. "Why did you do it, Bea?"

She pulled the ashtray closer and stubbed out her

cigarette. A few specks of ash drifted across the desk on to her Jaeger pants trousers suit. "It was a question of you being arrested either for forging wine documents or for murder. I chose the former."

"Murder?" Kennedy's face turned crimson. "What are you talking about?"

"You know exactly what I'm talking about." Beatrice scoffed. "You set up Davis Hart and Jason Findley to take the fall if your money-making scheme was discovered. But you screwed up, as you always do. When that document you signed went missing, you decided Sarah Bennett had taken it. When the loser you hired failed to recover it, you asked Hawke for help. Next thing you know, Sarah and the little girl were attacked and a policeman was murdered. So what exactly did you think would happen when you told Hawke that Jason had had it all along?"

Kennedy spun round and wandered past the sofa and chairs to the window. A steady drizzle painted the sky a dismal grey. A few brown fronds had fallen off the palm trees, littering the path from the car park to the entrance. He noticed someone approaching the building. A sharp stabbing pain started in his left arm and moved to his chest. He pressed a hand to his heart but the pain persisted.

Beatrice took out another cigarette and put it between her lips. After a quick flick of a tiny silver lighter, she took in another lung-full of smoke, observing her husband closely as he left his post by the window. "You knew damn well that Hawke would take care of Jason the same way he tried to take care of Sarah, by hiring Julianna and her thugs to murder him. I thought once Jason had handed over the document he'd be safe. But it didn't work, did it? He's dead, Angus."

Kennedy heard the familiar creak of the office door and saw his wife's eyes narrow. He turned as Julianna came in, wearing a skintight animal-print dress. Keys dangled from her right hand, jingling as she glided towards him.

Snuggling her free hand into the crook of Kennedy's arm, she glared at his wife, who was leaning against the desk. "I need to talk to you, Angus. Let's go to my office."

"Ms Porter." Beatrice stood up. "We no longer require your services. Please hand over the keys to the office and leave the premises. Your personal things will be collected and sent with your final cheque."

"You can't fire me! Tell her, Angus!"

Kennedy wondered if his wife had lost her mind. In a soothing tone, he said, "Actually, Beatrice, she's right."

"Take the keys from her this instant, or I'll call the police," Beatrice insisted, with icy calm.

Julianna released Kennedy and flew at Beatrice, keys in hand, points out. She rammed into the older woman and forced her backwards pinning her to the desk. Beatrice's cigarette flew out of her hand and landed on the floor. Julianna pressed a forearm arm to her neck. "You dried-up old bitch. You want the keys? Here they are!" She held them a hair's breadth from Beatrice's right eye.

"Please, Julianna, stop this." Kennedy had found his voice. "I can straighten it out."

As if in a trance, Julianna lowered her fist and removed her arm from Beatrice's neck, staggered backwards and collided with him.

"Good girl." Kennedy caught her.

"You pathetic old man. Fucking you was the most

disgusting thing I've ever had to do." Julianna's lip curled as she swatted away his hands. "If you report this to the police, I'll finish what I started." She pointed the keys at Beatrice, then waved them in his direction. "And if you ever go back on your word about us being together the night Jason Findley died, I'll tell the police exactly how you and Mac Hawke planned Somers's murder – and Sarah Bennett's. Not to mention Jason Findley's."

Chapter Fifty-one

Swathed in black, wearing rubber-soled shoes, Wicky Riley followed the stream running through Dunwoody, a neighbourhood directly north of Atlanta's Perimeter Highway. Careful of the slippery footing in the mushy Georgia clay, he advanced towards Sarah Bennett's garden. She lived in one of the older sub-divisions, where houses stood on half-acre plots, their gardens sloping down to the brook. Most had been left wild.

Holding his breath against the whiff of mould and decay, he took up a position in a shed filled with ancient gardening tools. It stood on the property directly across from Sarah's home and was hidden from view by overgrown bushes. Nearby, a small bridge crossed the brook. He felt around in his pack, glad he'd remembered bug spray. The mosquitoes had eaten him alive over the last few nights. That done, he took out his binoculars. Sarah was standing in the kitchen, talking on the phone, her dinner guest in the dining room. On the deck he could see the policewoman who'd been staying with her since her return from Australia. Wicky considered himself a patient man. Sooner or later he'd get his chance.

Sighing heavily, Sarah hung up and wandered across the kitchen, her high-heels clattering on the tiled floor. At the stainless-steel refrigerator, she filled a glass with filtered water, then turned to the two-tier island and the bar stools upholstered in sage green. Her jade and black tweed jacket lay across one. She frowned. Elliott had purchased it for her in London. Reminders of him surrounded her, at the office, at home, even in the clothes she wore.

She drank the water and left the glass in the sink. The french windows leading to the deck were open a crack. Outside, Sergeant Helen stood at the railing, smoking and staring down the staircase that dropped two storeys into the jungle that was Sarah's garden.

She went back to the dining room, where her friend Clare was standing by the mahogany table, holding a platter with the remains of pork tenderloin in hot mango-chutney sauce. She'd been hawking her watercolours to local galleries all day and had shed her black shoes, which were under her chair.

"That was Bernie. He finally tracked Jake down." Sarah said, glancing to the three tall windows with a view of the garden. The striped curtains were open, but there was nothing to see. The sun had set long ago, leaving an opaque night sky made darker by the absence of stars.

"Where was he?" Clare balanced a few more plates on the tray and padded into the kitchen.

"New York City. At the Park Central. Tomorrow he's off to Baltimore." Sarah picked up a bowl and followed her friend. "I can't understand why Jake's being so secretive. He refused to tell me why he's meeting with his distributors when they'll all be at the Wine and Spirits Wholesalers of America convention is this weekend."

"The nerve of that man, not discussing his business with you." Clare placed the dishes on the counter next to the sink, her smile fading at Sarah's bleak expression.

"Did Jake remember who recommended the perfume he bought his mother? What was it called again?"

"Oceana is Julianna Porter's signature scent." Sarah rolled up the sleeves of her blouse and started to load the dishwasher. "Bernie asked him about it, but all Jake could say was that he heard about it at a wine event in Adelaide. Stephen Randall, Macquarie Hawke, Andrew Dunne and Graham Blackwell were there, but he can't recall who mentioned it, which gets us nowhere." She picked up a paper-thin crystal wine glass and washed it by hand.

Clare pushed back a strand of salt-and-pepper hair. "Why is the perfume so important?"

"I'm not sure it is. It's just one of my wild hunches." Sarah dried the glass, set it aside and started to wash another. "Everyone agrees someone other than Julianna is calling the shots. So, she wears this three-hundred-dollars-a-bottle perfume. On her salary, a lover must be buying it for her. What if he's the one? I know it's a stretch, but neither Stabler nor O'Connor seemed at all interested." The glass hit the tap and shattered. "Damn it! What's the matter with me?"

"Did you cut yourself?" Clare asked, waving away Sergeant Helen, who'd dropped her cigarette and raced into the sunroom, gun drawn.

"Not badly." Sarah plucked a microscopic piece of glass out of her finger and blood gushed. She peeled a paper towel off the roll under the cabinet, and wrapped it round her finger.

"Sit down. I'll finish clearing up." Clare nudged her aside, fished the larger pieces of glass from the sink and threw them into the bin, then washed the remaining slivers down the drain. "Sarah, I hate to say it, but the recommendation could have been completely innocent. Maybe Taylor Robbins wears Oceana. You said she and Stephen Randall were an item. Maybe he buys it for her and mentioned it to Jake."

"As far as I know she only wears So Sweet by Cartier." Sarah walked round the island and climbed on to a barstool.

Clare glanced over her shoulder with a grin. "So Sweet?"

Sarah burst out laughing. "Please. Don't say it."

"I swear I don't know what you're talking about. The day I met her in your office, she seemed, well, so sweet after she'd got over her hissy fit." Clare rolled her eyes as she put the plates into the dishwasher. "On the other hand, maybe Randall bought the perfume for Julianna. He might be sleeping with her behind Taylor's back."

"Possible, but I don't think so. He and Taylor were going at it pretty hot and heavy when I saw them at Adelaide airport. Besides, I don't think he's involved." she said. "Neither he nor Oskar Hallgarten is connected to Southern Valley or Macquarie Hawke. If they were, I'm sure Jake would have mentioned it."

"What about Macquarie Hawke?" Clare poured detergent into the dishwasher dispenser, closed the door and switched it on. It began to hum.

"Strangely enough, a neighbour of Hawke's identified a picture of Julianna and said he often sees her leaving Hawke's house early in the morning." Sarah jumped off the stool, went to the wine rack and selected a tawny port from a number of bottles standing upright on the shelf above it.

Clare nodded.

"But when O'Connor questioned him about it during

the Wharf's Winemaker Dinner," Sarah put the bottle on the island counter and took down two glasses from a group hanging upside down above the rack, "Hawke trotted out his girlfriend. She was the spitting image of Julianna."

"So? Hawke likes a certain type. That makes it more likely he's Julianna's lover too, and he does have a strong motive." Clare picked up a tea towel and wiped her hands, as Sarah began to open the port.

"True. If Sam Somers had published the retraction, then Hawke's sales would have gone down the tubes, permanently. No brand could recover from something like that." Sarah's shoulders sagged as she tugged at the stopper. "Then there's Andrew Dunne. He was very friendly with Julianna when we visited Southern Valley, but I have a hard time buying his involvement. I mean, he's such a goofball. His idea of fun is playing stupid jokes on people. As for Graham Blackwell, I think we can safely strike him off the list. Maybe I'm totally off base, thinking Julianna's lover is behind the murders. Talk about grasping at straws."

"Doesn't Bernie always say it's important to throw everything into the mix?" Clare hung up the towel, then turned as Sarah covered a yawn with her hand. "When this is over, promise you'll take some time off and come to Tybee. Our new place is right on the beach, and I know how much you love low-country food!"

"Sounds wonderful." Sarah fingered the small scar on her neck, wondering if it would ever be over.

"Might that be my favourite Bluestone Cellars tawny port?" Clare asked.

"Of course." Sarah showed her the label. "Bring the glasses and we'll sit outside. I need some fresh air."

Sergeant Helen came in. "I'm going to check on O'Reilly," she said, and went out through the back door. They heard her striding away to the squad car parked at the top of the driveway.

The night air was cool, surprising both women as they stepped on to the deck. Bypassing the rectangular dining-table and six chairs, situated in front of a built-in gas grill, Clare went to the two reclining chairs and placed the port glasses on the small glass-topped table that separated them. She brushed pine needles off the cushions, then sat down. Sarah poured two generous glasses of port, put the bottle on the table, handed a glass to Clare, took one for herself, then curled up in the other chair.

Clare took a sip of port. "Are you going to tell me about Jake, or should I mind my own business?"

Sarah cleared her throat. "Is it that obvious?"

"Only to someone who knows you both as well as I do." Clare tucked her feet beneath her.

Sarah's eyes swivelled to her. "Before I left for Australia, you said something about letting things happen. Did Jake ever mention how he felt about me, other than us being friends?"

"He didn't have to." Clare said.

"Damn it." Sarah stared into the blackness of the garden. "Why didn't I see it before?"

"You weren't ready." Clare had infused her voice with optimism. "Now you are."

"I'm not sure that's true." Sarah frowned. "But it's too late to go back now."

"Back to what?"

"Being friends." Sarah stopped, diverted by the rustle of branches in the breeze, followed by the sound of twigs snapping. She cocked her head towards the stairs.

Was it her imagination or were they creaking? The wind gathered, and a forceful gust caught the french windows, slamming them with a resounding bang. Sarah vaulted out of her chair and seized Clare's arm. "We need to go inside. Now!"

Her hand was shaking as she twisted the door handle. It was locked.

Twenty miles south, at Police Headquarters in downtown Atlanta, Lieutenant Bernie McDermott sat at his metal desk, the sleeves of his white shirt rolled up to the elbows. "Unbelievable! Un-fucking-believable!" Hanging up, he yelled, "Watson! Get in here!" "

Watson appeared. "Yeah, boss?"

"O'Connor lifted Macquarie Hawke's champagne glass at that Winemaker Dinner in Sydney. The fingerprints on it belong to Malcolm Hawkins, born in Leeds, England. He was tried on fraud charges, one in conjunction with a UK brewery. No conviction."

Watson let out a low whistle, then lowered his bulk into the dilapidated chair across from McDermott. Stretching out his long legs, he grinned from ear to ear. "Macquarie Hawke. Malcolm Hawkins. Rather tidy, don't you think?" Watson was good at imitating his brother-in-law's English accent. "Is he perchance acquainted with Wicky Riley, another former English citizen?"

"Knock off the accent, Sergeant," McDermott huffed. "And no. No connection's been established, yet, but O'Connor gave me a heads-up on Hawke. He's on his way to Orlando for the Wine and Spirits Wholesalers of America convention. I want you to look for anything we can use to haul that fucker's ass in, and I want it as of yesterday!"

Watson heaved himself off the chair and strolled out of the office.

McDermott winced at the sharp pain in his lower back as he reached for the telephone and dialled Sarah's number. "Helen, why are you answering the phone? What the hell's going on. Let me talk to Sarah."

"But nothing happened!" Sarah insisted after McDermott had reprimanded her for a good ten minutes. "I panicked when I heard footsteps, but it was Helen walking down the driveway." She didn't add that the sergeant had crashed through the gate into the garden, shouting and brandishing her gun at a shadowy something she was convinced had been about to climb the stairs to the deck.

"Don't give me that crap. It might have been Slattery. You were lucky this time!" McDermott paused, his heart beating double-time. "Which brings me to the point of my call. I phoned a buddy of mine in Orlando who's familiar with the ins and outs of WSWA. Quite honestly, Sarah, even if I had a battalion of officers and you miraculously decided to comply with my security measures, there's no way I can keep you safe there. You're not going. That's final."

Chapter Fifty-two

The nervous young woman arrived early on Wednesday morning from an Atlanta secretarial agency to work at Cornerstone Wine Imports while Sarah Bennett and Jim Barnes were out of the office. Her duties included answering the telephone, typing letters, and helping out generally in the office, but no one had said anything about working in the Excel program.

She'd been asked to make some minor corrections to a lengthy document, but a few minutes ago, she'd accidentally erased the entire thing. She was grateful that the rest of the staff were at lunch. Looking at her watch, she realized she still had at least ten minutes to resurrect the file before anyone discovered what she had done.

When the phone rang, she nearly jumped out of her chair. "Cornerstone Wine Imports."

"Good day." The man's voice sounded pleasant. "I'd like to speak to Sarah Bennett."

Forgetting the orders she'd received not to give out any information on her absent employer, other than to Cornerstone's existing distributors, she replied, "Ms Bennett is at a convention in Orlando this week. May I take a message?"

"I'm supposed to meet her in a few minutes, she isn't answering her phone and I'm having a devil of a time trying to get her room number."

Anxious to return to the deleted document before the

others came back from lunch, she glanced at the bulletin board next to her desk. There was the letter Cornerstone had sent to their US distributors. Pencilled in at the bottom were the suite and phone numbers that Jim Barnes had called in earlier. "You can reach Ms Bennett at the Orlando International Hotel, suite twelve twenty."

Chapter Fifty-three

In the bowels of the Orlando International Hotel, a staging area the size of a football field had been set up by WSWA to accommodate shipments of wine, beer and liquor for the convention. The room's low ceiling was discoloured by water stains, the concrete floor strewn packing materials, and the fluorescent light fixtures were crowded with dead bugs. Cartons of display materials and cases of product had been stacked in aisles and were waiting to be claimed. The entire place was bustling with people trying to locate their goods.

Sarah had spent the better part of thirty minutes searching for two missing cases of wine. McDermott was one aisle away, bent over, studying a stack of boxes. Straightening briefly to rest her back, Sarah looked around the room. There was Jake. A blonde woman walked up to him, put a hand on his neck, and kissed his lips. Sarah averted her eyes, stepping over a lone case of wine to join McDermott in the next row.

"It looks like the two at the bottom are ours." McDermott adjusted his beige windbreaker over the gun clipped to his belt.

She leaned over to inspect them. "Good work, Detective," she teased, although her heart wasn't in it. "I'll let the union guy over there know we're ready to go."

* * *

"Fine." McDermott watched her walk to the end of the aisle. A moment ago, she'd seemed energized by the hubbub of the convention, even though they'd had an exhausting day, chasing down display materials, special-order furniture, glassware and an extra refrigerator. His eyes drifted to the opposite end of the room and came to rest on Jake Malone removing a woman's hand from his neck. Maybe he'd said something to upset her because the next moment she bolted through a side door. At once, a man with white-blond hair made his way over to him and began an animated discussion.

"Sarah." McDermott said, as she returned with a union worker pulling a wheeled cart. "Look over there and tell me who Jake's talking to."

Without bothering, she replied, "Melissa McNair. She owns Southern Cross Traders, Macquarie Hawke's importer."

"She left," McDermott said. "He's talking to a man. Macquarie Hawke? Right?"

Sarah glanced in Jake's direction. "It's hard to tell with his back to us, but it looks like Peter Vine."

She turned back to the worker, thanking him as she handed over the paperwork authorizing delivery to their suite on the twelfth floor. "Bernie, let's get going. I'd like to finish setting up by five so we can break before the opening night reception."

"OK, but I think we're about to have company."

"Hey, Sarah." Jake said, his smile fading at her cold expression. "I've been looking all over for you. Hello, Lieutenant." He held out his hand.

McDermott shook it. "It might be better if you leave off the title for the time being. Tell me, was that Peter Vine you were talking to just now?"

"No. Macquarie Hawke." Jake's lips thinned. "Sarah, do you have time for a quick cup of coffee?"

"I don't think –" Sarah was interrupted by Stephen Randall.

"Jake, I need a word." he said.

"Bernie McDermott meet Stephen Randall, vice president of Hallgarten Vineyards." Jake's jaw pulsed. "And of course you know Sarah."

Randall's lips contorted into what might have been a smile. "We need to talk. Now. In private."

"Actually, I set aside time later this afternoon, based on your message. You wanted to meet in your suite, right? I can be there at, say," Jake looked at his watch, "four o'clock?"

Randall's angular face tightened. "This is extremely important."

"I understand, but that's the earliest I can get there."

"Up to you." Randall stalked away.

"Charming." Sarah muttered once he was out of earshot. She turned back to Jake. "I wish I had time for coffee, but I have to finish setting up. Besides, Bernie won't let me out of his sight."

McDermott watched Randall walk to the escalators that led up to the main lobby. Macquarie Hawke seemed to have been waiting for him there. They had a brief conversation, then Hawke bounded on to the escalator with Randall at his heels.

"Why don't you come to our suite, Jake?" McDermott said. "You two can brew some coffee while Jim Barnes and I unpack the wine."

Cornerstone Wine Imports' suite was one of six on the twelfth floor, all a good hike from the lifts. The door opened into a sitting room with two beige sofas, two armchairs and a coffee-table. Along the right wall, an eight-foot table displayed Bluestone Cellars wines and point-of-sale materials.

Directly behind the sitting room, a four-panel sliding door opened on to a narrow balcony with a view of a golf course. A fabric display covered with scenes from Bluestone Cellars' wineries stood to the left.

After he'd exchanged greetings with Jim Barnes, who'd been opening cardboard boxes, Jake followed McDermott into the kitchen. Sarah remained with Barnes to confer about updates to the distributor meeting schedule. It wasn't long before angry voices drifted to them from the kitchen. Excusing himself, Barnes hurried out, saying he'd be back after he'd had a bite to eat at the hotel's café.

Sarah headed for the kitchen. Tight with suppressed rage, Jake was pressed with his back against the refrigerator, McDermott just inches away from him.

"Your meeting this afternoon is with Randall and Macquarie Hawke, isn't it? I knew you were hiding something from me. Do you want to tell me about it now?" McDermott prodded Jake's chest with his finger.

During the flight from Atlanta to Orlando, McDermott had admitted to her that he'd picked up Jake at Atlanta airport on his return from Australia, and questioned him for several hours before releasing him. No wonder Jake had barely acknowledged him downstairs. She could only imagine what McDermott had put him through. "What's going on in here?" she asked.

"He's lying to me." McDermott said, running a hand through his shorter-than-short hair. Glowering at Jake, he stepped aside to make room for Sarah. "He refuses to admit he's involved with Macquarie Hawke."

Sarah moved between the two men. McDermott's face reminded her of a bulldog who'd sunk his teeth into an intruder's arm and wouldn't let go until he'd ripped it to shreds. "Maybe that's because he isn't. Now, if you don't mind, I'd like to talk to Jake. Alone."

"I don't think being alone with anyone is a good idea." McDermott growled.

Sarah sent him a blistering look that warned him to back off, then stalked out of the kitchen. Jake picked up the two cups of coffee he'd poured and followed her into the adjoining bedroom. It was dominated by a king-size bed and a large dressing-table with a landscape mirror. A tall armoire stood open, displaying a thirty-six-inch TV. Jake put the coffee mugs on the desk by the picture window, while Sarah drew the curtains, filling the room with the late-afternoon sun. In the distance, the sky was obliterated by greenish-black thunderclouds.

"I'm sorry about the way Bernie's acting. He's only trying to protect me," Sarah said, releasing the drapery cords.

"Why do I get the feeling he's trying to protect you from me?" Jake came up behind her and touched her shoulder. "He mentioned that you saw Melissa kissing me. I'm sorry if it upset you. She is –"

"Oh, please!" Sarah interrupted. "Who you see is your business."

"I'm sorry you feel that way." Jake reached down and seized her left hand. "Is that why you're wearing your wedding ring again? You haven't worn it for over a year."

Sarah jerked her hand away, then walked over to the bed and sat down. Jake joined her, the springs buckling under his weight so that he fell into her, their thighs touching. "Please, Sarah. Talk to me."

"The ring – it's not what you think," she said. "The nightmares about Elliott are back. Sometimes when I wake up, I think he's still alive."

"We've been through this before," Jake said. "Elliott's father identified his body."

"Elliott is dead, I know that, but seeing him in the dreams brings back, all the things between us that were unresolved." Sarah faced Jake, her eyes boring into his. "I never intended to tell anyone this, but you need to know." She took a deep breath. "Elliott went to England to sort out whether or not he wanted to divorce me. I never told anyone because I kept hoping he'd come to his senses. Three months later, he left a message on my answering machine to tell me he was coming home. That's it. No mention of a divorce. Nothing about reconciliation. The next day he was dead."

Silently damning the man to hell, Jake put an arm round her. "It's all right. I know."

"What do you mean, you know?"

"Elliott came to see me before he left and asked me to look after you," Jake murmured. "He made me promise not to say anything about it, unless you brought it up first."

"You knew all along?" Sarah felt the room swirl and dip as if she'd been struck by vertigo. The sensation increased when she shut her eyes. Jake's friendship had sustained her in the days and months after Elliott's death when it had been all she could do to get out of bed, much less run a business. She'd come to rely on him, trust him, as she did Clare and McDermott. "I don't know what bothers me more – you and Elliott deciding I couldn't take care of myself or you pretending all this time to know nothing about Elliott leaving me. It seems so dishonest."

Jake hoisted himself off the bed, went to the desk, picked up a mug and sipped the lukewarm coffee. He moved to the window and looked outside. The storm had blotted out the sun, darkening the room. A flash of lightning sparked, followed by a rolling boom of thunder.

"What about Clare? Does she know too?" Sarah asked.

"I never discussed it with her." Jake replied.

"Of course not. We both know how seriously you take your promises," she muttered, flashing back to the night at the Rose, Jake standing by his suitcase, a white towel wrapped round his waist. "How far were you willing to go this time? Were you 'taking care' of me in Australia?"

Jake flushed. "I should walk out of this room right now, but I know how strung out you are otherwise you would never have said such a horrible thing. Besides, I don't run away from the people I care about."

Sarah's head jerked up. "Like Elliott, you mean?"

"Yes, as a matter of fact."

"So tell me." she said, unable to stop now that she'd started, "what if I'd never confided in you? How long were you prepared to continue this sham?"

"I think you're forgetting something." Jake's voice had an edge. "I gave Elliott my word, but there was nothing to stop you confiding in me."

"He was my husband! It was none of your business."

"Elliott was my friend. He made it my business," Jake pointed out.

There was a knock on the door to the suite. "Sarah? Phillip Dwyer's here," McDermott called.

"I'll be there in a minute." Sarah stood up and went to the door.

"You're wrong about one thing," Jake said. "I know exactly why you're wearing your wedding band again. I've seen you do it often enough. That damn ring comes out any time someone gets too close. You push them away, like you're trying to push me away now. This argument is part of it. Please, Sarah, I love you so much, we've always shared everything, don't shut me out now. Talk to me!"

"I can't deal with this right now. I have to go. I don't want to keep Phillip waiting."

"OK, but I'm not finished." Jake gritted his teeth. "Just so you know, there's one more promise I made. It concerns you, in a roundabout way, but I won't be at liberty to discuss it until this evening. Meet me at the reception. After that, you have to decide where we're going. It's up to you. I can't take much more of this."

Chapter Fifty-four

The chrome and neon restaurant on the outskirts of Adelaide, modelled after an American diner, was packed out. Although stools were available at the counter, Julianna had waited for a booth. After she'd had a big, American-style breakfast of bacon, eggs and hash browns, she sat quietly, sipping bitter black coffee and wondering if she should try calling the Orlando suite again. Setting the cup in its saucer, she reached into her purse, drew out her phone and hit redial. This time an operator with the kind of flat American accent Julianna detested answered on the tenth ring. "I called a minute ago and was put through to the wrong bloody room. Could you try to get it right this time?" Twirling a strand of hair round her middle finger, she listened to the phone ring.

"Hello?"

That one word, spoken by the same female who had answered, "Wrong number," a few minutes ago, was like fingernail screeching across a blackboard.

"Who is this?" Julianna demanded, squeezing the phone in a death grip.

"I told you before, you have the wrong room." The woman's voice hardened. "And if this is some kind of joke, I don't find it amusing."

"Neither do I." Julianna was teetering on the edge of hysteria. Her heart palpitated and dizziness swept over her. "You bloody bitch!"

"Wait a minute. I know who you are!" the woman said contemptuously. "My fiancé warned me about you. Why can't you get it into your head that just because he slept with you, it doesn't mean he ever intended to marry you? Quit harassing him." She slammed down the phone.

Julianna was infuriated. She wanted to smash something. Hurt someone. She shoved the phone into her handbag, then took out a compact and inspected her face in the mirror. Amazing. She looked exactly the same as she had a few minutes ago. She took her time powdering her nose, then slid a tube of lipstick out of her handbag, and applied it liberally. Reflected in the mirror, she saw a movement behind her. Every nerve in her body was alert as she observed two hulking policemen approach her waitress. The three were murmuring, heads together, then the waitress threw a guarded glance in her direction.

Gut churning, she tossed the compact and the lipstick into her handbag, took out her car keys, inched across the bench seat, then glided quietly towards the exit at the far end of the restaurant.

"Lee Stout! Stop right there!" A policeman bellowed, as Julianna opened the door, setting off an alarm. "You're under arrest!"

Julianna ran down the steps, and leaped into her SUV. Her heart beat frantically as she switched on the engine, jammed the gear lever into reverse, and hit the accelerator. Squealing tyres were followed by a horn blaring as her car careened backwards into the busy street. Her door was open. She leaned over to close it as she shifted into drive with the other hand.

"Lee Stout. You're under arrest! Get out of the car!"

the young policeman barked, sprinting across the shallow car park into the street. He grasped the handle of the half-open door as the car lurched forward. Swept off his feet, he latched on to the wing mirror with his other hand, his feet finding the SUV's narrow running-board.

Julianna kept the accelerator on the floor, swerving through the traffic, but the officer held on. They were approaching an intersection. The stop light changed from green to red just as the SUV shot into it. Julianna screamed as vehicles on both sides rushed towards her. Wrenching the steering-wheel in a futile effort to avoid a collision, she sent the car into a spin. The policeman lost his footing and was flung into the air. Crashing to the pavement, he rolled over until he hit the kerb. Moments later, a red car smashed into the SUV's passenger side while a white van went straight for Julianna, crumpling the metal around her as if it were aluminium foil. More cars ploughed into the wreckage. A few moments passed, then dazed people emerged from their cars to the sound of horns and alarms. A few good Samaritans ran to the pulverized mass to help.

At the side of the road, two men helped the bruised policeman to his feet, his uniform torn and bloodied. They supported him as he limped to Julianna's SUV, which was crushed and smoking. Someone was trying to prise open the door with a crowbar, but it wasn't budging.

The policeman peered into the front seat and groaned. The airbag hadn't inflated and the woman, Lee Stout, a.k.a. Julianna Porter, lay inert, *sans* seat-belt, splayed across the front seat. She was covered with blood.

Chapter Fifty-five

Forty minutes into the WSWA opening-night reception, the cavernous Grand Cyprus ballroom was bursting with people, their conversations spiralling in volume over the music provided by a five-piece band playing from a raised stage in the centre of the room. Decorated to look like a *tiki* hut on a tropical beach, it was surrounded by wooden poles topped with buckets of fake flames. White-hot spotlights illuminated tables at which roast beef, shrimp and pasta were being served. Uplights in each corner showed the way to straw-thatched bars offering beer, wine and spirits. Exotic palm trees in terracotta pots lined the walls.

Trailed by Bernie McDermott, his phone pressed to his ear, Sarah made her way through the nearly impenetrable crowd, edgy after her quarrel with Jake. She moved closer to McDermott to hear his end of the conversation, bumping into him when he stopped suddenly.

"What's that? I can't hear you . . . Hawkins . . . Fowler . . . No shit . . . Atlanta? What about last week? . . . I see. Chicago, New York and Baltimore? Crap!" McDermott swore as his call disconnected. The display read, 'Searching for Service". He flipped the phone shut and shoved it into his jacket.

"Was that O'Connor?" Sarah yelled over the music.

"Yeah. Hawke's been travelling under his real name,

Malcolm Hawkins. He was in Atlanta the day of the murder and in Chicago, New York and Baltimore last week. Monday, Tuesday and Wednesday."

Sarah went cold. "That's where Jake was last week."

"I know. I don't think it's coincidence, but let's talk about it later. I can hardly hear myself think in here." McDermott pointed out three men with distributor badges heading their way. When she gave him the all-clear signal, indicating she knew them, he stepped aside and focused on the masses streaming round them.

It wasn't long before another importer butted into their conversation. Soon, Sarah excused herself and broke away. McDermott followed, close behind.

The heavy thump-thump-thump of drums was making Sarah's head ache, and the hordes of people stalking the room, checking badges, like animals in search of prey, were oppressive. In rapid succession, she was accosted by two winery representatives, using the event to make contact with any US importer they could find. After deflecting the Chilean supplier, citing a conflict of interest with one of her existing brands, she handed a South African a business card, asking him to contact her after the show. At that point, she removed her badge and stuck it into her purse, wedging it against the gun McDermott had insisted she carry.

As she passed a table at which a spotlighted chef was carving a side of beef with a wicked-looking knife, her stomach growled. She was hungry, but she didn't want to waste time queuing, not with McDermott pressuring her to leave. She didn't blame him. The unrelenting collisions were making her nervous too, as was the thought that anyone, including Slattery, could get into this reception. Although official WSWA badges were required for entry to all events, they were not photo-IDs, and anyone could use them. Loaning them was common practice. The purple badges were the most plentiful and consequently the easiest to obtain.

Pushing through the multitudes, Sarah found a bar that wasn't jammed and ordered cranberry juice for McDermott, tonic water with lime for herself. McDermott gulped his drink, and during the fraction of a second that his eyes left her, a man sporting a purple badge crashed into her.

"Watch it, buddy!" McDermott shouted, catching a glimpse of the man's ill-fitting khaki suit and odd, flat-top haircut before the crowd swallowed him. "Damn it, Sarah, that's it. We're outta here."

"Five more minutes. I need to find Donald Stoilas." Sarah left the bar, walked along the wall and stopped by a palm tree close to the ballroom's entrance. Slinging the gold chain of her evening bag over her shoulder, she scanned the crowd. At six feet six, Stoilas shouldn't be too difficult to locate. As the most senior member of his family, he ran Federated Distributors from his Jacksonville office, controlling the Pensacola, Orlando, Tampa and Miami operations. For a number of years, Federated had been one of her strongest Bluestone Cellars distributors. How long that would last was anyone's guess, now that Stoilas had gone back on his word and agreed to represent Macquarie Hawke. Indicative of problems to come, he'd been avoiding her attempts to set up a meeting during the convention. She laid a hand on McDermott's arm, "Look. Over there. It's Stoilas. Come on – before we lose him."

* * *

The man in the ill-fitting khaki suit ducked behind a cluster of people to avoid a head-on collision with Sarah as she propelled herself into the mob. Keeping a close watch on her wasn't difficult. Her spun-gold dress caught the light. He'd managed to run into her at the bar a few moments ago, but the cop dogging her step had been too fast for him. She was on the move again, headed for a man with a hooked nose, darkish complexion and coarse black hair peppered with grey.

". . . I'll see you at four, then." Stoilas smiled at Sarah, then wheeled round to confer with his younger brother, George, Federated's director of wine sales.

"Looking forward to it." she replied, her smile faltering as Macquarie Hawke glided up to her.

"Sarah, what a surprise. I didn't expect to see you here under the circumstances." His blue eyes roved up and down her body. "Have they caught the man who attacked you?"

"No. Not yet." Sarah gritted her teeth, her hand going to the wound on her neck. There was still a thin red line on her skin, but it was almost invisible now.

Donald Stoilas greeted Hawke with a hearty clap on the back. "You and George need to get together tomorrow to set up the introductory sales meetings before our three containers arrive." He lowered his voice: "I assume we're still OK for the free goods to be Coonawarra Shiraz. Three per cent, right?"

A stream of people bulldozed into the group, splitting it in two, engulfing the Stoilas brothers and an Italian supplier whose name didn't match the one on his purple badge. Macquarie Hawke was left standing beside Sarah and McDermott.

"Malcolm Hawkins? Bernie McDermott." He held out a hand, purposely allowing his jacket to fly open, revealing the snub-nose thirty-eight clipped to his belt. He smiled at the furtive look on Hawke's face. "Does the name Fowler mean anything to you? Biggest bad-ass motorcycle you've ever seen? Member of the Kawasaki Kamikaze Club in Adelaide?"

"Name's Hawke, if it's all the same to you." Hawke kept his hand at his side. "And I suggest you mind your own business and look after Sarah. You wouldn't want anything untoward happening to her, would you?"

Before McDermott could react, a group of revellers swarmed around the two men. Using it to his advantage, Hawke slipped away.

"Oh, Mr Hawkins, one more thing!" McDermott called loudly as the Stoilas brothers reappeared. "Detective Superintendent O'Connor wanted you to know that your girlfriend, Julianna Porter, was arrested for assaulting Mrs Angus Kennedy, resisting arrest and the attempted murder of a police officer." He spoke at a decibel level that ensured everyone in the vicinity could hear him. He didn't mention that Julianna was in hospital, fighting for her life. "And Angus Kennedy is no longer providing her with an alibi for the night Jason Findley was murdered."

"Get away from me, you crazy bastard!" Hawke stalked away and vanished into the crowd.

"If your intention was to rattle him, it worked." Sarah took McDermott's arm and steered him to the exit, relieved they could leave. "Why were you asking him about Fowler?"

"O'Connor said Doolan had been trying to get in touch with a friend of Fowler's, a member of his

Kawasaki club. The guy finally returned from a road trip and contacted him. He swore Malcolm Hawkins had hired Fowler to get the document back from you," McDermott said.

"Sarah, wait up!" Jake Malone shouldered his way through a stream of people to them.

"Busy night," McDermott said noncommittally.

Jake nodded in response, then moved closer to Sarah, leaning into her to be heard over the music. "Could you come outside with me for a few minutes? I made a promise about Macquarie Hawke –" He broke off. Someone was pushing towards them through the masses, agitating them, forcing them aside. Eventually Melissa McNair thrust herself in front of him.

"Jake Malone, you son-of-a-bitch," she shrieked, her glossy pink lips contorted. She produced a piece of paper and shoved it under his nose. "Do you know what this is? It's a letter granting the new importer for Macquarie Hawke wines the right to use my label approvals. To think I trusted you, you worthless piece of shit." She threw the paper into his face and stormed out of the ballroom.

It floated to the floor. Sarah stooped to pick it up. Squinting in the dim light, she studied its contents, unaware that Jake's entourage was hustling him out of the ballroom.

"What does it say?" McDermott peered over her shoulder.

"Southern Cross Traders grants the label use-up rights for Macquarie Hawke wines to their new importer, Malone Brands International, Ltd."

Two lone figures strolled along the winding path adjacent to the first hole of the golf course circling the

Orlando International Hotel. The lush tropical plants, accentuated by strategically placed ground lights, were so tall and dense that they shielded the towering hotel and the golf course from view.

Hawke ducked to avoid a palm frond. Hot and sticky, he unbuttoned his jacket. The warmth and humidity, even at twilight, was making him sweat. It had to be at least ninety degrees, he thought irritably.

"We've gone far enough." Randall stopped at a gap in the trees that allowed a glimpse of a well-manicured fairway across the shimmering water hazard.

The light was fading fast as Hawke went on a few yards to a concrete bench facing the water. A lamp behind it was switched on, attracting a cloud of insects. "Damned bugs." He slapped the back of his neck. "Why did you drag me out here? It's like a sauna."

"Why do you think, *Malcolm*?" Randall scowled. "You and Julianna."

"Oh. I see. You heard Rent-a-cop?" Hawke laughed dismissively. "You must be mad if you think I'd get involved with that conniving bitch. As for changing my name, don't you think 'Macquarie Hawke' is more marketable than 'Malcolm Hawkins'?"

"You think this is funny?" Randall's anger showed. "That cop accused you of being involved with a murderer and you're laughing about it?"

"Lighten up." Hawke walked to the water's edge and stared at the fairway. "You know, Stephen, you really are a fool. Why bring me out to this isolated spot and accuse me of being involved with a murderer? Aren't you the least bit concerned for your own well-being?" He swung round with a grin.

"Maybe you're the one who should be concerned."

Hawke snorted. "I have no quarrel with you. Besides, why kill the goose that laid the golden egg?" He slapped a mosquito on his arm. A bright spot of blood appeared. "Pull your head in. I'm not about to lie to you. Everything's all right."

"You lied to me about Melissa. You said she was on board." Randall removed his jacket, folded it over the back of the bench, and joined Hawke at the water's edge. Picking up a flat stone, he threw it with a quick flip of his wrist. It skipped across the water and disappeared. "The old man's getting nervous. If you want the rest of your instalments then you need to convince me there won't be any more unpleasant surprises."

"Such as?"

"Don't play dumb with me. Your wines are made at Southern Valley where Angus Kennedy is suspected of fraud. You've been linked to a woman arrested for murdering the winemaker there." Randall was incensed. "And Melissa! What a screw-up, allowing her to get hold of the use-up letter."

"You're the one who wanted to keep everything quiet. I was waiting to tell Melissa after the announcement because she has a very big mouth." Hawke snickered. "If your office hadn't faxed her a copy of the use-up letter . . ."

"What?" Randall's eyebrows went up in disbelief.

"I gave you the one and only copy of that letter, and some bloody idiot in your office faxed it to her," Hawke said. "Your office fucked up, not me."

"That remains to be seen. Then there are the samples we presented to Malone's distributors. They were plonk. If you hadn't already sworn you weren't using Southern Valley's cheap blends in your wines . . ."

"I didn't move five hundred thousand cases in the US alone by selling crap and you damned well know it," Hawke said, deadly serious now. "If the samples didn't show well, you only have yourself to blame. You should have shipped them in advance, like I suggested, to avoid bottle shock. The wine didn't have time to settle down."

Randall faced Hawke, with his back to the water. "I paid a bloody fortune for your brand, and because of you it's going down the crapper."

"Whoa, mate! You didn't spend a cent. It's all Hallgarten's money." Hawke thought he saw something move by the water's edge. An alligator. "Besides, what do I care? It's your problem, not mine. I don't own the brand any more."

Wiping a stream of sweat off his forehead, Randall moved close to him. "I want my cut by Monday, deposited in the Cayman account."

So that was what this was all about, Hawke thought. Randall's "fee" for jacking up the price Hallgarten had offered for his brand. The man was fishing for excuses to change the terms of their deal. "Forget it," he said. "You aren't getting anything until the last payment clears my bank. That was our deal."

"I'm changing the rules." Randall advanced on him. "I want my fifteen per cent or I'll make sure you never get another cent out of Hallgarten."

"You do that, and I'll send the old man the tape I made of you agreeing to my terms." Hawke's laughter echoed across the water. "I assure you it exists. Once I get my money, you get the tape. If you behave yourself, I'll throw in your exorbitant 'fee'. So I guess we'll have to put up with each other for the time being. Of course, what's to stop me pushing you backwards into the water where that alligator's eyeing you for a late dinner?"

Hawke placed his hands in the centre of Randall's chest and playfully pushed him backwards. "With your untimely accidental death, all my problems would be solved." But for Julianna.

Randall charged, his fist flying out and catching the other man squarely in the eye. Hawke bellowed and threw a round-house punch at Randall, who jumped aside, the blow glancing off his upper arm. Hawke lost his balance and stumbled forwards. Tottering precariously on the slope, he wobbled, lost his footing and slid into the water.

The creature on the bank came to life with a roar.

Later that evening, Sarah and McDermott were sitting at a table in the Wellington Seafood Bar and Grill. It was on a raised platform with an aerial view of the Orlando International Hotel's lobby. Sarah was toying absently with a glass of Marlborough sauvignon blanc, selected from an extensive range of New Zealand wines by the glass. They'd ordered blackened grouper and baked potatoes.

Someone below called up to Sarah. It was Roberta "Bobby" Wagner of Coastal Beverages, in a flowing, embroidered shirt, a wide belt and tight trousers. "Hey, Sarah, is it OK if I stop by tomorrow? Around five? I want to see your new labels."

Sarah came alive. "Any time's fine. Look forward to it!"

After Bobby had strolled away, McDermott angled towards Sarah. His hair caught a ray of light, turning it gleaming white. "We need to talk about Hawke. He was in Atlanta the day Somers was murdered and –"

"I've been thinking about that," Sarah interrupted. "Yesterday, in the receiving area, I thought Jake was talking to Peter Vine, but it was Hawke. What if I made the same mistake the day Somers was murdered?" She grasped the stem of the wine glass, and swirled it. Because of her, Peter Vine had been dragged into Police Headquarters and accused of killing Somers.

Reading her consternation, McDermott said, "Once we found out Somers was going to dump him, we'd have picked him up anyway. Actually, I wanted to talk about Jake. The use-up letter explains why he was travelling with Hawke last week. And why he tried to persuade you that the man you overheard in Southern Valley's passageway telling the winemaker to forge Nathan Smyth's documents wasn't Hawke. He didn't wait for you outside the ballroom because he's up to his neck in this."

"No, he isn't!" Sarah's apathy lifted. "Something's not right. Didn't you see Jake's reaction when Melissa threw the fax at him? He was confused. No, he was shocked." She removed the fax from her purse and held it up to him. "Look. At the top. This letter was faxed from Oskar Hallgarten. It doesn't make any sense unless . . ."

McDermott, who was facing the restaurant's entrance, vaulted out of his chair. "What are you doing here, Malone?"

Sarah returned the fax to her handbag, laid it on the table, and stood up. Jake came towards them, hands in his pockets. "I've been waiting for you outside the ballroom. I don't know how I managed to miss you." He arrived at the table, took his hands out of his pockets and straightened his jacket.

"We waited, but when we didn't see you, we left." Sarah was unable to meet his eyes. "How did you find us?"

"I saw you from the lobby. Listen, I'm sorry you had to find out this way." He trailed off as McDermott moved round the table to stand shoulder to shoulder with him.

"Why did you lie about being involved with Macquarie Hawke?" McDermott demanded.

"Back off, McDermott!" Jake warned, a deep furrow appearing in his otherwise unlined forehead. "I'm not involved with Hawke and I sure as hell don't like being called a liar."

"Then explain the use-up letter. And the trip you took with Hawke last week."

"You were checking up on me? Oh, never mind." Jake took a long, deep breath, and spoke to Sarah. "That's what I was trying to tell you before Melissa showed up. Oskar Hallgarten bought Macquarie Hawke. Randall offered me the brand, but I declined. I have no idea why the use-up letter names me as the importer. As for the trip, I told Randall it was a mistake to put two top Australian brands with one importer. To prove me wrong, he went behind my back and set up meetings for Hawke with my Hallgarten distributors. I had to go along for damage control. I couldn't tell you about any of it because I promised Randall I'd keep the acquisition secret until it was made public."

McDermott's eyes blazed behind his glasses. "Jesus H. Christ! Hawke is a suspect in the attempts on Sarah's life and Randall's company is buying Hawke's brand, but you couldn't tell us because of a fucking promise?"

"How was I supposed to know Hawke is a suspect?" The last vestiges of Jake's composure dissolved and he took a step back, clearly overcome by an urge to punch McDermott in the face. He focused on Sarah. "Please, you have to believe me." he said. "If I'd had any inkling Hawke was a suspect, I would have told you about the acquisition."

"What other secrets have you been hiding from us, Malone?" McDermott goaded him.

"Bernie, this isn't getting us anywhere," Sarah said. "Let's sit down and talk about it."

"I wish I could, but Randall insisted on announcing the acquisition tonight, at my Hallgarten dinner, and I don't trust the bastard on his own," Jake said. "There is one other thing, though. I remembered who told me about Oceana. It was Stephen Randall."

"Randall?" McDermott screwed up his face in disbelief. "Are you sure?"

"Absolutely. Would either of you care to tell me why it's so important?" Jake asked.

"Oceana is Julianna Porter's signature scent," Sarah answered, when McDermott excused himself, pulled his phone from his breast pocket and began talking quietly. "We're fairly sure she hired Wicky Riley to murder Sam Somers, and Clive Slattery to . . ." she hesitated ". . . come after me. The consensus is that someone else is behind the murders, telling her what to do. Maybe a lover. Someone who likes buying her expensive perfume."

"Damn this hotel!" McDermott cursed, flipping his phone shut. It was dead again. "That was O'Connor. Julianna's cell phone showed a call to this hotel. He thinks she may have been calling her accomplice, but we got cut off. I may be able to pick up a signal closer to the front door. I'll be a hundred yards away. Jake, stay here until I get back. Sarah, keep your bag handy." McDermott gave her a meaningful look. "Yell if you need me."

"Does this mean I'm out of the doghouse?" Jake asked.

"Not even close," McDermott snarled.

Sarah shrugged. "I'm sorry, Jake. I'll understand if you need to leave."

"No. My distributors can wait. We may as well sit down." Jake was holding out Sarah's chair when a man strode towards them, an angry set to his shoulders. It was Stephen Randall in a green-striped shirt, black blazer and tan trousers. He had a small laptop under his arm and was limping badly. His cheek was cut and his knuckles bore ugly purple bruises. "Stephen! What happened to you? Are you all right?"

"If you think I look bad, you should see the other guy." Randall laughed mirthlessly. "I hate to break up this tête-à-tête, but a hundred and twenty distributors are waiting to have dinner with you."

"Didn't you get my message?" Jake asked.

"Yes. I can certainly see the important business that detained you." Randall snapped, staring at Sarah with contempt.

"Hello, Stephen," Sarah said, engrossed in the revelation that Randall had recommended Oceana. It didn't make sense. She couldn't imagine a beautiful girl like Julianna falling so much in love with this man that she'd commit murder for him. Macquarie Hawke, on the other hand, possessed a dangerous sexuality that might seduce a young girl into doing almost anything. "I understand you recently acquired the Macquarie Hawke brand. Congratulations."

Randall's hooded eyes settled on Jake. "That was privileged information."

"Actually, Stephen," Sarah said, "I heard about it from Melissa McNair, at the reception. She created quite a stir."

Jake glanced from one to the other, concerned by the pulsing vein on the side of Randall's head. "Stephen, why don't you go ahead? I'll be there shortly."

"Dinner is scheduled to start in ten minutes, with the PowerPoint presentation I put together for you." Randall tapped on the small computer. "I need your help setting it up. I'm not leaving without you."

"Fine. Wait here. Sarah, I'll be back in a moment." Jake took off towards McDermott, who was facing away from them, his phone glued to his ear.

While Randall drummed his long, thin fingers on the back of a chair, Sarah picked up her handbag. The urge to reach inside for the comforting cold steel of her gun was strong. "Stephen, you must be concerned about the investigation at Southern Valley. I understand they've been accused of blending red and white grapes and selling the result at a premium. I do hope Hawke's wines weren't affected."

Rage showed in Randall's face. "Taylor was right about you. If I ever hear you imply that Macquarie Hawke or his wines are somehow involved in the problems at Southern Valley, you'll be sorry."

That was when Sarah noticed that the laptop tucked under Randall's arm carried an Addison Group nameplate, which read, 'Property of Taylor Robbins'.

Chapter Fifty-six

The boxy but spacious Palmetto Ballroom at the Orlando International Hotel, with its white walls and polished wooden floors, was saved from being totally devoid of character by a beautifully finished ceiling studded with crystal chandeliers. Capable of seating over four hundred people, it accommodated half that number tonight: a mobile stage, required for the evening's entertainment, occupied the other half of the room. Behind it, a movie screen flashed images from Jake's PowerPoint presentation, operated by a laptop on a podium at the back, where the standing-room-only guests were milling around.

A famous comedian, host of a late-night TV talk show, was scheduled to appear on stage shortly. At the moment, though, the owner of a celebrated San Francisco restaurant, who had been flown in to prepare the five-course gourmet dinner, walked on to scattered applause.

The noise level in the ballroom escalated as the restaurateur, a short squat man, described the meal's preparation. Someone dimmed the lights. Glasses clinked. More wine was poured. The waiters removed the dessert plates and offered coffee with after-dinner drinks. Others took matches to the candles at each of the hundred-plus tables where the Oskar Hallgarten distributors, their wives and uninvited friends waited impatiently for the main event to get under way.

At the table closest to the stage, Jake was relieved when Stephen Randall's assistant, a mannish woman in her forties, left for the ladies' room. She was drunk, having consumed an entire bottle of wine. Passing the next table, wobbling unsteadily on her feet, she laid a hand on Randall's shoulder, but he was too engrossed in answering his dinner companions' questions about the Hawke acquisition and didn't acknowledge her.

The evening had been the disaster Jake had feared. Instead of showing the Oskar Hallgarten distributors a good time, Randall had usurped the master-of-ceremonies role, turning the evening into a forum for his newest acquisition, Macquarie Hawke. Now the crowd was restless with boredom. Randall had to get rid of the chef. Jake signalled to him, but Randall pointedly ignored him.

Jake was about to take matters into his own hands when, without warning, the lights went out. A spotlight was trained on the stage, illuminating the chef. The pictures on the screen ceased and, amid cheers, a man appeared and ushered the chef away.

Now Randall was supposed do a stand-up routine with the comedian that included roasting a few distributors, then relinquish the stage to him. Jake estimated he had just enough time to accomplish his own task, if there were no slip-ups. He left the table and headed for the back of the room, praying that the spotlight would blind Randall to everything beyond the edge of the stage. All at once, the audience broke into rapturous applause, wolf whistles and cheers. The comedian had arrived.

Jake circled the podium, hoping he wouldn't trip on the wires. Pausing, he glanced at the stage where Randall appeared stiff and awkward. The comedian was picking up on it, making fun of him to the delight of the audience, who howled with laughter. When the howls turned to cat calls, Jake unplugged the laptop, lifted it off the podium and left the ballroom.

In the corridor, he raced across the marble floor and round a corner to a cluster of sofas, chairs and tables in front of a coffee bar that had closed for the night. He would have preferred a more secluded area, but his time was limited and this was the best he could do.

He sat down, put the computer on a coffee table, the Addison Group nameplate facing him, and turned it on. He accessed a list of files, then stared blankly at the screen, unable to resolve what he was about to do with his image of himself as an honourable man. But someone was out to murder Sarah. If her suspicions proved correct, the culprit might be Stephen Randall.

A few minutes later, he slipped back into the darkened ballroom. The comedian was alone on stage. Where was Randall? He made for the podium and as he placed the laptop on the stand, he saw something out of the corner of his eye. He spun round. Stephen Randall was a few feet away, his face taut with suspicion.

"What the hell are you doing with that laptop?"

Sarah screamed soundlessly. A tall, thin man clothed in black, a hood hiding his eyes, approached her bed. She was paralysed. He stood over her, a long, curved knife in his hand and raised his arm. The hood fell back. Moments before he slammed the knife into her chest, she woke up.

Trembling, she searched for the bedside light, and flicked the switch. Her alarm clock showed it was one a.m. She was in the bedroom of her Orlando

International Hotel suite. Someone was tapping on the door.

She put on her dressing-gown and wrapped it around herself, tightening the belt. Then she smoothed her hair, looked through the peephole and opened the door.

"Sorry to be so late. The show went on for ever." Jake stepped inside, his jacket slung over his arm, his tie and the top two buttons of his white dress shirt undone. "McDermott asleep?" He glanced at the door connecting her bedroom to the rest of the suite, half expecting the cop to burst in, gun drawn.

"I hope so," she said, detecting the faint scent of a woman's perfume on Jake as he passed her on the way to the bed. Despite the hour, he appeared bright-eyed and alert. In comparison, she felt ancient and worn-out, still shaky after the nightmare. "Don't worry. We had a long talk. He understands you aren't involved with Hawke. I don't think he's liable to rush in and shoot you!"

"He might if he found us here alone." Jake laid his jacket on the bed, then straightened the covers and sat down. "I gather he wasn't successful in finding out who Julianna called or we'd be celebrating."

"No. The manager refused to release any information, so Bernie has no idea if they can trace which suite the call went to. Bernie's friend, James Cameron, is working on getting a warrant. How about you? Were you successful?"

"You were right. Your Australian itinerary was on Taylor's laptop, hotels, flights, dates and locations of your meetings. He had access to everything. No wonder Slattery . . ." Jake put his elbows on his knees and lowered his head. "If only I'd told you about the acquisition. God, Sarah, what if . . ."

Sarah had seen an unusual brightness in his eyes. She went to the bed and stroked the hair behind his ear. "Don't blame yourself. Bernie and I should have told you what was going on. I'm fine. Everything's fine."

She sat beside him and put an arm round his shoulders, reminded of the months after his wife died when he'd drive Cassie around late at night, hoping the car would put her to sleep. If their lights were on, he'd come in, exhausted, to drink coffee with Elliott, while she looked after Cassie. And he had reciprocated many times when, sick with grief over Elliott's death, she'd called him at all hours of the night. But he'd been less than honest with her. He'd known all along that Elliott wanted a divorce. That was Jake. He kept a promise. She swallowed hard. For that, she had insulted him, argued with him, then belittled his feelings for her. However, unlike Elliott, Jake hadn't abandoned her. She cleared her throat and punched his shoulder playfully. "Any chance you could stop making these damned promises? Just don't promise me you will, or I might have to strangle you."

Jake raised his head. "I promise."

"You're impossible! What am I going to do with you?" Sarah shook her head in mock dismay, a twinkle in her eyes. She stood up. "I could use some water."

She went into the bathroom and filled two glasses at the tap. When she returned, Jake was by the window, the curtains open. She went over to him, sensing he was suffering from the revelation that he'd played a part in protecting Randall. She handed him a glass and saw that the night was aglow towards where she knew Disney World was.

"Thanks." He took a long drink, eyes still trained on

the window. "I saw something else in Taylor's computer. The pricing and sales figures for the entire Addison Group portfolio. At least, that's what the file names indicated." He put the glass on the desk beside him and rubbed his eyes. "No wonder Randall's price war has been so effective."

"Maybe they're password-protected, which doesn't mean she isn't helping him." She drank most of her water, then put down the glass. "Ever since Taylor became brand manager, she's done everything in her power to sabotage me and my Bluestone Cellars sales. Indirectly it benefits Randall." Sarah gnawed at her lower lip. "And she's at it again. She called me tonight. The extension on the payment for those two containers of old-label shiraz was cancelled. She actually sounded happy when she told me."

"I'm sorry." He came to stand beside her. "Maybe she's happy because, with the Hawke acquisition, Oskar Hallgarten takes over the top spot from the Addison Group, which means her lover gets a seat on the board of directors, and a bonus of one point five million dollars. That's according to Randall's assistant. She was drunk tonight, out of control, but I believe she was telling the truth. For her sake, I'm glad Randall didn't hear her, but he did catch me replacing the computer."

"Oh, no! What happened?"

"I told him I was taking it somewhere safe, so it wouldn't be stolen." Jake shook his head. "He seemed to accept that, but who knows."

"I shouldn't have asked you to access her files. It's all my fault," she said. Initially Jake had resisted, insisting it was unethical. She'd prevailed, but at what cost?

"No, it isn't. It was my choice. And, frankly, at this

stage I don't give a damn about Randall. I'm more interested in keeping you alive. If only I'd never made that promise. Maybe if he hadn't sprung it on me while we were playing golf at Bottlebrush Creek, then again, he'd only just signed the contract –"

"Oh, my God! I've been assuming all along –" Sarah stopped, agitated. "Tell me, exactly, when it was signed."

Jake blinked. "Let's see. We played on Friday. Randall said they'd signed it the day before. Why are you so upset?"

"Randall signed the contract after Somers had been murdered. Why would he have had Somers killed for a brand he didn't own? Why not just refuse to sign the contract?"

"You don't know Randall like I do. He's driven by two things, money and power. I wouldn't put anything past him, he's so unbalanced," Jake said. "Whoever sent Slattery after you had your schedule. Randall had access to it through Taylor's computer, whether she's involved or not. And how would Hawke know where you'd be? The only other people with access to your itinerary were Addison Group management and your staff. Don't be so quick to rule Randall out." Abruptly he broke eye-contact and walked across to the bed. He picked up his jacket, and slung it over his arm. "We both need to get some sleep. Please, Sarah, be very careful. I'll see you tomorrow." He walked to the door. She trailed behind him.

"I hope Randall bought your story," She stood next to him at the door, arms across her chest. "You risked so much. I feel terrible. What if it's all for nothing?"

Jake brushed back a strand of hair that kept falling into her eyes. "Just so you know, I have no regrets. I can handle Randall, whatever happens. Besides, I'd do anything for you. Anything."

Before she closed the door, she picked up the pile of wine and spirits trade publications and lifestyle magazine that appeared periodically outside the rooms of every WSWA delegate. She locked the door and threw them on to the dresser, then saw that the magazine on top, *Viva Vino!*, had Macquarie Hawke's Coonawarra Shiraz label on the front cover. Something about it wasn't quite right. It was a riotous swirl of bright colours in freeform shapes, except for a perfectly formed dot over the "M" in "Macquarie".

Sarah looked at the magazine from several angles. It has to be, she thought. Then, taking the magazine with her, she went to the sitting room. The faint smell of coffee from a pot of decaf McDermott had made a few hours ago lingered in the air, mingling with wine from the empty bottles in the bin.

There was just light enough for her to notice McDermott's computer on the table. He'd been working on it this evening, studying the Somers crime-scene photos. At the time, she'd been writing up meeting notes on her own laptop, while Jim Barnes straightened up before he left for his room on a lower floor. Later, when she'd asked to see the photos, McDermott had adamantly refused.

His computer was plugged into the wall, the batteries recharging. She went to the table, lowered herself into a chair and lifted the computer's lid. It was on. She tapped a few keys, attempting to get into his files, but they were password-protected. She was feeling a little guilty. From the beginning, McDermott had shared almost everything about the investigation with her or, at least, she assumed he had, so why not the photos? Whatever, she wasn't about to wake him up to ask his permission. She thought for a few moments, then typed in "Oreos". That didn't work. OK, what next? She entered "Oreocookies" and in seconds, she was viewing the photos. There were hundreds – no, thousands.

Fifteen minutes passed before she found photographs of the empty bottles in the recycle bins behind the red-brick building. They had been removed, lined up and photographed. Using the zoom feature, she homed in on one particular set of bottles.

Excited that her hunch had been correct, she began her next search. Melissa McNair had carried a bottle into the red-brick building on the day Somers was murdered. She'd put it on Somers's desk. Sarah prayed that the bottle had survived intact. Another fifteen minutes passed before she discovered what she'd been looking for. Once again she blew up the labels, then, satisfied, she escaped from the crime-scene photos.

She accessed another file, searching for shots of Somers's home. Again, her luck held, but this time it took more than half an hour to find images of the two cases she'd been seeking. There were photos of the boxes and the eight bottles Somers hadn't opened. Leaning back in the chair, she rubbed her eyes. Her brain was fried. She had to get to bed. But before she could stand up, she felt a hand on her back and let out a shriek of sheer terror.

Chapter Fifty-seven

Once again, an afternoon storm rolled in, obliterating the sun with thunderclouds. It was a wide front, forecast to hit the Orlando area around eight or nine that evening. Sarah had been studying the cloud formations from inside the Cornerstone Wine Imports' suite and estimated the rain would arrive sooner than expected. Pity those caught outside when the heavens opened, she thought, moving away from the windows, two glasses of red wine in hand.

Although it was only five o'clock, Sarah was ready to collapse with exhaustion. McDermott had scared her almost to death last night, his hand coming down on her shoulder as she was finishing up with his computer. They'd exchanged heated words, but she'd promised to explain herself when she'd found the last piece of the puzzle, then gone straight to bed. That had been at three this morning and he'd been giving her the evil eye all day. She needed something to reinvigorate her after eight hours of distributor meetings during which she'd never once stepped outside for fresh air. When George Stoilas had arrived, in place of his brother, thirty minutes ago, she'd put on all the lights to wake herself up.

Now he was on the sofa, facing away from the balcony door. She handed him a glass and sat on the sofa across from him, pulling her skirt over her knees. "That's the lot, the new labels, new vintages, new products, and sales incentive and marketing dollars."

"The new labels are very striking," Stoilas took a sip, swishing the wine round his mouth, "and this is excellent. Very spicy and peppery. The perfect shiraz."

"I'm glad you think so." Sarah said, her nerves on edge. This was an important test of Bluestone Cellars' ability to compete with Macquarie Hawke after revamping the brand identity. "We're focusing on the Coonawarra Shiraz with the new packaging as a way to take Bluestone Cellars to the next level. There are extra sales incentives available on container loads. Would you be interested?"

Stoilas raised his heavy eyebrows. "How much money are we talking about?"

"Five dollars a case." Sarah said, cutting the promotion dollars in half. "You'll get three per cent samples, and new point-of-sale materials that tie into the advertising campaign introducing the new packaging." She mentioned the names of several top wine publications scheduled to run the ads.

"If you'll consider doubling the sales incentive, I might be able to order two containers."

"Tell you what," Sarah said, excitement taking over from exhaustion, "if you offer your sales people ten dollars per case on a sixty-day programme, I'll provide seven dollars of it."

"Let me call Donald." Stoilas put his wine down, took out his phone, stood up and walked to the far corner of the suite.

Sarah remained on the sofa, looking out of the balcony door to the golf course. If Federated approached this programme properly, one container might turn into four or five. But how many Australian wines could they promote at once, especially with three containers of Macquarie Hawke on the way?

"Donald wants to know if you'll personally conduct the sales meetings introducing the programme," Stoilas said, as he returned to the sitting room. "Not that your salesperson isn't capable, but my managers have been asking for you."

"It would be my pleasure." She'd worked with all five wine sales managers years ago before George had promoted them. It was nice to know they hadn't forgotten her.

"Then you've got a deal!"

Later, when the details for an early autumn programme had been confirmed, Stoilas stretched his long legs. Holding up a flute of Bluestone Cellars sparkling wine, he said, "Here's to you, Sarah, for persevering with us. I'm glad we can finally do your brand justice."

"Thanks, George." She leant over to clink her glass against his.

"Forgive me if I'm out of line," he went on, "but is the man outside your door with hotel security or does he work for you?"

"His name is Bernie McDermott. He's a lieutenant with the Atlanta Police Department and an old friend of my father's," Sarah said.

"Last night Donald and I overheard him talking to Mac Hawke about a murder. It was disturbing, considering we're getting ready to introduce his brand. Quite frankly, I find it hard to trust the man, especially after he didn't keep his appointment with us this morning. I understand he never showed up at his suite today, either. Do you have any idea what's going on?"

Sarah sipped some wine to hide her dismay. Had McDermott overdone it last night? Was Hawke on the run? She looked Stoilas in the eye. "From a strictly personal perspective, I believe your instincts about Hawke will serve you well."

"Thank you. That's all I needed to hear."

After Stoilas had left, Sarah asked McDermott to lock the suite, then retreated to the bedroom. Although the bed looked inviting, she jumped into the shower, redid her makeup, and fixed her unruly hair. Then she put on a dress in her favourite emerald green with an antique gold necklace inherited from a distant English cousin.

When she returned to the sitting room, with a cup of coffee and a magazine, she was pleasantly surprised to find Graham Blackwell sitting on the sofa across from McDermott. On the table a jumbo bag of Oreo cookies had been ripped down the middle. It was almost empty. Blackwell was dunking one in a tall glass of milk.

"Hello, Graham, I see Bernie's taken a liking to you. He doesn't share his cookies and milk with just anyone!" She grinned, placing the cup and the magazine on a side table. "What happened to you last night?"

"Sorry I missed you. I was waiting for a call from the chairman and didn't get to the reception until fairly late," Blackwell said. He wiped his hands on a napkin and stood up. "By the way, you look great."

"Better than the last time you saw me, at any rate." Sarah gave him a hug and kissed his cheek. "From the number of cookies left in that package, it appears you two have been at it for a while. What did I miss?"

McDermott mumbled something about "cookie police", then went on, "We were comparing notes.

Graham's been conducting an investigation into Karl Kingsley's dealings with Macquarie Hawke."

Blackwell lowered himself to the sofa. "I was pledged to secrecy by the chairman until I had enough evidence to bring in the police. I'm sorry I couldn't tell you earlier, Sarah."

Sounds familiar. Sarah walked round the coffee-table and sat beside McDermott. Abruptly he propelled himself to his feet, his hand going for his gun. He reached the door as it swung open. Jim Barnes walked in, red hair slicked back, carrying a bottle of Macquarie Hawke Coonawarra Shiraz, Bobby Wagner behind him. She put down a bottle of wine and embraced Sarah.

After introductions had been made, Barnes said, "I hope this is what you wanted. It came from a wine shop round the corner." He handed the bottle to Sarah, then looked at his watch. "Half an hour to Taste of the Future. I guess I'd better start setting up. See you later."

Bobby pointed to the bottle she'd brought. "This one's from Hawke's suite. He wasn't there, by the way. I also emailed you a copy of his distributor contract, and I forwarded a photograph taken at the warehouse of a sample bottle. My boss Matt will have a hissy fit if he finds out so, please, keep it to yourself." She shifted her bag, loaded with shiny buckles, to the other shoulder. "The contract is fairly boilerplate except for two things. All wine-writer samples must be shipped directly from the winery. And we can't bill back for any samples. We receive three per cent of every shipment as free goods to be used strictly as samples. They're stickered with a 'Samples Only Not for Sale' label that's impossible to get off. Trust me, I've tried."

"Bobby, you're a gem. I can't thank you enough. Can you stay for bit?" Sarah asked.

"I wish. I'm off to Disney World for another over-the-top Albion Corporation extravaganza – you know them? London-based mega-company with every major spirits label in the world. Not going isn't an option. Besides, Matt loves these things," she said. "You're a doll, Sarah. Take care of yourself, ya hear? And call me tomorrow. I want to know what you're up to."

By the time McDermott had returned from showing Bobby to the door, Sarah had poured three glasses of each wine. This time, he sat next to Blackwell. Sarah sat across from them. "I want you to taste both of these wines before you say anything," she instructed, and handed them each two glasses.

"The one from the shop is okay, but it doesn't taste like shiraz. More like a generic red, a house wine blended to be unobjectionable," Blackwell said, after he had tasted both wines twice. He picked up the bottle from Hawke's suite and studied the label. "This one is superb. Spicy. Rich. Loads of fruit."

"I agree. The first is like watered-down grape juice," McDermott said, smacking his lips. "This one tastes like pepper and . . . toothpicks. Woody. It's much better. So, what the hell's this all about?"

"Red dots," Sarah and Blackwell said in unison.

Blackwell looked at her in admiration. "You figured it out, didn't you? You go first."

"OK. Every time I tasted Macquarie Hawke's wines I thought they were awful. I couldn't figure out why Sam Somers raved about them." Sarah picked up the copy of *Viva Vino!* she'd left on the end table and handed it to McDermott. "Then I saw this red dot, above the

'M' in 'Macquarie' and remembered that Hart told his friend Ray, 'If anyone sees the red dots it's all over.' Which is when I . . . uhm . . . borrowed your computer, Bernie. Sorry. But the only way to prove my theory was to view photos from the Somers crime scene and his home."

McDermott frowned and put the magazine down, jostling Blackwell, who appeared surprised by her disclosure.

"It all makes sense, now," Sarah said, her face lighting up, "especially the strange things that happened during one of the judging sessions at the Peachtree International Wine Festival competition. It was supposed to be blind, but Melissa McNair and I accidentally saw the label on her Hawke Coonawarra Shiraz when it was being poured. The wine was appalling, so the panel requested another bottle. Every winery had to submit three, so it was no problem. Unfortunately the second was as bad as the first. I found images of the two empty bottles in the recycle-bin photos. The labels did not have red dots. Before I left that night, I saw Melissa scribbling on something that might have been the panel's forms." She picked up her coffee cup, and took a sip, welcoming the jolt of caffeine.

"The next day, Melissa brought in a bottle of Coonawarra Shiraz and put it on Somers's desk. The crime-scene photos prove it had a red dot. I think she changed the panel results and gave her wine a gold medal, which meant it would be tasted again in the best-of-show competition. And she wanted to make sure it was a red-dot wine."

"So the bottle Melissa took with her was the third from the initial submission, without the red dots, right?" Blackwell asked.

"I would have to assume so." Sarah replied, noticing McDermott looking at his watch. She glanced at hers. There wasn't much time left before the next event. "So, my guess is Hawke produced superior wines especially for competitions and identified them with a red dot, then shipped lesser-quality wines to his customers. I think the tasting we conducted proves my point. Compare the labels. The bottle from Hawke's suite has a red dot and it tastes wonderful. The bottle from the shop doesn't have a red dot and it tastes, well, ordinary at best."

McDermott and Blackwell compared the labels.

"I think Hawke also used the red-dot wines for the media to ensure good reviews," she continued, "counting on the fact that most wine writers accept samples without bothering to authenticate a product by buying it in a shop. And he made sure the distributors didn't accidentally send out samples to the writers from stock without a red dot by including a clause in the contract stating samples must be sent directly from the winery. Unfortunately Somers broke the mould. He bought two cases of Macquarie Hawke's Coonawarra Shiraz from a shop. The photos showed they didn't have red dots."

Blackwell leaned forward. "We were pulling random samples from shipments, and I noticed the same thing. The wines Hawke submitted to us and the ones he shipped to his customers bore no resemblance to one another. When I compared them I noticed the red dots, so with the chairman's permission, on Hawke's next application, I substituted the same wine and vintage minus the red dot. The wine was rejected. The following morning Hawke came to the office and told Kingsley to get the wine certified or else. The following day, it showed up as approved. Unfortunately, I haven't been able to prove Kingsley changed the records or that Hawke paid him to do it."

"I'm sorry, guys, but this whole scenario is absurd," McDermott complained. "If Hawke shipped cheap wine to the US, the consumers would know it didn't rate a ninety-eight."

"Five hundred thousand cases says you're wrong," Sarah said, pleased that Blackwell had corroborated her theory. "Hawke guessed correctly that people would question their own palate before they questioned a ninety-eight rating by the great Sam Somers."

"I don't buy it, no pun intended." McDermott said. "Your distributors use samples and charge a portion back to you. Their salespeople taste the samples with retailers and restaurateurs. They must have done the same thing with Hawke's wines. Surely those people would question the quality."

"Wait a minute." She went to the desk in the sitting room and returned with her laptop. "OK. Here it is. The photo of the sample bottle that Bobby sent me. Yes! There's the dot. See? Every US shipment contained three per cent samples, free of charge. I'll bet all the samples have red dots. Hawke's wines were so popular that the distributors were stingy with samples. They'd never use more than the three per cent they were provided with, especially if they weren't reimbursed for wines they used from their own stock."

"I'm still not buying it," McDermott countered. "Someone was bound to wise up sooner or later."

"You're right," Sarah responded, after a moment. "The sale to Hallgarten suggests the venture was never meant to be long-term. Hawke planned to sell his brand before anyone discovered the scam. But Somers ruined everything. To ensure his deal with Hallgarten went through, Hawke had to get rid of Somers before he printed the retraction."

There was a moment of silence, then Sarah said, "But I have one problem with Hawke. I can understand how he found me in Adelaide. The Addison Group's used the Stamford Hotel for aeons. And I think Fowler and Slattery followed me from the hotel to the Australian Wine Bureau, then to the Barossa Valley. But no one could have followed me to the Pyrenees. Graham, is it possible to find out who was working as a wine inspector the day I missed my appointment with you?"

Using Sarah's computer, Blackwell accessed the AWB's records on the Internet. "Here it is. Stephen Randall, Andrew Dunne, Nathan Smyth and Macquarie Hawke."

Sarah paled. "I was downstairs, talking to Hawke, Randall, Kingsley and Inga, the receptionist. Later, I went upstairs to the conference room and called Detective Doolan. I remember giving him my entire schedule for the remainder of my trip. The light on the line I was using didn't go out after I hung up. Now, if Hawke was working that day, he was still in the office when I made the call. I think he must have listened in on my conversation with Doolan."

An hour later, Taste of the Future was in full swing in the Grand Cyprus Ballroom, host to yesterday's opening-night reception. Now, the room was filled with hundreds of eight-foot rectangular tables with white plastic tops and blue fabric skirts, set up in rows, back to back, suppliers facing outwards, pouring their products.

Circular tables covered with trays of cheese, fruit and light snacks stood in the centre. The aisles teemed with people moving from table to table, tasting new releases ranging from sparkling water to spirits.

Sarah, Bernie McDermott and Jim Barnes were pouring Bluestone Cellars wines at the third table from the entrance, affording them a perfect view of everyone coming in. Sarah bent over, careful not to bump into the person pouring wine at the table behind her. She rummaged in a case and selected another bottle. The pressure to keep up with fresh samples was relentless. People were standing three deep in front of the table, holding out their glasses.

When Sarah stood up, she gasped. She had come face to face with Julianna Porter. No – it wasn't Julianna, although the young woman standing before her could easily have passed for her twin sister. "This is Bluestone Cellars Coonawarra Shiraz." She poured wine into the young woman's glass as she tossed her hair back over her shoulder. On her lapel was a blue 'spouse' badge identifying her as Nicki Timms, Macquarie Hawke Wines Ltd. The flash of a two-carat diamond on her left hand caught Sarah's eye.

Sarah followed Nicki's progress as she walked to Hawke's stand, across the aisle and three tables down to join a ruddy-complexioned man. Stephen Randall stood in front of the next table, which displayed Oskar Hallgarten's wines, a glass in his hand. He didn't acknowledge Nicki.

Sarah's gaze returned to the mob in front of her just as Taylor Robbins strolled up, in a tight black dress with spaghetti straps. "Hello, Sarah. Uh, hi . . . Jim. How's the convention going for you?" she asked, eyeing McDermott.

"Great!" Barnes grinned, then busied himself pouring wine at the other end of the table.

"Hello, Taylor." Sarah poured wine into her glass. "I guess we'll see you and Phillip at five tomorrow. Your suite, right?"

"Haven't you heard?" Taylor shifted from one high heel to the other. "Phillip's been called back to Australia."

"Does that mean he won't be at the tasting tonight?" Sarah asked, unable to miss the smug satisfaction on Taylor's face.

"No. He's already left." Taylor shrugged "He said he'd get in touch with you next week."

Sarah just managed to stop her mouth dropping open at the sight of a three-carat marquise diamond on Taylor's left hand.

"Taylor? Bernie McDermott! I'm a friend of Detective Superintendent O'Connor's." He leaned over the table and held out his hand.

"O'Connor? Should I know him?" Taylor asked. Her eyebrows knitted as she shook McDermott's hand.

"He's Detective Inspector Stabler's boss." The chilly façade cracked. Breaking into a roguish smile, McDermott held her hand fast. "That's a wonderful perfume you're wearing. If I'm not mistaken it's Oceana, isn't it?"

"Absolutely not." Taylor attempted to pull her hand out of McDermott's steely grip. "This is a French perfume by Cartier, So Sweet."

McDermott seemed sheepish as he released her hand. "You don't wear Oceana? I must have got it wrong. I could swear Stephen Randall said his girlfriend always wears that scent."

Taylor glared as she backed away and fell into Stephen Randall's outstretched arms.

Chapter Fifty-eight

The cramped hospital room in Adelaide was closing in on Julianna Porter. It was too hot and there were too many people in it. She was thirsty. Her head hurt. The light on her face made her eyes ache. "Get those people out of here! And turn off that light!" She shielded her eyes with a hand.

Detective Danny Doolan shooed the non-essential people out, whispered to the technician recording the interrogation to adjust the light, then grabbed a metal chair and dragged it closer to the head of the bed. It screeched across the floor. Julianna cried out and put her hands over her ears.

The plump nurse glared at him, then poured a glass of water and added a straw. "Here you are," she said.

"I don't want it." Julianna pushed away the nurse's hand.

The nurse took up a position next to Detective Superintendent Sebastian O'Connor, who stood next to the door.

Doolan ran his finger round his black wool turtleneck, his sunken eyes grave. "Let's continue – that is, if you're up to it."

Julianna shrugged, then wished she hadn't. The doctors had been conferring in whispers, poking and prodding, running test after test, scanning her brain, her skull, her chest and every other body part. When she'd asked what was wrong, they'd hummed and hahed. "I'm fine. Let's get this over with."

Doolan's bleary eyes were riveted on her. "Who asked you to hire Slattery? Was it your lover?"

Her head jerked up. She put a hand through her hair. It was a good thing he couldn't see her now. Dirty hair, no makeup, cornered like an animal. She clamped her mouth shut.

"Oh, I see. You think he loves you." Doolan chuckled. "Did he say he wanted to marry you? Did he give you a ring? Set a date?"

Julianna tore at the sheet. The medication was messing with her brain. She felt sluggish, muddled. She put a hand to her forehead.

"No? I didn't think so. Yet you risked everything to help with his 'problems' – Sam Somers, Sarah Bennett and Jason Findley." Doolan's voice hardened. "He left you to face the consequences while he's in Orlando. Who is it, Lee? Who did you call at the Orlando International Hotel?" When she didn't answer, he stood up, sending the chair crashing to the floor. "Who did you call?"

"Oh, God!" Julianna moaned, her brain reeling at the noise.

The nurse attempted to rush to her patient's side, but O'Connor restrained her.

"When we took a break, I received a call from a friend of mine who's at Taste of the Future," Doolan said. "Macquarie Hawke and Stephen Randall's girlfriends are sporting magnificent diamond engagement rings. Your lover is making plans for a future that doesn't include you."

Julianna moaned, "I'll kill the bastard. I swear I'll kill him."

"Lee!" Doolan's thin fingers curled round the bed rail. "Did he ask you to have Sam Somers and Sarah Bennett murdered?"

"No. He arranged it!" Julianna's hands flew to her head. "Oh, God! My head feels like it's going to explode!"

The nurse broke free and rushed to check her pulse.

"Leave me alone!" Julianna shrieked in agony. She slapped the nurse's hand away, then collapsed into the pillows, her body limp.

Chapter Fifty-nine

Taste of the Future was winding down, but a few people still straggled into the Grand Cyprus Ballroom, wandered over to the precarious tower of glasses, picked one up, then moved off down the aisles. Tables once overflowing with food were no longer being replenished. Many suppliers had abandoned their stands, unwilling to stay to the bitter end. Officials were walking up and down, making a note of those who'd left early. They wouldn't be invited back. Behind the tables, the remaining suppliers were chatting idly with one another, throwing empty bottles into the boxes under their tables, counting the minutes until they could go.

Sarah studied Donald Stoilas, who stood with his brother George across the table from her, tasting Bluestone Cellars' new Coonawarra Shiraz. Donald was taking an interminable amount of time, swirling, sniffing, swishing and spitting. What if he changed his mind about the two containers?

"It's a real winner!" His eyes lit up and he patted George on the back. "I always said the Bluestone Cellars Coonawarra Shiraz was one of the best! Everyone's looking forward to you launching it, Sarah. Let's go out for dinner when you're in Jacksonville." He held up his glass in a mock-toast, then said goodbye and moved into the aisle, heading for Macquarie Hawke's stand. George grinned and gave her a thumbs-up before he joined his brother.

"Hey, boss, good going!" Barnes deposited an empty shiraz bottle in a box below the table. "When can I put the orders in?"

"Right away. George already signed them off." Sarah was scanning the aisles as she answered him. She added, "Jim, why don't you take a break and get a bite to eat? Bernie and I can take care of things here."

As Barnes squeezed between the tables, McDermott jerked his head in the direction of the Hallgarten booth. "That looks interesting. The Stoilas brothers are getting into it with Stephen Randall. Trade places with me so I can hear what they're saying."

All evening, Sarah had observed people flocking to the Macquarie Hawke table as word of the acquisition spread. Because Randall had made the announcement at the Hallgarten dinner, many existing Hawke distributors had been left in the dark. Sarah had heard some heated words when, unable to find Hawke, who had yet to make an appearance, they moved to the next table to confront Randall, who'd become noticeably agitated as the evening progressed. She glanced at him now.

Sensing a movement, McDermott turned as Jake Malone slid behind their table, then returned his attention to the argument, which was attracting a great deal of attention as it rose in volume.

"We can't take that risk, Stephen." After years of public speaking, Donald Stoilas had an authoritative voice that projected over a distance. "Until the situation at Southern Valley is resolved, the quality of Hawke's wines will be in question."

"I hope you're not giving credence to the vicious

rumours being spread by my competition," Randall said, his eyes sliding to Sarah. "Besides, Hallgarten will be producing Hawke's wines and I personally guarantee the quality of every bottle."

Donald Stoilas rarely lost his temper, but this man was testing him to the limit, insulting his intelligence. "I know for a fact that Southern Valley is being investigated for fraud, and Hawke's existing stock, which is what you would ship me, was made there. Do you dispute either of those statements?"

"Macquarie Hawke's wine received a nearly perfect score of ninety-eight from Sam Somers. Last year five hundred thousand cases were sold in the US alone. That's proof enough Hawke's wines are top quality," Randall countered. "If you act on rumours, you'll be the one who loses out."

"I don't like discussing business in public, but since you insist, I'll make my decision now. I'm cancelling my order for three containers. Perhaps things would have been different if either you or Hawke had bothered to contact me about your purchase of the brand before we found out about it by accident," Stoilas said sharply. "You're welcome to find another Florida distributor. Good evening."

"Sarah, did you see Randall's face when he looked at you just now?" McDermott muttered, as she and Jake moved aside to let Jim Barnes back behind the table. "I know he's one of your major suppliers, Jake, but I don't want that man anywhere near Sarah, especially after what he said to her last night."

"He's no friend of mine," Jake replied. "Besides, he's had more than his share to drink, which isn't a good sign."

"Bernie, I'm ready for a break," Sarah said. "Unless you object, I'm off to the ladies' room. Jake, will you walk me over there?"

"Of course, if Bernie doesn't object," Jake said.

McDermott looked around. The aisles had started to empty. Hawke was nowhere in sight. The ladies' room was a few feet to the right of the entrance. He couldn't come up with a good reason not to let them go. "Fine, but just there and back. No detours!" he warned. "And take your handbag."

Strolling past the tower of crystal glasses, Sarah and Jake came to billowing curtains that disguised the cloak-room doors. From what they could see, the curtains formed a corridor that zigzagged, then split off at a junction, creating separate paths to the men's and ladies' rooms.

"You don't need to walk me to the door. I'll yell if anyone jumps out at me," Sarah joked. There was so much more she wanted to say, but now wasn't the time. She squeezed his arm, then let it go. Although they hadn't nailed Hawke, she was happy they were on the right track. It was only a matter of time before she had her life back.

"I'll walk part of the way." Jake smiled. Once they were out of sight, he spun her round, took her in his arms and kissed her soundly.

When he let her go, Sarah burst out laughing. "I can't believe you did that! And Bernie thought I was safe with you!"

In the ladies' room she washed her hands, then touched up her makeup. She outlined her lips with a nude pencil, then filled them in with a delicate pink lipstick. Under the harsh fluorescent lights, she looked a hundred – well, maybe not that old, but certainly too old for Jake Malone. Why couldn't he see that? She threw the lipstick into her bag. It hit the gun with a ping.

Sarah opened the door, stopped to check the curtained area, then hurried towards the exit. At the junction she cried out as someone crashed through the curtains and rammed into her.

It was Stephen Randall. His lips curled back in a snarl. "What did you say to the Stoilas brothers to make them cancel their Macquarie Hawke containers?"

Adrenalin was rushing through Sarah's system. Randall was a good five inches taller than she was, wiry but strong. His eyes were abnormally bright and he reeked of booze. "I have no idea what you're talking about." Clutching her bag, she felt the comforting weight of the gun and quietly opened the clasp. At this moment, if someone had identified Randall as the cold-blooded murderer manipulating Julianna Porter, she'd have had no trouble believing them. "If you don't mind, I need to get back to my table," she said, and pushed past him.

"Oh, no." Randall's hand snaked out and clamped on her arm. "You aren't going anywhere."

Chapter Sixty

Hunched in a white plastic chair in the bland white hospital corridor outside Julianna Porter's room, Detective Superintendent Sebastian O'Connor brushed aside a strand of red hair. In the distance, the cleaning crew finished polishing the floor and began to stow their equipment. The floor had a high sheen and the sweet-smelling polish temporarily masked the odours of illness and death.

O'Connor glanced at his wristwatch. It was mid-morning on Saturday in Adelaide, making it Friday evening in Orlando. McDermott was still at Taste of the Future. Unzipping his beige windbreaker, O'Connor pressed redial on his phone, then held it to his ear.

"You have reached Lieutenant Bernard McDermott's voicemail. Leave a message at the tone."

O'Connor swore softly. This was his fourth attempt. He decided to leave a message. "Julianna fingered her lover for the murders, but I don't want to leave his name on your voicemail. He's with you at WSWA. Call me immediately."

He hung up, then shifted in his chair, his navy corduroy trousers whispering against the white plastic. He consulted the notebook that lay open on the chair beside him, then dialled the main number for the Orlando International Hotel. He scanned the corridor for Detective Danny Doolan, who'd taken a break from their vigil outside Julianna's room.

On the tenth ring, the operator picked up. "Orlando International Hotel. One moment." Without waiting for a reply, she put him on hold.

"Goddamn it!" O'Connor fumed.

"Who are you holding for?"

"This is an emergency. I need to speak to hotel security – *now*!"

"Ringing," she said, in a sing-song voice.

The phone rang and rang, then switched to syrupy music. O'Connor looked at his watch. It had been five minutes since his first call. He punched end, then redial.

"Orlando International Hotel."

"This is Detective Superintendent Sebastian O'Connor calling from Adelaide, Australia. It is imperative that I speak to the manager immediately. This is an emergency."

"The manager is off-duty, sir." The operator's voice had an inhuman, mechanical quality.

"Who *is* on duty?" O'Connor was in danger of losing his temper.

"Uhm, the assistant manager."

"Put me through to him."

"Hello, you have reached the voicemail of –"

Detective Doolan strolled up. He looked as though he hadn't slept in days. "I got the paperwork started on lover-boy. Any word on Lee?"

"No. The doctors haven't come out yet," O'Connor answered.

Doolan took off down the corridor, phone in hand.

O'Connor was worried. After Julianna's collapse, the doctors had begun frantic efforts to revive her. Before he and Doolan had been ejected from the room, her eyes had fluttered open, giving him hope they'd be able to prise the rest of the story out of her. That had been some time ago. The doctors were still with her. His optimism was fading.

Now, setting aside his concerns, O'Connor looked up the main number for the Atlanta Police Department. When the sergeant on duty answered, he identified himself, then said, "This is an emergency. I need to get in touch with Detective Leroy Watson."

"I'll have to put you on hold for a minute."

O'Connor was annoyed, but there'd been shouting and scuffling in the background and the sergeant had sounded agitated.

While he waited, he glanced at his watch. It was around eight thirty or so in Orlando. When did Taste of the Future end? He jumped when a voice came back on the line. "Sorry about that. Busy night," the sergeant apologized. "Watson's off-duty. Do you want his phone number?"

"Yes. Thanks."

O'Connor dialled and was put through to Watson's voicemail. He left a message and hung up.

What was he going to do? Who did he know in Orlando? James Cameron, of course. O'Connor put a call through to the Orlando Police Department.

"It's Lieutenant Cameron's day off," the operator said

"This is an emergency," O'Connor said. After what seemed an interminable wait, he was given Cameron's mobile and home phone numbers.

He called Cameron's mobile, but was put through to voicemail. He left a message, then rang his home. A woman with a soft, pleasant voice answered.

"Lolly, I'd love to chat," O'Connor said, "but I need to talk to Jimmy urgently. Is he there?"

"I'm afraid he and our grandson went out for dinner and a movie, I don't recall which. Let me give you his mobile number."

Chapter Sixty-one

The billowing blue curtains that camouflaged the cloakrooms in the Grand Cyprus Ballroom clung to Jake's face. He shoved his way through them blindly, batting them aside, but they were full of static electricity and encased him like cling-film. He'd heard Randall's voice raised in anger, the words slurred. This was a nightmare.

Now he heard thunder and knew the storm was closing in on them. The lights flickered, then held. Thankful for that, he rounded the junction and came upon Randall clutching Sarah's arm. From the look on her face, Jake knew this wasn't a friendly encounter.

"Hello, Stephen, Sarah. What's going on?"

Randall released her and stepped away. "We were just chatting." He smiled.

Jake went to Sarah's side. She appeared to be fine, except for the tension in her jaw and the tightness round her eyes.

"No, we weren't." Sarah pulled her sleeve above her elbow and rubbed the indentation Randall's fingers had made in her arm. "You accused me of being responsible for the Stoilas brothers cancelling their Macquarie Hawke order, which is absolutely ridiculous. I wish I had that kind of power. If I did, I'd make sure I had no competition whatsoever." She glared at Randall. She'd have a huge bruise tomorrow, thanks to him.

"You underestimate yourself." Randall's smile was ghastly. "Because of you, the Australian wine industry is in uproar, some of the most respected families in the Barossa Valley are under suspicion, and the reputation of my newest acquisition, Macquarie Hawke, has been ruined. None of this would have happened if you'd minded your own business."

"Wait a minute!" Jake was appalled by Randall's outrageous accusations.

"No, you wait a minute," Randall countered, with renewed viciousness. "I know you turned down Hawke's brand because of her. She convinced you, like she did the Stoilas brothers, that something was wrong with Hawke's wines, didn't she? What proof did she offer? None! She couldn't, because none exists. Don't you see what she's doing?"

"I've heard enough. I'll talk to you later," Jake said. "Come on, Sarah."

"I've not finished! She made sure everyone at the Addison Group knew that Taylor and I were seeing each other, just to get Taylor into trouble. Then she convinced the Australian police that Taylor was involved in the attempts on her life. The harassment didn't stop there. You told her I recommended Oceana – for God's sake, my mother wears it! But Sarah got her rent-a-cop to insinuate to Taylor that I'd bought it for a girlfriend. Do you think I'm going to let her get away with that?"

Suddenly, with less than half an hour to go before Taste of the Future closed for the evening, legions of people were arriving. They crammed into the aisles and swooped on the tables to sample the products. Within minutes, the ballroom was as packed as it had been when the doors opened earlier that evening. Near the front, the Cornerstone Wine Imports' table was mobbed.

"Where the hell did all these people come from?" McDermott asked Jim Barnes, who was crouched beneath the table, getting out unopened bottles he'd put away.

"Heck if I know." Barnes slicked back his curly red hair, then dug in his pocket for a corkscrew. Once he'd opened a few bottles, he poured with both hands to keep up the pace. "Man, this is really crazy."

The multitudes obscured McDermott's view of Jake. As they closed round the table, he kept his eyes on the blue curtains. When the crowd parted, he glimpsed Jake disappearing into the curtains. Cursing, McDermott scrambled past a startled Barnes, slid between the tables and plunged into the crush, feeling as if he were swimming against a raging torrent of water.

Clambering round people, elbowing them out of the way, he had made it past two tables, beyond which was an open space, then the main entrance. To his left was the tower of crystal glasses, and beyond, the curtains leading to the cloakrooms. He shoved someone out of the way, and saw Sarah and Jake materialize. Stephen Randall was on their heels, shouting and gesturing. McDermott couldn't hear what he was saying, but Randall was red-faced and agitated. He hit Jake with his palm, but Jake grabbed Sarah's arm and kept walking.

As the three headed towards the tower of crystal, McDermott directed his gaze to the main entrance just as Macquarie Hawke limped in, his white-blond hair a beacon of light, the pockmarks on his face as deep as craters. McDermott's gut tightened. Hawke's left eye sported varying shades of black, green and blue, and the lid was puffed. He paused for a moment, then turned towards Sarah and Jake, who were still followed by Randall.

Stuck behind a wall of people, shouting for them to move aside, McDermott was forced to watch as Melissa McNair rushed into the ballroom. She veered past the crystal tower, grabbed Hawke from behind and spun him round. "You lying scum! You sold the damned company out from under me and didn't even have the guts to tell me!" she screamed. Then, apparently, she noticed Hawke's black eye. "So, someone beat me to it!"

McDermott was within a foot or so of Hawke now – *"Police! Move aside! Police!"* he yelled, as Hawke held up his hands and attempted to back away from Melissa. But the solid mass of curious people crowding behind him stopped him dead. McDermott was beside himself. Sarah, Jake and Randall were being pushed forward into Hawke and Melissa.

Melissa sniggered when she noticed Randall peering out from behind Hawke's back. "You fell for his act too, didn't you, Stephen? You bought his lousy brand! Do you know this scumbag asked me to sleep with Sam Somers to get a good review for his shitty wines? It worked! Mac got his precious ninety-eight for a Coonawarra Shiraz that's nothing but rotgut!"

"Shut up, you fool!" Hawke grabbed her shoulders and shook her so hard that her teeth rattled.

"Don't touch me, shithead!" Melissa slammed her handbag into Hawke's black eye.

Hawke yelled in pain and his hands flew up to his damaged eye. Melissa continued to hit him, howling like a madwoman. Close by, another woman was being pushed forward – she tripped and fell. There was screaming, then angry words. A fist met a face and, without warning, the crowd had become a mob, pushing and colliding with each other. Someone fell into a table, which collapsed. Bottles went crashing to the floor.

"Police! Police! Out of my way!" McDermott roared, bulldozing through a few hardy souls striving to keep their front-row position.

Sarah was crushed against Jake. She reached for his hand, but people shoved her aside, poked her in the ribs and pounded her back. Someone was yelling about a knife. The crowd swept Jake away. For a moment she was headed towards Stephen Randall, but then she was forced against a door. She pushed on the handle, but it wouldn't move. An ear-splitting alarm went off and she felt suddenly faint.

She shook her head to clear it and turned back to the room just in time to see McDermott reach Hawke, but not in time to stop him punching Melissa in the belly. She folded over and Hawke landed another blow on her jaw. When she reared away from him, he fell forward into her. She reeled, tumbling into McDermott and the three collapsed into the tower of crystal glasses, which tottered, crashed and showered everyone with shards.

People crowded round Sarah like stampeding animals, pushing her against the door. Now her face was wedged between it and someone's shoulder. She gasped for breath and suddenly the door burst open. She was thrust into the foyer, then through another door and outside into the car park. The night air was thick, the pavement wet. A low rumble of thunder sounded in the distance. There were lights around the perimeter, but otherwise it was pitch black.

Sarah clutched her handbag, closed her eyes, and bent over to catch her breath as the crowd melted into the darkness. Then she heard footsteps and saw a pair of brown lace-up shoes in front of her. When she stood up, she was facing Stephen Randall.

In the Grand Cyprus Ballroom, McDermott brushed glass off his jacket and gave a hand to Macquarie Hawke, who was unable to stand on his own. Barnes appeared and McDermott sent him to get help, then searched the room desperately for Sarah. Most people had gone, with the exception of some suppliers at the back of the ballroom, closing their stands, unaffected by the débâcle. Nearer the entrance, however, tables had been overturned. Broken bottles and glasses lay on the floor in puddles of wine.

McDermott stood to one side, watching Jake, who was kneeling and pressing a paper napkin to a gash in Melissa's forehead. "Where's Sarah?" McDermott barked.

"Oh, my God, I thought she was behind me. Hey, you!" With his free hand, Jake gestured to a man who'd been standing at his other side, gaping at Melissa, to take over. then stood up and scanned the room.

McDermott lowered Hawke to the floor, stepped over him and grabbed Jake's arm. "Let's go. We have to find her."

"McDermott!" someone called from the entrance. "What the hell happened here?"

Surrounded by a bevy of uniformed officers, Lieutenant James Cameron, in civilian clothes, approached McDermott and slapped him on the back. "Looks like the party got a little rowdy. Hey, do I have some wild news for you. We're here to arrest Stephen Randall for Sam Somers's murder."

McDermott grabbed his shoulder. "Jimmy, I can't find Sarah. And I haven't seen Randall either!" He outlined the situation in a few terse sentences.

"Is Randall armed?" Cameron asked, as his officers spread out behind him.

"Unknown. But Sarah has a gun."

Just then, they heard a shot, which was followed closely by a second. Cameron ordered one of his officers to take command inside, then caught up with McDermott, who was already racing through the door on his way to the car park. A bevy of police trailed behind them. Jake attempted to follow, but was stopped at the door by a policeman who refused to let him pass.

McDermott felt as if he'd plunged into a vat of molasses, the atmosphere was so thick and unyielding. The car park was dark except for lights around the periphery and the officers' torches, which whirled in crazy patterns. A thin rain had begun to fall. He reached for the gun clipped to his belt and flipped off the safety.

Sweat poured down his face as he and Cameron raced among the parked cars, guns drawn. When the formation of officers reached the middle, one called to the others, who formed a tight circle around their discovery. As McDermott approached, he noticed that the torches were trained on something or someone on the ground, but all he could see were the officers' backs. His heart stopped as he neared the area, praying he wouldn't find Sarah's body.

Close on Cameron's heels, he stepped into the centre of the circle as a flash of lightning was followed closely by a roll of thunder. Seconds later another flash showed

Sarah standing stock still with a gun in her hand. It was pointed at the head of a prone figure: Stephen Randall.

"Give me the gun, Sarah." McDermott entered the circle of officers and moved towards her. Her hand, holding the gun, was shaking.

McDermott knew that anything could happen. The gun could go off at any second and he was afraid that if that happened someone might try to shoot her. He felt a hand on his arm as he pushed towards her. He shook it off, his heart about burst.

Chapter Sixty-two

At Adelaide Hospital, in Julianna Porter's room, Detective Danny Doolan sprawled on a padded armchair he'd brought in for the final interview. Turning, he gave a thumbs-up to the departing Sebastian O'Connor. They'd learned from his friend Bernie McDermott that Stephen Randall was in custody, having hit the ground when Sarah Bennett fired her gun into the air. He'd cowered there until the police had literally picked him up. Macquarie Hawke was also under arrest, but in hospital under observation. Sarah was safe and sound, although there'd been a few tense moments before she had given up her gun.

Doolan nodded to the technician to begin recording once more. He'd have to hurry. Her condition was deteriorating. She kept sliding sideways off the masses of pillows propping her up. He referred to Somers's notes on his trip to Australia, emailed by McDermott. "Tell me about the morning Somers went to Oskar Hallgarten Vineyards to taste wines with Stephen Randall."

Julianna smiled groggily. "Somers typed tasting notes on his laptop and, like an idiot, he left it in the winemaker's office when he took a tour of the vineyards. Stephen has all the keys so he unlocked the door and rummaged around in Somers's computer to find out what he thought of Hallgarten's wines. That was when he found the notes on Hawke's Coonawarra Shiraz.

Somers had bought a couple of cases. It wasn't the red-dot kind. It was the plonk."

Her fingers twitched at the blanket covering her. "The same day, Somers showed up at Southern Valley. Davis Hart was drunk and said some stupid things to him. I called Stephen to let him know. The next day, Stephen was doing his wine inspector bit at the Australian Wine Bureau and needed to use the phone. He accidentally punched into the line that Hart and Karl Kingsley were using. You know – when Hart reported the fraud. What happened after that was Randall's idea."

Doolan frowned. She seemed to be getting progressively more woozy and confused. "What idea was that?"

"To kill Davis Hart. Shut him up." She closed her eyes. "But the next day Hart died anyway and the only loose end was Somers. Randall asked if I knew anyone who could steal his computers. I mentioned Wicky Riley."

Doolan leaned over his notes and a lock of black hair fell over his forehead. He brushed it away. "Why not simply kill Somers and be done with it?"

"With the reviews Somers had given Hawke's wines? But he didn't have much choice after Wicky accessed Somers's files and found out he was going to retract the ninety-eight rating. Randall ordered him to kill Somers and make it look like an accident."

Doolan lifted his eyes to hers. "You called Wicky Riley from Southern Valley to give him the Somers job."

"Randall hired him."

"You did. But we'll come back to that later." Doolan uncrossed his legs. "So, Hart was dead, Somers was dead, and Peter Vine was under suspicion for his murder. Randall must have thought he was in the clear until

Sarah Bennett went to your office. You thought she'd lifted the SV888 document as proof of the scam. Right?"

"Sure. I mean, why would Jason take it? He was up to his bloody neck in it." Julianna's eyelids fluttered weakly. "Randall asked me to find someone to get it back after the losers failed. The ones Angus Kennedy and Macquarie Hawke had hired. I gave him Slattery's name."

"And you called Slattery to kill Sarah Bennett?" he asked.

"Randall did." She seemed very sleepy now.

Doolan rolled his eyes, not bothering to hide his scepticism. "How did Slattery track Sarah Bennett?"

Julianna put a hand to her head and a moan escaped her. "Stephen gave him her schedule. He got it from Taylor Robbins. She'd had it in for that bitch from the beginning."

The oak-panelled elevator in the Orlando International Hotel swooshed up to the tenth floor. Jake and Sarah were alone and she was wrapped tightly in his arms. He'd waited while she was interviewed by Cameron and McDermott. Since Randall and Hawke were in custody, and Slattery had been traced to New Guinea, McDermott didn't object when they took off by themselves. Jake smiled to himself. He'd seen McDermott following them. Once the doors had closed behind them, he guessed that the lieutenant would take the express lift so that he arrived at the suite ahead of Sarah to ensure it was safe for her. Just in case.

"I've changed my mind. I'm walking you to your suite, then I'll go to my room to change." Jake wondered if he was being ridiculously protective, but he couldn't bear to let Sarah out of his sight. Besides, she felt so good.

"I'll be fine. Come to my suite when you're ready." Sarah lifted her head to kiss him, then began to laugh.

"What's so funny?"

"You ambushing me by the ladies' room" She was laughing so hard that tears had come to her eyes. "Don't you think we're a little too old to be doing things like that? What if someone had seen us?"

Jake found a handkerchief and wiped away the tears. "I'm so proud of you." He drew her close and kissed her again, this time more insistently to make sure she got the message.

The lift chimed, and the doors opened at the tenth floor, where Jake's suite was located.

"See you in a few minutes," she said, as he stepped out.

On the twelfth floor, the corridor was empty and Sarah heaved a sigh of relief as she headed for her suite at a brisk pace. She hadn't been alone for some time, and it felt strange. In fact, she hadn't been alone since . . . since Slattery had attacked her in the Pyrenees. She fingered the scar on her neck, then clutched her bag to her chest. *Don't be absurd. He's on the other side of the world. Just keep walking,* she cajoled herself. But something about the corridor bothered her. The monotonous pattern of the carpet and wallpaper, repeating without relief, reminded her of a long tunnel. The recessed doorways, with lights above the numbers, stretched for miles. Was it her imagination or were the walls narrowing? Her chest felt constricted. The carpet muffled every sound, except the thunder. It reminded her of being in the drives in the Pyrenees when the ceiling had collapsed. Oh, God.

Her mind was playing tricks. She kept seeing Stephen Randall's face as he approached her in the car park, threatening to kill her, saying she'd ruined his life with her meddling, he'd make her pay. She'd fired the gun into the air twice. Would she have shot him if he hadn't hit the ground? Probably. But she didn't want to think about that now. She was safe now, safe but alone –

She heard a metallic click.

What was that?

She whirled round, and peered down the hallway.

She was imagining things again. The corridor was empty. She reached into her bag and took out the key card. Her gun was there. Lieutenant Cameron hadn't taken it away from her when he'd learned it was properly registered. But she didn't need it now. She was safe. McDermott wouldn't have let her come up here alone unless he was sure. Then again, he'd thought Jake would be with her. Oh, damn it, just keep walking.

An explosive crash of thunder made her jump. The lights flickered and went out, leaving her in darkness but for the exit signs. That was the last thing she needed. Disoriented, she stood still. The hotel was very quiet. There was another rumble of thunder. The lights came on, but they were dim. Had to be a back-up generator. She picked up her pace, vowing to get over her paranoia, starting right now, this minute. She wasn't going to live in fear for the rest of her life.

Her suite was two doors away. She slung her bag over her right shoulder. Taking the key card, she turned the magnetic strip down, ready to push it into the slot – and someone clamped a hand over her mouth. She felt hot breath against her ear.

The man pressed a knife to her throat. "Scream and

I'll kill you." Keeping the blade in place, he took his other hand from her mouth, ripped the bag off her shoulder, breaking the thin gold chain, and threw it to the floor.

It snapped open, and the gun fell out. Sarah bent her elbow and thrust it backwards into the man's ribcage, then butted his nose with her head. There was a grunt of pain. The knife nicked her throat. She felt blood running down her neck.

"Bernie! Help!" she shrieked, loud enough to wake the entire floor. God, what if McDermott wasn't in the suite? If not, she didn't have a chance.

She screamed as the man put an arm round her waist, lifted her and rammed her head into the wall, opening a gash in her scalp. He threw her to the floor and straddled her back. Her cries escalated. She swatted him with her hands. He sliced one with his knife. She kicked him with her heels. He grabbed a handful of hair and pulled her head back, exposing her neck. She felt the cold steel of a knife at her throat. That was when she knew she was dead.

A door opened. Out of the corner of her eye, she saw a gun appear, followed by Bernie McDermott, shirtless, shaving cream on his face. Without hesitation, he crouched, aimed and fired. Once, twice, three times.

Epilogue

Three months later: Peachtree International Wine Festival Awards Dinner, Atlanta, Georgia

The dining room at the Buckhead Ritz Carlton was illuminated by silver candelabra, which gave an air of elegance to the Peachtree International Wine Festival Awards dinner. Spectacular flower arrangements in a riot of colours adorned twenty-five tables covered with pristine white cloths. The hotel's finest china, crystal and silver had been pressed into service. Everything was perfect for the guests who'd paid several hundred dollars each to attend the banquet, held on the eve of the festival's opening day.

Peter Vine surveyed the glittering company from a tall podium, proud to play host to some of the world's most famous winemakers and winery owners. A host of importers and distributors, who'd made a superhuman effort to replace the wines destroyed on the day Sam Somers died, were also in attendance, with the volunteers who'd spent many long hours recataloguing. Others had served as judges, assembling as late as yesterday evening to finish off the gargantuan task of retasting each category. Vine had been up all night, tabulating the results. He stifled a yawn. Later this evening, he would pay special tribute to those who'd worked so hard to make the evening possible.

Of those attending, however, he was most grateful to the people who'd come to his aid when *Newsday*'s management had attempted to wrest the wine column from him after Somers's death. They'd taken out a number of full-page advertisements, encouraging the readership to write in, supporting him for the position. Without their help, he wouldn't be here tonight, addressing them as *Newsday's* new wine columnist. One of those people was Jake Malone.

Vine scanned the crowd until his eyes rested on Jake. It was only three months since the appalling events at WSWA, but he seemed to have recovered. Just then, a pretty blonde strolled over and struck up a conversation with him. Gentleman that he was, Jake rose and introduced her to the people at his table, among them Vine's staunchest supporters, Judy Russo, owner of Atlanta's premium wine shop, and Bobby Wagner of Coastal Distributors.

Vine's eyes drifted round the room. Dessert had been served with the Bluestone Cellars Liqueur Tokay, donated by Cornerstone Wine Imports in Sarah Bennett's honour. It was time to start. He was proud that the awards had remained secret until now, a feat unequalled by the legendary Sam Somers.

Once the murmuring had died down, he smiled benevolently. Over the years, the Peachtree International Wine Festival had been transformed from a sleepy event into a major international show, gaining recognition and stature in the world wine community. Every medal winner would experience a huge surge in sales, and the best-of-show wine would sell out immediately, no matter how many cases were available.

Vine cleared his throat. "Ladies and gentlemen, your kind attention would be appreciated. It's time to announce the award winners of the twentieth Peachtree

International Wine Festival." He smiled broadly as the crowd clapped, whistled and hooted.

The young woman standing next to Jake smiled. "Oh! The awards are starting. Do you mind if I sit down?"

"That seat happens to be taken," another woman said, coming up to the table.

The girl flushed, stammered her apologies, then fled.

Jake stood up and pulled out the chair out with a flourish. "Sarah, you have the most exquisite sense of timing."

"Just as well I came back when I did." She gathered up her emerald-green evening dress so that she could sit down. "It appears I was in danger of losing my seat."

"Never," Jake said, as the others at the table chuckled, among them Bernie McDermott.

Once they were seated, Jake took her hand. The cut had healed, but the scar was still prominent. "I'm so glad you came out tonight." He kissed her cheek, searching her face to ensure she wasn't too tired. She'd had several operations since that night in Orlando when Wicky Riley had attacked her in the hallway of the Orlando International Hotel. Riley was dead and Sarah had been hurt. But she was fine now. That was all that mattered. He hadn't lost her.

"I wouldn't have missed this for anything." Sarah smiled. "And neither would Bernie. Right?"

McDermott, who had been griping good-naturedly about having to wear a black 'monkey suit', grinned. "You bet!"

After ten minutes of announcing the winners in various categories, Vine reached the Australian wine division. "Winner of the gold medal in the 'best

Australian shiraz over ten dollars' is Bluestone Cellars Coonawarra Shiraz, also nominated for best-of-show."

Her table companions cheered and Sarah clapped, delighted. She was rewarded with wry smiles from Jake and McDermott. Somers's computer notes contained the review of the Bluestone Cellars Coonawarra Shiraz, the same vintage that had just won a gold medal: he'd pronounced it almost undrinkable.

Sarah tuned Vine out as he continued to announce the winners. Jake's kiss had prompted memories of her recuperation. He'd taken turns with Clare and McDermott, fixing meals and running errands, kissing her chastely on the cheek every time he'd left. The last few times, he'd brought Cassie along. She had been the best remedy of all. Sarah loved hearing about the things that made up the life of a seven-year-old. And, through it all, Jake had never mentioned the night they'd spent in the Pyrenees. It was as if her wish had come true. She and Jake were good friends once more.

"Oskar Hallgarten Chardonnay, gold medal and best-of-show nominee," Vine announced.

"Hallgarten" caught Sarah's attention, drawing her back to the present, "Congratulations, Jake!"

Vine cleared his throat. "The coveted best-of-show award goes to . . . Bluestone Cellars Coonawarra Shiraz!" He continued, over thunderous applause, "Congratulations to Sarah Bennett of Cornerstone Wine Imports. Thank you, one and all, for celebrating this special anniversary event. See you tomorrow at the Peachtree International Wine Festival."

McDermott let out a piercing whistle; Judy ran over and gave Sarah a hug, as did Bobby Wagner. Jake kissed her lips. Everyone grabbed their phones and raced for the lobby to spread word of the awards. Within minutes, the room had cleared, except for a few people who had stayed to savour their after-dinner drinks.

Peter Vine approached Sarah's table. "Good to see you, Sarah. Hello, Jake, Lieutenant McDermott. I have a confession to make." He laughed when McDermott perked up. "Not that kind of confession, Lieutenant. I think you should know, Sarah, that if it weren't for Jake, the best-of-show award would have gone to the Macquarie Hawke Coonawarra Shiraz."

"What do you mean?" Sarah raised her eyebrows.

"You tell her, Jake." Vine smoothed his dinner-jacket.

"Remember the judging session, when Melissa McNair dumped wine all over George, and later, when we saw her through the window writing on something?" Jake asked.

Sarah remembered that night vividly.

"I took her to TJ's. She'd had too much to drink, and confessed that she'd changed the results. I don't think she ever remembered telling me. Anyway, I dropped her off and went back to the building. Peter was still there and promised to retest the category. Your wine won, fair and square."

After Peter Vine had left, McDermott stood up and helped Sarah out of her chair. "It's time I took you home. We need to get going early tomorrow."

Sarah put a hand on McDermott's arm. "I hope you don't mind, but Jake offered to drive me home."

"That's perfectly all right with me." McDermott shook hands with him. "Best-of-show. We'll be busy tomorrow. Get some rest, Sarah."

* * *

Sarah's smooth skin gleamed in the moonlight as she stood on the deck of her Dunwoody home, still in the gown she'd worn for the banquet. She wrapped her arms round her rib-cage, laughing so hard that her sides hurt. "Jake, if you don't stop telling me stories about Cassie, I'm going to burst something!"

"Nothing important, I hope?" Jake rolled his eyes in mock-horror. In the pale light, he saw the scar on her neck and took a deep breath. He'd come so close to losing her.

The shrill ring of the phone startled them.

"I can't believe someone's calling at this time of night – or rather morning." Sarah looked through the windows to the clock on her sunroom wall. It was midnight. "It has to be Phillip Dwyer. I'll bet he got my email about the shiraz winning best-of-show and figured I'd still be awake."

"Go ahead and answer it. I'll stay out here." Jake watched her walk carefully into the sunroom and sit down on the wicker sofa facing the deck. When she signalled that it was Dwyer, Jake turned back to the railing and stared into the blackness of the garden listening to the breeze ruffling the trees.

He thought again Wicky Riley, who'd died instantly of the gunshot wounds inflicted by McDermott. No one had reckoned he would return to Orlando, intent on murdering Sarah, undoubtedly to prevent her identifying him as Sam Somers's killer. Jake shivered, although it was warm. Riley's attack had devastated McDermott almost as much as it had Sarah. He remained unable to forgive himself, although Sarah had reassured him time and again that she didn't blame him or anyone else.

As for Sarah, her injuries had been serious, but she

was strong and on the road to recovery. Which was just as well. Cornerstone Wine Imports needed her. He smiled. She was determined to go to Jacksonville next week to launch Federated's programme. Maybe he'd tag along – just to make sure she didn't get too tired, of course.

As for the Addison Group, Sarah's troubles with them had been resolved when Paul Burnside received a vote of confidence from the Addison Group's board of directors a week after WSWA. He had fired Pym Noonan and Taylor Robbins, although officially they'd "resigned". Rumour had it that Noonan was driving a taxi in Sydney. No one was sure what had happened to Taylor, who'd been found innocent of conspiring with Randall – he had printed out Sarah's schedule from Taylor's computer without her knowledge.

Burnside had promoted Phillip Dwyer, who'd immediately extended payments on the two containers of old-label shiraz for six months, giving Cornerstone plenty of time to pay for the inventory, which was likely to fly out of the warehouse now that the succeeding vintage had won best-of-show.

That brought to mind his own situation with Oskar Hallgarten, who had begun proceedings against Macquarie Hawke. There was little hope of getting their initial five-million-dollar payment back, but Hallgarten had nullified their contract to purchase Hawke's company by defaulting on the remaining payments.

Hawke had posted bail and skipped the country. With no one to press assault charges against Melissa McNair, she'd been released. Last he'd heard she was selling life insurance on the west coast. Hawke was still missing, although he was being vigorously pursued by a number of US and Australian police departments. No leads had surfaced as yet. McDermott mentioned that the trail they'd been following from the Cayman Islands, where Hawke had deposited the five million dollars, had gone cold once it reached Switzerland.

Stephen Randall was locked away in a maximum-security jail in Orlando. The state of Georgia was fighting for the right to prosecute him, but he'd petitioned the Florida courts for extradition to Australia, where there was no death penalty. As of yet, no decision had been made.

Julianna Porter, or rather Lee Stout, would spend the remainder of her life in jail. She'd confessed not only to murdering Jason Findley in self-defence after he had attacked her late on the night she had killed his cat, but also to castrating, then murdering her brother as retribution for his physical and sexual abuse. Jake shuddered. And in one of the more bizarre twists, the Oceana perfume lead had panned out on the day after Julianna had come clean. Randall was her lover, and, for all his smarts, he'd used a company charge card to have a department store send the perfume directly to Julianna's apartment.

Angus Kennedy went to trial for fraud, but the case against him was weak, and he ended up paying a personal fine, which his wife covered for him as well as the fine levied against Southern Valley. She had shut down the operation, sold the winery buildings at auction for a small fortune and begun divorce proceedings.

As for Karl Kingsley, he'd resigned and left for South Africa where he was starting up a winery in the Breede River area with a group of Australian investors. Neither

Graham Blackwell nor the Adelaide police had found any hard evidence to prove he had been paid off by Macquarie Hawke or Angus Kennedy to facilitate the fraud at Southern Valley. However, an investigation into the source of funds Kingsley had used to purchase the land for the winery had been traced to a Swiss bank account.

Blackwell had been appointed head of the US office of the Australian Wine Bureau, and was now in New York. He'd had a rough start dealing with the US media's frenzied focus on Stephen Randall's arrest at WSWA for the murder of Sam Somers and the possibility that Macquarie Hawke wines, as well as those of some top Australian wineries, had been adulterated with cheap grapes fobbed off on them by Southern Valley.

Initially sales of Australian wines had plummeted but Blackwell's masterful handling of the situation had staved off disaster. Once the public had been made aware of the limited scope of the fraud, sales bounced back. Blackwell was considered something of a hero by anyone with a vested interest in Australian wines. Jake knew that Sarah had been in regular contact with him, and wondered about the nature of their relationship. His musings were interrupted when she returned to the deck.

"What did Phillip have to say?" he asked.

"He's over the moon about winning best of-show. He called Andrew Dunne. Now they're both hot to do that vertical tasting of Bluestone Cellars wines they discovered in the drives, using the best-of-show as a draw."

"I guess that means there are no hard feelings between you," Jake said, glad for her sake that Dunne had not been involved in the attacks on her life. The wines he'd taken her to see in the drives had been found untouched in another section.

"I don't know about that," Sarah shrugged her shoulders, "but at least he's making an effort." She covered her mouth to hide a yawn.

"Have I told you how beautiful you look tonight? I'm so happy you came out for the awards dinner." He enveloped her in his arms and kissed her. He didn't want to let her go, but he had no choice. "It's probably time I left. We have a big day ahead of us."

"I know it's late, but there's something we need to discuss," Sarah said.

He stepped away, anxiety striking him. This had been one of the best evenings of his life. He didn't want anything to spoil it. "This is about us, isn't it?"

"Yes." She propped her elbows on the railing, avoiding his eyes.

The wind had died down. Jake joined her, listening to the chirping crickets and the rush of water from the stream below. When she remained quiet, he moved closer and put an arm round her shoulders. "You know I love you, Sarah. I think I always have. Whatever you want to do is fine with me. We don't have to talk about it right now."

"No. You deserve the truth. After we made love, all I could think about was losing your friendship, that something between us had been destroyed and what was in its place was destined to end badly. Then you'd be gone. For ever. I didn't know if I could handle that. Then somewhere along the way, I realized I didn't want to lose you because . . . I love you. I can't imagine my life without you. But it scares the heck out of me."

She twisted towards him. His blue eyes were shimmery,

like the sea catching the pure rays of the sun on a cloudless day. She smiled and touched his cheek, then kissed him as he put his arms round her.

Soon she broke away and, grasping his hand, led him through the kitchen, past the den, up the stairs to her bedroom. She flicked on the crystal bedside lamp. It cast a warm glow on the walls and bedspread as she unbuttoned Jake's dinner jacket and flung it on to the chair next to the bed. She undid his black bow-tie and cummerbund, and tossed them on to the floor, then his shirt. She ran her fingers through the hair on his chest.

He unzipped her dress, which fell to the floor, he took her hands in his and stared into the glittering emerald eyes.

A few hours later, Sarah woke to the gentle rhythm of Jake's breathing. She was in his arms, her back to his front. To be in her own bed with him gave her a wonderful sense of peace. This was the happiest she could ever remember being, but she wasn't going to fool herself. The disintegration of her marriage had been devastating. The thought that Jake's love for her could fade as Elliott's had done weighed heavily on her mind. For their relationship to work, she'd have to trust him and, more importantly, herself.

She was turning over, careful not to wake Jake, when Slattery popped into her mind. In that second, her sense of safety vanished. Slattery had eluded the New Guinea police and disappeared without a trace. She recalled that night in the Pyrenees and the horrifying things he'd vowed to do to her the next time they met. She knew he intended to keep that promise.

Acknowledgements

One rain-soaked day in New York City, my husband, Richard Gupta, sat down at a deli counter for a quick bite to eat and struck up a conversation with a stranger, David Kotick. That brief encounter lead to a lasting friendship, without which, this book might never have been published. My eternal gratitude goes out to David, who introduced me to Betty Anne Crawford of Books Crossing Borders and Annette Crossland of No Exit Press, two remarkable women whose constant encouragement made all of this possible.

A special thanks goes to real life detective, Bernie McDermott and my uncle, Lawrence W. Passow, who gave generously of their time and expertise and to Hazel Orme, my editor, whose insights were invaluable. And to all my friends in the wine trade – you know who you are – many thanks for your support.